SHATTERED

by
Rebecca Guy

Also by Rebecca Guy:

Ruin

For you, dear reader.

Whoever you are, wherever you are, whatever you are.

Keep your eyes open and your wits about you… you never know who you may have upset in the past.

Enjoy!

Chapter One

Charley Costin sat with her elbows on the table, chin resting in her hands. She watched the ripple of alternating yellow and blue as the curtain tugged gently in the breeze from the open kitchen window. The April day had been stifling. Static. Sun filling a cloudless sky. But now, a cool easterly breeze graciously lent the day some air. She closed her eyes and inhaled deeply, letting the light breeze caress her face and tug her hair.

Ah, that's more like it.

A swift, sharp pain exploded through her ankle and her eyes flew open at the sharp slap of a hand on wood.

'Ow!' she yelped, scraping the chair back across the tiles.

'Daydreaming.' Evelyn spat, gaze sharp and indignant over red rimmed glasses, her arms folded firmly across her ample bosom as Charley leaned to rub her ankle, eyes on her eldest sister across the table.

'I wasn't day-'

'I should *not* need to remind you,' Evelyn cut in sourly, 'that this is a serious matter, and one that I want clearing up within the next few minutes so I may retrieve my kitchen for domestic purposes.'

A chair creaked as Rue, born two years after Evelyn, shifted in the seat next to Charley.

'Why can't you just say you want to make your dinner?' she said in a small voice, pushing overly large tortoiseshell glasses self-consciously up her nose.

Evelyn fixed her with a gaze that could melt iron and Rue seemed to lose inches as she shrank back into the chair. Lank mousy hair fell to conceal her face as her gaze dropped to her hands.

'I'm sorry, Evelyn,' she whispered.

Charley reached for Rue's hand under the table and gave it a squeeze. The room was silent, pensive. Then Evelyn's shoulders relaxed, and she pursed her lips.

'Apology accepted. Thank you. Now shall we get back to business? This has taken quite long enough.'

There was a collection of sighs and a rumble of agreement from around the table. Kate, the final Costin sister, falling between Rue and Charley, pulled the used china teacups into the middle of the table with a scrape.

'Well, I can't go, that's obvious.' she said, wild blonde curls bouncing as she stood, 'I have four children who need their mother at home, and I have a business that won't run itself.'

'You also have a husband...' Charley pointed out.

Kate shot her a scathing look.

'Nick is a great man, Charley, but superman he is not. How can he run both sides of the business and look after four children? He won't manage. We are a well-oiled machine until one cog slips out of sync. That cog would be me, and let's face it,' She threw her hands in the air, 'there's not even a timescale to work to. I need deadlines!'

Charley rolled her eyes. 'I am so sorry they couldn't put a *timescale* on an old lady's life for you Kate.'

Francesca, the girls' mother and the final person sat around the large wooden table, reached a hand across to pat Charley's.

'You know what she means, Charlotte, pipe down.'

The touch was brief and awkward, and Charley felt a small blush rise up her neck as she pulled her hand away too quickly. Kate gave Charley a smug smile.

'Thank you, mom.' she said, 'Look, Charley, if I knew the time that I would need, then I could sort something out, but from where I'm standing it's just not possible.'

There was a sharp clink as Kate picked the cups up by their handles.

'Just for the record,' she continued, 'Mom shouldn't go either. She shouldn't have to travel all the way to Northumberland to look after anyone, she's an old lady herself now, she's far too frail.'

Kate threw a protective glance at Francesca, and Charley felt her mouth fall open, as Evelyn hummed agreement.

Frail? Yeah, so weak and frail she can look after your feral kids most days, which is probably more the issue.

Snapping her mouth shut, Charley swallowed the comment. Evelyn would expect her to argue, and would take great delight in shutting her down, so instead she watched Kate place the cups on the counter-top and the moment passed with the flick of the kettle.

There was a raising of hands for all those in agreement with Kate. Charley kept her hand firmly down, but noticed a sprightly, and very able-bodied, Francesca, raised her own to the vote, with a vehement nod.

Charley stared in disbelief as her mother called for quiet.

'Kate's right,' Francesca stated. She pushed her chair back and stood, short grey hair lifting off her lined forehead in the breeze. She looked at each sister in turn, a doleful expression on her face. 'I *can't* go. I'm sixty-seven years old. I should not have to look after a sick relative at my time of life, I'm a pensioner. If I travel all that way it will kill me. I'll get a blood clot; I know I will. You will be orphaned. I'm so, so sorry my darlings, it *has* to be one of you.'

She sighed dramatically putting one hand to her heart and clutching at the table with the other as she sat down again. Charley snickered, a low, unintentional sound but one that caught the attention of her mother all the same.

'Is something funny, Charlotte?'

7

Charley blushed as everyone turned to her. She forced her eyes to Francesca's.

'No mom, it's just... I mean... well, *orphaned* sounds a little dramatic at our ages doesn't it? I'm the youngest at twenty-seven. Evelyn is forty-one for God's sake!'

The room exploded into a collection of sighs, huffs, bangs, and tuts. Only Rue sat quiet looking downcast into her lap as the others began talking over each other.

'Losing a parent hurts whatever age...'

'... appalling Charley, just appalling...'

'I don't need my age bringing into this...'

'... think before you speak...'

Charley rolled her eyes and let go of Rue's warm hand as she stood, scraping her chair back on the tiled floor.

'Well, it's obvious I'm far too immature to look after anyone. I have a head full of fluff and daydreams, which counts me out, so I'll leave you all to it. Thanks for the tea.'

There was a loud scrawp as Evelyn rose, pushing back her own chair. She held both hands in the air as she simultaneously quieted the room and motioned Charley to sit back down. Charley hesitated for only a second before she complied with a sigh. She always did when Evelyn commanded an action. They all did. It was like an ingrained family trait.
Evelyn towered silently over Charley with a hard glare, willing her to make another move.

Go on, try again, have another go, Charley, see what you get. All it costs is a small piece of ego, not too much to lose.

Charley dropped her gaze to the table.

'Listen.' Evelyn said, 'I can see where Kate is coming from, and I agree with her. Mom can't go. It wouldn't be right, and I too have a very important job with time constraints. I am a headmistress...' She paused for effect, looking smugly around the table as though none of them

8

knew, which was horse shit. It was pushed in their faces at every opportunity.

Charley restrained a frustrated sigh and looked back to the window.

'I have staff and children to care for in a busy school.' Evelyn continued, 'It will not function if I have a length of time away. I know that I would, otherwise, be the perfect choice, and I would gladly take that responsibility, but I just can't. And anyway, Rue needs me here.'

All heads turned to Rue, who squirmed uncomfortably under the attention, her magnified eyes blinking back.

'Actually, I don't mind going,' she said, her voice barely above a whisper in the quiet that had descended.

Evelyn laughed, a harsh, clipped sound.

'You can't go, sweetie, look at the state of you. You can't even look after yourself, never mind a dying old lady. You have a disorder, Rue, and regardless of whether you like it, you need help.'

Francesca and Kate murmured their agreement, and Charley looked at Rue, taking in her thin frame, and pale pallor, as Kate turned her attention to pouring the tea.

Rue had Anorexia - well, maybe. There was no professional diagnosis. The Doctor confirmed her weight and BMI were low, although still within the normal range, but Francesca knew better. The medical profession had let Rue down, and it was decided, in a meeting not dissimilar to this one - minus Rue - that they knew exactly what was wrong, and exactly what to do about it.

Between them they ruled as much of her life as they could, and while Rue wasn't much to look at, and she *was* unbearably skinny, she was also holding down a full-time job as a legal secretary with none of their help.
They should give Rue a little more credit, and I think I'll wait for the professional diagnosis before jumping to conclusions.

Rue met her gaze, and Charley flicked her eyes toward Evelyn, giving an internal whoop of delight as Rue sat upright and pushed her large glasses back up her nose.

'I... I don't have a disorder,' she said, looking straight at Evelyn, 'and I would like to go. I live alone and I have the least to lose, I'm sure I could get the time off work.'

Rue lift her chin, but her fearful gaze gave her away. She wasn't strong enough against the three of them, and she knew it. Still, she seemed to find the courage to glance around the table. 'I will manage fine,' she said, 'and I... I think I'd quite like to see the sea again.'

Charley wanted to get up and applaud. It was the most Rue had stood up to any of them in a good many years, but no-one else seemed to notice - they didn't give her a beat before they shot her back down.

'We can take you to see the sea when you're feeling better,' Kate said, stirring the tea, 'You won't be able to manage Aunt Elizabeth. She'll flatten you like a bug.'

'Correction, 'Evelyn said, forefinger in the air, 'She *flattened* you like a bug. Every single time we went to visit, and that was when you were well. Who knows how far down the dementia spiral Elizabeth has gone now, she likely has no idea who she is herself, let alone any of us. She's probably worse than a witch, Rue, she's probably a *monster* by now.'

Rue shrivelled back into her seat, casting her eyes back into her lap, all fight shut down in an instant.

'Well, that's settled then.' Evelyn said, smug smile firmly back in place.

Charley narrowed her eyes, a spark of anger igniting in her gut, not only for Rue, but for her Aunt too.

'Where's your compassion?' she said, 'Aunt Elizabeth has been given a month left to live, she's an old lady at the end of her life Evelyn! The witch stuff was childish stories. *Your* childish stories that you liked to scare us all witless with.'

Evelyn folded her arms back over her chest.

'Says the only one of us that never knew her. I experienced her first-hand. I know how bad she was, I know what she did, and how well she guarded that cellar. What do you remember, Charley?'

Charley opened her mouth to respond but realised she had no answer. She couldn't remember her Aunt; all visiting had halted abruptly when Charley had been three years old. Kate had then been ten, Rue fourteen and Evelyn sixteen. She shook her head and sat back in her chair with a huff.

'It doesn't matter what I remember...' she tried, but her words carried no weight. She tailed off as Evelyn smirked and Kate covered her smile with a hand.

Charley worked her jaw in frustration.

What the hell is up with this family?

'Look,' she said, leaning forward 'Whatever she did, even if she's not a nice person, she's mom's sister and our Aunt. She's family. Elizabeth Kane is just an old lady who needs our help, can't you see that?'

Francesca afforded Charley a brief acid stare.

'Do not speak that name around me, Charlotte. I don't want to hear it.'

Charley huffed and spread her hands wide.

'Well, that's fantastic, mom, but that's exactly who we're here to discuss.'

Evelyn gave a loud tut as Francesca sat back, stony faced. She stared at the clock on the kitchen wall, conversation closed. Charley narrowed her eyes. She didn't understand what had driven a wedge so deep between the sisters, but even with Elizabeth at death's door Francesca wouldn't go to Northumberland, that much was obvious. 'Not so sure, now, are we Charley?' Evelyn said, eyebrows raised and with a smile that Charley wished she could wipe from her face. 'Keep your mouth shut when you have no clue what you're talking about.'

Charley bit back her anger as Evelyn turned away, and the discussion as to who would go continued. She dropped her gaze to the table with a frown.

Bloody witch! This is ridiculous, Aunt Elizabeth can't be that bad, surely.

She thought back to the stories, always led by Evelyn, and always told after dark. Back then Charley had been terrified, shaking under

Evelyn's duvet as her sister whispered stories of the witch and all she did to small children down in the cellar. In fact, all of her sisters had fed the fear at every opportunity, scaring each other even as they scared Charley, until their Aunt had become a monster in their fertile imaginations. Ugly and crooked.

A monster who had killed her husband to prevent him from exposing her secret. A monster who would live forever, casting secret spells alone in the cellar and feeding on the souls of small children for immortality.

Charley's frown deepened as a thought occurred to her.

Here's a fact, the witch won't live forever. It has been medically proven. Elizabeth Kane is just an old lady with dementia at the end of her days. And if eating children was part of her diet, they haven't given her the power of eternal life we afforded her, which means the stories are rubbish.

The shifting blue and yellow dance of the curtain edged back into Charley's gaze as a breeze tugged gently at her hair.

Blue. Yellow. Yellow. Blue. Twirling and whirling, tugged and pulled back and forth.

Lulled, Charley rest her chin in a hand and wondered how she could capture the motion, and the sentiment, with her camera. Her photography so far comprised landscapes, and more recently sunsets. These were selling well online, not only as prints, but as anything from notebooks to phone cases. But she wanted to go further. To go from capturing beauty, to capturing emotion, real feeling, within her pictures. She wanted to get away from the gimmicks and get into real art. The sort that was so profound it reduced people to tears.

A voice nudged at the edge of her thoughts, and she found herself pulled back into Evelyn's kitchen.

'It's agreed then,' Evelyn was saying, 'by a four-vote majority. Charley will go.'

Charley blinked and snapped her head toward her sister, eyes wide.

'What?'

'It's been agreed. If you weren't present when the vote was cast I can't be held accountable.'

'If a vote was cast Evelyn, then surely I should have been included. I have a vote too.'

Evelyn gave a superior smile as she peered over her glasses, eyebrows so high they almost reached her hairline.

'Oh, you have a vote, darling, of course you do. But whoever you vote for will still only have one vote to your four. If you do the math, you can see that-'

Charley slapped her hands on the table as the temper that she had been holding in flared up and spilled out.

'I'm not stupid Evelyn, but it's not a fair system. Aunt Elizabeth would know any of you better than me, I last saw her when I was just three years old. She won't have a clue who I am!'

Evelyn gave a shrug and cast her a pitying glance. Charley looked around the table, but no-one, with the exception of Evelyn, would return her gaze. Kate got up and busied herself with the kettle without a word. Francesca immediately dropped her eyes and pursed her lips. Rue simply stared down at her hands.

Anger spreading through her Charley threw her hands wide fingers still tingling from the sharp contact with the table.

'Mom? This is ludicrous, say something.'

'Charlotte, she has dementia. She probably won't remember any of us.'

'But... she's *dying*!'

Evelyn gave a dramatic sigh. 'Oh, for goodness' sake Charley, isn't that the whole point of the meeting?'

Charley snapped her head back to Evelyn, feeling the heat spread through her cheeks as she struggled to hold her temper.

'Well, surely you can't expect me to go. How am I supposed to cope? I know nothing about dementia, and what do I do when... well, you know... when the inevitable happens?'

Kate brought yet more tea to the table and Charley felt her stomach turn over, they were tea drinking machines, she couldn't touch another drop.

'How would *any* of us cope?' Kate said. 'None of us have had to deal with this sort of thing before, have we? You will manage, I have full confidence in you.'

She placed a hand on Charley's shoulder which Charley promptly shrugged off.

'Well, that just makes it all better doesn't it.' She snapped.

The table fell silent and Charley's blood boiled as she watched Evelyn take a sip of tea. The china clinked as she placed the cup back into the saucer on the table.

'It makes no difference Charley.' Evelyn said, 'Whichever way you look at it you are the only person with the flexibility to go. There can be no other choice.'

'If Charley doesn't want to go, I said I can go.'

Charley glanced at Rue, small and meek, and realised that Evelyn had been right about one thing. Rue couldn't go either. If she had anorexia, then she really did need the help. She was about to thank Rue anyway, the only one of them willing to take the baton for her, when Evelyn cut her short.

'I said no, Rue.' She snapped, 'You are too ill. It's a ridiculous idea, and it is *not* happening.'

Rue placed her gaze back where it had been most of the meeting, in her lap, and Charley caught Evelyn's satisfied smile as she turned back to her tea. The boiler hummed in the silence. No one spoke.

Charley found herself shaking with anger.

'So that's it? All the help I'm going to get?' She huffed an indignant breath as she scanned the faces around the table. 'Thank you. All of you.'

Evelyn raised her eyebrows, placing her cup down, as the smile slipped from her face.

'Oh, just stop.' she said, 'It was a democratic vote, Charley. The outcome would have been the same if you hadn't been staring into space. One of us has to go, and you are the obvious choice. You're the one who has nothing to tie you here.'

Evelyn gave Charley a hard look, all niceties and control gone from her voice. She rarely lost control, and Charley would ordinarily have backed down long before now, but the gloves were off. Her anger surged like a tidal wave and she met Evelyn's angry stare with her own.

'What do you mean by that?' she said.

'Well, let's face some facts, shall we?' Evelyn said, 'Your last fling left you over six months ago. Your flat is rented, if needs be you can give it up and rent somewhere else when you return.'

Charley felt the heat rise from her stomach, her hands shaking under the table. She worked her jaw until it ached as Evelyn continued.

'Your little picture shop is online, and let's face it, you can take pictures wherever you are in the world. The cogs of your little venture won't need to stop turning like Kate's. Kate has built a very lucrative and very busy...'

Charley snapped. She could take no more. She stood, sending the chair toppling to the floor behind her. Evelyn also stood, in imitation, across the table, her face etched with shock. Charley leaned forward until she was as close to her oldest sister as she could physically get, She heard Kate gasp and Rue whimper next to her. Only Francesca sat quiet.

'First, my flat is my home, Evelyn, It has been for the last eight years. I could no more give it up than you could give up being such a self-righteous idiot. Second, Joe was not a fling, we were together for four years. For the record he did not leave me, it was a mutual decision to call time, we were both ready to move on. Third, if you think I have to put any less into running my business than Kate does, you are sorely mistaken. An online presence is possibly harder to build up in the constant noise of web traffic than her livery yard. Which, incidentally, sits at the bottom of a posh housing estate, where every little girl has a pony.'

Charley's hands curled into fists as rage swept through her every fibre. She looked at the people sat around the now silent table.

Her family.

Every face but Rue's made her sick. These people were supposed to be there for her, to protect her. Instead, they were happy to send into her into the - apparently real - witches' coven with no qualms. It was a democratic vote after all. So what if she hadn't had chance to put her case forward? Anything was game in this family. Well, maybe she would give up her flat. Maybe she would go to Northumberland, and when her poor Aunt finally passed, maybe she wouldn't bother to come back.

The silence swelled, and she felt the tension pressing against her. The air was thick with unspoken accusations, Charley knew that if she opened Pandora's box the kitchen would descend into chaos. She felt herself teetering on the edge of the chasm that would force it open wide.

Not today. They're not worth it.

She picked up her satchel bag from the floor and put it on the table in a controlled movement. Her hands shook and her heart thumped in her chest. What she really wanted right now was to shout and scream, to tell them all how pathetic they were. How, when they were on their deathbeds, their stupid lives would seem insignificant, and she hoped that someone would want to sit with them when the end came.

She wanted to tell them that person wouldn't be her.

She wanted to reiterate just how terrified she was of what she would find in Northumberland, not just confronting a childhood nightmare, but facing death, and dealing with a person close to death. She knew a little about dementia, but nowhere near enough to know what to expect when she arrived tomorrow.

But she would go anyway because that was the kind of person she was.

Clenching her jaw, she took some deep breaths, pretending to occupy herself with the contents of her bag. No one moved, but she felt four pairs of eyes on her as she checked her phone and replaced it carefully. When she felt she could speak with enough control, she looked up at her family.

'Well, that's sorted then, I'll go. I won't argue don't worry.'

Evelyn's shoulders fell at least three inches as she released a breath and Charley fought down another surge of anger.

'As it happens,' she continued, 'you're right, I'm the obvious choice. I'm the only person in this room with an ounce of empathy. Aunt Elizabeth is just an old lady who doesn't have long to live. She is not a witch, and not a monster.'

There was an uncomfortable shuffling around the table as Rue shrunk further into her chair and Kate reddened. Even Evelyn had the decency to look away. Charley jabbed a finger at them.

'If you lot still choose petty feuds and childhood stories over the responsibility of looking after a dying family member, whatever may have happened in the past, then you have to live with that, not me.' She shot her mother a disgusted look, but it was lost on Francesca who was busy inspecting her hands in her lap. Charley shook her head. 'Well, it's a good job she doesn't have to look at your sour faces for the last of her days, she may wish to end things a little sooner.'

Before there could be any backlash Charley swung her satchel over her shoulder and left, catching the sound of indignant voices as the door slammed shut behind her. She didn't stop until she reached her car, flinging the bag inside she climbed in and locked the doors.

Heart pounding, she let rip.

The obscenities that flowed from her mouth got progressively louder and finally turned into a full scream, her hands white knuckled as they grabbed the steering wheel. When there was nothing more to come she sat, panting hard, head resting down on the wheel.

She would do this; but not for them, for her Aunt, who had probably been wrongly accused of so much as they had grown up.

Who knows, maybe I'll find out what really happened between mom and Elizabeth to stop us being able to visit.

Anger beginning to fade, she turned the key in the ignition and drove home to pack what she would need. It didn't escape her attention that not one member of her so-called family had followed her out to see if she was okay.

Strike one guys. On three I won't be coming home, I really don't need this shit anymore.

17

Chapter Two

There were five calls from Evelyn before she left the next morning. She informed Charley what she would need to take, the best way to deal with their Aunt, and explained the ins and outs of dementia and how it presents - a disease she knew nothing of yesterday, but was now suddenly an overnight expert. She went over the directions to Fortwind House, the traffic report as of seven minutes ago, and finally, said that Charley really *ought* to be on her way by now - *did she know how long this journey would take?*

At that point Charley stopped answering the calls, her mood descending further into darkness with each one. If Evelyn wanted to control so much, she should have gone herself.

But... oh, wait, she has a very busy school to run remember... that's why she's able to call every five minutes on a Monday morning.

As a saving grace - and a symbolism of freedom – the April sun shone with vigour for the whole two-and-a-half-hour drive from Harrogate to the coast of Northumberland. With the windows down, and the stereo up in her little yellow Mini, Charley's mood improved with each mile she put between herself and her shambolic family. By the time she reached Fortwind House she was in good spirits.

Turning through the iron gates, she slowed as the long gravel driveway climbed among immaculate shorn grass, shrubs, and trees, before rounding a bend at the top of the hill. Charley slowed further as the building came into view, finally pulling the car to a stop in front of a large two storey, double fronted house.

Leaning forward onto the steering wheel she assessed the building with awe. It was a million miles from the small three bed terrace that she had been raised in. At the centre of two large bay windows sat a tall solid looking green door, flanked by equally tall, thin panes of glass, etched with stained glass. The sandstone brick seemed to gleam golden in the late afternoon sunshine, and the dark windows shone, as though all dust and decay was repelled. Mature borders and spring flowers were in full bloom, their vibrant colour giving the imposing building an uplifting, and welcoming feel.

Turning the stereo down, Charley grinned and opened the car door, stepping out into the sunshine. A brisk coastal breeze pushed from behind, fanning blonde hair into her face, forcing her to hold it back with her hand. She leaned an arm on top of the open driver's door feeling the hum of the engine beneath her as she surveyed the house further.
It certainly didn't look like a witches' lair, and she hoped the well-kept, friendly facade meant that everyone was horribly wrong about the sole occupant inside.
Well, this is where the truth will out either way. Aunt Elizabeth: old lady or monster? One lucky lady gets to brave the domain of the legendary Witch and uncover the truth. Will she survive to tell the tale?

A cloud passed over the sun, dulling the landscape and sending a chill around her shoulders. She shuddered as an uncomfortable feeling jumped in her gut. Now she was here the suppressed tales that scared her as a child clambered to the surface. Elizabeth Kane, the witch, the children in the cellar, the haunted mansion. It all stood in front of her, as real as the gravel she stood on.

She swallowed hard as the sun reappeared.

Except the house doesn't look so haunted, and they were just stories Charley, get a grip.

Reigning her thoughts in before they galloped off riderless, she scanned the large driveway for a place to park up, but as there were no other cars here for guidance, she leaned in to turn the engine off where it sat. The immediate crash and roar of the sea below filled her ears. She turned to look over the roof of the car, shielding her eyes against the glare of the sun, and let out a small gasp.

The driveway she had climbed to the house hadn't seemed all that high, but from up here it seemed they were on top of the world. Spread below her lay the red roofs of the small village of Fortwind Bay, a scattering of houses, along a handful of roads that reached from the bottom of Aunt Elizabeth's driveway to the edge of the beach.

A large sandy bay swept away to the right, interrupted a mile or so down by large black rocks which broke through the sand like surfacing whales in the distance. To the left, on the edge of the village, sat a small fishing harbour with a handful of boats and small buildings, and just out to sea was a small island with the remnants of an old building. Beyond the bay, the rough blue-grey sea seemed to stretch forever before meeting the pale horizon. White horses crest the waves, the breakers further out to sea glittering like diamonds in the lowering sun.

Charley felt her open mouth stretching into a wide grin.

What a spot! I think this move may be fantastic for the business, I'm going to capture some amazing stuff up here. Maybe this wasn't such a bad thing after all, and I'll bet Aunt Elizabeth is lovely too. How can anyone feel mean when they live somewhere like this?

Heart swelling with both excitement and apprehension, Charley was still squinting out to sea when her phone pinged from the passenger seat. She leaned in to grab it and turned back to the sea, leaning on the roof of the warm car as she opened the new message. Evelyn.

Are you there yet? Let us know you've arrived safely x

Charley rolled her eyes. Having given up trying to call, she was on to new tactics. Evelyn would be desperate to be proved right that Aunt Elizabeth was nasty and mean, and it would only be to say 'I told you so'. As her thumb hovered over reply, it hit her that Evelyn had absolutely no hold over her up here. Charley held all the cards.

Hah! And guess what? I'm not playing Evelyn. And you're not here to make me play, how about that? I bet that will drive you insane, won't it, honey?

She grinned as she text back.

I'm here. x

The reply came immediately.

How is Aunt Elizabeth? x

Charley chuckled. Ah, there it was, Evelyn was so transparent it was almost comical. Well, she wouldn't grace her with another reply, she could stew a little longer.

Shaking her head, she locked the phone screen, and was placing it in her pocket, when the large front door swung open behind her. She turned to see a plump dark-haired lady in a blue tunic step out into the sunshine. Charley assessed that she was probably in her late fifties as she crossed the bay window, placed a black bag into one of the bins lining the side of the house, and turned back, feet crunching on gravel. She stopped short as she spotted the car.

Finding her manners, Charley shut the car door and stepped away from it to introduce herself.

'Hi, I don't know whether you're expecting me? I'm...'

'Charlotte? Ms Kane's niece?'

Charley smiled.

'Exactly. But call me Charley, please, no one calls me Charlotte.'

Except the mother from hell, but I've decided she doesn't count.

The lady gave a warm smile. She closed the gap between them quickly and grabbed Charley's hand, shaking it vigorously, along with her ample bosom. From here Charley could see faint slithers of grey among her dark hair and the creasing lines around brown eyes filled with life.

'Ah, lovely to meet you Charley, I'm Glen, Ms Kane's nurse.' She motioned around Charley to the car, 'Can I help you in with anything?'

'Oh, gosh no, I only have a couple of suitcases, I can get them later.'

'No time like the present. The sooner you're settled, the better.'

Glen bustled around the back of the car and popped the boot revealing the two small suitcases that filled the rear space. She dragged them both out and pulled up the handles offering one to Charley and taking one herself. She glanced back into the boot before shutting the lid.

'Anything inside the car?'

Charley smiled at her forthrightness.

'Nothing major. Is the car okay here?'

'It'll do for now, when you get five just park it alongside the bins. Come on, I'll show you to your room and you can start getting yourself comfortable. How was the drive?'

Charley followed Glen to the door, shouting to make herself heard over the noise of the suitcase on the gravel.

'Great, no real traffic, so I made good time.'

'Well, that's good news.'

Glen smiled as she held the front door open for Charley to step through.

The front of the house faced west, and the descending sun had warmed the structure for a good few hours now, but it was the coolness of the hallway hit her first. The waning day not quite warm enough to make it feel refreshing, she shivered.

Ahead of her the hall was small and dark and she quickly saw the reason. Mahogany.

Everywhere.

Mahogany stair rail, Mahogany dado rail, cabinet, hallway desk, mahogany framed mirror, mahogany framed pictures on the wall. It didn't help that the wall itself was adorned with old wallpaper lined with large dark flowers. Even the carpet was dark with an obscure pattern running through it. Now that her eyes were adjusting, she could see that it ran along the hallway and up the stairs.

Crikey, I don't know about a witch, this house would be better suited to a vampire.

Charley wondered if the darkness was intentional, or whether it was just her perception after being in the sun. She blinked a few times letting her eyes adjust further.

'You'll get used to it,' Glen said, shutting the door behind them, 'The hallway is always dark and cool. Kind of hits you doesn't it? Follow me, I'll give you a whistle-stop tour as we head to your room. Ms Kane is very particular about some rooms in the house, one of which is on our left here.'

Glen opened the door, flooding the hallway with light and warmth. She poked her head inside before inviting Charley to do the same. The decor was much the same as the hallway, although Charley realised now that the pictures and mirrors were probably the same tarnished brass, and not the dark mahogany she had first thought. Long heavy green curtains hung from the bay window and the green three-piece suite sat around the edges of the room. The fabric looked plush, almost velour. Charley had the urge to stroke an arm to find out if it were as soft as it looked. A small rug and a poof had just enough room to sit in front of the mahogany fireplace.

'This is the drawing room.' Glen said, 'I suppose it's a living room really, but it's one Ms Kane reserves for guests. This room is always pristine. Ms Kane doesn't like people in here unless she is entertaining, or the cleaner is in, and believe me she seems to know if anything has been moved to within a fraction of an inch, so touch *nothing.*'

Charley nod her head as her eyes fell on the large chandelier that hung from the ceiling. Gold, with at least fifteen bulbs. This house screamed opulence, but not modern opulence, this was older. More like the heavy fabrics, greens, and golds of the eighties. Charley remembered her mother once saying Aunt Elizabeth had been a millionaire before her husband died twenty years ago, and this house was like a time warp. It would have been the height of money and fashion back in those days, but since then it seemed she had updated nothing. The house standing still in time.

A gentle hand on her shoulder pulled Charley away. Glen shut the door and crossed to the one opposite, at the bottom of the stairs, opening it with a small key that she pulled from her tunic pocket.

'This is the other room that Ms Kane doesn't like people inside. There are only two keys, Ms Kane has one, I have the other. When I leave you will get this one, purely to let the cleaner inside once every two weeks. No one is to enter it otherwise. It is strictly off limits.'

Charley nodded again as she peered inside. This room was smaller, although it still housed a heavily curtained window, and a large mahogany desk. Behind the desk sat a high-backed captain's chair which appeared to be red leather. Dark bookshelves lined the walls behind and ran down each wall to the window and door.

'This was Mr Kane's study.' Glen said, 'He did a lot of his work from here when he was alive, and, apparently, it is exactly as he left it. Ms Kane managed a lot of the financial affairs from here until very recently, and although she can't do much now, she will occasionally come into here to 'work' if she is having certain hallucinations. What she does in here is anyone's guess, but as long as she doesn't hurt herself, you'd be best leaving her to it until it passes. Monitor her from a distance. Some hallucinations are quite violent. Speaking, or touching her through them only seems to exacerbate the situation. Hopefully, there won't be too many of those when I'm not around to help.'

Time seemed to stop and Charley felt her stomach turn over.

Did I hear that right? Violent hallucinations?

She pulled her head back out of the small room allowing Glen to lock the door and pocket the key again.

'I thought dementia meant losing her memory,' she said, 'why would she have hallucinations?'

'Dementia is a lot of things.' Glen said with a smile, 'It all depends which type as to which symptoms arise. Hallucinations and confusion are a big factor of most, but especially the type Ms Kane has.'

The floor seemed to shift under Charley's feet.

'What type does she have?'

Glen stared at Charley, bright smile slipping from her face.

'Have you been told nothing at all about the environment or disease you will be living alongside?'

Charley shrugged apologetically as her heart thumped. A lump of cold lead seemed to sit her stomach, if only she had been less ignorant of the disease, she would have sought information beforehand. As it happened, she had just thought dementia was, well... dementia.

Glen blew out a breath and placed a hand to her brow, raising her eyebrows.

'Right. Well, it will take some time to fill you in, and no doubt you will have questions. Come on, we'll go up to your room, I'll let you sort out your stuff, and we'll meet in the kitchen when you're ready.' She pointed at the door down the hall, opposite the front door, before starting up the stairs. 'Ms Kane is taking a nap in her room right now, so let's keep the noise down as we go up.'

Noise won't be a problem, Charley thought as she took the stairs after Glen. The carpet was plush and springy underfoot and they took the stairs in near silence, even with the suitcases in tow. Either the carpet wasn't as old as the rest of the décor seemed to be, or it had been well looked after. Then again, Charley remembered, Aunt Elizabeth had never had children to run up and down them (unless you counted the ones that lived in the cellar- and Charley really didn't want to count those).

Upstairs was more of the same plush darkness. There were three spare rooms up here alongside the bathroom which was roomy and housed both bath with a shower and separate shower – for who knew what reason. One of the back rooms Glen was using herself until she had to vacate next week. The other back room was used for the storage of a single bed and yet more dark furniture. The front room, above the drawing room, belonged to Aunt Elizabeth. Charley would like to have met her, but after a quick check inside Glen said she was still sleeping. She quietly shut the door again and motioned to the door opposite which sat above the study.

Glen nodded at Charley to go in and she pushed the door. The lowering sun was making its way into the room, which was surprising bright and airy, despite the window being a lot smaller than the ones downstairs. The room looked comfortable; there was what appeared to be a soft double bed, a double wardrobe, two sets of drawers and a dressing table which Glen told her to use as her own. She dragged the suitcase she had brought upstairs into Charley's room.

'Make yourself at home. I'll have the tea on,' she said, as she disappeared to descend the stairs.

Charley didn't intend to hang around. She wanted to know more. The situation her family had thrown her into both intriguing and scaring the hell out of her in equal measure.

She took a moment to wheel the suitcases neatly into the corner, as a cool breeze pulled her gaze to the open window. There was a long window seat against the wall underneath. She crossed to it, resting a knee on the plush covering and leaning her arms on the windowsill. She basked in the lowering sun, taking in the view.

From here she could see all the main points she had spotted from the car. The harbour, the island and ruin, beach, and the village below. She felt a tingle of excitement as a closer inspection of the window revealed a double-hung sash which meant she could open the top or the bottom to leave a wide opening good for taking photographs. At night she may just be able to stand the tripod on the deep windowsill too.

With a satisfied grin she closed her eyes and let the breeze lift her hair from her face as she thought of the sunsets she would photograph along with the back-lit island ruin and harbour.

The clink of crockery from downstairs brought her back into the room and she decided unpacking could wait, she was desperate to know more about her Aunt and it sounded like tea was almost ready.

Chapter Three

Down in the large kitchen Glen filled Charley in on the major points of her Aunts illness which had a strange name; Dementia with Lewy Bodies. Lewy bodies, named after the Doctor who discovered them, were tiny deposits of protein in the nerve cells of the brain. Symptoms included, not only memory loss, as Charley had thought, but a long list of complications. Speech problems, sleep disturbance, trouble with movement, depression, confusion, and hallucinations.

Charley was horrified, and more than a little overwhelmed as Glen explained the day-to-day life of her Aunt. There were no patterns to the symptoms and complications Elizabeth experienced. One moment she could move around with her walking stick, play cards, and hold a coherent conversation. The next she could be confused and violent, with slurred speech, unsteady on her feet, or lost in hallucination.

Glen went on to describe that during some hallucinations Elizabeth would seem to play a part, like an actress. She would be completely inside the scene that played in her head, seeing it as though she were wearing a virtual reality set, which is why it could be dangerous to intervene. During others there would simply be a person, animal, or object, in the room with them, she may become upset, but she would still know exactly where she was and what she was doing.

'So, I guess the hallucinations where she knows what is going on are a little easier to deal with?' Charley asked, her hopes raising that some of this may be straightforward.

Glen shook her head. Lips pursed, and Charley's stomach flipped over.

'I'm afraid not, each episode has to be assessed as they come. No hallucination is fun to watch or have to deal with, most of them leave Ms Kane genuinely distressed or frightened. Some days are good, and some are bad,' she said, 'Each day requires a fresh approach, and fresh observation of her behaviour. No two days are ever the same.'

As Glen talked on, the sick, weighted feeling in Charley's stomach was slowly turning into a flicker of anger at the situation her family had happily thrown her in to. If Francesca had been any sort of sister to Elizabeth, or a mother to her, she would never have allowed Charley to be here at all. At least not without knowing the full extent of what she was walking in to.

Charley closed her eyes and rubbed the space between them.

Aunt Elizabeth needed a nurse, not a niece. Francesca should have dipped into her savings and damn well paid for one. She had spent the last few years gloating that she was now the one with the money, making a show that Elizabeth had squandered her millions, but it was obvious the last of Elizabeth's money had gone on the private care she so obviously needed.

Shame sent heat to Charley's neck and face.

Not only at her mother's ignorance and complete lack of care for her only family, but at Evelyn and Kate's behaviour too. The self-absorbed, queens of the self-righteous, who were quite happy to leave a dying relative up here alone with no consideration of the very real situation.

Out of sight, out of mind.

Aware of Glen still talking, Charley opened her eyes and swallowed hard, emotion swirling in her chest. A firm resolution settled in her heart as Glen went over Elizabeth's medication. Aunt Elizabeth needed help, and Charley promised herself that she would do the best she could.

This family sucks, Aunt Elizabeth, you can't count on them, but I'll do what I can to make it easier for you. I promise.

Tears welled, encompassing the shame, embarrassment, and fear that threatened to consume her. She took a deep breath forcing them back down, and sniffed, blinking as her vision swam. Through the blur small pictures stuck onto the front of each cupboard door swam in and out of focus. She frowned, glad of the distraction from the emotion.

Then Glen put a hand over hers, and Charley looked back into kind deep brown eyes.

'It's a lot, I know it, and I'm a nurse. But listen, I will be around for a few hours over the middle of each day after I leave on Monday. I'll help you as much as I possibly can before I go, and I'm trying to get my boss to agree to a couple of full days, but I'm not very hopeful without payment. If I help you try to put together a case through official channels, maybe we can wing it together.'

Charley could only nod, Glen's kindness only making her feel like crying more. Why was that always the case?

'That would be great, thank you.' She managed without breaking the tear dam, 'I'm not entirely sure what my family were thinking, sending me up here alone.'

Glen smiled, big and warm.

'Probably the same as you. It's just dementia.'

Charley rolled her eyes and blew out a breath with a nod.

'I feel so stupid.' she said as a single tear finally let go, rolling down her cheek. She swiped it away with her hand.

'Don't. It's one of those things, unless you're in contact with it, you can never fully know any degenerative disease.'

Charley swiped at a second tear, glad of Glen's kind words, but being in an unfamiliar place, with unfamiliar people and now an unfamiliar disease, made her want to curl up into a ball and sob. Hard.

How in the hell am I supposed to manage all of this?
She pulled in a breath, trying to keep calm, pushing down the urge scream, run to the car and drive all the way back to Harrogate without another word.

You can't, you just promised Aunt Elizabeth you'd help, and who knows what help she would get from the others if you refused.

She clenched her jaw, pictures on the cupboards catching her eye again. Eager to get away from the feeling of helplessness, unease, and discomfort that were now putting every nerve on edge, she motioned to them.

'What are the pictures for, Glen? Her memory?'

Glen glanced at the cupboards, following Charley's line of sight. 'Yes, that's right. You'll find them in various places around the house. On the toilet door, the study door, on certain cupboards. Ms Kane is a fiercely independent woman when she is feeling well. You get a real glimpse of the woman she was in those moments. She likes to do things for herself, and the pictures help her remember. That way she can make herself a drink, or a snack, or go to the toilet without the need for help. It's important to keep that dignity for her as long as we can.'

Charley looked to Glen as the nurse pulled in a breath and re-placed a hand over hers.

'It's also important to remember that when things go wrong, and she can't find something or do something for herself, she will get frustrated. Keep calm and encouraging, try not to be critical. It will be hard, she can get very personal and sometimes a little violent if she thinks you are mocking her.'

Charley tried to react with logic, not emotion. A tactic that hadn't gone so well in the last half hour. She forced down her fear, narrowing her eyes as she nodded.

Here was something she could manage. Her sisters always said she had to be pushed as far as the precipice of a cliff before her patience ran out, and they, themselves, were clear evidence of that.

It's okay, you can do this. Violence, hallucinations, frustration, memory loss - no problem!

She half-smiled at her own optimism, wishing she felt calmer for it.

'You won't have to bother with cooking her meals or cleaning,' Glen continued, 'There's a couple of ladies come in to do all that, Avril and Nell. And the gardener is still here too, he is here a good few hours of every day. All you have to do is look out for yourself and Ms Kane and make sure she has what she needs, but if you need help and there is no-one else around, just call me. I'll help as best I can even if I can't get up here. Okay?'

Charley gave Glen a small smile and took a sip of lukewarm tea.

'I think so. I guess I'll have to be, anyway.'

Glen leaned forward to pat Charley's hand with a smile.

'You seem switched on, Charley, I think you'll be fine. You will come to know the signs when she is changing. Say, for example, she shakes continually, a little like she has Parkinson's disease, when she is having problems with movement. On the days you notice her shaking she will probably experience speech problems too, but she is usually placid enough to use an excuse to keep her upstairs. The one thing she insists on is sleeping in her own bed but getting her up and downstairs when she is so unsteady, is nigh on impossible for one person. If you can keep her upstairs it will save your back, and a possible accident, or even a violent interlude when she needs a nap and can't get to her bed. There are other little things I'll try to alert you to over the couple of days we have together too. It's hard to remember when you've been here so long. It becomes automatic.'

Charley hoped that one day she would be as fluent in her Aunt's disease as Glen. As caring and thoughtful as she was about it, and Aunt Elizabeth's welfare and dignity too.

'It's a real shame we hadn't the money to keep you on here.' Charley said, with a sigh 'Why doesn't Aunt Elizabeth sack the cook, cleaner and gardener, surely she would have enough money to keep you on then?'

Glen sat back with a wide smile, hands to her heart.

'Oh, I'd love to stay, I've grown quite fond of Ms Kane. She's a very regal lady. Don't get me wrong, she can be bloody hard work, but the woman underneath is really quite inspiring. On her good days she can regale you with tales from her past that will leave you in awe. If nothing else she has had quite a life. But that's beside the point, these people are her friends, they're not paid staff. They do these things for her out of the goodness of their hearts. They stay and help even on the days Ms Kane is hurling abuse at them. It must be so sad to see a dear friend disappear into a disease like this, but they never moan.'

Charley finished her tea and placed the cup on the table, toying with the next question before she let it out.

'How long do you think she has left?' She said quietly, appalled that she was half wondering when she would be able to get back to her normal, comfortable life, before she had even started.

Glen sighed, smile slipping from her face.

'Well, you've heard the medical diagnosis I presume? The scans show her episodes are getting worse, and her brain is becoming greatly affected. The tests proved that her function has debilitated from the last hospital visit too. They think a month to six weeks, eight at the most.'

Glen paused looking past Charley with a small frown, forefinger and thumb pulling at her bottom lip. Charley watched her, a sinking feeling pulling at her stomach.

'Okay. but what do you think, Glen?'

Glen shook her head a little and smiled taking her hand away from her mouth, recovering her poise.

'Well, that doesn't matter does it. I'm not a doctor, I just help with symptoms and medication.'

'I'd still like to know your thoughts.'

Glen looked at Charley, eye to eye. Charley held her gaze, intuitively knowing what was to come, and yet dreading it all the same.

'Well, there's no time limit with dementia, and to be honest over the seven months I've been here she's not seemed to get any worse. On her good days she seems perfectly well. Her bad days haven't been bad enough to constitute even one hospital visit yet. Her symptoms are pretty consistent, they don't seem to be much worse than they were when I arrived. Even so, scans and tests rarely lie. Maybe she handles it well internally. I suppose you can never tell. I've seen far worse than Ms Kane, I wouldn't have been putting a time on her life at this point, but there you go.'

Glen shrugged and pursed her lips.

'Have you seen the test results yourself?'

'No, she's got private healthcare. Her friend Nell, the lady who cooks, takes her to her appointments. I'm just hired privately though an agency to care for her, but I have worked in the NHS on and off for the last twenty-two years. I've tried to dig around for her file unofficially, through people I know, but so far nothing has come up. I'm not sure what hospital is doing the work for her, I've never been told, but with private care it could just be a clinic. Anyway, I'll keep digging. I'd love to know what they've found to make them so sure she won't be here long because I just don't feel it's so.'

Charley frowned, a stab of worry running through her. On one hand, it was nice to know that a nurse thought Elizabeth had longer left than they thought. On the other, it meant she may be here a lot longer than expected in a situation she really didn't think she was capable of handling. What if she was stuck here for the next two years looking after a deteriorating old lady? And not only that, but badly to boot.

Charley's thoughts returned to Francesca's stash of money and a steely resolve fell over her. There was no choice. She would have to make a call to her mother later and persuade her to hire Glen, or another nurse, for at least a while longer. Especially now that Charley knew the situation better.

* * * * *

Three hours later Elizabeth still wasn't awake. The cook, Nell, had been and gone. She made a soup with a crusty roll, and an elderberry pie for Elizabeth's tea if she woke. Charley had found her easygoing and friendly, and the three of them had chatted and laughed together as Nell worked. Nell had left just before 6pm and a couple of hours later, after trying to stifle a yawn, Glen had told Charley to go up to her room and get some rest. Elizabeth may or may not get up tonight, it would be better to meet her fresh tomorrow morning.

In truth, Charley was glad of the reprieve. She was utterly shattered, not only from the earlier drive, but from being in a different location, and from discovering what lay ahead with her Aunt. The unknown had a habit of draining energy.

Upstairs, she flopped onto the bed, face down, relishing the clean smell of the sheets, and the soft mattress which cradled her body protectively. She took a few deep breaths inhaling the fresh scent, and then pulled her phone out of her pocket, flipping over onto her back as she pressed the screen.

Six missed calls and sixteen messages, all from Evelyn. She raised her eyebrows and pushed out a breath.

Christ, this is bordering on stalking.

The room was growing red, along with the sky, as the sun dipped below the horizon and Charley was drawn to the window, sitting up on her elbows to see the view.

Come on Charley focus – Call mom about hiring a nurse or answer Evelyn?

Neither she decided. She would undress ready for bed, sit on the window seat with her camera, and watch that spectacular sunset instead.

She could make the calls tomorrow.

Chapter Four

Charley's eyes flew open, and she felt her heart pound behind her ribs. It was dark. Too dark, and the sense of a presence close to her was stifling. There was a not altogether unpleasant smell, like perfume that had been worn a while, it's fading scent fusing with body odour. She lay still, listening, and picked up a slight raspy breathing close to her right side. Fear covered her flesh in goosebumps, but she didn't move. She didn't want *it* to know she was awake.

As her eyes grew accustomed to the darkness, she made out a form standing at the side of the bed. It was small and slightly hunched, leaning in toward her. Charley whimpered unable to help herself and tried to edge slowly to the other side of the bed under impossibly heavy covers.

A bony hand shot out and grabbed her by the wrist stopping her from moving further. It had incredible strength, fingers pressing painfully into Charley's skin as she screamed and tried to tug herself away. The grip only got tighter as she tugged. Then, finding its way out of the clouds, moonlight lit the room exposing the white, age spotted, skin of an old lady. Charley's eyes followed the bony hand to the bony arm and finally the face of what could only be her Aunt. The witch herself, Elizabeth Kane. Her eyes were pale and wide, red lips peeled back from exposed teeth, hair wild around her head, opaque nightdress hanging around her skeletal form. Charley's heart banged in her ears and she found the scream dying on her lips as terror flooded every cell in her body.

The lady leaned forward slowly, until she was right over Charley, her face next to her own. Charley closed her eyes against the veiny blue tinged skin, she wanted to scream but had no voice; she wanted to run but the grip on her wrist held her down.

Foul breath warmed her cheek. And then her Aunt spoke with a voice brittle as dry paper.

'You're killing me, you little bitch.' She hissed.

And Charley suddenly found she could scream.

Panting and covered in sweat Charley swung bolt upright in the dark room, a sense of deja-vu creeping over her. Or was it an old lady that was creeping over her?

Light, I need light.

With the speed of a dispensed bullet she threw back the covers and jumped onto the plush carpet, diving for the switch at the side of the door, while expecting a bony hand to reach out and grab her ankle from under the bed.

Three hits and she had it. Light flooded the room.

There was no old lady, nothing was out of place, and Charley released a breath she was unaware she had been holding. She looked at her watch; 2.10am.

Shit, that was some dream. Maybe I'll leave the light on for a while.

The night was cool, and she shivered in her damp pyjamas as she wiped the sweat off her face with the back of her hand. She crossed the room to the suitcase where she had a spare pair and quickly changed sitting on the seat under the window.

Wide awake and feeling more comfortable, she turned to pull the curtain back, folding her legs underneath her as she faced the window. Aware that the light from the room would both light her silhouette and obscure her view, she pulled the heavy curtain around her back, blocking the light from the room.

The swell on the sea was still heavy and moonlight lit the rise and fall of the ocean like a heartbeat. She could just make out the ruin and harbour in the darkness and dotted below her were the streetlights of the village she had yet to visit. She turned the window lock to raise the bottom sash letting the cool breeze caress her face. The salty, seaweedy smell of the ocean filled her nostrils as she heard the roar of crashing waves and the hiss of the retreating tide. She took a breath and grinned. Even with the dream, this was so much better than being in Harrogate in her little flat.

Like a little holiday… well, a working holiday anyway.

SHATTERED

Holidays had been few and far between when she was growing up, but the ones they had managed to get to were always by the sea. It was all they needed, their mother had said, and it was the one thing she had got right in Charley's view. Holidays were times of rest for Mrs Costin. There was no exploring the area, no outings to attractions, no walks in the countryside. Just the tent, and the beach, while Francesca sat for the week reading book after book.

The girls had the run of wherever their feet would take them. As long as they were back for lunch and tea, and in by their curfew at the end of the day, there were no limits. But ultimately, they would always end up at the beach.

Evelyn and Kate were sunbathers. Any amount of sun would see them lying half dressed, catching rays, putting up windbreaks to shield off unwanted cold winds. Rue would join them with a book, but always kept covered, and sat under a small parasol if it were too warm. Evelyn, feeling responsible where their mother couldn't be bothered, tried to keep them all together, but Charley quickly tired of her sisters' small talk and bickering, and always eventually took off on her own.

The sea held no pull for any of them. It scared Rue and Evelyn, and Kate always said she had no desire to swim in mucky, salty, cold water; but it pulled Charley. It seemed to physically hold her heart. It held her in awe with both its power and its gentleness, its vastness and its depth. There were parts of the sea that were completely unknown; that had never been explored by man, many parts of it, and that enthralled her even now. The water had never scared her, and as she got older she often swam, staying out at sea, floating on her back, staring at the sky. The sea had always been a friend. It comforted her, held her up, kept her safe, and best of all kept her away from her sisters, who she could ignore all she liked way out at sea.

If it was too cold for swimming, she loved to explore the rock pools and the creatures that lived in them, the cliffs and caves, or she would take off her shoes feeling the cold tickle and pull of the sea as she paddled along the shore. On really cold days she would climb to keep warm, using the rocks to get herself as far out to sea as possible. There she would sit until the cold seeped into her bones, watching the waves crash around her, pretending that she was shipwrecked, or lost somewhere - anywhere that didn't involve Evelyn and Kate.

Rue was okay, but she didn't have any *go* about her. The times Charley had taken her along to show her the rock pools, or to climb the bigger rocks, she had just got frustrated with her sisters' slow pace and lack of enthusiasm. Charley was a loner. She knew it, accepted it, and revelled in it. Herself and her imagination were all she needed for company. She was happy alone, never lonely, always entertained.

Now, as Charley watched the sea in the darkness, her heart swelled. It was like she had her closest friend right out there calling to her. If she hadn't been in an unfamiliar house with people she didn't know, she may well have dressed and gone to sit on the shore, even at this hour. She sighed, shivering a little as the breeze cooled her.

Another time. Hopefully, there will be plenty of time.

Saying a silent goodbye, she shut and locked the window. Pulling aside the curtain, she eased her legs from under her and gently massaged her now numb calves. As she rubbed a trickle of unease settled back over her like a gentle, unseen cloak. She looked up from her legs.

She could see the whole room from here, which made her heart want to start pumping again, although there was nothing out of place. In her mind she saw the old lady lean over the bed, wild hair and long nightgown, arms outstretched. Charley swallowed a dry hitch in her throat as her heart picked up pace.

It was just a dream, get a hold of yourself.

She glanced from the door to the bed and leaned down to check under it. The space was empty. Still something nagged at her.

 What if? What if her aunt had actually been in here? The doors weren't locked, it was certainly possible. Maybe it hadn't been a dream and Elizabeth had left just before she woke? Goosebumps littered her arms, and she shivered crossing her arms over her chest and planting her hands into her armpits.

What, and a lady in her seventies still has a grip like that? And I remember it even though I was asleep? It was a dream. Your imagination runs too wild. Get back into bed. You will feel better after you've met her in person tomorrow, then your mind won't be trying to piece together what the witch of your childhood looks like. You'll know, and you'll know she isn't a witch at all.

Charley sighed and got up off the bench. Drawing the curtains, she climbed onto the bed from the bottom and crawled up it, pulling the covers over her as she climbed inside.

Well, I'm leaving the light on. And, by the way, if she looks anything like the lady from my dream when I meet her tomorrow I may just scream and run back to Harrogate. Any objections?

Her mind had run quiet. She pulled herself down onto her back, comfort and warmth surrounding her body as a deep and dreamless sleep took her under within minutes.

* * * * *

Charley awoke to noise. The birds chirping far too enthusiastically outside the window, competing for the morning attention from the someone who was shouting downstairs. She propped herself up on her elbows. The curtains were open in the centre, letting in the early morning light. The day was dawning fine and bright, the promise of another glorious spring day, although Charley knew that she would probably be too busy to go out visiting the village or the sea.

She yawned, catching movement by the window, and noticed the bottom sash raised up high, the heavy curtains ruckling gently in the breeze where they had been parted. She blinked. But she had shut it after getting up last night, hadn't she?

Had she? She sat up fully, rubbed her eyes and frowned at the gap in the curtains.

Yep shut and locked it. I remember clearly, pulled the curtains across too.

So, someone had been in and opened them both as she slept. Fabulous.

Maybe it was just Glen trying to wake her gently as it seemed her aunt was already up and causing a fuss downstairs. Not ideal, but she supposed if there was any way to be woken by a stranger, maybe it was the nicest option. Still, she felt a little violated by the intrusion, if Glen could enter the room and open a window without waking her up, what else could she have done?

39

Okay Charley, that's enough. Glen is a nurse, she's used to looking after people and going into rooms without a thought. It doesn't mean she's a thief.

No, she probably wasn't. She was also probably waiting for her. It didn't look good if she couldn't even be up before her Aunt in the morning.

Charley quickly washed and dressed in the bathroom before heading for the stairs. A yell stopped her progress halfway down, uncertain she paused to listen to raised voices from the kitchen.

'Come on Ms Kane, you can't keep refusing your food, you have to eat.'

Glens voice was kind but firm. Aunt Elizabeth's was hard and firmer. Her words pronounced, spoken with a posh lilt that all people with money seemed to acquire as their social status moved into different circles.

'I do not have to eat this. I won't. It's poison. Can't you see what they're doing to me?'

'What who are doing to you? Who are *they*?'

'Them. They'll kill me. They'll do it right under your nose, you'll be sorry.'

Charley froze, remembering the lady from her dream.

You'll kill me, you little bitch.

Her heart bumped at the coincidence, and the reference to a dream she would rather forget. Or was it possible that it hadn't been a dream after all?

Glen's voice filtered into the roar that beat behind her ears.

'Why would anyone want to kill you, Ms Kane? Please, come on you need to eat.'

There was a crash, followed by the scrape of a chair, and a yell from Glen. Charley flinched and closed her eyes, her hand shaking on the bannister, legs going to jelly.

'Ms Kane, please.' Glen said, her voice level and calm, 'There was no need for that. Sit down and calm down.'

'I want toast. I can make it, I'm not an invalid. I don't know why you insist on being here. You're in on it, aren't you?'

The sound of a brush and the scraping of pottery on tile.

'I have no idea what you're talking about.'

'The conspiracy.'

'Don't be daft.'

Charley drew in a shaky breath. More than anything, she wanted to turn tail and go back upstairs, but she had to meet her aunt at some point. She was just going to have to man up and go in. If she saw Elizabeth at her worst now, it would only get better afterward, surely. Besides Glen may need help to clean up.

Almost silently, and slower than she'd later admit, she made her way down the plush carpet to the kitchen door which stood ajar. Her nerves still jangled at not only the heated exchange, but the reference to the dream, and the thought of the lady that had leaned over the bed in the night. Reaching the door, she peered through the gap.

She had no view of her aunt, but Glen was on her hands and knees cleaning up a broken bowl of something which looked like porridge. Remnants of Aunt Elizabeth's breakfast were now clinging to various cupboards and the floor where the bowl had hit and smashed.

Oh no, poor Glen!

Charley pushed the door without further thought and crossed the kitchen. She took the black bin liner, holding it for Glen to scoop the mess into as she picked up globs of porridge with kitchen roll. The bulk of the broken bowl was set aside out of the way. When most of the mess was safely in the bag Glen smiled at Charley.

'Thank you, did you sleep well?'

'I did thanks.'

Were you in my room this morning?

Charley returned the smile, the words lingering on the tip of her tongue. Now wasn't the right time. She shook the bag and stood up, turning to look for a bin.

The old lady stood silently at her side. Charley jumped, scrabbling backwards to the table as her breath caught in her throat.

'Oh! I... well... You scared me!'

The lady she could only assume was Elizabeth didn't move, she fixed Charley with a cold gaze as she stood, tall and straight, hands resting on the ornate walking stick placed just in front of her legs. She was a good head and shoulders above Charley, and she was immaculate. There wasn't a crease in her bottle green skirt, or cream silk blouse. Her face looked younger than her seventy-four years, possibly due to the perfectly applied makeup and neat chignon in her hair. She wouldn't have looked out of place at a Hollywood award show. Fortunately, that meant she looked nothing like the shrivelled old lady in her dream, and that was good, although if looks could kill right now Charley would instantly have fallen to the ground dead.

'Who are you? Speak.'

Charley, still in awe at the sight of the elderly lady she had been so afraid of all these years, tried to speak and found her throat had gone so dry it could have been packed with sawdust. She Swallowed hard.

'I... I... '

Glen rose from the floor and took Elizabeth's elbow.

'Ms Kane, this is your niece Charley. She has come to stay for a while, remember I've been telling you?'

'Impossible. I don't have a niece of that name.' Aunt Elizabeth swung her walking stick up into the air and jabbed it toward Charley. She shrank back against the table and the rubber end stopped just short of her nose where it wobbled as her Aunt became unsteady. 'She's an impostor. Call the police at once.'

'No, no, Ms Kane. I've been telling you. This is your sister's daughter...'

Elizabeth swung toward Glen thumping the walking stick back to the ground for balance.

'I don't have a sister.'

Glen quickly moved to some folders she had placed on the countertop and began shuffling through them. Charley held her breath as her aunt turned her attention back to her, sharp hazel eyes scrutinizing every detail. Glen came out with two small photographs one of which she showed to Elizabeth. Elizabeth looked away with undisguised disdain.

'Well, yes, you mean *her*. She's not my sister, she is only family by blood, I'm not interested in any part of her, or her offspring, being anything to do with me. I remember the little brats well, let me think, who were they now? Evie, was it? Yes. Evie, Catherine and Ruth.'

Charley swallowed the lump in her throat.

'Ev... Evelyn, Kate and Rue.'

Elizabeth swung back to her fixing her with a hard gaze.

'That's right! Do you know them?'

Only too well, I'm afraid.

Charley nodded as her aunt continued.

'Yes, little brats they are. Anything that ever came from Francesca lead to no good. She's no sister of mine, I really can't be bothered to deal with the fallout of her rubbish. She's gone and good riddance.'

Glen pursed her lips, possibly thinking it would offend Charley, someone speaking of her mother in such a tone. It didn't. Most of the time she felt the same about all of them. She smiled inwardly, she had the feeling that she and Aunt Elizabeth might get on just fine. Glen pulled Elizabeth's attention back toward her.

'Yes okay, but this is Charley. She's come to keep you company. Look.'

She showed Elizabeth another photo and Charley could only surmise that this was one of her. She vaguely wondered where it had come from. Who had given it to her?

Her Aunt's perfectly arched eyebrows shot up as she looked from the photograph to Charley.

'Oh! It's Charlotte! Well, why didn't you say so?'

Charley's stomach sank. Surely her aunts surprise would soon sink to the same scathing remarks. Instead, Elizabeth took two steps toward her and placed a gentle feather-light touch under Charley's chin.

'Ah Charlotte, let me look at you. The sweet, quiet, baby. I am old and we have so much to catch up on.'

Charley felt herself reel from a blow that didn't come. She blinked in shock as her Aunt placed both hands back on the walking stick and regarded her thoughtfully.

'Do you know I'm dying?'

Charley felt her eyes widen in surprise. Could she really be so blase about the impending end? But then Elizabeth leaned forward, close to Charley and whispered, 'They're poisoning me you know. They think I'm just a stupid old lady, but I know what they're up to. I know what they're after.'

Charley opened her mouth to respond but couldn't think of a reply. Then, nodding to herself, Elizabeth took Charley by the arm and using the stick with the other hand she escorted her slowly to a chair and motioned for her to sit down.

'We have a lot to discuss.' Elizabeth turned to Glen, 'Leave us please, I would like to speak to Charlotte alone.'

Glen looked from Elizabeth to Charley and opened her mouth to protest.

'It's fine, really.' Charley said.

Glen nodded.

'Okay, well I'll be sorting some paperwork in my room. Call if you need me. A pinch of salt remember.'

Charley nodded, realising that Glen was warning her to take what Elizabeth said lightly. Unfortunately, Elizabeth got the wrong idea. She laughed; a harsh, sharp sound.

'If you think a pinch of salt will kill me, you will be sorely disappointed. A pinch of salt! Hah! We used to have three pinches with each vegetable every day when we were growing up. I am immune to salt.' She swung to Charley, pointing a manicured finger toward her face, 'But I'm warning you Charlotte, you put salt in anything I eat and I'll have you sent away before the pan can boil.'

Charley shook her head.

'That wasn't what Glen meant. Really. I don't know of anyone who would go to the lengths of trying to poison anyone with salt, that's just ridiculous.'

Her Aunt leaned forward, speaking in low tones.

'That's as may be, but these people will try anything. Anything. Are you in on it?'

Glen left the kitchen shutting the door behind her with a small click, and Charley felt a tangle of nerves swirl in her gut as she shook her head. She chewed the edge of her lip as Elizabeth regarded her silently. After what seemed like an eternity, her aunt sat straight-backed in a chair at the end of the table, placing them at a right angle to each other.

Now that they were alone, Charley found she had no idea what to say. Did she chat as though Aunt Elizabeth was a normal person? Or did the chat have to be a certain way because of the dementia, and what she would understand? Or could she understand everything? Was it just the memory issue? She chewed on a nail.

Crap, I can't remember. What am I doing here? I have no clue what to expect, or how to deal with it. What I'm supposed to do? How I'm supposed to act. Do I correct her, or humour her? At least she seems to be okay with me being here.

At the sound of Glen's movements upstairs, Elizabeth turned her attention from the door and back to Charley. Charley's stomach dropped through the floor at the iciness in her expression as she lifted her chin, eyes cold and hard.

'Right, lets not priss around pretending.' She hissed. 'Out with it. If you're not here to finish me off, what are you doing here, girl?'

Charley felt herself physically reeling for the second time in the space of ten minutes, the complete flip of her Aunt's mood catching her off guard.

'I... I don't understand...'

'Don't play coy with me. You don't turn up on my doorstep after all these years for no reason, I know you're after something, and I know it's for your mother. What does she want?'

'No, nothing. I... I came to look after you that's all... We heard-'

Elizabeth snorted down her nose loudly and thumped the end of her stick onto the floor with a muffled thud making Charley jump.

'Look after me?' She spat, 'That is ridiculous. I may walk with a stick but I'm the most able-bodied woman of years I know. I am respected and revered here in Fortwind Bay. Why would you suddenly think I need looking after when the last time you darkened my door you were just a small child?' Elizabeth narrowed her eyes and then they widened with recognition. 'Ah, now I get it. Of course. Francesca wants her fair share of the loot when I keel over, eh? Well you're in for a shock because there's none. It's all gone. Everything. So you can take your pert little backside back to the rock you crawled from under and tell that despicable human being you call your mother exactly what the situation is. She will not get her mucky little fingers on anything of mine. It isn't my fault she couldn't make anything of herself. Always wanting what everyone else has got. Jealousy is an ugly trait, and she is full of it.'

The breath felt sucked from Charley's lungs and she felt her mouth hanging open. She attempted to shut it, and for a second she understood where Glen was coming from. For a woman who was supposed to be on her deathbed Elizabeth was acting a lot like a very normal, very capable woman. A woman who seemed much younger than her years.

'You have nothing to say?'

Charley swallowed thickly.

'It… it's not true, I...'

Her voice sounded meek and small in the large kitchen and her Aunt shook her head, cutting her off as she rose from the chair.

'I would say it was nice to see you, Charlotte, but under the circumstances...'

Elizabeth huffed a sigh, both hands placed elegantly on her stick. Charley sat not knowing what to say, while also realising the irony that she hadn't got a word in yet.

Touché, Aunt Elizabeth, Tou-flipping-che.

'Well,' She continued, 'Now that we're clear I expect you out of my house by midday at the latest. I won't have you vultures trying to take my dignity on top of my life. Out. Do you understand?'

'I do.'

Christ, Charley, that's the best you can manage? You're not taking wedding vows. You're supposed to be looking after this woman, not breaking down at the first hurdle, the others will be furious.

Charley rose from the table, hands shaking and heart thumping, she met her Aunt's clear hazel eyes with her own. Charley recognized the steely stubbornness, and tilt of the chin that she was often capable of herself, but this was a gaze she instinctively knew she wouldn't win against. In front of her was a woman used to getting exactly what she wanted. Charley dipped her head, nodding lightly, and left the kitchen to go to her room and pack. There was no other choice.

As she climbed the stairs, she heard the faint ping of her phone from where it lay on the bed. She rolled her eyes.

Fabulous, the only thing that could make this morning any worse is Evelyn, and there she goes, bang on cue.

Chapter Five

Elizabeth Kane stood by the kitchen table thinking that it had been a good many years since she had been caught so off guard. To come face to face with Charlotte was both wonderful and disarming. To have seen any one of Francesca's girls again would have been a pleasure she could only have hoped for, but under these circumstances it was obvious that something was amiss.

Why now? It was a huge coincidence that just as she suspected foul play, Charlotte should turn up on her doorstep. Had Francesca done this on purpose? Was the girl in on the whole conspiracy? It didn't bare thinking about, and yet, Elizabeth had to think of it. She thought her life quite possibly depended upon it.

She knew she had been hard on Charlotte, saw how upset she had been, but it was for her own good. She must be removed from the picture. If she was in on it, then to be sent away was for the best for Elizabeth. If she wasn't, then she was better off out of the fray. It was a shame, but necessary.

Leaning her right hand onto her walking stick she made her way to the French doors and gazed out across the trimmed lawn and blooming spring colour. Axl was doing a good job out there, as he always did. They all did. Nell, Avril, Axl, it was just a shame that none of them could be trusted any more.

Her hand shook a little on the stick, the remnants of yesterday's episode, which still had to be recorded. Elizabeth had intended to go into the study this morning when she had awoke feeling fine, but between Glen and Charlotte they had interrupted her plans, resulting in them catching the tail end of her poor temper. It was unfortunate, but it was done now. She looked back out to the garden, feeling her anger melt away as daffodils, irises, and snapdragons blew gently in the breeze.

In the silence there was a low click, followed by a prolonged creak from the corner of the room. Elizabeth turned to see the cellar door swing partially open. She could just see the top of the stone steps leading down as a cool breeze found its way up into the kitchen. She turned toward it, placing both hands on her stick as she watched the door which was now still.

These days it took some time to determine whether she was hallucinating, but today she felt none of the other symptoms that usually preceded and accompanied an attack. Indeed, this morning she felt more awake and aware than she had in the last three days. There was also the fact that the cellar door seemed to be doing this a lot when she was alone.

She cocked her head, considering the door as Glen's disembodied voice called from upstairs.

'Ms Kane? Are you alright down there?'

'I'm absolutely fine, why wouldn't I be?' Elizabeth said without taking her eyes from the door.

'Okay, I'm just seeing to Charley, she's a little upset, and then I'll be right with you.' Glen was now leaning over the bannister about halfway down the stairs. Elizabeth glanced through the open hall door, pushing down a small stab of guilt.

'No need to rush, I'll be in the study working.' she said.

Glen hesitated, and Elizabeth smiled. She always worried about the study as Elizabeth liked to lock herself in. In the end it was the reason she had relented and given her the spare key, with the proviso that she wasn't to enter unless there was an indisputable reason that she believed that something was wrong, or to let Avril inside to clean.

'Well, all right, give me a shout if you need anything.' Glen's head disappeared back over the bannister.

Cellar forgotten, Elizabeth turned back to the garden, to the sway and dance of the flowers. What she would really like to have done this morning was take tea, and a scone out onto the patio and feel the sun on her skin. It had been a long, harsh winter, dark, wet and gloomy, but now the sun was finally starting to show up again. It was a ray of hope that everything would work out. That everything would be all right.

SHATTERED

Is Charlotte's arrival a sign of hope or doom?

She hoped it was the former, but either way she would leave before there was any consequence from her appearance.

The slow creak was back and Elizabeth sighed. She turned to see the cellar door now swinging wide to bump gently against the kitchen wall. She eyed it before making her way to the entrance where a cool breeze lifted goosebumps under the sleeves of her blouse. There was just one tiny window down in the cellar and peering down the steep steps Elizabeth could just make out a few lonely bottles on the shelf and a sprig of something still hanging from the roof. An earthy, herby smell reached her nostrils, and a stab of nostalgia ran through her gut. She pushed it down firmly with a shake of her head.

'Well, I don't know what you want me to do about that.' she said into the murky light, 'I keep telling you I can't get down there any longer with my stick. You'll just have to keep swinging open until hell freezes over, I'm not what I used to be.'

She shut the door firmly and went to the study to write.

Chapter Six

Two hours later Charley sat on the blackened rock, feeling the barnacles dig into her legs and hands, watching the sea swirl and crash around her. Each time a large wave crashed against her little rock jetty she closed her eyes as the spray cleansed her face and wet her clothes.

The blustery wind and beating sun dried the salt onto her face almost immediately, making her skin feel tight and gritty. She felt herself relaxing, growing calmer with each crash of the surrounding ocean.

She had made her decision. She couldn't go home. Here was better than home, even with her disastrous welcome. And with the sea on her doorstep she could handle the worst of her aunt with more patience and tolerance than she could handle dealing with her family in Harrogate.

I suppose if I go home now there may even be bloodshed.

She rest back on her hands, turning her face into the sun thinking of the messages that had been on her phone when she had got up to her room, and the response after she had informed Evelyn of recent developments.

Evelyn's messages had been mostly sarcastic enquiry as Charley hadn't been in touch since she had arrived yesterday. But as Charley had recounted the exchange with their aunt and told her she would return to Harrogate this afternoon, Evelyn had been on the phone immediately.

Charley had answered reluctantly, listening as Evelyn informed her - with a calmness that told Charley she was actually furious - just how selfish she was to leave. How pitifully weak to break after one conversation, how she had to bury the ridiculous childhood fear, how hurt they were that she had let them all down. Her dirtiest card was how their mother, who was already breaking her heart over her sister's condition, would now have to find some money for care, or come up to look after Elizabeth herself. Which was the smelliest kind of bullshit.

Charley had tried to fight her corner, but in true 'holier than thou' Evelyn style, she had continued to talk calmly over the top of everything Charley had tried to say. In the end, it was Charley who had broken down, shaking, and crying, more from frustration and anger than anything Evelyn said. It was even more frustrating that Evelyn had thought Charley was crying because she knew what she had said was right.

When the condescending tones of her eldest sister made her want to throw the phone up the wall, she had finally ended the call. Right in the middle of Evelyn's speech about handling Elizabeth with kid gloves and treating her like a naughty child.

Evelyn knew shit about Elizabeth, or her condition.

What had made the whole phone call so much worse was that Kate and her mother had been in the background, ranting and raving as much as Evelyn. There was no-one, not one of them that was on her side, or willing to believe that Aunt Elizabeth could be that domineering and intimidating when she was on her deathbed.

Glen had knocked softly on the bedroom door after hearing Charley's sobs, and Charley had found a caring and patient listener in the nurse. She spilled everything she was feeling, from her conversation with Elizabeth, to the conversation with her family that had brought her to Fortwind house, and finally the conversation that she had just had with Evelyn. She rarely had someone so willing to listen to what she had to say that hadn't been able to stop. In fact, she had cried her way embarrassingly through all of it.

Glen wasn't bothered, she had simply listened, adding 'um' and 'ah's' at the right moments, while handing out tissue after tissue. She had been much more consoling than her family, and at that moment Charley felt Glen was more of a mother than her own had ever been. Glen explained that Elizabeth would probably be completely different next time Charley saw her, and not to take what she said to heart.

'I told you she could get personal, and that's why I said to take it with a pinch of salt. In those situations it is best to walk away as you did, she will usually be different again when you've collected yourself and gone back to her. You've seen now when she gets nasty, it rarely gets any worse for your pride than it did this morning. It's a shame she jabbed at you so soon, but really, at least you've had a taste. Now you just need to learn to put what she says aside. It's the illness, not the lady.'

By the time Glen had finished she had convinced Charley to stay, without directly saying anything to stop her from going. Charley had felt that the choice was her own, and that Glen would have respected any decision she made. When the tears had dried, she told Charley to take herself off into the village for a few hours.

'Get out, take time, and see how you feel. Come back when you're ready and we'll take your decision from there.'

At that point Charley had already known she would stay, but the break was certainly welcome. Tired and emotionally battered, she felt like she had been here for weeks already, and she already knew the perfect antidote for her mood. She had driven down to the village and parked in the small harbour car park. There was no other place that was better for her to think things through than the sea. She had walked from the harbour side of the beach right around the bay to the rocks. She climbed, welcoming the exertion, and found herself somewhere to sit, as close to the water as she could get without being washed out to sea.

Now, another wave crashed around her, wetting her trainers as the water rose. She pulled her legs higher up the rock scooting back a little and turning her face back up to the sun high above her.

Tide is coming in, I'll have to move soon. Just give me a little longer here though.

She was fully aware of how fast a tide could move if you turned your back on it. She had been caught out more than once, and it was a good job she was a strong swimmer, because her sisters had done nothing to help but shout angry insults from the shore, as if their harsh words had been ropes to pull her in.

Her eyes were still closed when she heard the voice.

'It's okay, see Ted? We can climb away from the witch. Engage super sticky shoes.'

Charley opened her eyes turning toward the sound. There was a slurping that ended with a smacking of lips which she supposed was the youngster's super sticky shoes engaging.

She could just make out the blonde head of a small girl as she climbed one handed over the steep rocks. In her other hand she held a small bear who Charley supposed was Ted. Charley frowned and stood to see her better.

The child was a little further out and obviously oblivious to the incoming tide. Shielding her eyes with her hand, Charley scoured the bay for the adult with her, but she could see no one.

The little girl was now trying to scale a large wet rock, and that was all it took to set Charley into motion. A wet rock was one that a wave had very recently covered. In this choppy and unpredictable water, the girl would be swept out to sea and drowned in an instant.

'Hey!' she called, but the girl didn't seem to hear through her own chatter.

Charley started across the rocks toward the water. She moved quickly, sure-footed on the barnacle-encrusted surface, rubber-soled converse, and all the years of climbing and exploring rock pools, giving her confidence. The young girl was now on top of the wet rock and turning toward the flattest rock ahead of her, which happened to be just that little further out to sea.

'Hey,' Charley called again. Her heart started to pound as she noticed a particularly large swell out on the ocean that was headed for shore, and the rocks. The little girl turned toward Charley. She had heard, thank god, but now she had her back to the sea.

'Come here, honey, the waves will sweep you off the rocks out there.' Charley cupped her hand and motioned for the girl to come toward her, but the girl just bowed her head and tucked her chin into her chest. She brought the bear up into a hug as she eyed Charley, who continued to move nearer.

Shit, this is not the time to be coy.

The swell was travelling quickly toward them now and Charley feared for herself and the small child. She eyed the gap between the rock she was now on, and the one the girl was standing on. Between them was only around two feet but the height difference would make the jump awkward. There was also seaweed where she would need to land. The swell rolled closer and Charley realised that there was no choice. Moving quickly, she took a stride and jumped.

Her feet hit the seaweed which slid underfoot. Her arms outstretched for balance, she managed to stay on her feet and lunge forward to grab the girl's arm, as the swell hit the rock and broke around them. The girl screamed, but Charley couldn't do anything for her as the wave washed over them.

It was all slow motion. One moment it felt like the heavens had opened, dumping a flood of heavy rain down onto them and then water was rising up her thighs pushing her backwards. The larger rock behind slammed into her back knocking the wind from her lungs. She was hyper aware that she still had a grip on the small girl but that she had no visual of her, her eyes shut against the water's salty sting. The girl screamed again, her voice sounding far away and muffled, and then the wave retreated, pulling Charley back out toward the sea. She tried to grip the rock behind with one hand as the muscles in her left arm strained to hold on to the girl, the force of the sea trying to rip her away from her grasp.

And then as quickly as it had appeared, it was gone. The wave retreated and the pressure and weight of the water left her body. Wiping water from her eyes she looked for the girl and saw her lying on her side on the rock. Her eyes were wide with shock and her face crumpled as she started to cry. Relief flooded through Charley, but she knew they were far from danger.

Her legs shook as she moved to the girl and feeling like she was picking up an entire football team, she pulled her up into her arms as the next wave crashed at the rock. Charley hadn't been watching the swell on this one and she knew if it was anything like the last one it would drag them both back into the water. She planted her feet, holding tight to the crying child and tried to keep still against the spray. Mercifully, this one was smaller, only covering her feet, and she moved quickly to the higher rock behind, pushing the girl up as much as she could. The girl climbed, and after waiting for the next wave to pass, Charley followed, using the barnacle-encrusted edge as a foothold.

Up on the higher rock, with only spray to wet them Charley flopped onto her back and closed her eyes, panting heavily. Her lungs burned, and her limbs were so fatigued she felt like she had run a marathon. Her heart thumped wildly in her ears.

When she could finally catch a breath, she opened her eyes and saw the small girl sat next to her eyeing her warily, legs tucked up and encircled protectively by her arms. Miraculously she was still holding the small bear.

Charley saw a small gash in the girl's arm and wondered how much more damage had been done. She was also soaked from head to foot. They both were. Charley tried to smile as she pulled herself up. The girl pulled her legs in tighter.

'Are you okay, sweetie?'

The girl nodded and continued to stare.

'Good. I think we may just be the luckiest people on earth right now. What's your name?'

The girl seemed to squirm before answering in a near whisper.

'Belle... I'm not s'posed to talk to strangers.'

The girl dropped her eyes to the rock.

'Well, that's good advice, Belle. I'm Charley, it's nice to meet you.'

Charley held out a hand which shook uncontrollably between them. Belle eyed it and crossed her arms tighter.

'It's okay, sweetie, I just want to make sure you're safe. You shouldn't be on the rocks. Are you here alone? I don't want to go and leave you out here.'

Belle shook her head.

'My dad.'

'You're with your dad?'

Then where the hell is he? Maybe he should be the one pulling you out of the path of dangerous waves.

'He's on the beach. I ran away.'

'Oh, why would you run away from your dad?'

56

'I was playing. We were running from the witch, not daddy.'

Charley nodded, she guessed Belle was around five from the way her nieces and nephews had been at that age.

'Well, you shouldn't stray quite so far from your dad, honey, and especially not up onto the rocks. They can be dangerous especially when the tide is coming in. When the sea comes in- '

'I know, the water eats up all the beach fast so I can't play where I was before.'

Charley nodded. Maybe her dad wasn't quite as neglectful as she had first thought. He had taught her something of the dangers of the sea.

'That's right, and the sea will eat up these rocks too. It's safer to play on the beach where you can get away from the water quickly if you need to.'

'But I like the rocks, that's where we hide from the witch. I like the pools too, the water has funny creatures in. I like crabs, have you seen a crab?'

'I have. I like crabs and the rock pools too, and that's fine, but not on your own, Belle.'

A large wave crashed below them sending up a barrage of fresh spray and Charley glanced down to see the rock below now completely covered.

'Come on, we need to get off these rocks before the sea eats *us* up. Lets go find your dad, he will be worried about you.'

Belle nodded as she got to her feet. Charley got up too, clothes hanging coolly against her skin in the breeze.

'Who will be worried about you?'

Charley turned to Belle who was looking up at her.

'Me? Why would anyone worry about me?'

'You're up here all alone.'

Charley smiled.

'I am, but I'm bigger. I'm okay up here alone, I watch for the water to keep myself safe. Ready?'

Belle nodded and dropped quiet. Charley started over the rocks, surprised to feel Belle reach for her hand as they made their way carefully back to the sand.

At the foot of the rocks Belle shouted.

'Look, there's my dad!'

In the distance a dark-haired man was shouting and waving. As Belle waved back he began to run across the sand toward them.

Charley felt as if someone had removed a weight from her shoulders. She sat on a low rock, feet on the white sand.

'Let's wait here Belle. My legs are like jelly.'

Belle sat beside her pushing at a small piece of dried black seaweed with her wet shoe. They sat in silence for a while as Belle's father came closer and then Belle turned to Charley.

What were you doing up on the rocks, Charley?'

Charley huffed an ironic laugh.

'Same as you Belle, hiding from the witch.'

'Really?'

'Really.'

'It's a good place to hide.'

'One of the best for sure.'

Belle laughed delighted before running to meet her dad who dropped to his knees and scooped her in a big hug covering her little face with kisses.

Chapter Seven

Axl parked the black Range Rover beside the bins of Fortwind House. He rubbed at his tired eyes and ran a hand through his thick dark hair, letting it travel down to a beard of almost the same thickness and just as dark. He rubbed at his chin before hauling his large body out of the driver's seat.

Shutting the door, he stood looking at the driveway with a deep frown. Something wasn't right, but he couldn't put his finger on what it was. He waited, listening, drawing his bushy eyebrows together, but there was nothing out of the ordinary.

Raising them back up in resignation, he walked to the back of the car and opened the boot. He leaned in to retrieve a couple of potted plants, a bag full of slug pellets, bug spray and rat poison. He set them down beside the car and reached back in for the wire mesh that would protect some of the vegetables from birds and bigger predators. He leaned the mesh against a bin, turned to shut the boot, and that was when he saw it. The something that wasn't right.

There were tyre tracks in the dirt by the bins.

Tyre tracks that weren't his, these were too fresh, too small. His eyebrows drew back together as his eyes narrowed. No one had been up here in a car for the last several months, ever since the nurse had been drafted to live in. Both Nell and Avril lived just at the bottom of the hill, they walked up daily, and in the last year since Elizabeth had been in decline not a soul had visited that he hadn't known about.

No-one.

So who was this?

He stared at the tracks, mind whirring.

Was there something she was having checked in the house? Boiler service? Gas meter read? Was it a hospital day? On those days Nell would drive up to take her, but he was certain that there were no hospital appointments due yet.

There wasn't much Axl didn't know about Elizabeth's schedule, he made sure of it, but his short term memory wasn't what it used to be, and he was coming up with nothing that explained this right now. He wiped a hand across his sweaty brow and unzipped his padded coat.

Well, he would find out soon enough.

With a quick sniff up his nose he picked up his things and headed for the wooden back gate, set into the wall of the surrounding garden, just in front of the Land Rover. He unlocked the gate with the large cast iron key from underneath a ceramic pot. It was one of the latest in a long line of decisions that Elizabeth had made that showed just how much her mind was in decline.

Elizabeth was a strong woman, worldly, and not easily intimidated. Axl had never known her to have made a decision that wasn't wise or fully informed, and when her mind was made up, it was set firm. The decision to keep the key under a flowerpot by the door where every Tom, Dick and Harry kept their spare key, was just poor judgement. Especially when the back of her house was so secluded, but in true Elizabeth form she wouldn't be swayed. Axl was beyond trying to change her mind, the arguments were pointless.

As a frustrated last-ditch attempt to keep her safe he had taken the key home with him one evening not long after her decision, fearing that Elizabeth was vulnerable with such easy access to a secluded position, but she had known. Oh god had she known. She had torn a strip off him when he had arrived the next day. Accused him of stealing. He had restrained himself, using all of his self-control not to retaliate as she had chastised him like a schoolboy, and threatened to involve the police if he tried anything like it again.

It had taken all of his willpower not to throw the key at her, tell her to stuff her garden, and that she was a nasty old bitch. But this wasn't the woman he had known, and she wouldn't be around for much longer, so he had forced himself to apologise. It still grated when he thought about the incident, but it wasn't worth arguing about.

On the other side of the gate he put the items down and looked around the garden, immediately feeling his mood and suspicions lift.

Gardening was his passion, his escape. His salvation from a life spent behind a desk, or at the mercy of a woman who was happy to take him for all he was worth and give nothing back, on a daily basis. There was nothing like gardening for quieting the mind and giving instant gratification.

The central patch in front of him was a small ornamental garden with a small fountain bird bath. The grass was short, and edged neatly, small, clipped trees and spring blooms. Around the edges of this centrepiece were many varieties of rose, and beyond them to the far walls of the garden were larger ash, rowan and oak trees and mature rhododendron, elderberry, choisia and belladonna bushes, all of which shielded the garden from the worst of the coastal weather. Beyond the picture-perfect garden lay the allotment, with large greenhouse and a small orchard from where most of Elizabeth's daily fruit and vegetable intake came. Everything was checked, watered, weeded, sown, picked, pulled, hung and frozen daily. He took his time, there wasn't much to go home for.

Axl took a breath, filling his lungs with the scent of spring flowers, and gave a satisfied nod as he scanned his eyes over the large area. From here the garden sloped gently downhill, and he was just able to see the whole area from wall to wall. It was beautiful, colourful even at this time of year, and stood proud in the uncharacteristic heat of the spring sun.

Leaving the things he had brought on the ground, he walked to the French doors at the back of the house and let himself inside, mopping sweat from his brow as he grabbed a cup from the cupboard and ran the tap to get a drink.

'Ah, you're here. I suppose you know about the girl already.'

Elizabeth could move as stealthily as a cat, it didn't matter where he was or what he was doing, she would be absent one minute and by his side the next with seemingly no motion. Axl turned, surprised more by the question than by the lady herself.

'The girl?'

He surveyed her as she surveyed him, eyes narrowing under a flawlessly made-up face. She was in good form today, he saw, and he understood that the paranoia was part of her sharp mind going over whether his reaction was genuine. She was unduly suspicious of everyone and everything these days. Maybe it was the disease and maybe not. Maybe she had reason to be suspicious, even with the doctor's diagnosis he could never be certain that a mind such as Elizabeth Kane's could ever be over-ridden or taken down by something as demure as dementia. Maybe that made him suspicious too.

He waited as she scrutinized him. Finally, she took a breath and sat down at the table, ramrod straight as she addressed him.

'The girl, Charlotte, my niece. They've sent her here to check on us.'

Axl felt himself reel. The tyre tracks. Charlotte of course. Another finger in the pie, and a dangerous one at that. He placed the glass back onto the countertop but his hand still grasped it, knuckles white. He tried to remain nonchalant.

'Ah, yes, Nell did mention her. Who has sent her here, Elizabeth?'

'They have. But she won't find out, I won't let Francesca get her grubby fingers on anything left of me, and if she thinks Charlotte will win me over now just to get a share, she will be sorely mistaken.' Elizabeth leaned toward him and lowered her voice to a conspiratorial whisper, 'Our secret will be safe, don't worry.'

Axl felt his heart jump as he tried to keep his expression neutral. He wondered how tight he could hold the glass before it shattered under his fingers.

'Elizabeth, we said we'd never mention that again, remember?' his voice was tight and controlled.

Elizabeth sat back in her chair bringing the fingers of one hand toward her lips. Her eyes were anxious, fearful, and he knew her well enough to know that she was questioning her own behaviour and how easily she had let this slip, even just to him. Walls had very keen ears, and they both knew it well.

'Well, of course,' she said, 'I've never spoken of it before now.'

Axl mopped more sweat off his brow with a shaky hand.

'Elizabeth, please, It's important. And dangerous...'

'I am well aware. I may be old, but I am not stupid.'

Axl watched her, heart thumping behind his ribs. How could he make her see?

She may not be stupid, but there were other forces at play now. If she had almost slipped so casually just then, how long would it be before it came out entirely? It had worried him for a while, as Elizabeth's health had declined. Of course, there was always a chance that no-one would believe a word she said now, but he couldn't take that chance. He couldn't allow it to happen. It would destroy him.

He brought his attention back into the kitchen where Elizabeth scraped back the chair to stand was now firmly ranting, offended by his pressing her to keep her mouth shut.

'I'll have you know, Mr Maddox, that I am more than aware of what is going on here. They may tell you I am losing my mind, but I can tell you with confidence that I most certainly am not. When I meet my end it will be via bloody hands, not a disease of the mind.'

Axl felt his grip loosen on the glass. So much of the lady Elizabeth once was hung in that statement and the way she delivered it. It almost made him smile. But he didn't. These days she wouldn't have taken it the way it was meant, so instead he tried to calm her with a tactic he frequently had to use.

It often helped when she was confused to train her mind elsewhere, and almost always she would instantly forget what had been said as little as two minutes before. It was a tactic that worked well on her better, or more lucid days. When she was extremely confused, hallucinating, or forgetful, however, it didn't make a spot of difference. Nothing seemed to.

Today he saw that she was more of her former self than she had been in a good while. He wasn't sure if it pleased him or unnerved him. He let go of the glass and crossed to the table where she now stood, tall and straight, glaring at him. He glanced at his watch. 12.45pm. perfect.

'Calm down, Elizabeth, please.' He took an elbow, and sat her back down, which was surprisingly easy today. Then he placed a hardened hand over her soft one. 'It's lunchtime,' he said, 'are you hungry? What did Nell leave for you? I can sort you lunch before I start on the garden if you like?'

He moved to the counter, filled a glass with orange juice and placed it before her.

'I already ate.' she said.

He ignored her, and as Elizabeth frowned, he crossed to the fridge and peered inside. Bingo. Elizabeth's favourite, sitting on the middle shelf.

'Ah, here,' he said. 'There's some pie left. It's your favourite isn't it? You can have it for dessert. Cream or ice cream?'

'Pie? I already told you I ate.' Elizabeth looked confused.

'It's dessert. Elderberry pie, you always say it makes you feel better. Remember? Like a slice of-'

'Heaven, yes.' Her eyes glazed as she cut him off. 'Now that you mention it I have quite the appetite for a piece of pie, although the way you're acting, I'm starting to think elderberry wine may be more the ticket. Anyway, however frustrating you are, it's always lovely to see you, Axl, won't you join me?'

Axl heaved his grunt that stood in place of a laugh and smiled.

'Not today Elizabeth, I have far too much to do in the garden.'

He warmed the last piece of pie in the microwave and placed a small spoon of carte-dor next to it on the plate, placing it on the table in front of her.

'I'll pick some extra berries for you today if you like. Maybe Nell knows how to make wine?'

Elizabeth raised an eyebrow. The spoon clinked on china.

'I should think she does, she was a master of home brew back in school.'

Axl nodded, there wasn't a lot Nell couldn't whip up.

'Then you shall have it, Elizabeth. And please remember not to say anything more.'

'About what?'

She put a piece of pie into her mouth and chewed daintily.

'Never mind.' He said as she swallowed.

'Oh, do stop talking in riddles Mr Maddox! Either say what you mean or say nothing at all.'

He smiled as she tucked into the pie like the previous conversation had never happened. Heaving a relieved sigh, he filled the glass with water, took a drink, and went back out into the garden.

Chapter Eight

Around the time Axl Maddox was pulling up at Fortwind house, it was becoming clear to Charley that Belle's father should have known to be a lot more careful about how far ahead the girl had been.

Theo was a local fisherman, working a boat from the harbour for up to fourteen hours a day. He would have known the tide was on the turn better than most, but Charley was beyond chastising him. He looked utterly devastated and embarrassed as she recounted what had happened. She didn't have to say it – he knew the sea, and he knew only too well that he could have lost his little girl this morning.

He fussed over Belle, checking her over for cuts and bruises, while Belle fussed over talking to a stranger, her near fatal accident forgotten. She whined and apologised, flinging her arms around his neck repeatedly. He gently removed them each time, reassuring her she had done the right thing, before continuing his check with a care and patience akin to the Dalai Lama.

He checked under one small arm and placed it at her side. Charley grinned, as Belle immediately threw both arms back around him in a tight hug.

'I'll never speak to anyone, ever again.' she said kissing his face as he moved her arms away.

'That would be impossible, Belle,' Theo murmured, lifting her other arm. 'You are the world's biggest chatterbox.'

'I'll just chatterbox to you,' she said, cupping his chin with a small hand and forcing him to look up at her.

'I'm not sure my ears will take it.' He replied with a smile, removing her hand and brushing her damp clothes straight. 'I think you'll live, Skipper.'

He grimaced at his own choice of words and stood with a sigh, wiping sand from the knees of his jeans. Belle asked if she could run ahead and Theo seemed to pale a few shades. 'Well, not too far and keep to the sand. We're heading back to the car, so this way.'

He pointed to the harbour and Belle turned toward it, skipping ahead, a soggy Ted hanging from her hand. Theo turned to Charley, placing a hand on her arm with more pressure than he probably realised.

'Charley, I can't thank you enough for today, Belle certainly has a guardian angel in you, doesn't she?'

Charley laughed, trying to make light of the serious situation.

'Well, maybe the angel sent me to watch for her, sounds more realistic.' She gestured to the harbour. 'I'll walk down with you, my car is there too and I suppose I should get back.'

She let out a longer sigh than she intended, and Theo looked at her bemused, brown curls blowing back off his forehead to expose brilliant green eyes.

'Is getting back that bad?'

Charley pursed her lips, nodding her head. 'Could be.'

They walked. She chastised herself for being melodramatic, especially under the present circumstances. 'Probably not, I'm sure it'll be fine. I just don't know what to expect that's all. I'm staying with my aunt, but I don't really know her that well. It's always a little uncomfortable at first isn't it?'

Theo raised his eyebrows as he glanced at her, his attention quickly returning to Belle ahead of them.

'Ah, I thought you were a tourist. So, you're staying here then?'

'Yeah, just for a few weeks I think.'

Just until my Aunt dies.

Charley wrinkled her nose as a stab of fear ran through her stomach. She pushed it down.

'Maybe you know of my aunt if you live in the village? Elizabeth Kane? apparently she was quite prominent here before she got ill.'

Theo, who'd had most of his attention fixed on Belle, turned to look at her.

'Your aunt is Elizabeth Kane? So, you're staying at Fortwind House then.'

'The very one.'

And it couldn't be in a nicer location, she thought, as she looked toward the harbour. They walked on the firmer damp sand, but to their left were long rolling dunes with tall tufts of grass and soft white sand. The kind of sand that seemed to make walking a high-performance sport and got in every crevice. It was a picture-perfect beach, and for now it was serene and quiet, just how she liked it. Only the warm wind in her face, the screech of gulls and the crash of waves to accompany her.

'It's a beautiful house,' Theo said, breaking into her thoughts.

Oh, and Theo of course.

'And you're right,' he said, 'she was prominent. She was a councillor here, did a lot for the community, but that was a good many years ago now, I was only a child. I remember she got the play park installed at the other end of the village, that was all I cared about back then.'

He grinned and Charley smiled back.

'So you're here looking after her?' he said, 'I heard she had a nurse?'

Charley stepped over a rogue sandcastle; half fallen in its battle with the elements.

'She did. A good one too, but Glen has to go. She's a private nurse and the family can't afford to keep her on anymore. It's a shame because Elizabeth has dementia, and it's quite advanced. They don't think she has long left.'

Theo swung his head to her, surprise lifting his eyebrows.

'Oh, really? Wow, that's a real shame. Doesn't sound like a nice reason for you to come and visit, if you don't mind me saying.'

Charley shook her head.

'No, and it doesn't help that I haven't seen her since I was about three years old. Elizabeth and my mother had some feud years ago and haven't seen each other since. I have some repair work to do, I tell you, because Elizabeth hates me just for being her sister's daughter. She's already ordered me to get out of her house.' she let out a sigh. 'Plus, I know nothing about dementia. I feel I'm already a good few steps behind before I've even started.'

Theo grimaced and placed a hand lightly on her shoulder.

'Sounds like you have your work cut out up there then. Families, huh?'

She laughed at the irony.

'Oh yes. Families indeed.'

They strolled amicably, and conversation turned easily to Theo's life as Belle ran on ahead, occasionally coming back before running on again, mimicking the motion of the tide. Charley didn't know if it was just that Theo was so chatty, but there was definitely something about him that made her feel instantly at ease. Something familiar, like talking to a lifelong friend, and God knew she could do with a friend up here right now.

She listened with interest as Theo told her about life on the boat, and the sometimes depressingly long days out at sea, but it was obviously a job he was proud of. His eyes shone as he spoke of bringing a large haul back into the bay, much of which was supplied to local businesses. Any time off work was spent with Belle, usually in a small motorboat that he had refurbished himself after spying it neglected on the rocks at the back of the island last year.

'Such a waste,' he said, 'I couldn't just leave it there, so I borrowed a friend's boat to tow it back to the harbour. It was a wreck, but I knew I could do it up, and when Belle got excited about it with me I knew I was on to a winner. Four months later we had a seaworthy boat, one I could never have afforded to buy, and it's given us priceless time and memories together. Perfect father and daughter bonding time.'

69

Belle ran back up the beach, blonde hair blowing back now it had dried in the sun. She showed them both a shell she had picked up which looked like a unicorn horn. Theo took it from her and held it aloft, twisting it in the light before handing it back.

'That's sweet, Belle.' Theo said, 'Keep hold of it, unicorn shells have magic in them.'

Belle's mouth dropped open, and he winked as he placed a forefinger to his lips. She pursed her lips tight and gave the shell to Theo to pocket without a word. With a grin she turned to run again but Theo put a hand on her shoulder.

'Hey, Belle, before you go tell Charley what we called the boat.'

'Our boat?' Belle said, her eyes lighting up. Theo gave her a nod.

'She's called Belle's Beauty.' She said, putting a hand to her little chest with a proud flourish, and then she began to chatter about the boat and the 'work' that she had done with daddy. Theo had called it perfect father and daughter bonding time, and from the excitement Belle was exuding Charley thought he was probably right.

'Will you come out in her with us one day, Charley?' Belle said, pulling on Charley's hand. 'Pleeeaaaaassseee!'

Charley laughed, glancing at Theo. 'If it's all right with your dad it's cool with me. I'd love to.'

'It'll be good to have you on board.' Theo said with a grin.

Belle whooped and ran off ahead, as Charley and Theo fell into an easy step behind. Charley watched Belle pick up more shells.

'So, where does Belle's mother fit into all of this, Theo, do you ever get time to see her?' She said with a grin. Theo heaved an exaggerated a sigh, eyes still on Belle.

'It's a very long story, but no, I don't see her. At all, actually.'

Charley's hand flew to her mouth, and she closed her eyes briefly.

'Oh, Theo, I'm so sorry, that was insensitive. And rude. It's none of my business, forget I asked.'

Theo grinned, placing a hand briefly on her arm.

'It's fine, don't worry. It's usually one of the first things that comes up when I meet people. Unusual to find a father with sole custody of his daughter, and no involvement of her mother. If I were a woman, of course, no-one would bat an eyelid, but that's life I suppose.'

Charley grimaced, and he laughed, placing his hands in the pockets of his jeans. His shoulders shrugged up toward his ears.

'It doesn't bother me what people think. If Belle is happy, I'm happy. She never knew her mom to miss her, and although we've spoken about her, she doesn't seem very interested in the fact she has one just yet. Maybe that will change at school and we'll have another battle to go through finding her, but until then, life is good.'

Charley frowned, perplexed.

'Oh, so she's still around? I thought-'

'What? You thought she was dead?' His eyebrows flew up and then he burst into laughter. 'Oh, no, she's still very much alive and kicking. I just don't know where, and as she won't get in contact it'll be a job to find her if Belle ever wants to see her.'

'But I don't understand. If she's still around then why would she not want to see her daughter? I mean, look at her.'

She gestured toward Belle as she came running back toward them along the sand, hair flying behind her, Ted flying in front.

'Yeah, well, we know she's cute,' he said with a shrug.

Charley smiled. All credit to Theo, Belle seemed a happy and carefree child, he was doing a good job. Charley found her admiration for him increase as he looked to her and placed a finger to his lips as Belle came nearer.

Let's not talk about this until she's out of earshot, the look said.

When Belle had shown them the shells that she and Ted had found, and Theo had placed more in his pocket, she ran back off in front. Theo stared after her and Charley wondered whether he would continue, but he was only checking Belle was far enough away before he turned to her.

'Are you ready for this? It's quite a story.'

Charley nodded, and Theo began.

He and Belle's mother had split when Belle was a baby, although, on reflection it wasn't so much of a split as an escape, on her side. Belle had been only five months old, and as far as Theo was concerned, they were a perfect little family. All was going well, and they were adjusting to life as parents. There were no signs that anything was wrong until she disappeared one night. Literally.

Theo had finished a long shift on the boat and had gone to bed tired at around ten leaving Ella to stay up watching television. She had been normal all evening, he said, and told him she loved him before he went upstairs. That was the last time he saw her.

The next morning Theo had woken with the alarm. Realising that Ella hadn't come to bed, he had expected to find her asleep on the sofa, but she wasn't there. And after checking Belle and checking the house, he found she wasn't *anywhere*. She had literally vanished. No clothes were taken, and her bag was still over the chair. As far as he could tell her coats were all still in place, even her phone was on the table.

Initially he'd been annoyed that she would make him late for work as he couldn't leave Belle alone, but as the minutes turned to hours, and then days, he became frantic, wondering if she had been hurt, or killed. Even thinking she had been abducted from their living room overnight. The police were called, and a lengthy search stretched for weeks before she finally got in contact. By letter. Not to say where she was, just to say she was fine and that he could stop looking for her. She had apparently been shocked by the level of coverage the case was given, especially when she didn't want to be found.

Charley gaped. 'So that was it? Stop looking, it's over, and by the way I want nothing to do with you or my baby girl? How could she do that?'

Theo pursed his lips and shook his head.

'I don't know. For a long time I tried to work out I'd done, what had gone wrong, but her letter was very clear. If I hadn't got the police involved, she wouldn't have contacted at all. She said she had been having an affair with a married man for most of our two-year relationship. He had finally left his wife, and they had gone to start a new life together. Apparently, that didn't involve Belle, or me, and I wasn't to try to contact her.

So I didn't. I wanted to keep a shred of dignity, especially as the whole village knew exactly what she had done. I kept my head down and gave up work for a while as I tried to figure out a routine that kept

Belle and myself happy. I wanted to work; I loved my job, but I didn't want Belle to feel that two parents had neglected her. I wanted her to know she could count on me to be there, and that still stands. So today I work on the boat four days a week, leaving the other three to look after Belle. I have a good friend who's a childminder; she has her on the days I work. The one thing I always aim to do is get home to eat tea with Belle and put her to bed on time, although that sometimes goes by the board too.'

They stopped walking as they reached the harbour steps, and Belle, realising that they weren't going to the car just yet, dropped to the sand a few feet away to build a castle with her hands. Ted was placed in a sitting position, back propped against the stone steps as she dug, and as horrified as she felt, Charley smiled as an inventive castle came together, complete with moat.

'Well, I don't think it's doing her any harm,' She said to Theo. 'In fact, I think you've done an awesome job so far. She's a really sweet, clued up little girl.'

Theo cocked a lip, worry crossing his features.

'Yeah, well, maybe at the times she isn't climbing the rocks out to sea as the tide turns.' he shook his head, his eyes on Belle. 'I always think she should know these things, she's out at sea such a lot with me, but then, things like today happen and I remember she's only five years old. She lives in her imagination a lot, and I need to be more aware.'

Charley touched Theo's arm which radiated warmth from the glaring sun.

'Hey, she's okay, and we all make mistakes.'

'It won't be one I make again.'

'And there's the lesson.'

Theo smiled at her.

'I suppose so,' He looked at his watch. 'Well, it's my day off, and it's after one. Are you hungry? I'll treat you to lunch if you have time, God knows I owe you at least that much.'

Charley's stomach rumbled at the thought of food. Lunch with Theo and Belle was a lot more appealing than going back to face the music with Aunt Elizabeth, especially as she was now late for her own departure from Fortwind House, but she couldn't take Glen's good nature for granted. Looking over the sand, her gaze was drawn to the imposing house, sat proud up on its hill.

'Lunch sounds wonderful, but I really should get back.' she said, with genuine regret. 'I'm just glad Belle is okay, and that I could help.'

Theo nodded.

'Okay. Another time then? I'm sure you'll need a break at some point.'

Charley huffed a breath through her nose.

'I'll probably need a break in the next twenty minutes, right after I get back up there.'

Theo grinned, moving the hair out of his eyes with a flick of his head.

'Well, that's settled then. What's your number? We can sort a date later on.'

Charley smiled as she pulled her phone from her pocket and they exchanged numbers.

'Great,' He said, 'I'll keep an eye on how Mrs Kane is treating you until you can get out too. She's not sending you away until I've sorted you out with the best food in the village.'

Charley laughed.

'Okay.' She said, 'It's a deal.'

Theo called Belle, who looked up, swiping her hair back with her hand before retrieving Ted from his perch.

'Time to go, skipper, but hey, how about we take Charley to our favourite restaurant-cafe one day?'

Belle grinned from ear to ear, Ted squashed between her chest and her arm. 'Now? Can we go now? Can we?'

'Not right now, but soon. Tell Charley what the food will do Belle?'

Belle rolled her head and her eyes like she was about to faint.

'It will blow your mind.' she said and started to giggle as Theo laughed.
Charley laughed with them. She was flattered that Belle seemed so excited that she would be joining them, and as they walked back to their cars, she found that she was looking forward to it too.

If there was something more to life up here than just the Witch of Fortwind Bay, then that was a blessed relief.

Chapter Nine

Elizabeth pushed the pie around her plate with a fork. Her stomach bubbled. It was happening again, she could feel it. What she didn't understand was what had caused it this time. The pie had been fresh, and there were usually a few days grace between whatever they were adding to the food.

She put the fork down on the side of the plate, and placed her fingers lightly to her temples, trying to stop the room from spinning. Closing her eyes, she took a few deeps breaths, although she knew she would be on a downward spiral until whatever this was wore off.

It was a shame, because both the pie and the ice cream were delicious, but she could no longer finish them. There would be terrible consequences if she did, she would be out of action for a day, if not more, and with Charlotte appearing out of the blue, Elizabeth had to keep her head straight and her wits about her so that she could assess whose side the girl was on.

As she fought to keep her thoughts in check, she wondered which it was this time. Ice cream, juice, or pie? There was no rhyme or reason to the episodes, no one person who seemed to be around when they happened, and she couldn't pinpoint it to a particular item of food or drink. It must be something they were adding into her meals at random intervals, and the very real trouble was that, unless she wanted to live on toast, she wasn't able to stand and cook for herself any longer. If she told Nell to go, she hadn't the means to pay for another cook. For the moment she was cornered.

Trapped.

It pained her enormously. She had been a trusted and revered woman in Fortwind Bay for most of her married life, and along with her husband, she had done much for the village over the years. However, when the time came that Elizabeth needed the help, not one of her friends believed that there was anything more than dementia at work.

If, indeed, they were friends at all.

Over the last year her closest so-called friends had managed to lock her away up here, in her house, without direct force. No one came to visit except Nell, Axl and Avril. They said that she must stay home for her own good, her mind was not her own, and they feared for her safety. Not that she could make it out alone any longer if she wanted to, she had never owned a car, and couldn't even get down her own gravel drive with the gradient and this damn stick. Other friends and acquaintances had stopped coming to the house altogether, and since she didn't go to town herself any longer, there was no-one she trusted enough to listen to her pleas.

Her three closest friends had effectively cut her off from the thrum of life. Possibly on purpose.

At first Elizabeth thought she *was* losing her mind. There were parts of her days that she couldn't remember, she saw strange people, objects and animals, and felt intensely irritated that they shouldn't be there; akin to stepping out of your door and seeing the marshmallow man from Ghostbusters flattening the village below. The visions made no sense, and at first she attributed them to vivid dreams, but she had known that something was horribly wrong when Doctor Glibb from the village, had come up to the house.

He had made her perform some small tests and asked lots of questions about her health and state of mind. Elizabeth remembered only bits of the conversation, but she did remember his precise diagnosis. Dementia with Lewy Bodies. She had thought it strange that he could do that with no further tests, she also thought it strange that he had been there at all as she hadn't been into town to see him with any complaints. But there he sat, large as life. There they had all sat, in the drawing room; The Doctor, Axl, Nell, and Avril. All wearing identical pitying looks as he gave his diagnosis and prescribed her medication. At the time she thought her friends must have contacted the Doctor out of the goodness of their hearts, but as she became more suspicious over time, she took matters into her own hands and hired Glen.

If her friends were up to no good surely a live-in nurse would spot the signs that didn't indicate dementia, and that would help to prove

Elizabeth's theory. However, as the episodes of confusion had come and gone, Glen had been as convinced as the next person. She shuffled around, treating her like an idiot, thinking she was losing her mind, and for a while Elizabeth began to believe it herself.

It had taken a day when Elizabeth felt relatively well to see beyond the cracks. She'd had a particularly violent vision that she had returned from quickly with more of her senses than normal. The vision had involved her late husband, Frank, and had both scared and upset her more than she wanted to let on. Afterwards she had spent most of the morning in Franks study, looking through old photographs, taking him in. Trying to commit him to memory fully before she lost it, as everyone told her she would.

She heard Nell arrive, heard her let into the hall by Glen, but she had no inclination to greet her, so she had simply gone back to the photographs. That was until she heard Nell say that she was to go for tests today as part of her ongoing care. This was news to Elizabeth, she hadn't been for any tests before, well, other than the ones the village Doctor had performed. Apparently, Nell would drive her to the clinic and bring her home afterwards.

As Elizabeth puzzled over the tests, wondering if she had missed or forgotten about them, she heard Glen tell Nell that she hadn't been well, that she had locked herself away. She also heard Nell reply that it was good, that the clinic being able to see her in a state would be beneficial, and that was when Nell had entered the room.

Her intuition now on high alert, Elizabeth had stayed largely quiet as Nell ran her through the itinerary for the day. She was to get into the car, go for some short tests, nothing that would hurt, and then they would be home. The infantile tone of her voice had stirred Elizabeth's anger, but she was feeling herself enough to know that it was better to stay quiet and assess this strange situation before confronting whatever was going on.

By nature, Elizabeth was an information gatherer. Forewarned was forearmed, she had used the strategy a lot throughout her working life to pass council motions and plans. Listen first, gather facts, and only then do you open fire. And so, as she looked at Nell's condescending face, she smothered her anger and lapsed into pretend nonchalance.

Elizabeth stayed quiet throughout the journey, refusing the sandwiches that Nell had brought for lunch when they pulled up alongside a beach. After an hour of sitting in the car, Nell eating, Elizabeth watching the ocean, Nell had simply returned home.

No clinic. No tests.

Intrigued, and feeling more herself again after having nothing more to eat or drink, Elizabeth stayed quiet and passive throughout, wondering what the hell was going on. Nell was still speaking in a condescending tone, and in a sudden surge of inspiration, Elizabeth faked a slight shake to her hands and slurred her speech just a little. When they had arrived home, she had returned to the study, demanding to be left alone.

Nell had fussed, but Elizabeth had insisted. As Nell left and went down to the kitchen, Elizabeth poked her head silently out of the study door. There was a conversation, Glen's voice in the kitchen, along with Nell's.

As quickly and quietly as she could she slipped upstairs to the bedroom that sat directly above the kitchen. The bedroom that shared a chimney with the kitchen fireplace. She had stood next to that fireplace and listened.

What she heard rocked her to the core.

Nell was precise. She gave Glen details of the tests Elizabeth had endured at the 'clinic', and from the rustling it appeared she had given Glen some paperwork to look through too. She told Glen that the tests were conclusive. The brain was deteriorating at such a rate that she didn't have long left. Maybe even just months.

Elizabeth faltered. She knew they hadn't been to a clinic. They had sat in the car at the beach, she would have testified under oath, but here was Nell telling Glen blatant lies. Or was she?

Still teetering on the edge of doubt, she thought hard. Had she imagined the beach? Had they been to the clinic after all?

They couldn't have, the beach had seemed so real. She had been well enough in her mind to fake illness so that Nell hadn't suspected she had worked anything out. But what excuse would Nell have to lie?

SHATTERED

A cold hand had encircled her heart, and the air had squeezed from her lungs. She knew there was something drastically wrong with what was happening around her, and she now knew she could trust no-one until the game was up, not even her closest friends. She would have to be vigilant, and she would have to do it alone.

She decided she would write things down when she felt well enough. Starting right at that moment. She took herself back to the study, found one of Franks leather-bound notebooks and began to write. Everything of the day, where she had been, what she had worn, and what Nell had said. She wrote it exactly as she remembered it and continued, in regimental fashion, from that day on. Whenever she felt well enough, she went to the study and wrote what she had done, what she had eaten, where she had sat, topics of conversation. On the days she was ill she could do nothing, but she remembered each vision vividly, and wrote them down afterwards with the clarity that she saw them.

Over time, she began to recount things back to Glen, what she had eaten three days ago, what she had been wearing yesterday, what part of the house they had sat in, what the weather was like yesterday. She even went into details of her visions up to a few days previous. Glen, who had a head for details, unknowingly corroborated everything Elizabeth said. Confirming the fact that very little error was occurring in Elizabeth's recollection.

Elizabeth was now not only certain, she became frightened.

Something was going on, and from what she could put together it looked like someone was trying to get rid of her, and if that were the case, she had to stay one step ahead.

As the only unbiased party, she confided in Glen. She went into detail, telling her she hadn't got dementia at all, but that she was being poisoned. She even confirmed to Glen that she hadn't been to hospital on the day Nell had taken her out, and that instead they had sat and had a picnic at the beach.

Each time she mentioned it Glen gave a small smile, and a *look*. She dismissed everything Elizabeth said as paranoia, confusion, hallucinations, and each time she finished Glen smiled and patted her arm gently.

'No-one is trying to poison you Ms Kane,' she always replied. 'Why would they want to?'

From that point on, Elizabeth knew she was on her own.

So, she had monitored. She had monitored when she felt well and when she didn't. She wrote fastidiously, keeping the book hidden at the back of the Victorian fireplace in her husband's study, where she hoped it would be safe enough. Glen had the only other copy of the key, and the fire was never lit. Sometimes she wondered if Avril ran the duster over the fireplace at all. She had no call to moan though. The rest of the house was spotless, it was only the study which fell short, and that was a good thing. It didn't do for people to be prying in there. At the time she had trusted Avril implicitly, nowadays, everyone was a suspect. And everyone comprised her three closest friends.

She was shaking now, and Elizabeth swiped the plate away from her. It skidded and rattled on the tabletop as she grabbed her walking stick. The cane shook under her grip as she stood, scooting the chair out from behind her. She held the table with her free hand for balance as Glen rushed in from the hall.

'Ms, Kane! Stay right there, I'm coming.'

She bustled up behind Elizabeth, taking her arm, and pushing the chair further away with her free hand. Elizabeth snatched her arm away with a glare.

'I don't need help.' she said.

Even as she spoke, the counter-top wobbled and bent in front of her and the words sounded as though they had come from someone else, someone a million miles away. She felt her body sway and Glen had her arm again.

'It's all right Ms Kane, come on we'll take you for a little lie down and you'll feel much better. Come on, up to bed now.'

Glen sounded like she was trying to speak whilst gargling soup. Disjointed and mushy. Elizabeth swiped her hand away again, but this time with less force. Her legs were shaking now too, and Elizabeth was becoming aware of her husband standing by the kitchen counter.

He looked as he had in his thirties, and although that would have been around the 1970's, he was dressed in an old green army uniform from many years before. His face was stern, his moustache neat and hair slicked back with oil as he pointed to the doorway leading to the hall.

'Go Elizabeth!' He shouted, 'Get to the shelter!'

A group of uniformed men ran in orderly formation in front of him kicking up dirt as they went. Frank swam out of focus as the orange dust swirled around him turning his uniform, and his hair, bright orange.

Elizabeth wanted to laugh. She wanted to tell him he had bright orange hair, and hear him laugh about it with her, but a soldier was tugging on her arm, pointing to the small hole that marked the entrance to the shelter. Heat seared around her and the dusty road was making her throat dry, her legs felt laden and jelly like. She tried to shout to Frank, but her voice wouldn't work. He was still shouting something to her though.

'... Elizabeth, don't let... keep safe... to the shelter.'

Elizabeth could do no more than nod, and then her eyes bulged, and she found her voice as a large bang reverberated through the air and Frank's face blew clean away. He teetered for a while, right eyeball hanging out of the socket, the only part of his face left intact. And then he fell, slowly, face first to the floor, with a thick thud. A plume of dust rose to cover him as Elizabeth's legs buckled and gave. With a shriek, she sank to the floor with him.

Chapter Ten

A black Land Rover was parked in the space at the side of the bins when Charley returned from the beach. She pulled up next to it, leaving space for the wooden door that lead through the wall in front of her. The door to the garden she supposed.

Stalling for time she checked her phone, turning the sound back on. No messages, and no missed calls. Not even from Evelyn. She drew in a breath and then blew out her lips as she pushed the phone back into her jeans pocket.

I don't know whether I should be grateful no one sent scathing messages, or upset that no one wants to check how I am. What is wrong with my family? Why can't they just be normal?

And speaking of family, there was an old woman that she had to deal with inside. An angry, intimidating old woman; one that had asked her to be out of the house more than an hour ago. On the beach it had seemed easier to stay here and fight Elizabeth than to go home and fight her family. Now, sat on the driveway of Fortwind House just meters from her aunt, she wasn't so sure.

Come on Charley, you need to be strong for this or she will reduce you to a blubbering wreck. Especially after the day you've had already.

She sat up taller in the driver's seat. No, there would be no more tears today. Aunt Elizabeth was very ill. Glen had warned that she could get personal, and still Charley had taken it to heart. She had to take a step back and remember that her aunt wasn't herself. Taking a deep breath, she got out of the car and headed for the house, her confidence faltering at the door which stood slightly ajar.

She blinked. Why would the front door be open?

Puzzled, she gave it a small push and a cool breeze rose to meet her on the step despite the warm sun still on her back. The house was hushed and dark, the air oppressive and charged, like it was about to throw out a storm.

There may well be a storm when I find Aunt Elizabeth.

Charley swallowed hard. The house remained silent, still, and she felt her heart knocking against her ribs.

Where is Glen? Why is the door open, and why is it so quiet?

She thought about calling out to break the tension. It wasn't like there wouldn't be anyone home, but her nerves were already protesting, her voice in this eerie silence may just push her over the edge.

Oh, for God sake Charley this is ridiculous, the hallway is dark. So what?

She stepped inside. Cool, oppressive air gathered around her, pressing, and a shiver ran down her spine. She scanned the stairs and the hallway, hearing the quiet tick of the kitchen clock as she let her eyes adjust to the darkness. The door into the kitchen was ajar, as it had been when she had first met Elizabeth this morning, a bright shaft of light fell onto the wall, but there was no sign of her aunt now. No sign of anyone.

Anxious for the warm light of the room ahead she started for the kitchen. Behind her the front door creaked and Charley turned to see it swing shut with a low click. She stared.

Wind. Just the wind.

The hair prickled at the nape of her neck.

Jeez Charley, why didn't you just shut the damn door? You'll scare yourself stupid. Nothing is going on here but your imagination. Get in the kitchen and find Glen.

Turning fast, she strode into the kitchen, resisting the urge to slam the door shut against the weirdness in the hall. A trickle of relief ran through her at the brightly lit room, and cheerful sunlit garden just beyond the French doors.

Which were also open.

Charley rolled her eyes and huffed a relieved laugh. They were outside in the sunshine, of course. That's why the house was so quiet.

Except they weren't.

Charley scanned the area outside the doors and came up with nothing but birdsong and the wind in the new leaves. Not Glen. Not Aunt Elizabeth. Not the gardner. No-one.

A prickle of fear crept back down her spine she re-entered the kitchen, shutting the door behind her as another door to the left of the hallway clicked and swung slowly into the kitchen with a long creak.

Charley blinked.

You have to be kidding me. What is this? A bloody game?

'Newsflash. It's not funny, it's freaking me out.' she whispered, voice sounding too loud in the quiet.

Chill out Charley, it's just the wind from all the doors being open.

With a shaky laugh she moved to the door to shut it, and that was when she saw the steps leading down. She froze.

Steps.

Down.

Unable to move, the breath caught in her throat and goosebumps littered her body.

The cellar.

The floor seemed to shift under her feet.

The cellar? Oh shit, I forgot about the cellar!

With a shudder she broke the spell, shut the door hard and pushed her back against it. Heart thumping wildly, she closed her eyes to images of small children and the witch, Aunt Elizabeth. What did she do down there in the dark?

The hall door opened and footsteps on the tiled floor almost made Charley cry with relief.

Finally, there's someone!

Swinging her head to the sound, she was shocked to see a large man enter the kitchen. He turned to face her, jet black hair and thick beard almost hiding identical shock on his features.

'Oh!' She said, more a breathless exclamation than a word. He gave a startled grunt and backed up to the table, tucking a small brown paper bag behind him. Charley simultaneously pressed her back to the cellar door, hand flying up to her chest.

'Oh! I... oh....' She tried, but the words wouldn't come.

The man only stared, looking flustered, and under his face full of beard she thought she saw him colour. It occurred to her that this must be the owner of the car outside, and she took a breath, trying to steady her thrumming nerves.

'I... I'm so sorry,' she said, forcing a smile with dry lips. 'I actually thought you were Glen. I'm Charlotte, Elizabeth's niece? I'm staying here for a while to help look after her.'

The man gave another grunt, still staring as he swiped his free hand across his forehead to wipe away beads of sweat. Charley stepped toward him, holding out her hand. He looked at it unmoving. Dread crept through her and her heart began to pump again.

Why didn't he answer? Was he even supposed to be in the house? What was he hiding behind his back? Had he broken in?

She craned her neck to see the bag, and he muttered something illegible moving to the counter by the sink and placing his hands on the worktop. His back now to her, bag between them, he heaved deep breaths. A nervous panic swirled up from Charley's stomach.

Who the hell is he? Why is there still no sign of Glen and Aunt Elizabeth? Has he done something to them?
Charley felt the panic begin to spiral as the man turned to her, looking more composed. He smiled and Charley wondered why the warmth didn't spread to his eyes, which flit around the kitchen as though he was looking for an escape.

'No, I'm sorry,' he said, his voice deep and gruff. 'I just... I wasn't expecting anyone. I'm Axl Maddox the gardener. I was just washing off some of the vegetables I'd picked...'

He trailed off and gestured to the fresh cabbage, potatoes, cauliflower, and carrots on the side of the sink. Quite a hefty amount of vegetables. Charley noticed that he didn't indicate what was in the bag, keeping it stowed behind his large frame as he stood leaning up the counter. He also made no move to come forward and shake her hand, which she now slowly lowered. She smiled stiffly and nod at him, keeping her eyes on his, but noting his hands which now writhed and twisted together in front of him.

'Elizabeth took a turn while I was in the garden,' he said. 'Glen has taken her upstairs. She mentioned that you were staying. I... uh... I was just up there checking on her.'

Colour deepened his cheeks as he looked down to his hands, but Charley barely noticed as the relief that Glen and Elizabeth were here and okay flooded in. Relief that was quickly replaced by shock as his words hit home.

A turn? But she was perfectly okay this morning as she was bellowing at me to leave. Did it happen that fast?

If she remembered what Glen had said correctly, she only took Elizabeth upstairs when she was showing signs that she would be unable to get herself up there later. Charley thought she had better check out those signs for herself so that she would be aware when she was on her own.

'Right, okay, I think I'll go and check on Aunt Elizabeth myself.' she said.

He nodded, keeping his eyes on hers and she faltered for the second time since she had got back. Was Axl Maddox the gardeners name? She couldn't remember now. What if this man was actually up to no good and she were about to leave him downstairs alone?

Don't be silly Charley, there are vegetables in the sink, a burglar wouldn't take the time to pick that lot before breaking in, and he wouldn't park his car by the door.

'Okay,' she said, 'well it was nice to meet you Axl, I'll probably see you around.'

He nod his head again, still twisting his hands, and she went into the hall, pulling the door close behind her but not shutting it. She moved to the end of the staircase and then quietly doubled back to peek through the gap, adjusting herself so that she could see him. He was facing the counter, leaning his arms on the worktop, bag just visible between them. He didn't move. He just leaned, and breathed, and again nerves swirled in Charley's stomach.

She had to get upstairs to Glen and find out if this man was coacher or not.

She also wondered just what the hell he had in that bag.

Chapter Eleven

Axl threw the small bag into the boot of the Land Rover a little too quickly, hoping he hadn't damaged the contents, but there was no time to check now. He lumbered to the driver's side, swinging his big frame inside, and slamming the door shut behind him. Pushing the start button, he sent up a silent prayer of thanks to the lord that technology had come on so much that he didn't have to insert a key into the ignition. His hands shook so much he wasn't at all sure he could have managed it.

The girl had scared him when she had appeared in the kitchen out of thin air, much like Elizabeth had a habit of doing, but it was much more than that. Coming face to face with her at that particular moment had shaken him far more than it should. Even armed with the knowledge that she was around he still hadn't been prepared. Still hadn't taken enough care.

It was stupid; she was just a girl, and he had been caught off guard. But even so, Axl knew he would have to be extra careful. From now on, he would need to keep his actions in check when he was up at the house. It would be better if he could steer clear of her altogether, but as she seemed to like to sneak up on him, it didn't seem likely.

His heart gave a jolt as he remembered her eyes travelling to the bag, the pounding in his head as he had tried to hide it, knowing that she had seen it already. She couldn't have known what was inside, but still, it was way too close for comfort.

He clenched his jaw and thumped a palm onto the steering wheel. Why now? Why did she have to come and interfere right at the end? He was almost there, almost free.

The thought hurt. He rammed the car into gear with a grunt, and reversed from the space, noting her yellow mini for the first time since he had got in the car. With a curse and a spit of gravel he lurched forward down the long driveway much too fast.

He saw Nell as he drove down main street, shakes still chorusing through his body. She sat on a bench overlooking the sea, not far from the clock tower at the north side of the village. Pulling the car up to the kerb he placed his hand on the horn to get her attention.

The blast rang out a little too long gaining the attention of passers-by, Nell turned with a frown short bleached blonde hair blowing onto her face which lit up with recognition. She held aloft a baguette with a shrug. Axl sighed and shut off the engine. Heaving himself out of the car he walked over to her.

'Axl,' she said as he sat his large frame at the opposite end of the bench. Not too near, not too far.

'Afternoon, Nell,' he replied, rubbing a hand across his beard. 'just thought you'd like to know that Elizabeth is out of action. Another turn. I'm not sure she'll need dinner tonight, seemed a bad one again.'

He kept his gaze out to sea as Nell frowned. This hadn't been part of the plan, he knew.

'Ah. Did you get her lunch?'

'I gave her some of the pie from the fridge.' he said.

Nell shrugged and took a bite of baguette, chewing and swallowing slowly, contemplating her answer.

'Ah well, it's done now. I'll go up and cook some more this afternoon anyway. I get more done when she's not around, bless her.'

Axl nod his head, pulling an agitated hand through his hair. Nell waited taking another bite as she watched him.

'I met the girl.' he said finally.

'And?'

He shrugged, 'She'll probably get in the way.'

Nell smiled. 'We're Elizabeth's friends Axl, we've been around a long time. we carry on as normal, she doesn't change that. We do the best we can until Elizabeth... until she goes.'

Axl heaved his big shoulders up again with a sigh. 'I'm nervous.' he said.

'Not long now.' Nell said, leaning to pat his hand as she looked back out to sea. 'won't be long.

Chapter Twelve

Elizabeth drifted between sleep and hallucination for the rest of the afternoon. There wasn't much that Charley or Glen could do, except make sure she was out of the path of anything that she may hurt herself on, or with, but she couldn't be left alone, Glen made that very clear.

Elizabeth seemed to spend most of her time either in some sort of war, where she shouted and screamed, often jumping out of bed and waving her arms around trying to get everyone to safety. Or at work, where she sat at her vanity table tapping the wooden top like it was a computer and shuffling non-existent papers. It was the strangest thing to watch, even more so when Elizabeth chaired a meeting, standing in the middle of the room and addressing non-existent people around her with incoherent babble. Her Hallucinations were hard to watch, but there was one vision that distressed Charley so much she had sat with her hands over her ears and her eyes averted for much of it. It had involved Elizabeth's late husband, Frank, being blown apart. By gun or bomb Charley couldn't be sure, but each time ended with terrifying screaming and shouting from Elizabeth, and finally sobs so heart breaking that Charley had had to wipe away her own stray tears.

Charley and Glen, who had placed themselves by the door to the bedroom, were never spoken to and never involved. It seemed to Charley that Elizabeth wasn't even seeing, her vision glazed and out of focus. Each time a hallucination tapered off, and Elizabeth's focus came back into the room, she would beg for water. Her speech low and slurred. Confusion evident.

At this point Glen would give Elizabeth a drink and try to settle her back into bed. Elizabeth would fall into fitful sleep, before emerging fully awake in a 3D imaginary world, where the torture would begin again. At first sleep would last only minutes at a time, but as the hours passed, the periods of sleep were longer and the hallucinations seemed to get less violent and frantic.

Finally, at a quarter to eleven that night, after sitting for an hour and a half in Elizabeth's room with no activity other than a few shouts and restlessness, Glen had reached up to a baby monitor which sat on a small shelf at the side of some books. The green light flickered on and Glen placed the mobile 'parent' end into her tunic pocket. They left the room in silence, Glen signalling to Charley to follow her downstairs. It had been over nine hours of constant care and observation. More for Glen, who had been at it before Charley had arrived home, and who now would be 'on call' with the baby monitor for the rest of the night at least.

In the kitchen Glen set the monitor on the table and made them both a hot drink as Charley collapsed into a chair at the table and put her head down on her arms. She was both physically and mentally exhausted, the extreme nature of the hallucinations played back on the screen of her mind in glorious HD like a movie - but with no stop or pause function. Not for the first time she had serious doubts that she could handle this alone. Glen reached to place a hand over one of hers, giving it a squeeze. Charley looked up and smiled weakly at her, noting how composed and in control Glen looked as she sat opposite, steaming cups of tea and a plate of biscuits between them.

'That was a particularly bad episode, one of the worst I've seen her have in a while. You did well, Charley.'

Glen smiled, but a ton weight seemed lodged in Charley's chest.

'I did nothing, we couldn't even make her more comfortable. I just wanted to take it away-'

The tears spilled up and over before Charley could stop them. Her chest heaved and hitched as wave after wave of emotion poured out. Glen sat quietly, letting her sob, but keeping a gentle hand over hers. By the time she was getting herself under control, her chest hurt, her eyes hurt, and she felt she could sleep for a week.

'God, I'm so sorry Glen, I know I should be stronger.'

'I don't want to hear it and being stronger won't help Ms Kane either. It's better you let all of this out when you need to, it'll do you good. Don't bottle it up or you'll end up taking your frustrations out on Ms Kane, and goodness knows she's frustrating enough on her own.'

From the baby monitor Elizabeth moaned and shouted. Glen looked from the monitor to Charley.

'It would appear she knows better.'

She grinned and Charley heaved a teary laugh, wiping at her eyes. Glen waited until Elizabeth had settled again, the monitor falling quiet.

'It is hard, I'm not going to tell you it's not, but today has been a particularly bad day here. To experience her wrath so forcefully this morning and witness one of the most distressing episodes of hallucinations I've seen her have this afternoon, is quite a test. Along with the pressure from your family it must be feeling tough on you right now. Did you manage to clear your head and have a good think while you were out?'

Charley nodded with a sniff, and Glen handed her a tissue from a box on the side.

'I did, and I felt much better until I arrived back to Aunt Elizabeth like she was.' Charley cocked a corner of her mouth at Glen, 'But I've decided to stay. That's my decision and I'm going to stand by it, whether or not she tells me to leave again. She is sick, and it's events like this afternoon that make me realise she really needs the help. She needs someone with her. If I leave, I don't know what my family will do. They will string me up for sure, but what bothers me is that they will leave Elizabeth up here alone. Or one of them will come up here and treat her like they think she needs treating, much like they do with my sister, Rue. Or they will come up in a pack, and deal with her as they see fit. She is going through enough, she doesn't need that.'

Glen nodded.

'Ah, there it is see? you're stronger than you think. I think you'll be able to manage this Charley, and like I said I can be around through lunch breaks if I get the time, and evening's if you need me. I heard from the boss earlier, and it's good news. For the moment I'll be filling the gap in a care home only a couple of miles out of Fortwind bay. Care homes mean the pressure is spread across all staff. Which means my lunch should be protected at least, and I will have a clocking off time too it won't be as full on as it is here. Obviously, that can change, so I still think we should sort out something official if we can.'

Charley nodded, a little sigh of relief escaping her mouth.

'I'll ring mom in the morning and see if she can use her savings to pay for a few extra hours, it's silly the money sitting down there when Aunt Elizabeth needs the care so badly.'

'Well, if there's money involved, I'm sure we can get my company to agree to a few days. We'll sort something out between us, don't worry.'

Charley looked at Glen. Worry was exactly was she was doing. Two days was all Glen had left and the first day had so far been disastrous. Charley didn't think she had learned anything from it but terror and a sense of responsibility that produced the most outrageous sense of overwhelm. She pursed her lips.

'It'll be all right,' Glen said with a smile, 'Come on, drink up. It's after eleven already and if there's one thing you're always short on in this house, its sleep. If there's a good night to be had then it should be taken with gratitude.'

With an almost debilitating tiredness Charley finished her drink and said goodnight, leaving Glen to tidy up. She barely had the energy to climb into bed before she was asleep. Deep and dreamless.

She remained unaware as just after midnight the curtain slid sideways revealing part of the window before her door creaked open. Something stepped out onto the landing, and downstairs in the kitchen the cellar door swung slowly open into the dark.

Chapter Thirteen

Caring for Elizabeth was both physically and mentally challenging, just as Glen had promised, but as April melted into July Charley felt she was getting into her stride. There was still a lot to learn, but she was definitely feeling more confident, more able to handle whatever Elizabeth threw at her. It had been a steep learning curve, and the hardest ten weeks of her life, but she had coped. She was still coping, maybe even enjoying it a little too.

Glen had left Fortwind House to start her job at the care home after that first weekend, but Charley had yet to feel completely on her own. Glen had returned most lunch times, and the occasional evening, to answer any questions Charley may have, and to see how she was managing. Charley was glad she was around. She appreciated Glen's help, dedication, and knowledge.

She also wanted to ask if Glen had noticed anything strange around the house. A presence of sorts she supposed, but up to yet she hadn't plucked up the courage. Charley was under pressure, and the things she saw out of the corner of her eye or woke her in the dead of night, could just be a figment of her own stress. As time passed, she hoped that her senses would settle down. It was disconcerting to believe there was someone else in the house – opening curtains, a bang from upstairs, an opening door, the doorbell chiming - only to find that there was no one there.

Sometimes Charley felt that Elizabeth wasn't the only one going mad up here.

Axl and Nell turned up daily to cook and tend the garden, and Avril twice a week to clean. Charley was getting used to their friendly smiles and chatter, and the company which meant that there was activity at the house. Avril, bustling around as she cleaned, picking up every ornament and placing it back just so before moving on to the next. Nell, red faced and sweaty, as she cooked and baked. Even Axl was starting to come out of his shell after that first encounter, he wasn't chatty like the women were, but he seemed nice enough, although she still hadn't found out what he'd been hiding in the bag that first day.

Elizabeth surprised Charley by getting steadily easier to manage each day, which may just have been Charley's awareness and ability growing each day too, she supposed. Little by little Elizabeth was opening up, becoming less suspicious, and she was finding her aunt good company. In fact, as time went on, she was starting to think Elizabeth was more switched on and remembered far more than anyone gave her credit for. In a funny way, she reminded Charley of Rue. Very able, but everyone batting her back down regardless.

On the days she was well Elizabeth taught Charley how to play poker and gin rummy with a deck of cards. They sat at the kitchen table, oblivious of the coming and going around them until well into the night some days. Once Charley had got the hang of both games, they played for matchsticks, in silence, eyes squinting at each other over the cards in their hands. Card games were one of Elizabeth's favourite pastimes, and she said more than once that she was glad Charley was turning into a good opponent. She said it helped to keep her mind quick and her wits sharp. Charley felt a twinge of sadness at the disease which was taking Elizabeth's mind and wits with it, however sharp she thought they were.

On warmer days, Elizabeth often asked Charley to sit outside on the back patio with her. They sat on two ornate cast-iron chairs, facing the large garden. The small cast iron table always held a selection of cakes and tea between them.

Colourful spring and emerging summer blooms offered their sweet smell on the breeze, and as Elizabeth admired the garden, she told Charley of the different plants, and the times of year they flowered. The flowers in the garden were heavenly; purples, reds, yellows, oranges, all shapes and sizes, perfectly put together. Axl truly knew what he was doing with horticulture, this Charley couldn't deny. Even not fully in bloom the garden was a feast for the eyes and Charley often got her camera out, snapping off pictures as her aunt watched. Elizabeth rarely joined her on the walk around the garden but watched her from the chair, stick propped at her side, waiting to appraise the photographs from the screen on the camera or the laptop.

Occasionally Charley snapped off a few of her Aunt too, causing her to scoff and wave a hand at her.

'Take the flowers Charley, they're much more interesting.'

When the garden talk and photography had been exhausted, Elizabeth often told tales of her time working on the council, the things she had done, and the scandals that had been over the years. She told Charley of her husband, Frank, the accident which left him paralysed, his fishing business, and the parties they used to throw each year at Fortwind House.

Charley was fascinated by Elizabeth's stories, especially about her Uncle Frank, and their life up here. Her aunt was always very regal. She held herself upright, and was always immaculate, even now. A glimpse into Elizabeth and Frank's life gave Charley the insight to know why, but the telling of the story gave away enough personality to reveal that her aunt was, in fact, very down to earth, and possessed a wicked sense of humour. The stories, told with irony and a sprinkling of straight-faced dry humour, would always have Charley in fits of laughter, and her aunt cocking an amused eyebrow at her in feigned disdain. Charley felt she had laughed more up here, in this situation, than she had laughed in the last year at home.

Elizabeth spoke often of the parties, with Charley's encouragement. Big parties, with important people in the fishing world, who always expected to be well entertained. Elizabeth had wrinkled her nose at mention of those people, they were tiresome, but she was very aware that she had to play ball on those occasions. These were some of her husband's biggest customers, and some of them lived in the village. She told how she and Frank often used to compare notes after the evening was done, sitting with a bottle of brandy between them, doing impressions, and laughing at how important their guests had thought they were.

One afternoon, as they sat in the sunshine at the back of the house, Charley persuaded Elizabeth to show her some of those impressions. Tears of laughter rolled down both of their faces as she perfectly imitated the most stiff and self-important guests.

'It's all a fallacy, Charley,' Elizabeth said, smiling as she dabbed at her eyes. 'Importance and entitlement. They aren't worth a dime. Most of the people at those parties were selfish and self-important. Me, me, me. Underneath, we are all the same, flesh and bone, some are just more fortunate than others. I remember a young woman at one party, very confident, and very self-important, but at home she had a husband who was not only domineering and forceful but also entertaining five mistresses. Five!' She raised an eyebrow at Charley, whose mouth dropped open.

'Did she know?'

'Oh, of course she did. She married for money, told others she didn't care what he did, but I know she was desperately unhappy. Unfortunately, money kept her with that same man until she died, she couldn't let go of the riches enough to see that a life rich in happiness is worth so much more.' Elizabeth shrugged and gave a small smile. 'In contrast, there was a man in the village hit by a car down on the beach road. The accident left him disabled, and he could only perform menial tasks. The council supported him work wise, Equal Opportunities were just coming into their own back then, but he had very little money to support his family. He had a wife and four young children when the accident happened, and it left them all but destitute.'

Elizabeth paused and took a sip of tea. Charley waited, her heart heavy with the unfairness. Elizabeth placed the cup back down and turned to her with a smile.

'Oh, but he was rich, Charley. Every day he counted his blessings, watched his children grow, loved his wife. He laughed, and lived, and loved. He died an old man, at home, surrounded by friends and family. I always think of him when I think of that silly woman and her monied husband. Such a waste of a life.'

Charley was enthralled. The irony was that her mother and sisters were sitting at home full of the same entitlement and self-importance. All bar Rue anyway. They may have good jobs and a little money between them but look at them. All of them spiteful and selfish. Charley wouldn't swap her life for any of theirs.

She looked to her aunt. Composed and peaceful. Her silver hair shone in the sunshine, hazel eyes sharp and intelligent, brimming with life. Charley thought it was a shame she couldn't have grown up here, with her aunt, instead of back in Harrogate with the family from hell. How could two sisters be so opposite in nature?

SHATTERED

On the inevitable days that Elizabeth became unwell, struggling with her memory, movement, or having hallucinations, Charley felt low and numb. Her aunt seemed so alive on the good days, and when those good days had a short run she sometimes completely forgot their situation. Now and then, usually when she was alone in bed, Charley thought of the moment that was creeping steadily forward with each passing day, and her heart would give a fearful jolt.

She didn't want her aunt to die just yet, in fact she didn't want her to die at all. She wanted months here, years even, to sit with Elizabeth and let her regale stories of the past and play gin rummy. She wanted to get to know her Aunt, to listen to stories of parties and Uncle Frank, and to know what had happened with her mother all those years ago.

And if she was being honest, death scared the hell out of her, and she was here alone.

The when and the how scared her. How did people die? Did they know it was coming, did they just take a breath and slip away? Or did they fight it, and struggle to hold on to life? Did they lie down, knowing it was coming? Or just fall down, taken by surprise? There were so many questions, and although Glen had come across death before, even she didn't have the answer to all of them. Some questions could only be answered by the dead, and Charley didn't have the luxury of questioning them.

The other dark cloud that hung over their days, was the extreme paranoia. Beside the good chats, the cards and the laughter, Elizabeth was still completely convinced that she was being poisoned. There were moments when she would become almost frantic trying to coax Charley into believing her. Charley had relayed the conversations to Glen, who said it had been a feature of the last year or so, and just to humour her. Listen, and then dismiss it.

But Elizabeth wouldn't let her dismiss it. Each day she became more convinced, and over time Charley noticed that she was getting thinner as she ate less and less. By mid-July she was begging Charley to cook her meals, pick everything fresh, and start from scratch. She was to throw away all of Nell's lovely roast dinners, pies and pastries.

Horrified, Charley had intended to sneak some aside to save it going to waste, but reading Charley's mind, Elizabeth had been adamant that she was not to touch it. All of it went down the garbage disposal under her aunt's stare. Every last crumb. Every day. Charley always felt some of her soul go down with it.

It was certainly an added pressure to cook but Elizabeth, who had been quite a cook herself until the disease really took hold, liked to be in the kitchen to watch her anyway. She advised and mentored Charley on each meal, tasting soups and casseroles for just a dash more parsley, rosemary, salt, paprika, balsamic vinegar, pepper, thyme, cumin, oregano. The list went on. The cupboards and garden were full of fresh and dried herbs, spices, ingredients and condiments, and Elizabeth was adept at using each one. She made Charley taste the mixture before and after each item was added so she could taste the difference herself, and Charley began to look forward to the time of day when Avril, Nell, and Axl left, and they could get down to some cooking.

From being a self-confessed take-out girl, she was slowly becoming a fruit and vegetable gardener. She learned what to pick and when, what was ripe and what wasn't, and she was becoming a good cook with a keen sense of taste.

Everything Axl picked went down the garbage disposal.

Of course, he knew the vegetables were going missing. He knew every inch of the garden and allotment, but Charley merely said she picked them for herself with Elizabeth's blessing. There was never enough gone for him to question it, Elizabeth was incredibly careful to tell her to pick only what they would need for each meal. She would send Charley with a list, six beans, four potatoes, one cabbage, two spears of broccoli. It was all very precise and calculated.

It was another thing about Elizabeth that amazed Charley. If this was dementia, then she had got the disease completely wrong.

Most days were full and busy, time went by quickly, and Charley enjoyed life up here. She continued with her business around Elizabeth's quieter times, fulfilling orders through third party sellers. It wasn't the way she usually worked, but up here she knew there was no way she could chase deliveries and post several orders per day. So she used companies who printed for her, arranging for them to send directly to customers hot off the press. It was costing her extra and she couldn't check the quality for herself, but it was the only way to keep working for the moment, and she'd had no complaints so far.

She found snippets of time to take photographs, sticking to the view from the windows and taking pictures around the house and grounds. She didn't go out. She didn't want to leave Elizabeth up here alone, much to Theo's disappointment. He was badgering her for lunch and Belle wanted her to go out in the boat.

Charley promised Theo that she would let him know when she got a chance, but for now it was a no go. Meanwhile, they kept in contact and Charley looked forward to his texts and calls, and hearing what he and Belle had been up to during the day. It was an unexpected friendship, and a break from the world at Fortwind House. She enjoyed it here, but she hoped to get out soon. Another visit to the sea wouldn't go amiss, even just for ten minutes, and she was excited to see Theo and Belle again.

The only other contact Charley received from the outside world was from her family. Mainly Evelyn, family spokesperson, who was still an expert in all things Elizabeth and dementia. And who still rubbed it in each time she called that *she* had been right about Charley staying.

It had been the noble and right thing to do. Didn't Charley feel so much better for it? Think how bad she would have felt if she had ran away and one of the others had had to come here, giving up lives and money when Charley had it so easy, it would have been selfish wouldn't it? Don't you think so, Charley?

Charley still prickled every time she saw Evelyn's name appear on the phone, via text or call, but the effect of the family was slowly waning as the time away from them increased. She found she was better able to deal with the patronising tones from up here and Elizabeth was a good listener when she wanted to let off steam.

In the garden with Elizabeth one day, at the start of July, Charley had put the phone on loudspeaker so that she could hear for herself. They had silently mimicked Evelyn so much that Charley had struggled to keep the laughter out of her voice when she'd had to speak.

For now, with them hours away, she could deal with it. She wouldn't bite, and she wouldn't let them think they were anything other than right. They would discuss how badly she was doing around Evelyn's table daily, for sure, but she couldn't be bothered to correct them.

Aunt Elizabeth was just the witch of their childhood. *Still* the witch of their childhood. They had no idea.

No idea about Elizabeth and the woman that she had once been - still was in snippets - and certainly no idea about dementia and the struggle it entailed for her on a daily basis.

No. They had no idea. It was a simple as that.

Chapter Fourteen

The weather had been changing over the last few weeks. After the warmth of a good spring and early summer, August had been wet and by the first week of September a cool nip was starting to appear in the air too. Today was blue skies and sunshine, but a brisk wind tugged and pushed, making the air feel cooler than it looked.

Charley stood at the front door of Fortwind House. The doorbell had been chiming at odd hours lately and had chosen that moment to go off again. Racing to the door so that whoever was playing pranks had no time to hide, Charley flung it open and stared at the empty driveway where there was nothing but the rumble of a car engine in the distance.

Impossible.

A small blue Fiesta came into view but coming *up* the drive. Glen.

Doorbell forgotten, Charley grinned as Glen parked and got out, coming to the door hunched against the wind, pulling her coat around her.

'Hi Glen, come in, come in.'

'You were expecting me?' Glen laughed.

'Not really, just putting some rubbish out and heard the car.' Charley wasn't even sure why she had lied.

She waved a hand at the doorway, stepping aside as Glen hurried through, running a hand through her greying dark hair, wild from the wind. She took off her coat as Charley shut the door behind them, shivering a little in the cool air.

'Woah, Summer has decided to come to an end early, huh? How are you, Charley? And how is Elizabeth?'

'Elizabeth is good… well, she's had a great few days, but she went downhill again this morning. She was shaking and slurring quite badly when I got her upstairs, and she was very confused. I told her to sit and watch the ocean while I got her a drink, but when I got back, she was on her bed asleep. That was around ten minutes ago, I've got the monitor in the kitchen just in case she wakes.'

Glen nodded and pursed her lips, a smile that started in her eyes spreading across her face.

'What?'

'There I was feeling guilty that I haven't been able to get up here lately, and you've been swimming along with no problems, taking it all in your stride.'

Charley laughed as they went through to the kitchen and she flicked the kettle on, taking a couple of scones out of a storage container on the side to join the jam and cream on the table.

'Oh, I wouldn't go that far, but I told you, she has been so much easier over the last month or so. It's been great, her bad days have been nothing like that first day, not by half, and she's making a lot of sense when she talks, she doesn't seem as confused. I was just having a scone you want one?'

Glen pulled out a chair and sat down with a nod.

'Please, I'm famished. Listen… Charley, I know she has long outlasted her prognosis, and I know what I said that first day too, but you mustn't get the wrong idea, Ms Kane is a very sick lady. She will have good and bad days, but she won't get better. You know that don't you?'

The smile slipped from Charley's face as she put the cups of tea on the table. She sat heavily in the chair opposite Glen.

'I know she won't, I'm not under any illusion. It's such a shame though, I think I'd have really liked to have known Elizabeth when I was growing up. I thought she was a witch you know, which is ridiculous when you get to know her, I've never met anyone with such a good heart and a great sense of humour, she's had me in stitches with some of her stories. I... I'll be devastated to see her go.' Her voice caught as she thought of the inevitable.

Glen gave Charley a sad smile.

'I know, she's very magnetic. Nell said people have always seemed to flock to her, even as far back as school. It's a terrible thing the way she is now, but she is seventy-four, she has had a good life, and that is to be celebrated.'

Charley pursed her lips, swallowing hard, as she cut into a scone. Glen picked up the other one to do the same, sensing the need for a change of subject.

'So, here is a story that intrigues me. Why on earth would you think Ms Kane was a witch?'

Charley smiled. 'Stories. That's all. My sisters mainly, although thinking about it, my mother did nothing to dispel the notion either, which probably only embedded it further into my young head. I don't know where it came from. My sisters said she used to brew potions down in the cellar all day and that she was horrible to them when they visited. She would shout and lock them down there with all of the children she was going to eat. Later she apparently killed her husband, my Uncle Frank, and ate him too, to stop him exposing her secret. As you do.'

Charley looked at Glen, who had paused with her tea halfway to her mouth and was staring at Charley wide eyed. Charley felt the laughter rise up from her stomach and spill over. And then they were both laughing hard.

Glen wheezed as her shoulders shook, and Charley had to hold her jaw to stop it from aching.

'I know it's stupid. It's especially ridiculous now that I know her, but it was very frightening as a child.'

Glen pulled a tissue from her pocket to blow her nose and dab her eyes.

'It sounds like one of Grimm's Fairy Tales,' she said.

'It was worse, believe me.'

'Well I suppose I can offer a little insight into those tales. Elizabeth used to be big into herbal medicine, even going as far as making her own using plants from the garden, which is why there's such a wide variety I believe. And I believe she did work down in the cellar, although I know of no children locked down there. And Frank? He died of natural causes years after an accident paralysed him down at the harbour. He was young when he died, in his fifties I think, but he certainly wasn't murdered as far as I know.'

Charley felt years of laden weight slide off her shoulders at the innocent explanation. She opened her mouth, but Glen held a hand up to her.

'That's all I know. You should ask Elizabeth about it. She loves to talk about the herbs and different plants that heal ailments. She'll probably tell you about your Uncle Frank too.'

Charley grinned. 'You know what, I'll do that thank you.'

They tucked into their scones, spreading them with jam and cream, and as the laughter wore off, Glen caught up on Elizabeth's situation. Charley told her how she was getting on with the symptoms and the medication, what she was doing when each symptom came on, how she was dealing with the hallucinations, everything she could think of until she had given Glen all the information she could.

'Good,' Glen said, with a smile. 'You're doing really well, Charley. Really well. Gosh these scones are beautiful, I know it's cheeky but is there another? I've not had lunch yet, and I'm sure Nell won't mind.'

Charley brought the box over for Glen.

'Nell won't mind at all, these are freshly made by me.'

Glen stopped spreading jam and looked up at Charley.

'You get time to bake too? I'm impressed. You don't just leave her in bed do you? Is that why she's been easier to handle?'

Charley grinned.

'Nope, she sits in the very seat you're in instructing me what to do from the table. I had no idea how to cook or bake anything before July.'

Glen pushed out her lips bringing her eyebrows together.

'Well, where has this come from? She was never interested in cooking when I was here.'

'To be honest, I think it's the paranoia. The only thing that she's still absolutely convinced about is that someone, well *they*, are trying to poison her. She has never said who she thinks it may be, or why, but she won't touch any of Nell's food anymore unless she has to.'

Glen's eyebrows shot up.

'So, she's told Nell to go?'

'Oh no, she still lets Nell come up and cook, she still chats to her as normal, she doesn't want to hurt her feelings I don't think. But after Nell has gone, I have to throw away everything she has made, she's so convinced the food is laced that I'm not allowed to eat it either. So, she instructs, and I have to cook everything in front of her. It's the only way she will eat. I only agreed because she was getting so thin, she needs to eat.'

'And Nell has no idea?'

'No, Elizabeth will eat bits and pieces to appease Nell if she is around but never much, only a few bites.'

'Wow, the brain is a funny thing, but I suppose if you don't mind, it saves fighting about food with Ms Kane, anyway.'

Charley nodded.

'I'm quite enjoying it.'

Glen finished the rest of her second scone and licked jam off her finger.

'They're really delicious, Charley, you've been busy up here, and with no break, which makes what I'm going to say all the more important. Listen, I have the afternoon off and I was going to ask you if I could hang around here if you didn't mind. I don't have anyone to go home to, and I've missed Ms Kane. To be honest though, with her asleep it doesn't need two of us so how about you take a break now? Get out of this house for a while. I know it can be claustrophobic.'

Charley's heart leapt, but she caught herself just in time.

'Oh, no, Glen I couldn't have you up here looking after Elizabeth on your afternoon off. I'd feel so guilty. You must have things to do.'

'I have nothing to get home for, honestly Charley, and like I say I've missed it here, and I've missed Ms Kane. You go and grab a few hours to yourself, I don't know when I'll get the chance to take over again. Take it, you deserve it.'

Unable to help herself, a large grin spread over Charley's face and she ran around to Glen's side of the table, grabbing her in a hug.

'Glen, I don't know what I'd do without you. Thank you so much, I really appreciate this.'

At Glen's insistence, Charley left her clearing away and rushed upstairs as quietly as she could, so as not to wake her aunt. Not that it was possible to make any noise on this carpet. In her room she text Theo. She had messaged him yesterday, so she knew it was one of his days off, she just hoped he didn't already have plans.

Hey, What you up to? Fancy lunch?

She threw the phone onto the bed and put on a jumper as she waited for his reply. If he had plans, she would wrap up and go down to the beach, maybe take a stroll through the village and see what was around. A flutter of excitement swirled in her stomach at finally being able to get out and knowing her Aunt would be safe with Glen.

Her phone pinged.

Well, it's about bloody time! I've almost forgot what you look like, wear purple so I can identify you. See you on the seafront in ten?

Charley grinned as she replied, before stuffing her phone into her pocket, and grabbing her hat – purple, in case he wasn't joking - and scarf. It was extreme, she knew, but it would be windier and colder down on the beach, and if there was one thing Charley hated it was being cold. Pulling on boots, and grabbing her coat, she headed back downstairs, checking on Elizabeth on the way.

'I'm off then,' She said to Glen in the kitchen, 'Elizabeth is still sleeping. Thank you so much for this, Glen.'

Glen smiled crossing her arms over her ample bosom.

'That's how much you need it, you've got a mile-wide smile. Enjoy pet, and take your time, I've got nowhere to be.'

Charley let out at a strangled screech of excitement as she headed for the door.

Within seconds she was in the car, music up, heading down the drive to the seafront. She had enjoyed being with her Aunt more than she could have imagined, but at this moment freedom had never felt so good.

Chapter Fifteen

The small ocean themed cafe was bustling with people. A queue wound its way from the red counter and around the blue and white striped wall adorned with seashells, fisherman's rope, and anchors. Paintings of seascapes, ships, sunsets, and beach huts filled every available space. Shouts, laughter, music, clinking of cutlery and crockery filled the small space.

Theo pulled Belle in front of him and, keeping his hands on her shoulders, steered her toward the only remaining booth until they were safely seated. Charley stayed close behind, taking the seat opposite.

'We made it through the storm skipper, time to relax.'

Belle grinned up at her father.

'Aye, aye captain.'

She slumped her shoulders dramatically and blew out a breath putting her head down to meet the polished wood of the table. Theo laughed and ruffled her hair.

'It's not too noisy here is it?' He said turning his attention to Charley.

'No, it's fine. You said this place did the best lunch, and it seems the whole village agrees with you. I'm excited.'

'Well, prepare yourself for a treat. Order whatever you fancy, nothing is too good for the saviour of skipper Belle.' He smiled and turned to Belle the mass of brown curls bobbing on top of his head. 'What'll it be Belle?'

Charley picked up the menu and began to scour through the lunchtime section as Belle chose her meal without looking.

'Haddock and chips, extra bread, but hold the mushy peas, and a strawberry slushy to drink, yum.'

Charley peered at her over the menu.

'Crikey, this girl knows what she wants.'

'She sure does,' Theo said, he grinned down at Belle. 'We have to eat at this place at least once a week. Belle would eat here every day if she could.'

Belle suddenly sat up, eyes wide.

'Oh, I forgot the Chocolate Brownie Sundae too.'

Charley placed the menu back on the table and looked at the slip of a girl, her eyes as wide as Belle's.

'And just where are you going to put all that food, young lady?'

'In here.' Belle giggled leaning back and patting her stomach.

'I'm not sure it will fit.'

'It will.' Belle said nodding.

She grinned as the waitress appeared at the table and Belle recited her order, word for word, as the waitress wrote it on her little pad. Theo ordered steak and chips with peppercorn sauce and a coffee. Charley, who hadn't even looked at the menu, quickly scanned it and chose the first thing she saw. A ham baguette. Which went down like a lead balloon.

'I'm not treating you to a ham sandwich Charley, I don't know when I'll get you out again, order some food for god's sake.'

She glanced back at the menu, but all the dishes were blending into one under the stares of the three people waiting for her.

'I can't choose. I just don't know what to have, there's too much choice.'

'Well ham is off the menu,' Theo said, he looked up to the waitress, 'what's the special today, Clara?'

'Pan fried sea bass.'

Theo looked back at Charley.

'You like fish?'

'Er, yes, in general. I've never had sea bass but -'

'Now is the time to try, it's delicious.'

Charley nodded and looked up at Clara who was smiling back at her.

'Ok, I'll give the sea bass a try. Why not?'

She ordered a coffee and the waitress slipped away into the seemingly never-ending bustle of customers. Charley smiled after her until she caught sight of the chalkboard on the wall behind the counter that announced that today's special was just £14.99. Dismayed, she looked back at Theo who was sorting Belle out with some crayons and paper from the little Peppa Pig bag he had dutifully carried here for her.

'Theo, I'm so sorry, if I'd known how much the sea bass was I would never have ordered it. I have some money on me I'll pay half.'

Theo looked up at her.

'Pay half?'

'It's fifteen pounds. That's a ridiculous amount for lunch.'

'You'll do no such thing. It's my treat. Belle's life means much more to me than a measly fifteen pounds.'

Charley opened her mouth to contest, but Theo cut her off abruptly, hand up, palm toward her face.

'No, I won't hear of it.'

Charley closed her mouth with a snap. She sighed.

'All right, thank you.' She said.

'That's better,' Theo said with a smile.

Charley grinned. 'So, what have you two been up to since I last saw you, anything exciting?'

Theo shook his head slowly, looking thoughtful, as Belle nodded hers eagerly next to him.

'I can't think of anything major,' Theo said. He ran a hand across his chin in thought.

Belle started to bounce in her seat.

'There is something, remember?' She elbowed her father in the ribs and he pretended to think.

Charley didn't have a clue what the news could be, but she grinned as Belle's eyes widened.

'You do remember, it's very important.'

Theo looked down at her, narrowing his eyes, and then looked back away.

'Nope, nothing springs to mind.'

'Daddy! I started School!'

Theo sat back mouth dropping open in mock horror.

'That's right you did, I forgot.'

Charley laughed as Belle cut her eyes at him, bottom lip jutting out.

'Wow, Belle, so you're a big girl now then? And how is school, do you like it?'

Belle nodded proudly, pout leaving her lips as quickly as it had arrived.

'It's good, I get to play and make things and have yummy dinner with my friends.'

The drinks arrived and Charley sat back with her coffee listening to Belle describe the important things she did all day. When it appeared that her list would go on indefinitely, Theo pushed the colouring book under her nose.

'Here, why don't you show Charley how well you colour now you've been practising at school. This mermaid picture is beautiful, look.'

'Okay, but I'll need to contrate.'

'Concentrate,' He corrected, with a grin and a wink at Charley 'All the better.'

Belle pulled out her crayons and studied them seriously. Finally she picked a purple and began colouring the mermaids tail, tongue flicking between her lips.

Theo raised his eyebrows at Charley.

'So how are you getting on with Lady Elizabeth?'

Charley smiled and put down her cup.

'Really good. She's not been too bad at all, she can still be frustrating but I'm actually getting to like her a lot, she's good company. I can't believe I had her so wrong. I wish I could have met her sooner without the dementia cloud hanging over us.'

Theo's eyebrows flicked together momentarily in confusion.

'What did you have wrong?'

'Oh, just silly stories my sisters used to tell me. Ridiculous now I know more, but I thought she was actually a witch brewing stuff in the cellar.'

Theo snorted a laugh as Belle stared at her, purple crayon hanging from her fingers.

'You were running from a real witch that day?' she said.

Charley shook her head.

'No Belle, I only thought she was a witch, but actually she's a real nice lady.'

'Oh.'

Apparently, it wasn't exciting enough because Belle was straight back to her purple tail as Theo put a hand over his mouth to calm his laughter. Charley looked at him.

'It really wasn't that funny.'

'Elizabeth Kane? A witch?' He leaned across the table toward her, lowering his voice to a whisper. 'Have you checked for a cauldron down in the cellar? They say there's a secret only three doors away from you at any one time... this could be mine.'

He waggled his eyebrows, and Charley rolled her eyes fighting to keep the grin off her face.

'Don't scoff, it was a scary part of my childhood! I was properly terrified coming up here, it's like meeting the boogie man of your nightmares. And no, I'm not going near that cellar.'

Theo cracked up again and Charley shook her head, laughing with him.

'It's not funny,' she said as his laughter tailed off.

'It really is.' he said, taking a sip of coffee. A man walking by outside raised a hand in greeting through the glass and Theo raised his in return before smiling back at Charley.

'So, I'm intrigued, how was it you that ended up here then? I just presumed you were the only one to do it. I mean, your mom wouldn't come if they've not spoken for years, that's obvious, but you have sisters?'

'Three, and I'm an easy target that's why. I'm quite a lot younger than they are, they're dominant when they get into a pack, and they like to think their lives are more important than mine. When my mother joins in, there's no option but to get steamrollered.' She smiled at Theo and took a sip of her own coffee. Strong, just how she liked it. Theo cocked an eyebrow.

'You make them sound like wolves.'

'That would be a fair description. It's nice to have a break from them, even under the circumstances.'

Theo gave an easy laugh.

'Sounds like you were stuck between a rock and a hard place then.'

'I was until I realised Elizabeth is really nice. Now I'm in the better place.' She grinned at Theo, 'I'm enjoying getting to know her, and getting to know a little more about her life.'

Theo sipped his drink and nodded.

'I asked my parents about her after I'd met you. We don't see her down in the village anymore but she is still a well-respected woman. As I said, I was too young to know much, but she and her husband Frank had quite a presence over the village when I was small.' He paused, taking another sip of coffee and narrowing his eyes in thought. 'I do remember seeing them in the street a few times, but that may have been more to do with the clip around the ear.'

He chuckled and Charley raised her eyebrows as her mouth dropped open.

'She clipped you around the ear?'

Theo burst into laughter holding his hands up in front of him.

'No, no, not Elizabeth, jeez you do have quite a vision of her, don't you? My mother always clipped me around the ear.' He became serious, cleared his throat and held his head high speaking each word properly and precisely, very much like Elizabeth did. 'When Mr and Mrs Kane pass you in the street, stand to the side respectfully, Theodore. You will stand up straight and greet them politely bowing your head as they pass.'

He let the accent go, grinning as he continued.

'At least in my house, anyway. I'm not sure many of the families around here went to the lengths my mother and father did to make a show of them. I was only around Belle's age. I didn't see what all the fuss was about they seemed like normal people to me. I'm not sure they'd have cared either way if we'd taken a bow and rolled out a red carpet, or carried on walking straight past with a nod and a 'Hi'.'

Charley leaned forward, intrigued, resting her chin in her hand.

'So how did your parents know her? Did they say what she was like? From what my sisters said she was quite intimidating and ferocious back in the day.'

A small frown passed over Theo's brow as he spoke.

'Hmm, only if you got on the wrong side of her I think. Dad worked with her, he said she did a lot of work on the council here, I've heard she could be quite ferocious in those situations, but only for the good of the town. Many dilapidated shop fronts have been overhauled, and the flowers you see in the hanging baskets today, all down the main street, were thanks to Mrs Kane over the years. Her involvement in keeping the village bright, neat, and cheerful seems to have carried through the years. You won't find an empty, disused, untidy, or unkempt shop front in Fortwind Bay now, the tourist industry is booming here, it's won the prettiest village award for the area six years running. Mrs Kane may be no longer in action on the council, but her work here is still very much present in the village.'

Charley nodded impressed.

'What about Frank, my uncle? Aunt Elizabeth has spoken a little of him, and I know of the accident, but she hasn't said much else really, did they mention him?'

'Ah well, Mr Kane I know more about. He owned a fishery and a small fleet of fishing ships which ran from the harbour, the company still exists, I work for it, but it was sold on after his death. He made quite a good deal of money over the years, millions, if the rumours are to be believed. They brought Fortwind House, which is obviously a prominent building, but they never splashed money about other than that. They actually gave a lot of it back to the village, dad said, creating the play park for the children at the end of the beach and adding the clock tower, and small garden around it, in the centre of town for people to admire and sit.

There were other things I'm sure, I'm only going by what I can remember, and dad didn't go into it much. I do know Mr Kane gave lots back to the fishing industry here, new equipment, boats, and the like. He even paid to extend the harbour here which, back in the day, only docked a couple of boats at a time. We can easily get six big trawlers in there now. Dad always says it's why the fishing industry here still thrives like it does. That Mr Kane's company had a reputation for being at the forefront of new technology and techniques that allowed for more, and better-quality fish and shellfish. I don't know how true that is, but I do know that the fish, from all of the trawlers here, is in high and regular demand. Fishermen here are paid better wages than further up the coast too. It says a lot for a small seaside town of around five hundred people really, doesn't it?'

Charley nodded enjoying the story, enjoying the company, and enjoying this bustling cafe, in this pretty little village.

'It really does. So, is this one of the places you supply to?'

Theo's eyes lit up with a pride for his job that just couldn't be hidden.

'Yep, all the fish sold in Fortwind Bay come from our trawlers daily, amongst going many other places too, of course.'

'I shall look forward to this sea bass then.' Charley said.

Theo grinned. 'Well, if you don't like it, just remember this lot wasn't my catch.' He laughed and winked, before glancing at Belle, who was colouring the mermaid purple and green in a world of her own. He looked back to Charley. 'So, where do you normally call home?'

The waitress appeared with the food cutting the conversation short and Charley's mouth watered as the smell of the sea bass and fennel filtered up from the fish-shaped plate placed in front of her. The fish sat atop a scoop of herb filled mashed potato and a few young broccoli stems. It looked and smelled delicious. Charley waited until the waitress had placed Belle's food before her and retreated to fetch Theo's steak before answering.

'Well, home is Harrogate normally, but for the foreseeable future I'll be living up here. Hopefully a while yet, I've already been here much longer than they said I would need to be, but I'm not complaining.'

Theo finished his coffee as the waitress brought his steak.

'Yeah, I remember you saying the prognosis was bad.' He said picking up the salt and shaking some onto his chips. 'She didn't have much long-'

He stopped shaking and stared at her, salt cellar still in his hand. 'But... woah! Hang on, she passed her date already, so soon?'

Charley nod her head as she swallowed more of the delicious fish.

'Yes, they had given her a month in April, but to be honest with you, Glen, her nurse, wasn't so sure that she was that bad, and now that I've been caring for her for a while I'm not either. She seems full of life when she's not having a bad day. I just don't think she's at death's door. But then, I'm not an expert, and Glen said just today not to get my hopes up as the tests were conclusive.'

Theo frowned as he chewed and swallowed his steak.

'No arguing with science, I suppose, You just have to enjoy the time you have left with her then. So, they said a month?' He shook his head slowly. 'Wow, and you're well over that already. Does that mean you have to get back to Harrogate soon? What about your job?'

'Oh, that's fine. I'm a photographer. I sell my stuff online so I can easily do that up here. There's probably a lot more inspiration here to be honest.'

Theo's fork clattered to his plate dramatically as he looked up at her eyebrows raised. Belle pushed her own battered fish into her mouth as she glanced at him.

'A photographer, eh? Charley! We have to get you out on the sea. The scenery, the island, the village. There's some fantastic sunrises and sunsets here, I've always said if someone could photograph here properly they'd make a mint...'
She grinned at his enthusiasm, cutting him short as she held a hand up.

'I know, I've seen them from the window, I really want to get out there too. I can't wait to photograph something a bit different up here. It's hard to explain but I want to try to go from taking pictures to capturing emotion. You know?'

Theo wrinkled his nose.

'Er, kind of?'

'I mean... like,' she paused, thinking of a way to explain, 'Well, the sea is the sea. And a photograph of the sea is just that. But what about the feeling behind it? The love for it, the swell, the heartbeat, the power. What I *feel* for it. What about capturing the *real* sea? Not just the surface. Depth. Emotion. I want people to be emotionally moved by my photographs.'

Theo grinned and picked up his fork with a cock of his head.

'Good luck with that. I have no idea what you're talking about, or where to start helping you out.'

Charley laughed.

'It's okay, I can't really explain it, but the boat will be a great start.'

'The boat I can do,' he said, pushing the last of his steak into his mouth.

Belle's head shot up.

'Ooh yes!' she said through the last mouthful of fish, her empty fork clattering back onto the plate. 'The boat Charley, you have to come on the boat!'

Charley nodded at Belle.

'I promise you I will definitely come out on the boat before I leave here. Whatever happens.'

'She has to,' Theo added, 'she needs to find emotion somewhere under the sea.' he leaned down to Belle. 'She doesn't realise that all there is in the sea are fish. I should know.'

Belle giggled as Charley threw her unused paper napkin at him, and then all three of them were laughing as talk descended into the much more exciting subjects of boat trips, the beach, the sea, and picnic's on the island under the shelter of the walls of what she now learned to be a ruined castle.

Chapter Sixteen

When Axl Pulled up at Fortwind House, he immediately recognised Glen's car, but saw no sign of Charley's. It was unusual now, but he wasn't about to ask why, instead he heaved a sigh of relief. His work would be a lot easier, and a lot more enjoyable, with Charley out of the way. Not having to catch her out of the corner of his eye or feel her eyes on his back.

He decided he would pick the fruit and vegetables Elizabeth needed first and take them inside. Then, when Charley arrived back, he would be out in the garden, where he could stay. No possibility of having to make chit chat or small talk.

Feeling better for his plan, he parked up and moved quickly to the back of the house.
Elizabeth was in the kitchen, chair positioned in the sunshine with a view out of the French doors across the garden. He smiled and held up a hand as he caught her eye, but her glazed look and lack of reaction showed that she wasn't good today.

He felt his mood sink as he entered the house and crossed to her.

'Hello Elizabeth, how are you feeling today?'

He put a hand over hers feeling the tremors in her body. Her eyes swung to him, her head shaking slowly and rhythmically. Her gaze was slightly off his and she tried to speak but her words wouldn't come. She simply made a 'zzz' sound with each jerk of her head her tongue pressed behind her top teeth. Eventually she turned her gaze back to the garden and sat unfocused on the view as she slowly shook from head to toe.

Axl swallowed hard. Sometimes he wished the process was faster, and that she would just hurry up and keel over. As time lagged it was getting harder for him to have to watch, and although Charley wasn't around at the moment, he now had to work with Elizabeth's unseeing eyes watching him from the window. Accusing. Rubbing it in.

He stood, taking his hand away from Elizabeth's, and mentally pulled himself together. He glanced into the hallway. There was no sign of Glen. He could find her to state his presence, but Charley may be back at any time, so instead he got to work. He checked the fridge and cupboards, noting what he needed, before going back out into the cool air with a few Tupperware boxes.

He reached the allotment and stood looking at the perfectly formed rows, irritation winding its way around his spine.

More gone.

There was a little something every day, and although he didn't begrudge Charley using the vegetables, he was getting increasingly annoyed at the amount she had stepped on, or broken, in her endeavour to pull things up. Things that were not yet ripe or ready, because she didn't know enough to see the section of them that were.

Everything was planted in orderly lines and planted at such times that a fresh supply was ready every few weeks, allowing Axl to pick and use the earlier plants before the next batch were ready. Charley was picking and digging all over the place. She clearly had no concept of gardening or growing vegetables. No concept of the care and conditions it took, but she was happy to traipse over the lot, and pull up what she cared to.

Axl heaved a sigh, grinding his jaw as he began to tend the patch, tidying and saving the trodden fruit and vegetables if he could, before picking fresh and placing them in the boxes. When he was finished, he lugged the boxes over to the wall and filled two Tupperware containers full of elderberries from the large bush. He replaced the lids before taking the stacked boxes back up to the house. His back groaned, and his arms ached, but he wouldn't take the chance of doing a double trip and bumping into Charley.

In the kitchen, Elizabeth was still sat as she had been for the last hour, and there was no sign of Glen. Axl didn't bother talking or calling out. He washed the things he had picked, before placing the vegetables into the cupboards and fridge, and the berries at the back of the cupboard nearest the sink where Nell knew to look for them. He worked quickly and methodically, shutting the last cupboard door as

Glen bustled in from the hallway. Lurching upright he swung round, his heart thumping as he stood to face her.

He tried to steady his breathing. He didn't know why he felt so jittery up here these days; nothing had changed. It wasn't like anyone suspected anything, even with Charley here.

He nodded to Glen and narrowed his eyes. The seemingly unflappable nurse was a little flushed and out of breath, which was strange. Out of character.

'Axl,' she breathed, her hand on her chest as she stopped in the doorway.

'That's me,' he replied, 'just picked a few vegetables for Elizabeth. I'm just going to do a little tidying outside now and then I'll be on my way. Is Charley out?'

Glen nodded quickly.

'Er, yes. Yes, she's gone to the village. I told her I'd look after Elizabeth for a while, I've nothing else on this afternoon. I'm not sure when she'll be back. I told her to take her time.'

Axl paused. There was something wrong here. Something wrong with Glen rushing in from the hall when Elizabeth sat two feet away, right here in the kitchen. The nurse had always watched over Elizabeth when she had been unwell, but for all the time it had taken Axl to pick the vegetables she had been sat in the kitchen alone.

He watched Glen's flushed face and rabbit in the headlights stance and felt something turn in his stomach.

'Everything okay, Glen?' he said.

'Yes, of course, why wouldn't it be?'

Axl stared.

'No reason, you look a little out of breath that's all.'

Recovering her posture, Glen smiled and gestured to the hall.

'Just changing Ms Kane's bed. Shaking on the sheet always gets me out of puff, that's all.'

He watched her, saying nothing.

'And you scared me,' she added, 'I could hear noises, but I didn't know there was anyone here. If I'd have known it was only you, of course, I wouldn't have been so bothered. Silly really.'

She tittered a little, hand over her mouth.

Strange. He dipped his head as his heart gathered speed. Did she know something?

'Right, sorry about that. I'll be outside then.' he said before he lost his own composure.

He stalked out of the doors not waiting for a reply, pulling in gulps of fresh cool air as he turned over the conversation. Had there been an inkling? An inkling that she knew?

Logic told him not. There was only Elizabeth to slip with information, and she was an unreliable witness. There was nothing else to give them away except the letters, which would be in his possession soon enough. Glen couldn't know, there was no logical reason to think she did.

Heaving a relieved breath, he crossed to the tool shed.

* * * * *

Glen watched Axl amble down the garden, her own heart thudding behind her ribs.

That had been close. Too close.

It wasn't like Axl normally announced himself, or for that matter, ventured into any part of the house. He usually let himself in the back and stuck to the kitchen and garden. That was his domain. But if he had chosen today to venture back into the hallway, he would have seen something that would have set him on red alert, and who knew what the consequences would have been then, or how the game would have changed.

Glen checked on Elizabeth, who was still in her chair staring unfocused through the window. This time she moved though. The rasping sound had stopped, and Elizabeth tried to swing her eyes to her.

Knowing the signs, Glen drew her a glass of water, holding it to her lips while Elizabeth took small sips. The shakes were slowing down, she was coming out, and soon she would be aware of what was going on around her again. Glen knew she had to finish up quickly.

'There we go Ms Kane. I'll just finish up and I'll be right back to sit with you a while until Charley returns.'

She pat Elizabeth's hand and went back into the hallway. Closing the kitchen door behind her, she crossed quickly back into the study, shutting the door and locking it from the inside with a small click.

Chapter Seventeen

The following day Elizabeth was back to herself as if she had fought off nothing more than a small virus. It was further proof in her mind. After taking only two bites of the cake that Nell had made yesterday morning, she had started to feel disjointed. Immediately stalling, she had declared that she felt unwell and Charley had taken her to her room. She decided in that moment that to eat anything not freshly cooked by Charley was dangerous. She was feeling more like herself every day, and the occasions where she felt ill were forming a little pattern in her mind. Not only the food she was eating, although there was still no pattern to what they added the poison to, but the amount she ate or drank which determined the severity of the attack afterwards. If it hadn't been obvious to her what was going on before Charley started cooking, it certainly was now.

What she couldn't understand is why her friends were involved. Nell she had known since they were both five years old, after they had bonded on the first day of school and been joined at the hip ever since. Axl and Avril had been friends since her days working on the council, and good friends she had thought they were too. It was giving her a headache wondering why these people, all wonderful in their own right, should have to come under suspicion. But the fact remained that they were the only ones around now, and one of them must know the truth, if not all of them.

Glen wasn't under suspicion, this had been going on before she started here, in fact it was the reason she had been here at all, and it had continued since she had left. Charley wasn't on her radar either. In fact, Charley may well be her saviour through all of this nonsense. She had been cooking fresh for Elizabeth for the last six weeks without incident, and over those weeks Elizabeth had finally started to feel less frail as her food intake increased along with her trust that Charley was clear of involvement too.

In fact, the only incidents lately were when Nell had been around and had enticed her to eat something at the table with her. As her oldest friend, and one she didn't want to believe was involved, she ate a few bites with Nell for old times' sake, but three out of the four times she had taken something from Nell, she went downhill within minutes.

Yesterday's episode hadn't been as harsh or lasted as long as usual, but it had still been harrowing. Elizabeth was glad she had felt the effects early and had known to stop. She saw only two snakes on the way up to the bedroom with Charley, one curling itself around the bannister with a hiss, and one slithering across the landing. After Charley helped her into her bedroom chair she saw two more, one curling around the chair legs and the other on the ceiling.

At that point she got up and climbed unsteadily onto the bed, laying her head on the pillow and closing her eyes to block them out. When she awoke they had gone, and Glen had appeared. Elizabeth felt a flutter of panic that Charley wasn't around, but Glen said she had merely gone out for a while and would be back later.

Elizabeth had been appeased but found she couldn't answer Glen. Her mouth felt full and heavy, filled with fur, and a sour coating seemed to line it from front to back. She couldn't seem to get any words out, the steady shaking of her whole body was taking up so much energy, she felt too depleted to try. It had lessened as the day and the evening wore on and after a good night's sleep and lots of water this morning to flush anything remaining out of her system, she felt revived. It had rarely been so quick a recovery.

Charley was in the kitchen when Elizabeth got downstairs. Her laptop was in front of her, paper at her side, and she was clicking away at something on the screen. Elizabeth watched her a moment from the doorway before clearing her throat.

Charley looked up with a smile.

'Ah there you are, feeling better?'

'Much better, thank you.'

She moved her chair back and started to rise.

'Do you want-'

Elizabeth raised a hand and shook her head.

'No, no, please don't let me disturb you. I have no appetite yet. I was just going to sort some business in the study. You carry on, I'll let you know if I need anything when I'm finished.'

Charley paused, looking at her with uncertainty. That was okay, Elizabeth merely smiled and turned to the study.

She opened the door and went inside, using the same key to lock it behind her, and then she stood, hands on her stick as her eyes fell on the contents of the room. The smell of mahogany and furniture polish reminded her of Frank. She imagined him sitting behind his desk, the steady ticking of the clock behind him, the steady scratch of his pen as it marked the pile of papers in front of him.

She smiled a little sadly, her heart pining for the man she had loved. She would do anything to have him back by her side, now more than ever. He would have believed her. He would have sorted this mess out, found out who was doing this, and why. It hadn't always been a smooth road or a smooth marriage, especially after the accident and Frank's disability, but he had always been on her side and they had always worked things out, no matter what it was.

Taking a steadying breath, Elizabeth crossed to the fireplace and bent to retrieve the little leather book from behind the flue opening. She put the book on the desk, found a pen and paper from the drawer, and sat down in the large desk chair. She wrote the letter first, taking her time, before opening the book to record the events of the previous day and this morning. The cake, yesterday's shakes, the people involved, and the hallucinations, in as much detail as she could.

Charley knocked the door at around 11.30am, interrupting her flow.

'Aunt Elizabeth? Are you okay in there?'

Elizabeth shut the leather book and quickly placed it in between other two books on a shelf, 'Healing Herbs' and 'The Home Remedy'. Noting it's place, she took her cane, moving to the door and opening it with a smile.

'I'm fine Charley, just a little longer and I'll be done.'

Charley stood in the hallway holding two small tupperware boxes.

'Okay, well I'm all finished. I thought you may be hungry. Do you want me to make lunch while you finish up? I thought sausage and egg sandwiches, and I could make us something sweet for dessert if you like?'

Elizabeth smiled down at her. This young lady was a godsend, and one she was incredibly grateful to have got to know, even if it had taken these circumstances, and Francesca's greed, for her to come.

'That would be Perfect. I shall be done in here soon, half an hour at most.'

Charley smiled and held up the boxes.

'Any idea? I found these in the cupboard, they had been pushed to the back.'

Elizabeth took a box from Charley and opened the lid to find the small, shiny, dark berries she loved so much.

'Elderberries.' She said with a smile. 'Fresh too. Axl must have picked them when he came yesterday. Maybe Nell mentioned making a pie.'

At the thought of Nell making anything for her Elizabeth's stomach clenched. The last few instances of feeling unwell had all been when Nell was around. If Nell was the culprit, then she would outwit her, she could use these safely before Nell had a chance to use them.

'Have you ever tasted them, Charley?'

Charley shook her head as Elizabeth lowered her nose to the box and sniffed. No unfamiliar smells, and they were complete berries, not much room for adding poison to them, and the bottom of the box was dry so it didn't appear that they had been soaked. There was only one thing for it.

'Berries aren't really my thing,' Charley said, wrinkling her nose, as Elizabeth picked up the smallest single berry and popped it into her mouth. The sweet sourness burst against her tongue.

She waited, pretending to savour the flavour, but really waiting for signs of any ill feeling. There was nothing so far, and usually the effect was swift. The poison was strong; she knew.

Her stomach rumbled. Yes, she was hungry, and it had been a long time since she'd had an elderberry pie, she thought she would take the chance. She popped another two into her mouth. They tasted wonderful and she almost closed her eyes with pleasure.

'Yum. You know what Charley? It's been so long since I've had an elderberry pie. It's one of my favourite things to eat and these seem fresh. You make the sandwiches, I'll finish off here, and be in to help you with the pie afterward.'

Charley nodded and grinned.

'Sounds good to me. Do you want me to pick fresh for you? I don't mind if you don't want to eat these.'

Elizabeth shook her head.

'No, they seem fine to use.' She popped a further two into her mouth for luck.

With a nod, Charley went back to the kitchen and Elizabeth shut the door. She didn't lock it, she wouldn't need long now, half an hour, just long enough to check the berries properly.

Sitting back at the desk she completed yesterday's entry before placing the book back in its spot behind the fireplace.

With everything safely hidden Elizabeth glanced at the clock. Almost twenty minutes had passed, and she was still feeling fine. She had thought she would divert Charley from the pie if she felt any kind of ill effects, but these berries weren't tainted, they could be used.

She breathed a small sigh of relief and brought her fingers up to the pearls around her neck. To be honest, she had never suspected Axl would be the one to be doing the poisoning, anyway. Women were always more spiteful and resourceful than men. They were also more careful. If these berries were okay, then Axl could be relied upon, she was sure. She may even start to keep the vegetables he picked, if they were okay, then he could be removed from the equation completely.

She smiled, feeling she was finally starting to get somewhere. Who knew, maybe she would beat them at their game yet. It was far from over but she was a small step closer to the culprit, she could feel it in her bones.

Feeling good, she picked up the small handwritten paper she had left on the desk and folded it in half. placing the cream paper into an envelope, she sealed it and wrote Charley's name on the front. She stared at it a while, thinking, before putting it into her skirt pocket, deciding to keep it on her. What she really hoped was that Charley would never need it, but every eventuality had at least now been taken care of, every possible loose end had been tied up, and with a bit of luck, the outcome would be in her favour.

Elizabeth smiled as her stomach grumbled. She was hungry today, but she would give it fifteen more minutes before going in to Charley, just to be sure.

Opening the door, she poked her head out into the hallway, and told Charley she would be a while longer before picking out her favourite book of short poems and sitting back in the captain's chair to read.

Chapter Eighteen

Charley sang along with the radio as she packed away her laptop and took it upstairs, she had done as much as she needed to. The time away from the house yesterday had revived her, and with her aunt better again this morning, she was feeling happy and relaxed.

This was the life. When the going was good, it was fabulous up here.

Placing her laptop case on the bed she walked to the window, the radio and the hum of the microwave defrosting sausages downstairs reached her ears as she leaned her arms on the sill. The day had started out grey with mist and drizzle that had now turned to a persistent drum of rain, she could just make out the harbour and the island through the murk, a far cry from yesterday's cheery sunshine. She was leaning into the glass for a better view when there was a loud thud from the kitchen, bringing her attention back inside.

That was quick, she said fifteen minutes. What is she doing down there?

Pushing off the sill Charley made her way back downstairs, walking into the kitchen with a smile. The room was empty, sausages still turning in the microwave, grill open as she had left it.

'Aunt Elizabeth?' she said with a frown.

There was no reply.

I must be hearing things, but that's nothing new here is it?

She huffed a breath and opened the microwave to check the sausages.

A thud came from behind her, followed by a low scrape. Turning, Charley's heart flipped, and the packet of sausages tumbled from her hands to the countertop.

The cellar door was standing open.

Oh crap.

She stared, and then closed her eyes, willing the door to be shut when she opened them. It wasn't. It sat open. Passive. The ominous silence growing oppressive. Charley shivered, the air seemed cooler now...

...From the open door of a damp cellar. Just shut the damn door and forget it Charley.

She crept toward it, listening, every hair standing to attention at the back of her neck as she put her hand onto the doorknob - and paused.

This is ridiculous. Maybe this stupid fear should be addressed? There is a logical explanation for the stories, and it is just a room in a house after all. How scary can a god-damn cellar be?

Peering down the stone steps, she shuddered in the cool breeze that rose to meet her... and frowned.

There was a light down there. Not daylight. The fluorescent glow of a strip light. Her heart thumped against her ribs.

'Aunt Elizabeth?' She called.

The air stirred, but no reply came back. Every hair seemed to stand on end as the light flickered, dimmed, and shone bright again with a low buzz and a metallic ping. Charley gulped around the lump that was holding firm in her throat.

I'm going to have to go down and turn the thing off, aren't I?

Was she? She debated shutting the door, but it wasn't her electricity bill to pay and Elizabeth was already running on air as far as money was concerned.

Then go turn it off it's just a light in a cellar.

But who turned it on?

Does it matter? just turn it off.

I don't want to go down there.

It's just a damn cellar.

What if I find something...?

Charley put her hands to her temples and clenched her jaw

STOP. Charley, just stop. The light could have been off by now.

The microwave beeped and she let out small yelp, putting a hand to her chest.

Idiot. Get this over with.

She rubbed the goosebumps down on her arms, preparing to launch herself down the steps, find the light switch and launch herself back up - preferably in under ten seconds - and then the scrape came again. Low and heavy.

From down in the cellar...

...just as Elizabeth called out from the hallway that she would be done in five minutes and the click of the study's door latch filled her ears.

Filled her *brain* as the realisation sank in.

Elizabeth wasn't in the cellar.

The goosebumps were back, along with a nervous lurch in her stomach.

'Okay,' she called back weakly.

Right here in the kitchen nothing was okay. Elizabeth and Charley were the only people here, and yet something was down in the cellar.

Another scrape, and a thud from below.

Nope, not possible. I'm hallucinating.

Charley closed her eyes trying to fill her constricted lungs with air.

135

SHATTERED

I'm shutting the door. When Elizabeth is in here I'll maybe turn off the light. Safety in numbers and all that.

She opened her eyes and began to push the door closed, catching the apparition at the bottom of the stairs from the corner of her eye. The light flickered again as the figure, a swirling blur of white began to ascend the steps, and then momentum from her hand finally slammed the door shut. Charley's breath caught in her throat as a quick retreat backward slammed her into the table. She stood gasping for air, every nerve on edge, as her wide eyes fixed on the door, which seemed to be alive. *To be breathing.*

The handle twisted slowly. Stopped. Twisted again. The door pushed against its hinges as pressure pushed from the other side, gently at first, and then harder until it swung out into the kitchen with a long groan. The rush of blood beat loud in Charley's ears, and there was a pulse behind her eyes. Her vision wavered. The door seemed to double, blurring, and she thought she may just faint right where she stood... which would be better than to have to face the thing that may or may not come out of the cellar.

In broad daylight.

She closed her eyes.

This is not possible. NOT possible.

'Bloody door.' A voice admonished. 'Sorry, Charley did I scare you? The door only opens from the outside, the catch doesn't quite draw back from the cellar side. It's hit or miss whether you get out. It's a pain in the rear. I should have called out.'

Charley opened an eye to see Nell close the cellar door. Nell who was as real as the daylight. Nell, who was wearing an oversized white jumper with her jeans.

'Nell,' she breathed, the relief came with the force of a tidal wave, and she plopped back into the chair behind her, letting her head fall to the table on her arms. Nell placed the tubs quietly back onto the table where she had found them with a small laugh, then she pat Charley's shoulder as she passed to the sink.

'I'm sorry,' she said, washing her hands with a squirt of liquid soap, 'I should have told you I was here. It's a flying visit, I dropped some

136

supplies for Axl, and he asked me to check the damp in the cellar. It was leaking in a little, but it seems to have stopped now. He'll be pleased to hear that. I'll give him a call shortly to let him know. It's a horrible room, full of filth, If I were Elizabeth I'd have it filled. Be done with it. Must be lots of nasty things living down there.'

Charley had no desire to find out if anything lived down there, nasty or not. From now on the cellar was off limits, she was about as interested in facing her damn fear as she was in letting piranhas gnaw off her arms.

Nell was still gabbling by the sink and Charley looked up at her back with a frown. Nell was normally chatty, but she was on a roll today. Charley hadn't so much as spoken a word before Nell was wiping her hands on the towel and crossing to the French doors.

'I'll be back later to do a little cooking,' she said, 'for now I really have to go. Things to do, people to see.'

Charley nod her head, mouth open with words that hadn't had time to form, and then a cold vice clamped her heart.

'Nell!' she yelped.

Nell turned, face red and flustered, her eyes held in question.

'The light... the cellar light was on.'

'Oh! I turned it off dear, can't have Elizabeth paying for all that waste in a room that isn't used now can we?'

Charley let out the breath she had been holding with a small laugh.

'Just checking,' she said. Waving a hand at Nell as she disappeared through the doors and was gone.

Charley ran her hands down her face with a small chuckle as she eyed the cellar door. Still closed. Thank God.

Christ, you need to get your shit together Charley. The stories were stories. Aunt Elizabeth is not a witch, and the cellar is just a damp unused room, as Nell just said. You are such a wuss, really.

Even so, as she moved the tubs full of berries from the table to the counter, and put sausages under a warm grill, she decided the cellar was a room she didn't need or want to be involved with. And she didn't intend to be. Ever.

Chapter Nineteen

Elizabeth came in a little after twelve just in time for Charley to plate the sandwiches. They ate together at the table, chatting amicably, before moving on to the pie, which Charley made easily under Elizabeth's instruction and watchful eye, using a good chunk of the berries from the two boxes. With the pie in the oven, she made them both a drink, and brought them over to the table.

Elizabeth wrapped her steady hands around the teacup. No shakes now, Charley noticed as she watched her aunt, she seemed in really good form today, possibly the best she'd seen her yet. Elizabeth met Charley's gaze with a smile that warmed her stomach. Her aunt really was one of the nicest, most intelligent, and funniest people she had ever known. She grinned back at Elizabeth, who's frail hand left the cup and grasped hers.

'I'm so glad you came, Charley. I am. It's been so long, too long, and I suppose I tarred you with the same brush as Francesca, but you've surprised me. You're a lovely young lady, very caring and more than capable. Life is so short, Charley. I won't be around forever but promise me something. Don't let anyone stop you from doing what you need to live the best life you possibly can. Don't be afraid, and don't get caught up in the little things. Rise above it all and chase those dreams down.'

Warmth swirled in Charley's stomach. She was so touched that couldn't seem to find a reply, and a lump filled her throat. She swallowed hard. It had always been a struggle to do anything she dreamed around her family who had a dozen problems for every solution. They had laughed at her photography idea until the venture had started to make some money. Charley was on her own with everything. Without realising it her aunt had touched a very raw nerve.

'What's the matter?' Elizabeth said with a smile, her hand going back to her cup to take a sip of tea.

139

Charley shrugged. 'No one's ever said anything like that to me before, I'm just touched, I suppose, thank you.'

Elizabeth met her eyes, the smile slipping.

'Not even your mother?'

Charley shook her head, her gaze falling back to her tea.

'I've never really been that close to her. She never really... got me, I suppose. I wish I could have a relationship like she and Evelyn do, but I just don't seem to fit in. My sisters, they're not even nice people, they're all so full of...'

Charley struggled for a word that didn't involve swearing, but Elizabeth caught her off guard.

'Shit.' She said firmly.

Charley gaped and a burst of surprised laughter surged up and out. Elizabeth chuckled along with her.

'Exactly.' she said. 'I can't stand it. They get around the kitchen table and just chat shit. I can't even be bothered to join in, they just seem to enjoy bitching, gossiping, and moaning. All of them. I feel like an alien, like I dropped down on this family from another planet.'

'Oh, I understand that feeling entirely.' Elizabeth said with a sigh, looking out into the garden.

The reference to Francesca was obvious, and Charley wondered if she would offer the information that her mother never had.

'Aunt Elizabeth, can I ask you something?'

Her aunt's gaze turned back to her. Bright, calm. Happy, Charley thought.

I hope I'm not about to blow that mood.

'Anything,' Elizabeth replied.

Charley smiled.

'Well, tell me if I'm speaking out of turn, but what happened between you and mom? why did we stop coming to see you all those years ago? She won't speak about it, she refuses to acknowledge that you exist, all she says is that it was all your fault.'

Elizabeth raised a hand to finger her pearls and turned her gaze back to the garden. Her clear hazel eyes, perfectly framed with mascara, formed pools of pain and emotion, and Charley was immediately sorry she had brought it up. She shook her head.

'No, I'm sorry, I shouldn't-'

Elizabeth reached to place a firm hand over hers.

'No, don't be sorry. Maybe it's time the story was told. I suppose Francesca is right, in the end it was all my fault. I don't even know where she lives now, you know, she could be in Timbuktu. Could have been there for the last thirty years and I wouldn't have known.'

She turned to the oven, watching the pie through the glass door. Charley waited.

'Well, let me start from the beginning. We were brought up in a small town not far from here, did you know that? We had a good childhood, thick as thieves we were, as close as sisters could get. It changed as we grew into adulthood. I met Frank in 1959 at a gig I suppose you call it, only a local rock-and-roll band but they were a hit around here. I was twenty-two, and he was twenty-four.' Elizabeth smiled wistfully. 'He was already the owner of a small fishing fleet at that point although he didn't earn big bucks until later.

'Anyway, we fell in love, got married, and I think Francesca just felt left behind. I saw her most days, and we got on, but there was a definite air about her. She would make remarks about my being lucky marrying into money, and that if Frank hadn't come along no one else would want me, amongst other things. Jealousy was always a big part of Francesca. It ate her up, especially as she grew older and found her own man who was a bully and a layabout. I ignored her comments; they hurt, but she was still my sister. Anyway, as life went on, she eventually gave birth to the three girls...'

Elizabeth waved her hand in the air and closed her eyes briefly.

'Evelyn, Kate and Rue.' Charley offered.

Elizabeth smiled.

'Yes, of course, so she had these three beautiful babies, quite close in succession, but Frank and I? We just couldn't fall pregnant. We wanted children of our own, we so desperately wanted it, but it just never happened.

'Over the years we pretty much gave up hope, but I counted myself lucky that Francesca had the girls and that I could be involved in their lives. I doted on each one of them as though they were my own, and I always made sure I had a gift when they came to visit, but Francesca had hated it. Hated that she couldn't afford to, I suppose. I don't really know, I just so wanted a child to love.'

Elizabeth smiled sadly, one hand going back to her necklace as she paused.

'I want to show you something.' she said. 'To try to explain, I think you'll understand.'

Charley was intrigued as her aunt rose and left the kitchen, returning a few moments later with a small figurine.

'Here,' she said, handing it to Charley, 'Be careful with it, it's quite old. It got knocked and broken a number of years ago when I had it upstairs in my room, It was fixed, but now that's why I keep it in the drawing room where no-one really goes. It's precious.'

Charley turned it over in her hand, it was smooth and white, a small fracture line running through the middle. There were no features to the figure, just accents of a head, a body, arms. And in the arms, enclosed in an eternal hug, was a small child. Charley swallowed.

'I always kept this with me until it was broken,' Elizabeth said, drawing Charley back to her. 'This was my child, my little girl, this was all I had, all I'd ever have. And so I cherished an ornament. Silly, I know'

Elizabeth smiled but Charley could see the pain etched on her face, and she struggled to produce a smile of her own. She placed the figurine down on the table in front of her and looked at it.

'Not silly at all. It's a beautiful ornament. I think you're very strong, Aunt Elizabeth.'

'Well, maybe.' Elizabeth sighed picking up the figurine and rubbing a thumb over the child's face. Charley placed a hand over Elizabeth's, the small ornament between them both. She had to change the subject, or she would be blubbing over her aunt's misfortune herself. Especially as the pain was still so evidently raw.

'If Francesca hated you giving gifts to my sisters what happened? Did she stop you seeing them?'

Elizabeth shook her head and placed the figurine down gently.

'No, but to be honest that was the worst of it. She was living on the outskirts of the village, when her husband finally left her,' she continued. 'He wanted nothing to do with the girls and gave her very little money. From that point on she was abominable, her jealousy of what Frank and I had here rose like a beast. Anger and spite poured from her when we were together, but both of us were between the devil and hells chamber back then. Francesca had no one else to rely on, and I desperately wanted the girls in my life.'

Elizabeth blinked a few times, she picked up her cup to sip her tea. Charley waited, appalled at how different the story was from what they had suspected as children. Or, indeed, guessed at as adults. She was also aware that her aunt was getting upset. Charley blinked back her own tears as Elizabeth sighed heavily.

'After you were born, Charley, Francesca got worse,' Elizabeth swallowed hard. 'You were unplanned, she was alone. She was contemptuous, angry, jealous, and nasty. Why should I be in this big house with my loving husband and no responsibility when she was having to bring up four girls alone in a council house with nothing? No life, no man, and no money. She blamed me, of course.'

Charley frowned.

'How could she possibly blame you?'

'I was a councillor, so it was all my fault that Francesca was down as low as she was. I had tried to keep in contact with housing to find her somewhere bigger, and constantly tried to assess her benefits to see if I could do any more for her, but it was useless. Meanwhile, she was bribing me for money in return for seeing you all, but when Frank found out I had to put a stop to it. The amounts of money increased with each visit, you see, and Frank was only ever going to find out when so much was going missing from a joint account. I could only explain away so much before having to tell him the truth.'

She shrugged her shoulders lightly.

'I had no choice. I begged him to let me carry on, to agree a set price with Francesca, I was devastated that it may jeopardize my seeing you all and I was right to be worried. Francesca was savage. She came to the house and we had the most terrible argument before she stormed out of here, and out of Fortwind Bay. For good. I've had no idea where she was, how she was, and more importantly how you all were, and I have seen none of you since that day, until now anyway.'

Charley reached across the table for her aunt's hand. Francesca *had* always been jealous of Elizabeth; that had been clear as Charley was growing up. There were always scathing remarks, especially where the money was concerned, but Charley hadn't realised just how deep the scars had run. For Francesca to be bribing Elizabeth so blatantly, using Charley and her sisters as bait, and then to rip them away, after what Elizabeth had been through trying for her own family, was nothing short of barbaric in Charley's eyes.

Elizabeth placed her other hand on top of Charley's, patting it with a sad smile, her eyes watery with emotion. Charley felt an overwhelming urge to both cry and to apologise for Francesca's behaviour. She saw the raw and painful emotion behind her Aunt's expression and wanted to get in the car, drive home, and confront her mother about how much she had hurt Elizabeth, and just how selfish she was.

'I... I'm so sorry Aunt Elizabeth, I really am. We had no idea what had happened, she never said a word, we couldn't even mention your name. I feel terrible, it was a horrible thing for her to do to you. And all over money? I'm ashamed to be her daughter, I really am, we were her kids, hers to raise, this wasn't up to you.' Charley shook her head and pursed her lips, anger and despair mixing to form a strange heat in her stomach. 'And she knew what you and Frank had been through... I mean, how could she do that to you?'

Elizabeth swallowed hard, and then smiled weakly.

'I understand your anger Charley, but you mustn't take this on yourself. These actions were Francesca's, and you were so very young, you couldn't have known, or done, anything. My only consolation now is that she has raised a caring, bright, and beautiful young lady and that is to her credit, not mine. I can't forgive her for what she did all those years ago, and I can't re-forge the relationships I had with all of you now. I don't have the time, especially with the situation as it is, but at least I got to meet you. I got to know you a little, and to tell you my side of the story. That means such a lot. If there is one thing Francesca did right it was to send you up here, and whether she intended it or not, she has given me a wonderful gift. I couldn't have asked for more.'

The fire in Charley's stomach dampened at her Aunt's words, and instead she felt the lump grow in her throat and the prickle of tears let go behind her eyes. She wiped them away as she stepped around the table and hugged her Aunt. Elizabeth also let go as she pulled Charley in, sobbing like an old lady should never have to. Charley cried with her, her heart breaking with every sob.

This kind-hearted lady, who gave so much to the village she loved, couldn't have the one thing she really wanted. Francesca had it all wrong. Elizabeth may have had a more privileged life, but money couldn't buy everything, and Elizabeth and Frank had been denied the one thing in life that would have made their family complete. But Elizabeth had carried on with good grace, accepting her fate. Unlike Francesca, who had four children and still couldn't be happy for herself. Her dealt hand was apparently so awful that she had to bring everyone down with her.

As she held on to her sobbing Aunt, Charley made a vow.

Never would she bow to her family again, never would she feel she had to answer to Evelyn and Kate, and never would she take their snide remarks and cutting comments.

That's strike two.

I'm not going home, that's done with, I'll find somewhere up here. And on three, I'll never speak to any of them again. Ever. And that's only if I can be bothered to wait for strike three...

Chapter Twenty

Elizabeth hadn't cried with such abandon in years, and she was eternally grateful that she'd had Charley to hold on to as she did it. Charley was the missing piece, the daughter she couldn't have, and it made her feel complete. One of the few times in her life she had ever felt so complete. She had felt both cleansed, and ravenous, by the time the pie had been ready.

She knew something was horribly wrong around the time she shovelled the fourth bite of pie into her mouth.

The time that had passed without her favourite food had left her with an overwhelming craving as the smell had permeated the kitchen. Confident that the pie would be good to eat, she had devoured most of it in just four bites, relishing the flavour as it slid down her throat.

But now Charley was talking funny. They had been laughing about the state of their faces, all puffy eyed, and all traces of make-up gone after their tears. But now Charley's words began to ebb and flow like a tide, one minute screeching in her ears, the next disappearing as if she weren't speaking at all, just moving her mouth.

Elizabeth's laughter died away, and she put a hand to her head. Charley moved round to her side of the table. She looked concerned, brow furrowed, but Elizabeth couldn't hear what she was saying. Her stomach grumbled, growled, and ached, and she suddenly knew this would be a particularly bad episode.

She had eaten too much, trusted too much.

But this wasn't Charley, the concern in her face was real, she'd had no idea about the berries. She had offered to pick fresh until Elizabeth had told her otherwise.

No, this must have been Axl after all. Axl having the last laugh after she thought she meant so much to him.

Her thoughts began to swim. She knew she had to tell Charley, convince her, before she was back in the world of pain and hallucination again. She tried to focus on her, tried to talk, but her mouth didn't seem to want to work. Charley was still speaking, yelling at her, although she couldn't hear anything but a dull whine.

Now Charley was starting to ebb and flow too, bending toward her and then bending back as though she was an inflatable girl, not a real one. Elizabeth made her hands go to Charley's shoulders although the effort was like that of lifting a tank. Her hands slipped as they tried to grasp, and then Charley had her hands in hers and was kneeling down at her side. Elizabeth desperately tried to talk but she couldn't hear her own voice, couldn't unscramble her own thoughts, the room was starting to take on a strange jelly like quality, everything moved, nothing was still, and it made her stomach roll over and over. Her mouth was fuzzy and sour and she felt the foul vomit rising just before she lost consciousness.

* * * * *

The spray of projectile red vomit just missed Charley. It splattered across the floor as she screeched and launched sidewards, careful to keep hold of her Aunt with one hand. As the spray stopped Elizabeth immediately flopped over like a rag doll. Charley moved quickly around her back and circled her arms under Elizabeth's armpits to hold her up.

Shit! Is she breathing? Is that blood? What do I do?

Panic surged in Charley's chest as Elizabeth became a dead weight in her arms. What the heck was going on? Keeping her hands around Elizabeth to keep her upright Charley moved around the chair and pulled her Aunt forward onto the table. She heaved and pushed forward until Elizabeth's chest was resting on the table, and only when she was sure she was stable did she finally unclasp her hands.

Heart thudding, her chest heaving in heavy, ragged gasps, Charley looked at the ominous smear of red across the floor, and then to her Aunt, sprawled across the tabletop. How had the last two minutes of time completely turned itself on its head? She put her hands up to her head pulling her hair back and clasping the back of her neck, her thoughts frantic.

One minute they had been laughing, and now... now what, what had happened?

Oh God, oh God. Is she okay, is she dead? What do I do?

Feeling sick, Charley leaned across the table and put a trembling hand close to her Aunt's nose. Warm air blew on her skin. The panic subsided a little as she saw the faint, but rhythmic, rise and fall of her Aunt's back. Elizabeth was breathing, thank God. Still with her. Charley closed her eyes and let out a shuddery breath of relief.

The back door crashed open, and Axl lurched inside.

'Elizabeth! Jesus, what the hell happened?'

Charley's eyes flew open, and she staggered a few paces back, pushed by the forcefulness of his approach. Axl took no notice. He bent to check Elizabeth, as Charley recovered herself enough to tell him.

'What do we do?' She asked him. She would later wonder why a gardener would know any more of what to do than she did, but right now, she ached for someone to lean on.

'Have you called Glen?' Axl said.

Charley kicked herself. Why hadn't she thought of Glen?

Ignoring his harsh tone, she did as she was told, happy to have someone here with her and taking charge. She pulled out her phone and dialled as Axl stooped by the red streak and confirmed with a murmur that it was berries, not blood. Charley almost swooned with relief.

Glen answered after the fourth ring and waited as Charley hurriedly explained what had happened.

'Okay, all right, stay calm,' Glen said, her tone soothing, 'I know it's frightening, but this isn't the first time Ms Kane has vomited and passed out. She'll be fine. Make her comfortable for now if you can. Can you get her to bed?'

'Axl is with me,' Charley said by way of an answer. 'I should think we'll be able to between us.'

'Good. Get her up there and make her comfortable. I'll be down as soon as I can, but my shift doesn't finish for another four hours yet.'

Charley swallowed, dismayed. She glanced at Axl who was lifting Elizabeth's eyelids gently one at a time.

'She will need close monitoring until she comes round.' Glen continued, 'I will warn you that it was quite some time before she woke the last time she did this. It's a heavy vigil, can you use the blood pressure machine?'

'Yes, I'm confident with that, but not the pulse thingy.'

'Well, not to worry. Take her blood pressure and record it in fifteen-minute increments. Don't worry about the pulse oximeter. Use the second hand on the clock to take her heart rate and note it the same.'

Charley nodded to herself.

'Right. Shall I call an ambulance?'

'No need,' Glen said, 'The worst is the shock of her vomiting and passing out, the rest will be working through the hallucinations after she wakes. If there are any notable changes in her blood pressure or heart rate call me right away. I'll talk you through what you can do, or we'll think about calling an ambulance then.'

A flutter of unease wound around her stomach.

'But Glen, I don't think...'

'Charley. Trust me. I'll be there in a few hours. She will be absolutely fine. This is unusual for dementia sufferers in general, but not unheard of for Elizabeth. Get her to bed. I'll be on my way.'

'Right. Thanks Glen. And please hurry.'

'I'll be as quick as I can.'

Charley said goodbye and ended the call. With a little reassurance that Elizabeth had done this before and would be okay, she felt herself kick into gear with more calm.

'Right,' She said to Axl, 'we need to get her into bed, and make her comfortable for when she comes round. Glen says it could be awhile, she isn't too concerned, but she is going to come down as quickly as she can to check her over and make sure she is okay.'

Axl nodded, and Charley saw the worry in his eyes. He picked up Elizabeth on his own, scooping her easily off the chair, and holding her like a baby as he carried her upstairs. Charley followed, for once wholly glad he was here.

In the bedroom they took off her vomit stained skirt and top together, Axl holding her up and averting his eyes when he needed to, and Charley struggling with the fancy buttons and zips. Axl had to stop her from strangling Elizabeth as she hurriedly tried to pull off her shirt over her head, not realising her pearls were still under the collar. Finally, Charley pulled a long nightgown over her head, Axl manoeuvring his hands gently to accommodate the cotton.

By the time Charley folded back the sheets on Elizabeth's bed she was in a sweat. Axl placed Elizabeth down on the bed with care, pulling her straight, and propping her head on the pillow. Then he pulled the covers up, tucking her in.

They stood watching.

Charley couldn't think of a thing to say, but Axl broke the silence anyway, his voice cracking in the silence.

'I thought she had gone then, Charley. I really did.'

Charley nodded. He'd echoed her own sentiments.

For a moment she had been scared to death that Elizabeth had gone too.

Chapter Twenty-One

They said that they would take turns to watch over Elizabeth for the afternoon, but it ended up being a double vigil, neither one willing to take their eyes off her.

Charley didn't leave her aunt's side, Axl only left twice to bring them hot drinks. Mostly they just sat with her together, watching. Waiting. The silence all encompassing.

Glen arrived a good three hours after the episode, earlier than Charley had thought, but she had apologised anyway as she bustled quickly upstairs.

'I'm so sorry, I tried to get out earlier but there wasn't a chance. How has she been?'

Charley told her that there was no change, that the readings she had taken and recorded, although a little high, had remained stable.

'Good. That's good.' Glen smiled. 'I'll check her over now, who's on tea duty? I've had nothing this afternoon. I'm parched.'

Axl moved himself back downstairs and Charley felt a little sorry for him. There were shadows under his eyes, which were etched with worry and tiredness. Charley knew she must look the same. Three hours merely watching someone who was ill, and not knowing the outcome, seemed like three years - with no sleep. Axl almost looked *older* somehow, and Charley certainly felt it.

Glen set herself to work checking, noting, and recording Elizabeth's state and vitals with a quick ease. She sat with her, taking her pulse frequently and syringing water into her mouth, which flowed red back out onto the towel that Glen had placed under her head.

Each time a smear of red appeared Charley's heart lurched. It looked too much like blood. Too bright, too ominous, and although

Glen seemed perfectly calm, Charley couldn't remove the lead weight from her stomach.

There was no movement from Elizabeth until the early hours of the morning. Charley had been dozing in a chair at her aunt's side, Glen sat in a chair around the other side of the bed, while Axl propped up the door frame. The atmosphere was tense and thick, each of their faces grave. It was as if they all knew deep down that something bad was coming.

It arrived with a long moan as Elizabeth woke, her unseeing eyes rolling to the back of her head. She grabbed at her throat slurring and writhing. Long steaks of red saliva pulsed trails down her cheek and disappeared into her silvery hair. Glen and Charley tried to calm her, fetching her hands down from her neck and trying to sooth her but it was too late. Much too late.

Elizabeth coughed, spurting a string of red out over her chin. Glen tried to clean it with the towel as she gave another long moan and began to fit, her frail body almost jumping off the bed with each twitch.

Charley grabbed her aunt's hand in horror.

'No Charley,' Glen said, 'let go, you may do some damage to her arm.'

'Glen?' Charley choked. 'This is bad right?'

Glen didn't answer. She clicked something on her pocket watch and began to write furiously in Elizabeth's medical notes.

The fit continued for three minutes and twenty-two seconds, there was nothing they could do but watch and wait. Charley thought the scene would be seared into her brain forever.

Finally, Elizabeth had lurched up on the bed, as though unseen hands had pushed roughly under her shoulders, throwing her into a sitting position. Glen had called out, and Axl had shouted Elizabeth's name, but Charley had been quiet, struck by the look of horror on her Aunt's face. Her mouth hung open, streaks of red flowed down her chin and stained her nightshirt. Her eyes were clear, wide, but unseeing. She teetered a moment before falling back onto the bed with a gasp. As she took her last shuddering breath Charley held her own breath. Fear and disbelief coursing through her.

That couldn't be it. It wasn't right. Glen had said that she would be all right. She needed to be all right.

Despite Glen's warning, Charley was still grasping Elizabeth's hand tightly, and she felt the moment her Aunt went. Elizabeth's hand had grasped hers briefly, just as firmly, before falling limp and lifeless. Dead.

Elizabeth Kane was dead.

The room erupted around her. Axl and Glen were here somewhere, noise and commotion, but Charley could only sit. There was only her and Elizabeth.

What the hell happened?

She held Elizabeth's hand until the warmth seeped out of it, and somewhere downstairs a doorbell chimed over and over.

Chapter Twenty-Two

Charley was sat on the bedroom window seat, watching the ocean, when the text pinged through. She forced her head to move toward the phone on the dressing table. After the last four weeks of chaos and grief, she just wanted to be left alone. She turned to look back outside watching the waves swell under thunderous clouds. Rain battered the window. There would be no visiting the sea today.

The phone pinged three more times, almost consecutively. She rolled her eyes.

Heaving a sigh and moving a body that felt stiff and heavy she picked up the phone and dropped onto the bed. One was from Glen, asking how she was and saying she would call in at lunchtime before her house calls started. The other three were Evelyn.

Have you found it yet?

Mom wants to know what's going on up there.

Charley, mom has a right to know, her sister just died, this needs sorting. Have you found the will?

Charley didn't bother to reply to any of them. She knew that Elizabeth hadn't passed a copy of the will to the solicitor before she died, but she had made one, she had phoned and told them the week before she passed. There was to have been a meeting at the house next Tuesday but that was now obsolete, and the executors couldn't go ahead until the will was found.

Charley supposed if it was going to be anywhere, it would be in Franks study, but she hadn't had energy or inclination to look yet. She flopped on her back and traced the aertex swirls on the ceiling instead.

SHATTERED

After Elizabeth had died, official diagnosis; convulsions brought on by brain deterioration as a direct result of Dementia, she had been moved to the morgue, until the funeral just over a week ago, when she had been returned home.

It had been a sombre affair. A horse and cart had pulled her from the house in her casket to the cemetery at the edge of the village. There had been no cars. A small procession had walked from the house behind the cart, including Charley, Glen, Axl, Nell and Avril. Theo sent his condolences, he had to work, but in his defence he had been on the phone at least once an hour that day.

Down in the village it seemed Fortwind Bay had literally shut down at the passing of one of its biggest ambassadors. Main street was lined with mourners, it seemed all the Bay had come out to pay their respects. The procession moved on through the streets and by the time they reached the wooden cemetery gates the small gathering following the cart had amassed to the hundreds.

Elizabeth was buried next to Frank in one of the most beautiful services Charley had ever witnessed. Not that she had witnessed many. People paid their respects in droves, and many offered words about Elizabeth's kindness and loyalty to the village. She was finally lowered into the ground as a lone violinist played Ava Maria. It was haunting on that cool, overcast day, with the silence broken only by the mournful sound of the bow on strings, and by the time they were covering the coffin Charley had felt her heart would split in two with pain.

She barely remembered the walk back to the house, or the wake that followed in Elizabeth's name. She felt numb, lost, and disjointed. Between them, Nell, Avril, Axl, Glen, and Theo - via calls and messages - had managed to keep Charley upright through the condolences and well-wishers. The people who should have been there to help her out and hold her together, were missing.

Francesca was apparently too ill to fly. Charley had heard her in the background of her conversation with Evelyn, and she hadn't sounded so ill from the noise going on at the other end of the phone. The conversation had thrown up another three excuses as to why Evelyn, Kate, and Rue couldn't possibly attend on her behalf, and so the whole affair had been left to Charley.

Half numb, and half expecting it, Charley couldn't have cared less.

As it happened, Elizabeth was well prepared for her death and had left strict instructions with a solicitor and a funeral director exactly what was to happen on the day of her funeral. She had paid everything in advance, long before the money ran out. The only thing that had stopped the well-oiled machine was the will.

The will.

Charley sighed and turned her head toward the bedroom door. It stood open, affording her a view out across the landing. Elizabeth's door was shut tight, as it had been since her death.

She hadn't sorted the room, never mind looked for the will. Nothing had been done since Elizabeth's death but the legalities. The dishevelment and chaos of that night still remained behind the wooden door.

Now, she found herself staring at it.

The room needs cleaning and sorting, Charley. It can't stay like that forever. You need to pick yourself up, get on with it.

No one had stepped foot in the room since that fateful night. She hadn't allowed it.

Avril had offered to clean, and Glen had told her she would feel better if the room was 'put back to rights', but Charley had refused. She was fiercely protective of her Aunt's things. She was Elizabeth's only family, and she felt a duty to be the one to tidy things and put them, or do with them, as Elizabeth would have liked.

So do it for her.

The doorbell chimed. Charley ignored it. It had been chiming a good many times a day for weeks. She had told herself it needed new batteries, but after changing them twice she no longer believed it.

It wants you to sort Elizabeth's things, find the blessed will, tie up the loose ends. It's time Charley.

Do it!

With a vigour and sense of purpose she hadn't felt for weeks, she swung her legs off the bed and started across the landing.

Elizabeth's door clicked open as she reached it. Not much, only a crack. But definitely open. Charley froze, watching the now still door, while trying to still her bumping heart. There must be a window open in there, even on a latch it would cause a breeze.

So why hasn't it opened before now?

Swallowing hard, she pushed the door slowly, and the moment was forgotten as she immediately found herself back in the horror of that night. Elizabeth's clothes were on the floor, where they had been dropped in haste, the chairs in disarray around the bed, the bedspread was still dishevelled, dark red stains still marred the sheets.

The room spun and Charley grasped the door frame, drawing in breaths until it steadied again.

Okay. you're okay, Charley. come on, get yourself together. Let's do this. For Elizabeth.

* * * * *

Charley blocked all emotion as she tidied meticulously, with fervour, until the room looked just as it always had. She picked up, put away, changed the bedspread, even rearranged the dressing table and placed Elizabeth's pearls on it. Finally, she looked at the heap of material that was the last reminder of that fateful night.

The bedspread and clothes were ruined. No cleaning would suffice. They would need a bin.

Charley picked up the bundle, with the now ruined blouse and skirt sitting on top. Trying not to think about what was in her arms, she took them downstairs to the outside bin. The doorbell chimed her out; she ignored it, lifting the bin lid with an arm and pushing it back with the bundle. The bottle green silk skirt fluttered from the pile and landed on the gravel as she pushed the other items inside. A bracing gust of wind forced the bin lid shut with a bang as she stooped to retrieve it, fingers closing on silk just before she had to chase it down the driveway. Its softness drew through her hands. She paused.

There wasn't much staining, she should probably get it cleaned. Probably.

But the thought of the skirt hanging in the house or going to charity made her feel sick.

No reminders. It's just one skirt, it doesn't matter.

There was an ache in her chest and a lonely tear escaped down her cheek. The wind whipped it away as she lift the bin lid, and something crackled under her hand. Charley frowned. Nothing in a silk skirt should crackle, should it?

Did she care?

She considered the answer, almost decided she didn't, but in a last second change of heart she ran her hands over the silk, avoiding the dried stain as much as she could until she heard it again.

Pockets. The skirt had pockets.

Putting a hand tentatively inside she withdrew a cream envelope. Her heart gave a jolt as she stared at the blue ink written in neat hand across the front.

Charley.

Swallowing hard she frowned at it, pulsing beat of her heart in her ears.

A letter? For me?

The biting wind snapped at her clothes and she shuddered. Pushing the skirt into the bin, she went back into the house.

She took the envelope to the kitchen where she placed it in front of her on the table and sat staring at her aunt's neat handwriting for almost an hour. Finally she took a breath and slid her thumb under the seal. Her hands shook, and a deep ache pulled at her heart, as she took out the letter and started to read.

My dearest Charley,

That was all it took. All she could read before her eyes filled, and the pain dragged through her heart. She closed her eyes, gathering herself, and swallowing the lump in her throat. Then she read through the rest of the note wiping at stray tears that blurred her vision.

SHATTERED

My dearest Charley,

If you are reading this, then my time has come, and hopefully I am with Frank in whatever is waiting for us after this world.

Charley, I want you to know just how much it means to me to have had you here and to have been able to get know the person you have become. Francesca wasn't able to take everything away after all was she? One up to us!

Remember what I said. Follow your heart and reach for your dreams. If that means breaking away from toxic people then don't be afraid to do so. I think you know where I'm going; you don't owe them anything. Believe me.

I need you to do me one last favour. Charley, please keep the study locked and collect both keys. I keep mine in a drawer of the dressing table in my room, the only other should be yours, if Glen gave it to you as I asked. The room holds possessions very dear to me, including many items of Frank's, and there are things in there I want you to have as my most trusted companion. All will be revealed, please don't worry about it now. You will know the time to open the study back up to all when affairs are settled.

For now, I don't want you to feel sad that I have passed; I have had a good life, even with the spite of family, but, if you are feeling melancholy I'll tell you a little trick that used to brighten my days, especially through this dreadful illness. Go into the study and find a book called 'A little pocket of goodness', It isn't a well-known book, but it is very light-hearted, the poem on page sixty-six with the maid and the fireplace is one of my all-time favourites, but there are so many more in that book worth reading.

Please humour me.

If you intend to light the fire, please don't forget to open the flue. Victorian fires have a door to keep out the cold but you will smoke yourself to death of you leave it shut, I do not need to see you in this world quite yet or I will be very disappointed!

Anyway, I digress, remember to open the flue, and sit back and read some of the funniest and most heart-warming poems I think you'll ever read.

I would love to tell you more but time runs out, all I can say is that I'm sorry, and that I loved you, all of you, I never stopped loving you.

I'm so sorry to have to leave you with such a mess. I hoped this would never come to pass, and that I would have much more time with you. Sadly, that was just not meant to be.

Until we meet again,

Much love,

Elizabeth.

Charley's tears had dried up by the end of the letter. Considering it was supposed to reach her after Elizabeth had died it didn't say much as a parting shot, and the ending was downright weird. As much as her aunt had appeared well over the last few weeks it was heartbreakingly obvious that the disease had taken her over.

Charley wondered whether the times she had appeared well were snippets of her aunt at all, or a persona brought on by the dementia. Why on earth would Elizabeth think she would want to read poems after her death? Especially as Charley had never been much of a reader and had never suggested that she was.

She looked over the letter again, only growing more puzzled.

Why would Elizabeth write this? And why talk about lighting the fire? The house had central heating. Something felt off.

With a sigh, Charley shook her head and folded the letter back up, placing it into the envelope. She would keep it close. Even with its strangeness, the letter with its belief in her was all she needed to go forward. Even in death Elizabeth had her back, she understood, and she had encouraged and supported her far more than Francesca or sisters ever had.

Maybe one day she'd look the book of poems up, for Elizabeth, but for the time being there were more important things to sort, such as the will, and the study keys.

She stood, running her fingers under her tired eyes and placing the letter into the pocket of her jeans. Across the kitchen the cellar door clicked open. Charley watched it creak to a stop, swallowed, and then sighed. Before she could talk herself out of it, she marched to the door and slammed it shut.

'If you don't quit, I'll buy a lock. I'm not going down there.'

The doorbell chimed half-heartedly and Charley rolled her eyes.

I'm talking to a house... and it's answering? This is getting ridiculous.

Chapter Twenty-Three

The next few days were quiet, and Charley was glad, Elizabeth's room and the letter had taken more out of her than she had expected, but after more messages from Evelyn this morning she finally felt ready to put Elizabeth's affairs to bed, especially as Evelyn had hinted at Francesca coming up to meddle in them.

The downside to the will being found was the division of the estate. Charley would need to leave, possibly to go back to Harrogate, and after spending the last few months here with her very caring and inspiring aunt, the thought hurt as though someone was trying to remove her heart through her chest with a blunt stick.

At the study door, which she kept locked at Elizabeth's request, Charley tipped the two collected keys out of the envelope where they sat with her letter. She unlocked the door and went inside.

The air was stuffy with central heating, and the familiar smell of wood and old books filled her nose as she scanned the room. She took in the tidy floor to ceiling shelves that lined the walls, the masses of books, binders, and trinkets, the large oak desk and leather chair, and finally the thin layer of dust that covered them all. Elizabeth had liked the study clean, but Charley felt protective over this room, much like the bedroom, and especially after the letter. Her eyes fell on the ornate cast iron Victorian fireplace behind the chair. *Don't forget to open the flue.* Charley smiled and shook her head to dispel the words from the letter.

I'm finding the will today, Aunt Elizabeth, the family from hell are driving me nuts. Fireside poems will just have to wait.

Leaving the door open to allow the stuffy air to circulate, Charley moved to the desk. It was large and cumbersome, but for all its bulky dark angles and ornate decoration, it only had one small lockable drawer at the front. Luck would have it that the key was inside the lock, however, the drawer was mostly empty. Just a few old papers pertaining to Frank's business. Receipts, invoices, letters. Nothing of interest, and no will.

Did you think it would be that easy?

No, she decided, she didn't. She stood, hands on hips.

If I was stashing a will, I would definitely put it in the study. So where else in here could it be?

After the desk, the answer was nowhere obvious, so she started from the left of the door with the first bookshelf, bringing the small wheeled ladders from the corner by the window. Working top to bottom, she ran her eyes over the titles of the many books that lined the shelves while running her hands over the dusty tops. She checked anything out of place, inspecting any gaps between books, pulling out and scrutinising any loose papers, and flicking through any book that looked like it had been moved out of place. She moved from the wall with the door, past the fireplace and onto the opposite side, continuing methodically through each bookcase, each shelf, each book as the hours passed.

She found 'A Little Pocket of Goodness' amongst a good number of books on herbal remedies and plants that heal proving that Glen had been right with her story that Elizabeth had been into herbal medicine. It sat right in eyeline on the middle shelf, halfway along the wall opposite the door. Curious, Charley pulled it free. It was a thin book, with a tatty green cover. A gold bordered glossed square on the front surrounded a faded picture of daffodils.

Looks like it belongs in the eighteenth century.

But a peek in the front confirmed that 1936 was its official publication. She flicked through the well-thumbed pages discovering well-formed and wordy poems, sometimes spanning a page or two. Closing the book Charley placed it carefully on the desk behind her. Then, she glanced to the ceiling, as everyone seemed to when they were talking to the dead.

'Okay, I can't promise it will be my thing, but I will read the poem on page sixty-six for you, I promise."

She turned back to the bookshelf with a smile, just as a dull thud came from behind her. She paused, hand outstretched, as she looked back over her shoulder. 'A Little Pocket of Goodness' now lay open, face down on the floor, a small plume of dust settling around it.

Charley stared at it, knowing she had placed it too far onto the desk to fall without help.

But that's impossible because there's no-one else in here to knock it off.

The back of her neck prickled.

Glancing around the warm study, her eyes settling on the open door which now unnerved her. The house was silent, but the feeling that someone was just beyond the doorway was intense. A shudder ran down her spine.

Leaving the bookcase she crept to the door and peered out. The stairs and hallway were still and quiet, front door shut. The ticking of the clock in the kitchen filled her ears and a trickle of relief followed the shudder, she pushed her swirling nerves down with it.

This is silly, Charley, there's no one here, the book fell, just pick it up and get on with finding the will.

Pulling in a breath she went back to the desk and stooped to pick up the open book. Turning it over she found herself staring straight at page sixty-six.

She huffed a breath.

Of course it would be. Where else? And you'd better believe that's only because it was Elizabeth's favourite poem or you'll never sleep in this house again.
Still stooped, she looked over the poem her aunt had recommended. It was short, much less than a page. A faded colour picture of a maid, in an old-fashioned black-and-white uniform adorned the remainder of the page. She held a feather duster over a fireplace not unlike the one right in front of her. Curiosity peaked, Charley kept place with her thumb, and rose to sit in the leather chair.

'Okay Aunt Elizabeth, 'she whispered, 'you have my attention. I'll read the damn poem.'

The sound of her voice in the empty room sent her nerves on edge and she moved her focus to the poem.

A MAIDS TALE

When the master is at ease, dust one to keep his peace.
When the master is tense, scrub four for recompense.
When the master is out, ensure ten more rounds of stout.
When the master is down, wash five to bring him round.
When the master is jolly, darn three for his folly.
When the master has a temper, clean eight, and remember,
When the day is over, if a kind word is spake,
Treasure it, lock it up, keep it safe.

Charley blinked, read the poem over, and raised her eyes back to the ceiling.

'Jeez Aunt Elizabeth, I have no idea what is supposed to be so comforting about that. In fact, this poem may just be the reason I don't do poems. Period.'
Guilt immediately climbed up her chest and she backtracked, just in case her aunt was able to hear as perfectly in the afterlife as she seemed able to pull books from desks.

'But I'll keep it with me.' she said. 'I may like some of the others I suppose and it will always remind me of you.'

Well saved, she thought with a grin, knowing full well that if Elizabeth Kane were listening, she had missed nothing. Charley put the book down on the desk, careful to place it right in the middle. She sighed and stretched.

Well, I feel better for the short break, anyway. Now let's get on with the search for this blessed will.
'Any help greatly appreciated.' She said aloud, hoping the will would drop to the floor in a plume of dust in much the same way the book had.

It didn't, and an hour later, frustrated and annoyed, Charley gave up. The study had been thoroughly checked, and the will was nowhere to be found.

Chapter Twenty-Four

Down the hill in a small semi-detached Axl paced the living room, realising that for all the planning he had done, he hadn't really thought this through. He had underestimated everything, but mainly the time it would take Elizabeth to go – he hadn't expected it to be so *fast* - and the depth of his feeling when she went.

He was more upset than he wanted to be, and that was dangerous because he hadn't tied up every loose end. The letters were still up at Fortwind House. He had been too complacent with his timing, too lenient with the evidence. Nell had said Elizabeth had plenty of time yet, the plan had been slow, and now that evidence was sitting in a house with the last person on earth he wanted to find it. Time was no longer short; it was almost out.

He wiped a sheen of sweat from his forehead and thumped his hands onto the windowsill, as he stared down at the harbour.

What the hell are you going to do about it?

He had no idea and, he realised he had more chance of building an igloo in the Sahara than of getting hold of them now.

Charley had told them all that they were no longer needed at the house - Axl, Avril, and Nell. Thanked them very much but she would take over while she sorted Elizabeth's things. Which meant that, although a welcome visitor, he would have no opportunity to be alone up there to search the study again.

A dull ache throbbed in his head, and he rubbed under his tired eyes with a finger and thumb, dragging his hand down over his face to his bearded chin. He was so sick of thinking, of watching his step, of watching his actions. Would this never end?

At some point Charley would find the will, and with it were the letters. At that point it was game over. But he was at a loss how to change it.

There was a creak from the ceiling above him, and he grit his teeth in frustration as his wife's nasally shriek pierced the quiet.

'Axl? Where is the goddamn tea? Are you picking the bloody leaves or what?'

He glanced to the ceiling, where his wife would be sitting up in bed, book in hand, scowl on her bulldog face that he didn't need to see to imagine. Maybe he could bump her off, there were plenty of berries in the garden at Fortwind now. A bumper crop.

He huffed a chuckle at his own wit and grabbed his coat from the peg by the front door.

'Axl? Axl! Don't pretend you can't hear me!'

'Ah, get it yourself,' he said as he opened the front door and stepped out into the grey morning. The wind bit at his ears, the nip at the change of the seasons obvious. Autumn was on its way.

Pulling his hood up and stuffing his hands into his pockets, he walked over the road and stepped onto the dunes above the harbour. A glance back at his house revealed Ann in the bedroom window, Pink nightgown draped off one shoulder as she bunched a fist at him. He watched with mild amusement as she flung the window open and screeched something that the wind thankfully took away before it reached his ears. She hung from the window further and as the wind died he was blessed with a 'selfish bastard' and a raised middle finger.

He turned back to the beach, nonplussed, he expected nothing more of her.

Knees and hips groaning, he made his way through the dunes and down onto the firm sand, where he stood watching the swell of the sea. It was rough out there today, as rough as the wind at his body, and the nip of the cold on his face, As rough as he felt trying to keep his life from collapsing at seventy-two years old.

Collapsing is not an option, what the hell do I do besides bumping Charley off?

As he worked his jaw in thought, his hand hit something hard and cold in his pocket. With a frown, he closed his fingers around it bringing it out into the grey light of the day. He held it in front of him, eyebrows pushing together before springing up almost to his hairline. Spluttering a laugh, he turned the object over with wonder and gratitude for his sheer good luck.

Charley had forgotten something when she dismissed him. Something very important, indeed.

With a widening grin, and a weight taken off his shoulders, he pocketed the small key to the French doors tapping it under his fingers in thought before zipping the pocket shut, sealing it safely inside.

Chapter Twenty-Five

'Still no sign of it then?' Theo said that afternoon as he tucked into a scone. Jam and clotted cream squirted from the sides.

Charley shook her head with a grimace as she watched him.

'That is heart attack material, right there.'

He looked at her, eyebrows disappearing up into his curls as he swallowed.

'Not having the will?'

'No, the amount of cream on that scone.'

He grinned, giving her an exaggerated wink as he took another bite and her stomach turned over. She'd had no appetite since Elizabeth died but the urge to cook and bake stayed with her. A slice of normality in a world that was still upside down.

'Glad you like them, anyway.' She said rolling her eyes at him with a smile.

'Beautiful,' he said, wiping cream from his chin with a finger and putting it in his mouth. 'You should have one, you've lost weight. So, the will?'

Charley shook her head again, ignoring his comment, 'Nope, no sign of it. I've turned the house upside down over the last week, and let's face it, if you have a study, the will is in the study, surely. Or is that too straightforward?'

He shrugged as he swallowed the last bite of scone and reached for another, running the knife through the middle to split it in half.

'Well, I'd say so, but most people aren't straightforward, are they? You sure you've checked everywhere in there?'

'Yep, twice. There's nothing. I just don't get why Elizabeth would write me a letter pointing me to the study for a dumb poem - sorry Aunt Elizabeth - but not give me any hint where the will is. I mean, priorities, right?'

She sighed heavily and ran a hand through her hair pulling it back from her face.

Theo paused to look at her, knife in the jam jar, which he held in his other hand.

'She *was* ill, Charley,' he said gently. 'She probably wasn't thinking straight. In fact, if dementia had her she hasn't been thinking straight for a while, has she?'

Charley shook her head, and rest her arm on the table, placing her chin in her hand as she watched Theo smother more jam and clotted cream onto the scone.

The kitchen was bright today, afternoon sunshine seeping through the French doors onto the table. It was all a fallacy, outside September felt colder than an arctic winter, and just as harsh with the wind chill.

'Let's see the letter again.' he said as he put the knife down. 'maybe there's something more to it.'

Charley grinned as he tucked into his second scone. 'This isn't Inspector Clouseau. I'm not sure there are any alternate meanings from the mind of a seventy-four-year-old lady with dementia.'

Mouth full, Theo stretched his arm toward her, and wagged his fingers for the letter. She took it out of its envelope and straightened it out on the table before passing it to him. He read through it and she waited, watching as his brow furrowed, his green eyes narrowed, and then his eyebrows raised. Finally, he shook his head.

'I think you're probably right. It's unfortunate that she didn't mention the will, but at least you know there is one. The solicitors confirmed that didn't they?'

'Yes, they were supposed to come here to meet just after Elizabeth died. She had told them it had been updated.'

Theo cocked his head.

'So it's most definitely here.'

Charley nodded. 'Tell me something I don't know, I wish she hadn't been quite so good at hiding things because I have no idea where it can be.'

Theo swallowed the last of the second scone, looking at his watch.

'It's a shame I don't have much time today. I'm off Tuesday though I could drop Belle with mom and dad and come up to help if you haven't found it by then?'

'That would be good,' she said, 'I probably just need some fresh eyes going over this place. I feel like I'm going insane and Evelyn really isn't helping messaging every two minutes with threats.'

'Ignore her,' he said, 'What's she going to do from Harrogate? Send a heat-seeking missile? It takes as long as it takes.'

Charley rest her chin back in her hand. If only it were that easy.

So, what is this poem she mentions?' Theo said.

'I found the book in the study, you can read it,' Charley said, reaching to her laptop bag and pulling the book from the pocket. She opened it to page sixty-six and passed it to him. He read through it and cocked an eyebrow.

'You know what I think?' he said.

'What?'

'That this isn't Inspector Clouseau. Where Elizabeth's mind was when she wrote the letter is anyone's guess, and I hate to say it but…'

'She did have dementia,' Charley finished for him.

He nodded his head with a small smile. 'I think you have to forget the letter and the poem and concentrate on the will.'

She grinned. 'I was. You asked to see them both.'

He shrugged. 'Hey, this is a small village, nothing ever happens. A little mystery here and there would be exciting you know?'

'Sorry I couldn't help you out.' she replied.

He laughed as he stood and shrugged his way into his coat. 'Oh well. I'll pop up Tuesday anyway and we'll see if we can solve the mystery of the missing will, eh? If that's as exciting as it's going to get around here, I guess I'll take it.'

'Yeah.' Charley said with a smile. She planted both hands in opposite armpits as she watched him zip his coat. It only took him a beat to notice her expression and engulf her in a big hug, one hand rubbing at her back firmly.

'Keep your chin up, we'll sort it, don't worry.'

She nodded at him, unable to speak as he stepped away.

'Right, I'm off then before I'm late to get Belle. I'll see you Tuesday.'

Charley followed him to the door and waved him off as he sped down the driveway with a loud honk of the horn and a hand out of the driver's side window in a wave. She stood watching him retreat into the distance, hearing the roar of the car as it disappeared out of sight and through the village. When her teeth began to chatter with cold she shut the door and leaned her back against it staring down the hall.

'Just you and me again then.' she said, shoulders dropping along with her spirits.

It was getting harder to be up here alone with the will and her family hanging over her. There were moments when she felt the entire world was going on as normal and she wasn't even part of it. She was the only one stuck on the outside, in this mess, unable to move forward.

Back in the kitchen her eyes fell to the small book of poems, still open on the table. The mother and child figurine sat next to it, where it had been since the night Elizabeth had died. Charley felt the familiar pain creep up her chest and shook her head, breaking the focus before emotion overwhelmed her again.

Elizabeth liked that in the drawing room, Charley, you really need to keep things tidy. If it gets broken again...

Irritated with herself, she scooped the figurine up, took it back into the drawing room and placed it carefully on the fireplace mantle assessing it's position before returning to the kitchen where the cheerful sun was falling through the back doors In a warm glow. It shined on 'A

Little Pocket of Goodness' in a golden halo, glinting off the glossy page sixty-six.

Bloody poem.

Charley pulled the book toward her and looked at the maid, doomed to clean the fireplace for eternity, holding the feather duster aloft to the writing above. As her eyes travelled up the page the fall of light exposed indents, as though someone had been leaning on the page as they wrote. No big deal, but what struck Charley as odd was that this wasn't writing that marked the page, it was short lines. Specifically, lines placed under certain numbers within the poem.

She tilted the book into the light with a frown. There were no other marks on the page, and nothing else underlined. No words, no imprinting through the poem itself, just underlined numbers.

What on earth...?

Tilting the book further into the sun Charley saw that the rest of the page was free from indentations.

Except that... no, it wasn't at all. There were also a series of indented numbers by the spine, she noted. One to five, in no order and in no correspondence to the number underlined in the verse it sat alongside. Charley's mind began to whir.

Numbered verses, with numbers underlined. On the specific poem that Elizabeth had instructed her to read.

Holding her breath, she stared at the uninspiring poem. If this was a breakthrough, and she felt like it should be, then why couldn't she put her finger on what it was?

The numbers. Write the numbers down.

She grabbed a pad from her laptop bag, jotted down the numbers by the spine, and finally the corresponding number underlined in the verse it sat alongside.

1-5, 2-8, 3-3, 4-1, 5-4

Chewing at the end of the pen, Charley stared at the row of numbers. What was this? Coincidence?

No. This is no coincidence.

Far from the ramblings of a diseased brain, Charley was now almost certain that Elizabeth had known exactly what she was doing when she wrote the letter. She was just damned if *she* knew what it was.

'Come on Elizabeth, give me a sign, some help,' she murmured. 'why would you lead me to this book, to this poem? And why on earth would you underline certain numbers? It has to mean something, doesn't it?'

Pulling the book back toward her across the table she read back through the poem only twice before the answer hit with the force of a sledgehammer.

Hang on! Underlined numbers in a poem, the last line of which is...

'...treasure it, lock it up, keep it safe.'

Charley's heart jumped as she slapped the book down on the table.

Safe. This is a safe code?

Five digits? It was certainly possible, and more than probable. So she was looking for a safe then, not paper? Is that what Elizabeth had been trying to tell her with the poem?

In that moment it seemed so obvious she almost slapped her idiot forehead in understanding.

'Of course!' she said, almost knocking the chair over as she stood. 'Clever, Aunt Elizabeth, bloody clever! And bloody lucky I noticed or the will would never have been found. It's in the safe. Of course it's in the bloody safe where else would it be? Jeez, Charley, you are an absolute idiot!'

In the hallway the study door clicked and swung open slowly, drawing Charley's attention with a long creak.

Chapter Twenty-Six

Book in the middle of the mahogany desk, Charley opened to page sixty-six, and started a new search. The search for a safe. Except that this wouldn't be so much of a search, she knew exactly where it would be. The fireplace.

It was a strange place for a safe, she supposed, but it was the only other insistence of the letter. The only other oddity. If the book told her the safe code, then 'opening the flue' must tell her where the safe is, especially as the room had already been turned upside down twice, with no sign of a safe.

Turning to the fireplace, she stooped. The back of the fire was closed, but a small cast iron handle sat at the top of an oval door around the size of a football. She pushed it, expecting resistance but finding none. The small door tilted back and sat on the outer wall of the chimney with an iron clang.

Sitting back on her heels Charley stared at the open fireplace almost willing the safe to fly out and land in her lap. When it didn't, she leaned forward, peering into the tiny gaps both sides of the flue door. Darkness concealed her view.

Surely a safe would never fit in this gap? It must be tiny.

She pulled her phone from her hoodie pocket, but the light didn't show much where she couldn't get her head to see, so she placed her hand inside feeling round the darkness into… emptiness. The chimney wall was uneven and there were a couple of ledges in the brick, but no safe. Repeating the process on the other side only brought up the same result.

Okay, well there's only up then.

Leaning into the fire she reached up the chimney into the darkness, sneezing as a layer of soot and dust dislodged and fell as she poked around, but there was only wall up here too, nothing more. The fireplace was empty.

With a frown she rocked back onto her heels, wiping a dirty hand across her brow.

No safe. But if Elizabeth mentioned the poem for the combination, then she mentioned the flue for the safe, surely.

Heaving a sigh, she stood, hand on hips, looking around the small room. The contents had been checked over and again, but she hadn't been looking for a safe back then she had been looking for paper.

I've checked everything on the shelves, so I suppose I need to look above and below the furniture too. At least a safe should be easier to find, in theory.

She followed her last search first, this time running her hands and eyes around all the nooks and crannies in the room, on the bookshelves, under bookshelves, under the table, under the chair, but there was still no sign of a safe. Coming full circle Charley grit her teeth and tapped her fingers on the desk.

I have a numbered code, I'm pretty sure there must be a safe, and if there's a safe, I'm pretty sure the will is inside it. How hard can this be? Think Charley, where would Elizabeth hide a safe, or rather where would Frank hide it?

The brass-framed pictures that adorned the walls caught her eye. Five of them, large and unassuming. Inspiration hit and with renewed vigour she checked each picture as though she were in some sort of Agatha Christie movie. Everyone hid their safe behind a large picture back then didn't they?

Not in this house though, the walls were intact behind each one. On a roll, anyway, she lifted the large rug as much as she could checking for loose floorboards, or even a trapdoor to another room, but to no avail. She ran her hands over the books she had missed before checking there was nothing behind them, or, indeed, that there were no false books hiding hidden niches.

She turned up nothing. Nothing at all.

With a grunt of frustration Charley flopped into the large leather chair, rubbing her dusty hands on her jeans.

Christ, this is not Nancy Drew, Charley, these were normal people, where would normal people put a safe?

The only place she hadn't thoroughly checked was the mahogany desk itself. The drawer was empty of a safe, she knew that from her earlier search, but the desk was bulky and well made.

Getting up, she checked over the desk, and finally crawled underneath. At first nothing struck her as out of the ordinary, but from down here a section at the back jutted down by at least a foot more than the front. On her hands and knees she crawled into the leg space running her hands across smooth oak and finally lying on her back to check the odd space.

She nearly missed it. The colour change of the wood was so subtle that from anywhere other than where Charley was lying you would never notice it. She pressed a hand to the lighter square and there was movement, a shifting sensation. Carefully, she pushed further, and the wood lift to reveal a false panel. Moving the panel aside she shone the phone's torch into the space and came face to face with a small cream safe, around a foot square and not very old by the look of it. Charley gave a hoot of surprise.

Ha! a false back, Nancy Drew had it right after all! Now please, please let the numbers be the code, and please let the will be in here, this is just not funny anymore.

She reached into the space, carefully pulling out the safe before crawling out from under the desk and lifting it on top. She left the panel open so that she could place the safe back inside. For safekeeping. No pun intended.

Wiping dirt, soot, and dust down her jeans, she stood beside the desk, gasping adrenaline fuelled air. Her hands shook as she used the book to enter the electronic code, and expecting it *not* to work, she almost whooped with joy as the mechanism whirred and the little safe door opened with a click.

Inside were papers, a fair few of them, a large, bulky envelope, and a fresh single piece of folded cream paper sitting on top, Charley could see the imprint of the Last Will and Testament wording even through the thick folded paper.

She grinned with relief.

Bingo.

She pulled the paper out. It was scant, and so pristine that Charley almost thought it was blank but opening it up revealed just a few lines of text. She scanned her eyes over the final wishes of her Aunt, hoping against hope that she wouldn't find that she had left everything to her sister. Heaven knows Francesca didn't deserve it, but Elizabeth had no other family, what else could she do?

The document signed just six weeks ago was to be upheld by the executors, Hampton solicitors, and had been witnessed by two people. One was Peter Harding, a name she had never heard, but the other was Axl Maddox. The chair creaked as Charley sat back into it to read.

The Last Will and Testament of Elizabeth Margaret Kane

I, Elizabeth Margaret Kane, presently of Fortwind House, Fortwind Bay, Northumberland, England, hereby revoke all former testamentary dispositions made by me and declare this to be my last will.

I direct my executor to maintain that the reside of my entire estate, and all items in it, to be left to my only daughter, Charlotte Elizabeth Costin.

Charley froze, her mouth dropping open.

Daughter? That can't be right. Elizabeth doesn't have a daughter.

Reading over it again with a frown, Charley finally processed not only that Elizabeth had a daughter, but...

'Charlotte Elizabeth Costin?' she whispered to herself.

Frowning, she re-read the name again. Disbelief giving the words a dream like quality, as if the letters were put together wrong, they were dancing on the page in the wrong order, spelling something foreign and yet so familiar that Charley couldn't quite grasp their meaning. And then the insinuation hit her with the force of a wrecking ball. The air forced from her lungs, her stomach flipped and the room seemed to drop ten floors like an out of control elevator, she involuntarily grabbed the desk for support.

That's my name! Me? Does she mean me? Can she just call me that out of fondness? But surely that makes the will void, If I'm not her daughter who does everything go to?

She re-read the document again, heart thumping in her ears, paper shaking in her hands so much that it finally freed itself from her grip and floated onto the desk. Staring at it Charley thought of Elizabeth's set jaw, and expression, how much she had thought it much like her own. Then she shook her head in denial. They were family, weren't they? Of course there would be similarities.

I don't get it. What the hell were you trying to do here Aunt Elizabeth?

Adrenaline surging Charley picked up the paper and headed out of the study. There had to be a simple explanation, and there was only one person who would have answers now.
It was time to call Francesca.

Chapter Twenty-Seven

The knock at the door came as Charley strode down the hall to get her phone from the kitchen. She almost left it, but as it was an exception to the doorbell, she supposed she ought to answer it and turned back.

It was Glen. She smiled, stepping inside.

'Hello Charley, how are you getting on?' She said, pulling a scarf from around her neck as Charley shut the door.

Emotion surged and Charley found she wasn't able to speak. Still shaking, she thrust the will at Glen, who read it and looked up at her, brown eyes wide but serious. She placed a hand on Charley's arm.

'I know, Charley.' She whispered. She cleared her throat before continuing. 'I didn't know whether it was the truth, but I found something. A book. She has written about you a fair bit.'

Glen looked away tugging at her coat and hanging it over the bannister, as Charley felt the elevator fall another floor. The hallway seemed to list to the right, as did Glen.

'A... a book? About me...?' she said with a frown.

Glen turned to face her with a sigh.

'I got suspicious after you said she had been so well. I'd had periods where Ms Kane had been better than others, but never a 'run' of clarity, especially for weeks, it's unheard of. After you said she was still adamant she was being poisoned, even in her good state, I became a little concerned. Especially as you were cooking fresh for her, and that seemed to link directly with her behaviour, as you'd implied.' Glen pursed her lips, 'I'm sorry to say that I did some digging around on the day you went out. I didn't want to alert you in case I was wrong and gave you false hope.'

Charley wasn't sure what response Glen expected. She wasn't sure what response she felt, so she settled for the first thing that arrived on her lips.

'What?'

Glen started again but the information was already sinking in and the anger began to seep upward.

'Why didn't you tell me?' Charley said cutting her off. 'What did you find? I can't believe you would hide this from me!'

Glen held her hands in front of her as though warding off Charley's accusations.

'It was all supposition Charley,' she said, 'and to be honest I didn't find much, I knew Ms Kane spent a lot of time locked in the study alone, so it was just a hunch. I found the book inside the fire of all places, but I barely had time to read before I was interrupted. Axl came in the back door without announcing himself, I got flustered that he should catch me rummaging in Ms Kane's personal things. Anyway,' She turned to pull a small leather-bound book from the pocket of her coat. 'This is the book. I took it to keep it safe, but obviously with what happened afterwards I forgot about it. I was popping up today to pass it back to you, and to say that you may have been right. That Elizabeth may have been right.'

The book passed into her hands; smooth, cold leather touched her skin, but Charley barely felt it. The noise coming from Glens mouth was like a strange ancient language she had to decipher. The words un-formable, thick and slippery.

Study... diary... fireplace... right about what?

The frantic thumping in Charley's chest stopped with her breath, suspended in the moment as her brain staggered and the world shattered around her, like sharp diamonds of glass, creating high pitched tinkling in her ears.

The fireplace.

*Shit! The book was in the flue! Which means it was the final part of the poem puzzle, which means Elizabeth wanted **me** to find it.*

A stab of irritation hit and festered in Charley's stomach.

Glen had poked around to the extent that she had not only found the book first, but read it through? Why would she do that? And why take it? Why not just pass it over?

Glen's words were tumbling over each other in a guilty haste to explain as Charley stared at her.

'…parts of the book I read completely match with what I remember of the days, which again doesn't sound like someone with dementia. Like I said before, I've never seen any specific test results and I've seen far worse cases than Ms Kane's was. I just... well, she wrote like a person completely in her right mind, she describes all the hallucinations, all the symptoms of her illness. Charley, she wrote with clarity, never wavering from her voice. The worrying thing is she also never wavers from the poisoning. She swears Nell, Axl or Avril were slipping something into her food, and with you cooking, she was noticing when the bad episodes came on and what she had to eat, never anything you cooked, always something Nell had. Now she didn't say that Nell was-'
A small sheen of sweat was forming on Glen's brow and Charley worked her jaw as her mind hit on something else disturbing. If Elizabeth had put the hiding place in code in the letter, then surely she didn't want just anyone to find the book and if it pointed to a poisoning by one of her three friends, it was no wonder... but Glen had said that Axl had seen her, did that mean he about it knew too?

'Did he catch you?' Charley said, breaking her silence.

Glen stopped mid-sentence, her mouth open, brown eyes wide. 'Who?' she paused, Charley waited. 'Oh, you mean Axl? Well, no, but I'm sure he suspected something. To be honest, he was looking a bit shifty himself, he was putting a couple of Tupperware boxes into the cupboard by the sink. I thought it was a strange place for fresh food, but I didn't ask, I just wanted him gone. It was probably nothing.'

Tupperware? They were discussing a possible murder and Glen was talking about Tupperware? A flutter of unruly giggles rose and threatened to force their way out.

'...Full of something dark, berries I presume,' Glen continued, 'but in the cupboard by the sink? It just seemed...'

The world slowed and stood still as the laughter died before it had been born. Charley's heart dropped through the floor and she felt the room disappear around her. A low buzz replaced Glen's voice, as though she were speaking in slow motion, sound extended and dragged.

Berries... oh, God, no... the berries!

Her hand flew to her mouth as the enormity of what she may have done circled her consciousness, threatening to push its way in and overwhelm her.

Glen trailed off, looking confused.

'What is it?'

Charley swallowed hard, her throat suddenly arid as the desert.

'The Tupperware boxes? I found them; they were full of elderberries. I checked with Aunt Elizabeth... I mean... I mean, she tasted them and confirmed they were good, so I made a... a pie for her.' she heaved in a breath trying to stop the hallway from its endless spin. 'Oh God. Oh God, Glen, I think they may have been laced with something. She had been right as rain all morning, but she hadn't even finished that pie before she keeled over vomiting. And th... that... was the beginning of the end.'

Horror crossed Glen's face. She opened her mouth but didn't seem able to find the words.

Tears let go down Charley's cheeks as she stared at Glen, the full force of the situation not only gaining entrance but hitting her head on.

'Glen, oh god, oh my god, Glen! I think I may have poisoned Aunt Elizabeth. I think... I think... I may have killed her.'

Glen composed herself and immediately began to backtrack, a hand on Charley's arm. Nurse mode well and truly on.

'Charley, no, no, this is not your fault. I saw Axl put the berries there, you couldn't have known-'

Charley pushed Glen's arm away, as she howled, and then she screamed.

Chapter Twenty-Eight

Axl worked his jaw and shook the paper so hard it ripped almost in two. This house was starting to feel as cramped and claustrophobic as the cage of a battery hen.

'There now,' Ann said from the doorway, a smug smile under pink rollers. 'The paper is ruined, I guess that's reading out for the day. Maybe now you can get off your arse and tidy the garden like I've been asking you for the last two weeks, huh?'

Axl said nothing. He snapped the remains of the paper in half with a grunt. Ann huffed beside him.

'I bet Elizabeth didn't have this trouble getting you to work now did she? Her garden was just dandy wasn't it? Loved the gardening you said, too bad you can't do your bloody own. Look at it, Axl, it's a bloody shit tip, and if you-' She jabbed a finger at him, Axl bit his tongue forcing himself not to react as her eyes scrunched into slits. 'If you think for one damn second-'

'I papered the hallway yesterday.' he said cutting her off as she jabbed a finger again. 'I'm having a break. I'll do the garden tomorrow, weather permitting.'

'Weather permitting?' Ann spat, 'You went up to *her* house come rain, shine, or bloody cyclone, but you'll only do ours weather permitting? It stinks Axl, how you treat me and this house. Yes, you papered the hallway. Was it worth it? I can't say the job was top notch, can you?'

'It's papered.'

'Papered!' Ann huffed turning from the doorway in a flounce of pink nightgown. The back door opened and he heard the click of the lighter before he smelled acrid cigarette smoke.

Axl put his head in his hands, scrubbing at his scalp with his fingers.

He would admit it wasn't his best work. He was beyond it these days. Each day he wasn't able to get the letters ate at him. Each day was closer to Charley finding the will – if she hadn't already. And each day scared the hell out of him.

He had a damn key for Christ sake, and still hadn't had an opportunity to use it. The thought drove him nuts, but Ann was on him every second of the day, and even when she wasn't Charley was at the house and he had no idea when she came or went. Everything was working against him.

His head ached. He pressed the heel of his hand to his forehead. When would he get a break?

The back door finally slammed shut and like a divine messenger Ann appeared offering an opportunity that seemed sent straight from heaven.

'I can't take another night in with your face. I've messaged Irene, we're off to bingo tonight. I'll be back late. Don't wait up.'

Axl looked up to the doorway in surprise but it was empty. His saviour gone as quickly as she had appeared.

'What?' he said, wondering if he had dreamed the whole scene.

'Bingo,' she snapped from the kitchen. 'I'm going, you can't stop me, I'll be back late, don't wait up. Clear enough?'

'Yes,' he replied. A slow smile curled across his lips. Bingo didn't finish until 1am.

Bingo.

Chapter Twenty-Nine

Charley pushed the little leather-bound book across the table toward Theo, he eyed her before picking it up and thumbing through. Pages of Elizabeth's neat writing tumbled under his hands, flashes of blue and black ink cascading on each page. Charley stared.

Aunt Elizabeth's writing... the witch... mom.

She had finally plucked up the courage to call her mother - her aunt - oh god, it was confusing, *Francesca* - with the news after Glen had shown her the little book three weeks ago. Francesca's only reply being:

'Codswallop, Charley, and if you think you're getting your hands on anything in that will by assuming connections via an old woman who was ill with dementia, and obviously not aware of what she was saying, then you are very much mistaken. I am her closest living relative. Don't flatter yourself, Elizabeth couldn't have children, it was the disease talking. Now get on with finding that will, Elizabeth would have wanted things settled as soon as possible. She was very meticulous.'

Because you know, Charley thought. But actually mom – Francesca - you know nothing. Charley had thought then of the will, and the sparseness of its contents. There would be a shock coming to Francesca Costin when it was processed.

Over the following days Charley had locked herself, and the will, away. She vetted calls and visits only answering the door to Theo and Glen who dropped in when they could. They were good to talk to, both of them calm and rational as she floundered for a grasp on any piece of her life that was still secure.

The Solicitors, a small firm who knew Elizabeth personally, rang often wanting to get her estate sorted, probably as much so they could cross it off their workload and get on with other things. Charley gave the same reply she gave to Francesca and her sisters in Harrogate - not yet. She was desperate to process what was going on herself first, it didn't matter how long the estate took to sort, there was only herself involved. But there would be fireworks, of that she was certain, and she couldn't handle the blow up just yet.

'Charley?'

A hand pat hers lightly and the cafe swam back into view as she looked back up to Theo.

'Did you hear anything I said?'

Charley shook her head.

'I'm sorry, I just can't seem to concentrate. My head feels like it's going to explode.'

'I know, it must be a lot to take in. I said this all seems very clearly written. I guess, she wanted you to know eventually, but why write it down? Why not just tell you? And why did she write down each day's events, and the visions and hallucinations she had? I don't get it.'

'She thought she was being poisoned, this may have been her way of trying to suss out who and why I guess.'

Theo's eyes widened so much Charley wondered if his eyeballs may just fall right out onto his cheeks.

'Right. Wow, okay.' He brought a hand up to scratch the back of his neck, 'What and you...?'

'Believe it? Well, the more of it I read, the more I don't believe she had dementia. Glen also suspects she didn't, she's a nurse but never had any access to scans, tests, reports, nothing. They never let her see, and she couldn't find out who her consultant was either. Nell used to take her to appointments and then bring her back with the news and results but look here.'

Charley reached for the book from Theo. She flicked to the first few pages, where Elizabeth had written about her fears being confirmed the day Nell had taken her to the beach instead of the appointment. Theo read the passage through.

'See?' She said, 'She heard Nell explaining the test and the results to Glen, even though they had only been to the beach front and sat in the car.'

Theo frowned and looked up at Charley warily.

'But couldn't she-'

He broke off discreetly as their drinks were brought over. A hot chocolate for Charley and a coffee for Theo. The waitress asked Theo how Belle was getting on at school and Charley turned to look out at the swollen grey ocean, hearing each booming crash of the surf as it hit the sand. The day was as grey and tumultuous as the sea; drizzle, wind, and cold air. Theo finished his conversation and Charley looked back to thank the waitress with a smile before she moved away.

Theo waited until she was out of ear shot, although the cafe was so noisy that Charley thought they could have used megaphones and still not have been heard.

'So, the tests, couldn't she have just *thought* that all of this went on? Couldn't it have been in her head from the dementia? You said she had frequent hallucinations.'

'I know, and we've been over that, of course, both Glen and myself. I might even believe it if there weren't another four instances just like this one in the book. And Glen can confirm that Elizabeth has written down almost exactly what Nell told her each time. If Elizabeth was okay enough to listen to Nell and write it down accurately, wasn't she also okay enough to know what she had been doing that day?'

Theo took a sip of coffee and shrugged. He looked unconvinced.

'I don't know. I mean, it just seems flaky.'

'I would think so too, but too much in this book matches up. The bigger, and more violent hallucinations were fairly few and far between, but Elizabeth recorded them with vivid detail and Glen remembers details of each from what Elizabeth was saying, shouting, or doing as the hallucination took place. It's all here. Loads of it, Theo. And most of it Glen can confirm was true at that time. She even recorded conversations she and Glen had, which Glen says were also recorded with accuracy.'

Theo wrinkled his nose.

'So maybe it wasn't dementia that killed her, Charley, what does it matter now?'

'It matters because I think she may have been right. She was poisoned, which, Theo, is murder.'

Theo pulled in a deep breath which he blew out as he ran his hands through his hair sitting back in his seat.

'That is a huge statement. Huge.'

'I wouldn't say it if I didn't think it was true. Elizabeth has written more than once in the book that she believes it and that she hopes she can find out who it is before they manage to get to her. The other thing is...'

Charley broke off, looking down at the table. She had spoken to no one of the berries that she had put in the pie, except Glen. She had been too ashamed, felt too guilty, and although she knew deep down that it had been a horrible accident, she still felt Elizabeth would have been around today if she hadn't made that damn pie. Theo still had his hands behind his head, his lips pinched together as he watched her carefully.

'What's the other thing?' He finally said.

'Charley glanced around, but nobody was taking any notice of the couple tucked up the far end of the cafe. She told Theo of the berries she had found and that she had baked the pie that had been the beginning of the end for Elizabeth.

'You're saying you think the pie killed her?' He frowned.

'I know it did, Theo. I only wish I still had some of the damn thing left, but it's long gone. It would prove I'm right. I can feel it.'

Concern crossing his face, Theo leaned forward resting his elbows on the table.

'How can you be so sure?'

'Because I know she was in good form. Very good form and had been for the period of time I had been cooking for her, until that pie.'

'Which you cooked...'

Charley felt the familiar stab of guilt flood through her, and tears suddenly pricked her eyes. Theo caught her hand across the table.

'No, I didn't mean it like that, Charley. I only meant you were cooking and she was alright, but you cooked the pie too, so how does that prove...'

She swallowed hard, pushing down the guilt.

'I had been using ingredients I had picked myself. The pie was made with berries that were already in the house. Someone else picked them and stored them in the cupboard. I already had an inkling she was being poisoned, but I still used the damn things. I checked with Elizabeth first of course, and she confirmed that they were okay to use, but they must have been laced with something. God, I wish I'd thrown them down the garbage disposal with the rest of the food.'

Worry was starting to form on Theo's face.

'So, Glen, her nurse, she believes this too?'

Charley nodded.

'She's almost as certain as I am.'

Theo sat back and turned to look out the window. Charley took a sip of her lukewarm hot chocolate. She hadn't eaten much over the last few weeks, and as Aunt Elizabeth unravelled more and more story that Charley had no idea she was so deeply involved in, she had lost more and more appetite. She didn't want the hot chocolate either, but Theo had insisted, and he was paying so she would force it down.

'Alright,' he said, swinging his head back to her, 'So we need to go to the police.'

Charley almost spat her chocolate across the table at him.

'With what evidence?'

'With what you've told me, and the book, they could start an investigation. Surely it's enough.'

Charley huffed a laugh.

'Of course it's not. The ramblings of an old woman, along with the word of her nurse, and freshly appointed daughter? They'd laugh us out of the station. If I'd got a bit of the pie, or the berries, we may have somewhere to start, but I don't even know who would be doing this or why. If there's no motive, and Elizabeth officially has dementia? Case closed, before it's begun.'

Theo nodded slowly.

'So if it's true then we need more evidence, and if the evidence we collect points this way too, then at least we're certain before we go to the police. It probably makes more sense that way.'

Charley nodded relief flooding through her.

'Okay,' Theo said, 'So, you've read the book, any theories to start us off?'

Oh, she had a theory alright, after the information Glen had given her, along with the book.

'Well, Nell faked her appointments, so she obviously had a hand in falsifying the disease, but quite possibly the actual poisoning was down to the gardener. Glen saw him putting the berries into the cupboard the day before I made the pie. Axl picked them, Nell would have cooked with them.'

Theo made to protest but Charley was on a roll.

'So I think between them, it was probably the cook and the gardener. The only thing I don't know is why, what their motive would be. They both seemed like good friends and ordinary people, but no one else was with her at all, ever, no one else had an opportunity.'

Theo was shaking his head vehemently.

'No, no that's not true, you've got it wrong and I'll tell you why. Axl Maddox is the gardener at Fortwind-'

'I know that, Theo.' Charley said cutting him off.

He held up his hand, his face serious.

'Charley, before you go throwing names into the pot, I know Axl Maddox did not poison anybody. He's a kind and gentle man and I know he thought a lot of Elizabeth, there is no way he would be plotting to poison her. Nell, I don't know at all, but I'm sure she's just as kind. Listen, we need to get some serious evidence together before you go batting names around.'

Charley nodded, feeling the blush creep into her cheeks.

'Okay, I hear you, it was stupid to name them, you're right. We'll see what we can uncover but I really can't see who else it could be at the moment.'

Theo looked down at the table, picking at the corner of a menu.

'I can't speak for Nell but it's not Axl, Charley. I guarantee that much.' He mumbled.

Charley looked at Theo who seemed to have paled three shades. She supposed murder allegations over coffee would hit anybody hard.

'You can't possibly know for certain; we need to be checking him out either way.'

Theo was shaking his head. His face as red as Charley's felt.

'He didn't do it, Charley. And I absolutely do know that for sure because he's my father.'

Chapter Thirty

The light went out in the front bedroom of Fortwind House, rendering the house completely dark. Axl checked his watch.

11.40pm.

He'd give it thirty minutes before making his move, just to make sure she was asleep.

Pulling up the hood of his coat against the cold wind he gave each leg a short shake in an attempt to get the blood moving. His knees clicked and popped their displeasure. His joints were stiff with cold, if he stood in this frigid air much longer he would have no feeling in them at all.

With a last glance at the darkened window he left the large maple he had been stationed behind for the last 40 minutes and moved to the bins at the side of the house. Half creeping, half lurching, and fully cursing the gravel which crunched loudly underfoot in the quiet of the night.

At the bins he crouched back against the wall, sheltering himself from the worst of the biting wind. He shivered and checked his watch.

11.41pm

It was going to be a long wait. He thrust his hands into his pockets where hand warmers were waiting for him. Warm hands were essential for stealth, he couldn't be fumbling with the keys, the back doors already creaked enough to wake the dead. Being gardener here for so long he knew from years of experience that the right door was much worse than the left, so he would use the left side to enter.

He managed until 11.49pm before making his move. If he sat much longer Charley would find him here in the morning, joints locked frozen. On the flip side he had barely an hour before Ann would find him missing when she returned home. Neither scenario filled him with joy so he took the cast iron key from under the pot by the gate and entered the garden.

Wispy clouds scurried across a clear sky, allowing the full moon to bathe the garden in silver light. Dragging his eyes from its filtered beauty, Axl replaced the key and shut the gate behind him, fetching the smaller silver key from his pocket to unlock the back door.

Slipping into the kitchen he stood listening. The house was still and silent. Comfortingly familiar. His thumping heart began to settle, and his eyes adjusted as the warmth eased itself into his joints. He let out a shaky breath, pocketed the key and crossed the kitchen, grimacing at the squeak of his shoes on the tile floor, until they fell mercifully silent on the thick carpet in the hallway. At the study door, he pulled the paperclips from his pocket, inserted them into the lock and twisted. It was an easy job, he had done it many times before, but with sweaty palms and shaking hands it took three attempts before the lock clunked over. He cringed at the sound, gritting his teeth as he wiped sweat from his brow. Upstairs all remained quiet and so he pushed the door, hope filling his chest as he pulled on his head torch and scanned the room.

Chapter Thirty-One

Charley sat bolt upright, trying to steady her breathing and calm her heart's frantic beat. There was enough moonlight to see that the room was empty, even if she hadn't known the lady with the veined skin and age spotted hands was just a dream. That dream. Again.

The bedside clock shone its red glow beside her catching her attention.

12.17am.

She rolled her eyes.

Still early. Fabulous.

Wide awake, she sighed and lowered herself down into bed pulling the covers up around her chin. She stared at the ceiling as thoughts of the day fired up in her head.

Showing Theo the book had been a mistake, his revelation about Axl being his father ended with his leaving the cafe furious. The worst of it was that, if he ever spoke to her again, she would have to be careful how much she involved him in her investigation. Glen said that Axl had been acting suspiciously in the kitchen, and that he had been the one to place the tubs of berries into the cupboard. In Charley's book, that made him the biggest suspect right now, whether he was Theo's kind and gentle father or not.

Her mind raced, chaotic with thoughts and feelings that stacked atop one another as she lay in the darkness. She still wasn't comfortable with the fact that her life had been a lie. If Elizabeth really was her mother, why had she not brought Charley up here at Fortwind? Why did she have to go and live with the family from hell? What was the story? What was the big secret?

And now there was a possible poisoning and falsified diagnosis in the mix too. What was all this about? Why would anyone want to poison Elizabeth? What could they want from her? She had no money left, all of her wealth eaten away by her care. Ironically, care that she may never have needed in the first place.

What the hell is going on here? Nothing makes sense.

Propping up on to her elbows, Charley could see the dark shapes of furniture highlighted in the low moonlight.

This is ridiculous, you need to stop getting wound up at night. You'll never sleep again.

She rubbed at her eyes with a sigh, and that was when she noticed the curtain ruckling in a soft breeze.

She hesitated.

I did close the window last night, didn't I?

She most definitely thought she had, but the curtain was proving otherwise as it billowed into the room on a gust of wind. Her heart gave a little jolt as she watched it. The material reminding her of the dream and the old lady's nightgown... which lead to thoughts of pale skin, wild hair and brown age spots... and then to thoughts of that tight clawed grip...

Okay Charley, that's enough, just stop it!

She threw back the bedclothes and crossed to the window pulling back the curtain in a smooth jerk before she lost her nerve. There was nothing beyond but the open bottom sash and a cold breeze. With a shiver, she leaned to shut the window, and let out a small gasp as she caught sight of the view below.

The sky was clear, the stars amassed like diamonds. The swell on the sea was immense, each heaving rise giving way to a tumbling crash before a splash and hiss of waves that reached her ears even up here. The village below was lit with the yellow of streetlamps and the bluey hue of the moons light. Heavy shadows flanked where the light didn't reach.

On the beach the sand emanated a silvery glow which reached all the way down to the turbulent water. A strip of silvery light bounced and scattered on the surface of the water right back toward the large moon itself.

A full moon, how appropriate with the day I've had.

She smiled as she took in the scenery. The dark harbour shone in the moons halo, and the black outline of the small island with the ruin of the castle was lit spectacularly. Where moonlight hit the castle walls they shone with a luminous quality, lighting the imposing dark shape like a hologram.

And that was the trigger.

It took Charley a mere second to set up the camera and tripod on the windowsill. She spent time adjusting the settings of the camera, taking a few test shots until she managed to catch the scene in its glory. She snapped different angles, shot close ups of the harbour, and the moon's light stretching across the ocean. She turned her attention to the ruin and snapped a few photographs there too, catching the light shimmering before it.

It looks so eerie, and yet so inviting!

She shivered as she grinned, clicking off a few more shots before finally closing the window against the cold. Leaving the curtains open she packed the camera back into its bag, cursing as she dropped the lens from her lap with a small bump. Picking it up she looked it over but there appeared to be no damage.

Thank god for plush carp...

The thought was cut short by a dull scrape from downstairs. Charley snapped her head toward the door, the zip on the camera bag only half closed. The silence lengthened and as her heart slowed Charley began to think she must have imagined it. With a small chuckle and a shake of her head, she closed the zip fully and put the bag back by the wall.

Idiot, you need some bloody sleep. These dreams are...

There was a muffled bump below, like something had fallen in the study. Charley's heart gave a jolt and immediately began to pound again. She swallowed hard as she swung back to the door.

Shit, is this just the usual craziness, or is someone in the house?

She rose and crossed to the bedroom door, opening it slowly onto the dark landing. Standing on the threshold of the bedroom she listened, not at all sure she wanted to confront an intruder. But the house fell quiet and the longer she stood in the darkness the more Charley was starting to think she had imagined it again.

You're tired, Charley, that's why you think you're hearing noises. Go back to bed and go to sleep.

As she turned back into the room the doorbell chimed, piercing the silence.

With a jolt and a stifled yell Charley reached a hand to the door frame for support and placed the other hand to her thumping chest. heaving shaky breaths she turned back to glance to the stairs. It was dark in the hall, pitch black, but as far as she could tell nothing moved.

I need light.

She flicked the light switch on the wall just outside her bedroom before she could think it through further. Light flooded the stairs and landing. Nothing looked out of place. The doorbell stayed quiet.

She waited a little longer in the doorway letting her heart return to its normal pace before going back to bed. Unsettled, she tried to sleep with light from the landing flooding the bedroom. It was normally a pet hate, but tonight it could stay on.

Maybe it would stay on for a few more nights yet too.

Chapter Thirty-Two

The shrill of the phone broke the silence of the warm kitchen and Charley put the little leather book and the highlighter down on the table to look at the screen.

Fantastic. Get lost Evelyn.

She swiped to end the call without answering and turned back to the book.

The phone rang immediately and Charley thumped the table with her hand.

'God damn it Evelyn, I'm up to my neck in shit here, I'm not interested!'

She almost swiped the red phone icon again before she realised it was Theo.

Her heart began to thump as relief flooded through her. She answered the call before he changed his mind.

'Theo, I'm so sorry about-'

'Charley, about the other day-'

They cut off abruptly together, Theo huffing a small laugh on the other end of the line.

'You go,' he said.

Charley bit her lip and swallowed.

'I'm so sorry about blaming your dad, Theo. Thinking it over rationally, now I've calmed down, to actually name names, especially people who have been so good to me since I've been here, was just wrong. Heck, I don't even have any evidence that this is what happened at all. It's just based on Elizabeth's book and Glens memory. It could just be dementia talking. I don't know, and that's why I need to apologise. Everyone should be innocent until proven guilty.'

Charley fiddled with the lid of the highlighter as the silence stretched, and then there was a sigh.

'Thank you,' Theo said quietly, 'Charley, I want to apologise too, I shouldn't have got angry and walked out, you have such a lot on your plate right now. It's enough to find out that your mother isn't who you thought and trying to get your head around that. This extra pressure must be putting you at breaking point. I do understand why you want to find out what happened and if you still want the help I'd be glad to come and give you a different set of eyes and a different perspective. If you still want me that is.'

Charley put her head on the table and closed her eyes.

'Of course I still want you, it's already obvious I can't do this objectively by myself. I need someone to be able to step back and look at things without the emotional ties. If you're willing, I'd very much like your help.'

'Okay, well, I've just got to get Belle her breakfast and drop her at dads, he's taking her out this morning, and then I'll come up to the house if you like, it may be easier there and we can talk more freely.'

Charley smiled.

'Okay, great, I'll see you in a little while.'

She ended the call and placed the phone onto the table where it immediately rang again. Grinning Charley answered, one eye on the leather book in front of her.

'What have you forgotten?'

'Forgot? Charley, I have no idea what you're talking about, and a hi would be nice actually. A little concern for how we're getting on down here if you can manage it.'

Charley cursed silently. Kate. If it wasn't one minion, it was another. If she didn't have to listen to Evelyn's condescending tone, she had to listen to Kate's.

'Hi, Kate,' she said rolling her eyes and propping her chin with her fist as she looked out at the garden.

'Thank you, hi, and yes were all fine, thank you for asking.'

I didn't doubt that you were, honey.

'You didn't give me chance.' she said.

'I prompted you.'

'And then you didn't give me chance. Look, I'm busy up here, what is it?'

'I hope you're busy looking for the will, and next time you want to ignore Evelyn's calls, just remember she has had to make a sacrifice in her day to call you in the first place, she can't keep chasing you around.'

'I didn't ask her to, what's your point, Kate? I need to get on with stuff here.'

'God Charley, stop with the attitude. I'm calling because mom is upset, she's making herself ill over this missing will. She says she can't take any more, and it will be the death of her if the situation isn't resolved soon. I'm really worried about her Charley, we need to move forward.'

Charley lifted the side of her mouth as she watched the wind ripple through the bushes along the wall of the garden.

Move forward? Elizabeth has only been gone a few weeks, and already you want to take her things and move forward?

An angry swirl punctured her gut at the injustice of what had gone on up here, not only recent events but also over the last thirty years. Charley eyed the stack of papers and envelopes from the safe ready to look through. The will she had tucked into the back of the book, keeping it close until she felt able to deal with the fallout. There were two mysteries to solve here and she wanted them sorted before Francesca had any input.

'Charley! Are you listening? Mom is ill, have you found the will or not? She is quite beside herself.'

'Nope.'

'Well, you need to look, this can't go on forever, eventually the-'

'Eventually nothing Kate,' Charley snapped. 'The solicitors know there is another will, it doesn't matter whether it is found this month or next, they will wait. Elizabeth was well loved up here and people want her wishes to be adhered to. If I can't find it, I can't bloody find it, Kate. There's a lot to sort here and I'm busy. Tell mother she would be best putting her efforts into feeling sorry for the loss of her sister, the one she couldn't be bothered to speak to for thirty years.'

Kate started to say something indignant, but Charley cut her off.

'Do you know Elizabeth only wanted to see us and to love us, Kate? To smother us with everything we ever wanted as she couldn't have children of her own? Mom took us away out of spite. *Spite!* She took us away without even telling Elizabeth that she would never see us again. Mom broke Elizabeth's heart. All these years we thought she was the witch when we were living with the real witch all along. Tell her to think about that!'

Again Kate tried to interject and again Charley barrelled right over her, the roll of her anger fast and furious.

'Tell her to grieve for the life lost before making herself ill over the contents of a blessed will. That was her *sister* Kate. Her flesh and blood. O*ur* flesh and blood, and not one of you cares! None of you could even be bothered to attend the funeral, none of you could be bothered to come up here and help me out. All any of you care about is the damn *will*.'

As the hurt and pain and injustice of the unanswered questions poured out at Kate, Charley heard her voice bounce off the walls of the walls of the empty kitchen, the crescendo loud enough to inform the entire village of Fortwind Bay below, she was sure – *no secrets here*. Breathless and flushed, she saw a drop of water fall onto the table beside her and realised she was crying. She brushed at her face giving pause enough for Kate to think she had finished.

'Charley-' she said, the condescending tone back, a mimic of Evelyn, and Charley's rage flared straight back to the fore.

'No Kate, I've had enough. Don't call me, I'll call you.'

Charley stabbed at the screen, cutting off Kate's indignant voice. Putting her head into her hands she grit her teeth trying to push the emotion down. There was work to do here.

But the family she had been a part of all her life was no longer hers and she had never felt the divide more than she did now. She wished to God she had Elizabeth back, just for a while, just so that they could talk this through, just to help her understand better. If she had been loved, why had Elizabeth let her go? It didn't make sense. Charley's chest physically ached with the hurt. She had never felt so alone.

When holding the tears back finally became too much she let them go, crying with abandon until her whole body ached.

* * * * *

A hand touched Charley's back and she gave a jolt of surprise as she swung round in her seat to see Theo behind her.

'Hey,'

Charley scrubbed at her eyes confused.

'Theo? How did you ...' Her horse voice broke and she tried again. 'How did you get in?'

He gestured back to the hall with his thumb

'The front door was open, I called out, but obviously you didn't hear me.'

Charley frowned, her head was pounding, eyes and throat sore. She couldn't think straight.

Front and back doors open? I must have been out of it last night, I'd swear I locked them.

'The front door?' she said.

Theo nodded. He squeezed her shoulder with a smile.

'Looks like you could do with a drink, shall I put the kettle on?'

Charley rubbed the last of her tears away as she told him where to find the cups and within minutes the room was filled with the aroma of strong coffee as he placed the cups in front of them.

She took a sip, burning her lips. The burn continued down her throat but it felt good. The pain soothing. Theo watched her.

'Are you okay?' He asked.

Charley nodded.

'I am now. I'm afraid a months' worth of grief and frustration was just vented at my sister... well not my sister, I guess. Anyway, it broke me, but I actually do feel better.'

Theo listened as Charley told him what she had said to Kate and how every conversation she had had with any of them since Elizabeth had died had been about the will. They weren't interested in her, or Elizabeth, just the contents of the will. He winced.

'Ouch, that's going to hurt when they find out where it's going.'

'I know, they'll want blood, that's why I'm stalling giving it up to the solicitors. I can't handle that on top of everything else right now.'

'I know, Charley, but it needs sorting. You can't delay it forever.'

'I'm just giving it another week, just to see if I can find anything else. If we have no solid evidence in a week then I think I'm just going to have to let it go, aren't I?'

Theo pursed his lips and raised his eyebrows nodding lightly.

'I think it would probably be best, it will eat you up if you carry on.'

Charley sighed and downed her coffee in one burning swoop before putting the cup onto the table.

'Another?'

Charley grinned and nodded.

'I'd love one, thanks.'

Theo made another coffee and joined her back at the table scanning his eyes over the papers.

'So what's all this then?'

'This was what I found in the safe, along with the will. I don't know what they are but if they're in the safe they may be worth going over.'

'Okay, shall I start with these and you can carry on with the book?'

'Perfect.' She said.

'What am I looking for?'

'I don't really know. Anything about me? Francesca? Anything that looks important I suppose?'

She shrugged with an apologetic smile. He reached over to squeeze her hand as he smiled back.

'We'll work this out, don't worry.'

Nodding, she picked the book and the highlighter back up as Theo pulled the papers toward him and began to read.

Chapter Thirty-Three

'Grandad look! The moats filling!' Belle squealed as a large wave sent the water right up to her castle. Axl stretched his mouth into a smile, his cheeks tight with cold.

'So it is. Now anyone trying to invade will have to swim.' He said, stuffing his hands further into his pockets. 'I hope they brought arm bands!'

Belle giggled, pulling her hat down over her ears, her blonde hair tugged underneath it by a snapping wind.

'Silly Grandad, they'll have boats!' she said batting playfully at his arm.

She watched the water travel around the little fortress, giving a little cheer when it met at the back forming a full moat, albeit a rapidly sinking one. Then she stooped to watch the water retreat and began digging again ready for the next wave.

Axl shuffled next to her, wishing he had thought to bring a wind break and a chair. They had started their beach expedition collecting shells up in the dunes, where they were a little more sheltered, and a lot warmer. But after a sand blasting that left Belle half laughing, half squealing in pain, and Axl with enough sand in his beard to make his own beach, they had moved down toward the water.

As the force of the wind hit, Axl suggested a walk. Belle suggested castles. Axl had told her that his legs wouldn't let him get down on the sand to help her today, her reply being that he could 'watch and learn' how to make a proper fortress. And so he stood, watching and learning, and wishing he was twenty years younger when he could tolerate the cold.

Or at least a week younger, when he would have been able to get down on the sand with her. Today his aching knees and hips screamed when he walked. If he managed to get down he feared he wouldn't get back up. His joints had caused him so much pain last night he had needed pills. It was his own fault, but there would be no mistake next time.

Axl's heart began to thud as his attention strayed from Belle.

And next time would have to be soon. No more waiting around, no more playing soft. There was too much at stake.

He grit his teeth as he thought about last night. He had come so close, found the safe, but Charley had been awake. After hearing her upstairs, he got flustered, dropping the safe on the desk with an almighty bang. In the silence that followed Axl had been sure she would come down and had quickly hidden the safe away again. After a few heart-stopping seconds, he had taken his chance and left via the front door where the key was left in the lock. He sprinted down the driveway in full view of the house, his legs complained and popped, and his lungs burned. He hadn't run so fast in the last decade, but it had paid off. If Charley had seen him, she hadn't come after him, and the police hadn't turned up at his door, so she hadn't known who it was. If sore legs were the only price he had to pay, he would take it.

Axl stared across the gloomy water, the swell was large and heavy today and there was a hint of rain in the air, He crossed his frozen fingers that it wouldn't fall just yet or he would be forced to take Belle back to the house, and however cold it was out here, it was infinitely better than the freezing temperatures of being within three feet of Ann, especially when he had to think.

So, think, how are you going to get back to Fortwind again?

He was thinking hard of excuses, assessing the situation from every angle when there was a piercing scream. Alarmed Axl swung toward Belle who was now standing further up the beach.

'Grandad!' she screeched, 'your shoes!'

She was jumping and pointing, a wide grin on her face as he felt the cold seep around his ankles. The shock of the water forced his gaze to his feet where he stood ankle deep in retreating tide.

'Oooh!, Ow, oof!' he yelled, pulling his feet from the sucking sand and clambering out of the water toward Belle who was clutching her stomach with laughter.

'Your feet!' she said delighted, 'your feet are *soaked!*'

'Bah,' he answered as he reached her, 'What's wrong with a wet foot eh?'

'Your shoes will stink.' Belle said holding her nose before peeling into laughter again.

'Your nana says they already do.' He said.

He watched her small face crumple with more laughter, and found himself chuckling along with her. Some of the tension slid from his shoulders. When her laughter had subsided, she slipped her hand into his and looked up at him seriously.

'Grandad, now we have to go home. You must watch the tide, silly. When it comes in it eats up the sand! If you don't move it will eat you up too.'

Axl smiled back down at her as they started to walk back toward home, the beach was done for today and his joints were certainly more than ready for a break. He winced as they made their way to the dunes.

'You're right, Belle. Grandad was very silly taking his attention from the water. That is good advice, your dad knows the sea, it's good you listen to him.'

'Not daddy! Charley.' Belle said beside him.

'Who's Charlie?'

'Daddy's new friend. We met on the beach.'

Axl nodded and smiled.

'Well this Charlie is a clever fellow, does he work on the boat too?'

'Not *he*, grandad!' Belle started to giggle again as she let go of his hand and turned to him. 'Charley is a girl. She lives in the big house. Daddy said he'll take me one day, I'll pretend to be a knight, riding up on my horse.'

She turned with a flourish and ran to climb to the top of the dune ahead, holding aloft an imaginary sword.

Axl's smile slipped as this new information moved around his mind.

Charlie... new friend... girl... the big house...

He staggered to a halt.

Charley! Elizabeth's Charley? Theo knows Charley?

The beach seemed to shift around him as his heart hammered in his chest.

*Theo **knows** Charley? No, this can't be happening... how?... how did this happen?*

You took your eye off the ball, Axl, you bloody idiot. Never, ever take your eye off the ball!

He dragged his hands down over his face. He hadn't thought it possible for this situation to get any worse, but it had increased tenfold in a matter of seconds.

As Belle did a victory salute from the dune, his own victory suddenly seemed impossible.

Chapter Thirty-Four

By the end of the afternoon Charley thought she may be getting somewhere. Using the highlighter in the little book she coloured all of the episodes that could be classed as confusion and dementia, and all of the events that preceded them. Elizabeth had been at the book for more than a year, and there were a lot.

The first few months were flaky and disjointed, with missing information, as Elizabeth tried to work out what was going on herself, but as it became apparent that what she was eating was making her feel unwell she started to write down not only what she had eaten, but when she had eaten. It was a shame because if Elizabeth had studied her own book as well as she had remembered the contents to write in it she would have seen a definite pattern.

Across the table Theo was pushing papers to one side as he looked through them. Most of them turned out to be legal affairs, there had been nothing of value yet, although he still had a small bunch to look through, and a fat envelope which looked like it contained more of the same. He had turned his nose up at that one.

'I'll deal with the separates before sorting that little lot,' he had said, waving the envelope at Charley before pushing it to the bottom of the pile. Charley had grinned.

'Whatever order you want is fine with me,'

He was reading through what looked like another legal letter when inspiration hit and Charley got up to fetch a pen, ruler, and paper, pushing the collection in front of him.

He looked up from the letter raising an eyebrow at her.

'What's this?'

'Paper. Listen, it's obvious what most of those documents are, would you help me make a chart? I need to cross reference everything, I think I may have found something we can go on.'

Theo put down the paper in his hand and leaned toward her with interest.

'What is it?'

'I'm not sure yet, but if I read out the info we can write it in a chart, I think it will make more sense if we can see it all together without all of the waffle around it.'

Theo snorted.

'Elizabeth would have your head for calling her writing waffle.'

Charley grinned.

'I think she'd agree most of it is worthless. She would go through this tooth and nail too. In fact, I'm not sure why the hell she didn't, she may have been able to change things. So, anyway, we need a column for the date and time, a column for what she ate, a column for how much she ate, and a column for the resulting hallucination etc.'

Theo began to rule out some lines onto the plain paper.

'She went so far as to record how much she ate?'

'Only over the last few months, the earlier stuff is a bit lacking but she has managed to note the things she ate sometimes in the earlier sections. The last few months are quite telling. Oh, and do a column for who was around too, she often names the people who were here at the time.'

The chart drawn and headed with titles, they worked through the book together. Charley finding the places she had hi-lighted and relaying the information back to Theo to enter into the boxes. For the early diary entries not all the columns could be completed but as the book went on the table could be filled in fully. It took a full two and a half hours, three cups of coffee, and four sheets of paper.

Charley taped the sheets together to make a continuous timeline of events before laying the large sheet on the table. She turned on the light against the growing gloom outside so that they could inspect it.

212

'There are some definite similarities here, especially along the severity of the episode and how much food she ate just before it. That was good thinking Charley.'

Charley nodded and set a pointed finger onto the chart running it down the column.

'Look at this too, it always the same sort of stuff, even over a year, it was always the same few things which gave her symptoms. Pie with ice cream, pie with roast veg, pie with chips, jelly and cream, jelly and sponge, jelly shots, jam on toast, jam and butter on scones, jam and coconut cake, elderberries on muffins, pancakes, porridge. The only anomaly is the wine which seems to have made her go downhill after drinking it six times over the last year, but she obviously drank wine at other times and was perfectly fine. There's also the sponge cake that she had...'

She trailed off as she counted the number of episodes that came after sponge cake specifically. Theo counted with her.

'Forty-six times,' he said

Forty-six!' Charley looked up at Theo, he looked back at her serious. 'But she never says whether it was the same sponge cake or not, it could have been a multitude of different flavours, and the same with all these pies. I wish she'd have put what they were.'

Charley heaved a sigh, trying to think.

'Okay, well let's count the pies anyway.' Theo said.

'Pudding or dinner?'

'I think a pie is a pie, but let's count them separately first, we'll have a total anyway. You do pudding, I'll follow down the chart with dinner.'

If Charley thought the sponge cake had been huge, the pies blew her mind.

'I get two hundred and fifty-six dinner pies! You?'

'Nearly three hundred. Two hundred and ninety-four puddings.'

Charley sat back into a chair and blew out a breath.

'So over five hundred pies? That's a lot of god-damn pie, Theo. I wish she'd have put the flavours or type of pie down, it would have made our job so much easier.'

'It is a lot of pie, especially as she only wrote the book over nineteen months. You've got to remember too that this wasn't just pie, it was pie that made her feel ill. There could have been more that didn't, although I'm not sure how many more pies you can fit into the year. Shall we do the jam?'

The jam came into play one hundred and fifty-two times in its various forms, and the jelly just twenty six. The few times she had had porridge, muffins and pancakes paled into insignificance with just a few instances each.

Charley felt a little overwhelmed.

'Okay, so we have these foods, and we have a link to them making her feel bad. I'm not entirely sure what I'm planning to do with that now, it doesn't really tell us anything does it?'

'Not as such. How about we look at the times or the people who were here? Or we could check whether there was a rhythm, how many times per week, or month this was happening? Was it regular or random?'

Charley was back on her feet.

'Of course, you're a genius.'

Theo grinned up at her.

'You asked to write all of this down, we may as well use it that's all.'

* * * * *

For the next hour they cross checked the whole of the chart against itself and came up with some sort of results, even if they weren't completely comprehensive.

'Okay,' Theo said, 'So we have a correlation between the times she ate something which made her feel bad as being usually early morning or lunch time. Strangely an evening meal is only party to the occasion once.'

'Right, and the one person always around is Glen, but then she would be, she was the live-in nurse, so that gives us nothing concrete. Out of eight hundred and fifty-ish episodes Avril was around for just two hundred and six. Axl was around for six hundred and fifty-four, and Nell for a whopping seven hundred and ten.'

Theo blew out his cheeks and ran a hand through his dark curls.

'It's a lot, but they worked here, they were looking after her. It's still not enough evidence for murder, Charley. And what about the remaining hundred that she was alone with Glen? If you're going to play it that way Glen was around for every single episode so she could be the one.'

Charley was shaking her head and pointed to the bottom of the sheet at the last few entries.

'No, Glen wasn't with her here, I was, in fact for the last seven episodes I was alone with her, or with Axl or Nell. Glen was working for a care home at this point, it took her a few hours to get away on that last day Elizabeth was sick. She couldn't have done anything from there, I'm sure.'

'You did say she was in Mr Kane's study that day.'

'I also said that Axl had put the berries that killed her in the cupboard that day, but along the same lines you know it wasn't your dad, I know it wasn't Glen. It just wasn't. Glen was drafted in because Elizabeth was already going through this, it says so in the book. She came in at half time. Someone was already up to no good, that's why she was in this position.'

Theo sat down biting at his lip, hands clasped behind his head as he leaned back in the chair.

'We're going in circles, Charley,' he finally said. 'None of this incriminates anybody, and although the food and times are a little suspect it could be complete coincidence. We don't know who did it, we don't know how they did it. She thought it was through food, if she was being poisoned at all, but this shows nothing does it?'

Charley looked at the chart frustrated. She shook her head. He was right, in a way it offered them nothing, no one person, no motive, no clear poison method, no evidence at all. And yet, it still bugged her.

Elizabeth had been so convinced that she had stuck to this book daily where she could and backtracked the days she had been ill. There was the situation where she had heard Nell lie about where she had been and test results, and Glen had confirmed most of the things she had written in the book were fact, as far as she could remember anyway. If she had been in her right mind when writing, there was a good chance she had been in her right mind when overhearing the conversations with Nell and recalling them perfectly as she wrote them down. It had been the medical details that had impressed Glen, Elizabeth had recounted what Nell had said almost word for word, as though she had taken notes.

But what Elizabeth had never offered, through all of the book was her feelings on motives and who she thought was involved. It was as though she was protecting herself, if it was found before she died it was to be seen as nothing more than the diary of an ill and confused woman. Charley couldn't even recall an instance where she had mentioned her fears throughout the book. Facts with no thought process behind the writing.

How I wish you were around to help me with this Elizabeth... mom.

It still felt strange to call her that.

'Open up, Charley. What are you thinking?' Theo said.

'I'm wondering what the hell Elizabeth was thinking when she wrote all of this down. If she was certain she was being poisoned and she had gone far enough to hide the book, then why are her thoughts not in here? How did she think someone would be able to get her justice from a bunch of facts with compromised and possibly coincidental information? I just don't know why she never went into why she thought someone would want to do it, and who she thought it was. What made her so sure? You're right, there's literally nothing in here to move forward with. It's useless.'

Theo pursed his lips.

'Well, there's nothing in these papers so far either. I don't know what else to say, but the police won't look at this, it's pointless, we'd need another angle.'

Charley looked at him. His eyes told her he was sorry, that he didn't think there was any way forward. His eyes told her to let it go, but she couldn't just yet, and she was thankful he hadn't voiced his thoughts out loud. She tempered her feelings so that he thought she was on the same page. She didn't want another argument. Some time was all she needed, if there was anything to be found she would devote her time to finding it.

'I know,' she told him, 'and I'll try to find one, here has to be something else if she was right. Surely there can't be no trail at all. Listen, just give me a week of madness so that I can focus on it properly, if I haven't got any further by then I promise I'll let it go and agree it was probably just the dementia talking.'

Theo gave her a lopsided grin.

'Done! And I promise I'll humour you for the week. And when the week is through I'm taking you out in the boat, Belle is driving me crackers to see you again, I couldn't even tell her I was coming up here today, she'd have wanted to come too.'

Charley grinned back.

'It's a deal. I'm missing Belle too, and I'd love to come out on the boat.'

'Good.'

Theo stood, pushing the chair under the table and resting his hands on the back.

'Speaking of Belle, I'd better pick her up, they'll be wondering where I am.'

Charley walked him to the door.

'I'll message you tomorrow,' he said, 'I'm working for the next four days so I won't be around but keep in contact and let me know if you find anything. Don't stay up all night on this, will you?'

'I'll try not to, dad.'

He laughed and shook his head as he walked to his car.

Charley shouted her thanks from the door, and he turned back.

'It's no problem. Remember to lock the front door tonight though, eh? I could have been anyone this morning.'

Charley nodded and waved as he got into his car and turned down the drive with a loud blast of the horn.

Chapter Thirty-Five

Back in the kitchen Charley fixed herself some tea, turned the radio off so that she could concentrate, and had another good look over the chart. The only noise now was the crackle of paper as she scanned through the book and the chart, attempting to find the connection, the missing piece.

She followed every lead, every angle, scrutinized every event, person, and food item she could think of. She was completely absorbed in her work when she absently scratched at a light prickle that began at the back of her neck. She carried on reading but the feeling persisted, light fingers tapping the top of her spine.

The air seemed to change in the kitchen, becoming ominous and heavy as a surge of insight gripped her.

*There's someone here. Someone watching... or **something**.*

The tap increased and travelled down her spine, cold as ice. Charley lowered the book scanning her eyes around the kitchen and into the hallway, waiting for the usual triggers - a door to open, a creak, the doorbell, a bang.

There was nothing amiss, nothing moved, so she turned back to the book, reading only a line before the feeling intensified. It pressed against her shoulders, light fingers through the base of her hair.

She turned to the French doors. It was now completely dark beyond the glass.

Are you sure you locked them?

She was. But she stood anyway, walking over to try both handles – which were locked. Of course they were, she had done it as soon as Theo had left, the front door too.

Feeling better she shook her edginess off, sat back down, and returned to the book.

But out of the corner of her eye the darkness pressed against the glass of the doors. Dark. Foreboding. Slowly she turned her head toward them, and what she saw sent a shudder down her spine. Reflected in the glass panes was a cosy kitchen, lights blaring. A young woman hunched over papers at the table, writing and highlighting as though her life depended on it. Elizabeth's had, but it was too late for her now.

Anyone outside in the dark has a full view of everything I'm doing. They could be watching right now, I wouldn't even know they were out there.

She moved back to the doors clicking on the outside light. Part of the garden was now illuminated, but the rest was still in shadow. She could still be seen from the bottom of the garden but she wouldn't see them, in the shadows. She looked at her reflection in the glass, fully exposed at the doors.

What if someone is out there, in the garden, watching from the shadows?

She not only felt exposed generally, but more so with them watching her trying to figure out the mystery of her dead aunt – mom - which may or may not have something to do with whoever was outside.

If there's anyone outside, Charley... If

And then they would come after her too wouldn't they? her mind countered ignoring the remark. She shuddered.

There were no curtains in the kitchen so she would have to suck it up or go into the colder drawing room or study where there were curtains to shut against the night. Or she could go up to her bedroom, no one would see her behind a curtained window upstairs, and the doors were locked, she was perfectly safe. Bedroom winning the vote, she turned to gather the book and paper just as the doorbell went, three times, stopping her in her tracks. Her heart thumped.

Answer the door?

Forget it, Charley, the doorbell is doolally. There's no-one out there. And if even there is just bloody leave them, it's late. The wall is

220

eight foot, and the garden gate is locked. I don't even know where the key is. No-one is outside. You're being paranoid.

She wished she could believe it but she was too rattled. She entered the hallway to check the front door was locked, only to see the study door standing open. Again. She stopped short.

'What the hell do you want from me?' she whispered into the emptiness, 'I'm trying my best!'

A cool breeze lifted her hair in some weird sort of airflow as she pulled the door shut and locked it. The scent of something sharp and spicy filled her nostrils. She sniffed with a frown, something about it was familiar. It was like... she sniffed again.

Aftershave?

Uncle Frank- dad?- entered her mind and the hair at the back of her neck lifted. It was the final straw. She had been planning to go to bed with a hot drink but that would go by the by now. There was no way she was returning to the kitchen to find the cellar door open too, not a chance.

Everything she needed was in her arms, upstairs her room waited warm and cosy. She would close the curtains against the night, and the door against the demons, and not emerge until daylight.

Chapter Thirty-Six

Axl crouched between a large choisya and an even larger rhododendron bush, sheltered by a mature apple tree. Today was a little warmer than yesterday, but he had added more layers anyway. After spending all day in the seeping cold with Belle the ache of his joints was driving him mad. At least the wind had dropped over the course of the day warming the air around him.

It was risky coming back tonight, but after Belle's revelation he had no choice. He was almost certain Charley was looking for something, and now he was aware that Theo was hanging around too, he would need to come back every night until he had the damning letters in his hands or he wouldn't rest.

On top of that Theo would have to be warned about Charley too. She was dangerous to be around, but without incriminating himself Axl wasn't at all sure what he could say to pull him away from her.

He rubbed his aching head with a sigh.

At least tonight had been easier to leave the house. It was darts night at the club. Not that he had been lately, and if Ann enquired she would find him missing from the game, but it was his only opening and she hadn't seemed to be interested. Bingo for Darts. Tit for tat. Theo had cut it fine not picking up Belle until gone 5pm and staying for tea, not leaving until 7.30pm. Axl had felt himself getting agitated, but it had worked out, he had made it here without suspicion.

He narrowed his eyes as he stared into the lighted kitchen. Charley knew something, he was sure, and if she didn't, she would know soon. She was digging hard at the table, paper surrounding her, and if she wasn't aware of anything yet, what else could she possibly be after? What was she doing?

He watched as Charley rose and came to the doors. She turned on the outside light and scanned the garden before her eyes settled on him. His heart gave a jolt and tried to jump right out of his chest.

The game was up. It was over.

He scrabbled for a story. A reason to be here, but just as he was sure she would come out and drag him from the bush she turned away, gathered a book and paper from the table and disappeared into the hall, switching off the kitchen light. Axl leaned back against the trunk of the tree, breathing hard, his heart thudding hard against his ribs.

For a moment he had been certain she had been looking right at him, like she knew he was there. Like she knew what he had done. He closed his eyes and rubbed his damp palms against his jeans before looking at his watch.

10.35pm.

He had a long wait. He couldn't chance being as early as last night. He would take his time and check properly before he entered again. There would be no more driveway sprints. His legs wouldn't take it.

'All this over one blasted woman.' He whispered into the undergrowth.

When he was sure Charley wasn't returning to the kitchen or watching from upstairs, Axl crept to his potting shed, keeping to the shadows. The familiar creak of the door accompanied him inside where the damp warmth and earthy smell filled his nostrils, encompassing him like a friendly hug. He let out a comfortable grunt and pressed on his head torch. There was a small stove and kettle in the corner. He sniffed at the now out of date uht milk and deciding it didn't smell too bad, he made a tea and sat in the dirty old wicker chair to wait, picking up an old gardeners world magazine for company.

* * * * *

It was after midnight when he decided to make his move. He had been dozing in the chair, and if he carried on it wouldn't be long before he drifted to sleep. Only the cool air around him kept him from being completely comfortable.

He made his way to the garden gate and stepped quietly through it, keeping to the edges of the house where he wouldn't be seen if she was still awake. The gravel was unbearably loud under his shoes, and he grimaced as he turned to the front of the house and looked up.

No light.

So far, so good.

He made his way back to the French doors and entered using the left side. He knew he had to be more careful after last night, but he also wanted to be quick, he didn't want to take the chance of being caught quite so closely again.

Ignoring the table where Charley had been working, he went straight to the study and jimmied the lock to enter. He had found the safe last night, and the code he already knew. It was one of the things he had helped Elizabeth to set up after Frank had died. He had brought the safe and he had set up the code, and although she had concealed it's hiding place even from him, he knew that she would never have seen fit to change it. Another slip up, like the gate key. He raised his eyes to the ceiling and thanked her with a grin as he stooped to the back of the desk, grabbed the safe and entered the code quickly. The door whirred open and the grin slipped from his face.

It was empty.

Axl reeled back on his heels, his knees screamed but he felt nothing, adrenaline forcing the pain away.

No!

His heart drummed in his ears. He wanted to be in and out, he didn't need this, and he certainly didn't want to come back again tomorrow.

He scanned the study with his head torch. Nothing but row after row of books - she could have hidden them anywhere.

Desperation brought him to his feet, and he began to rifle through the books as quickly as he dared. Perspiration lined his brow and upper lip and his hands shook as it became obvious the envelope wasn't in the books. He checked the drawer, but already knew it wasn't there from yesterday. He ran is hands around the bottom, but it was empty. He checked the floor, under the bookcases where a lip lifted in the wood and paper could be slipped, he checked under the chair by the window, the bottom of the chair, under the cushion and in the fireplace. No envelope. Not just his envelope but any envelopes or papers at all. He sat back heaving, his breath coming thick and fast, the armpits of his sweatshirt soaked under his jacket.

Where the hell...

His thought cut off as it hit him.

The table.

Charley had been sat with papers at the table. The air seemed to leave his lungs in one gasp and a weight landed in his stomach. If they were the papers from the safe then she had most probably already seen the envelope, hadn't she?

Although surely that would be all she needed, in there was everything that would destroy him. If she had that then what was she still searching for?

Hope welled as he crept out of the study, leaving the lock open to save the clunk of the barrel, and made his way back into the kitchen. He took the larger of the two piles, the ones face up, and sifted through them. The sheets cracked and snapped under his fingers, the noise sounding like gunshot to his ears. He grit his teeth trying to still his shaking hands and move with more care.

The envelope sat at the bottom of the pile, and Axl almost collapsed with relief at the sight of it. He took a quick look inside and saw it was what he was after. The bulging envelope full of the letters that would leave no doubt about his part in this. He knew there was only one. Elizabeth had kept them altogether, in one place. She had said so herself.

Meticulous as always. Thank you for getting me out of this, Elizabeth.

He squashed the envelope into his pocket with a grin. Now to get out of Fortwind house and put the past behind him. Elizabeth was gone, the evidence was gone, and with no proof, even if accusations came out, he was finally a free man.

Chapter Thirty-Seven

Four days later Charley felt as though she were living in an asylum. Going round in circles trying to look for a shred of information that would give her a clue where to go to next. Anything to give her a motive, a suspect, a clue to what the poison could be.

The papers downstairs revealed nothing, they were mainly financial, so Charley had put them back into the safe in case the solicitor wanted them at a later date.

Each day unfolded the same. Fresh coffee and fresh eyes over the little book and chart, which now wore messy red scribbles from links that amounted to dead ends. Always there would be a call from Evelyn or Kate about the will, she didn't answer any of them, but they left their feelings in long angry messages on her voicemail. None of the calls were ever from Francesca; she was apparently so ill that she was now dying.

Charley seriously doubted it, she had been in perfect health a few months ago, and she knew how this family worked. Bribery and lies designed to make her feel guilty, to shock her into action; they must think she was born yesterday. The only thing Francesca was dying to do was get her hands on whatever Elizabeth had left her.

Good luck with that, sunshine.

Charley pushed the chart and book away from her, across the table.

This is useless, it's going nowhere, and if there are no leads then maybe Theo is right, it was just dementia after all.

She leaned her chin on her hand with a frown. To add to the peculiarity, nothing had happened since Elizabeth's death. Nothing odd had come from Nell, Axl or Avril. Elizabeth was gone, and now so had they, without a word.

And these people are hardly in the prime of their life are they, Charley? Murder, really?

The phone shrilled and buzzed from the table. Evelyn. Charley left it to ring off, heaving a sigh when another voicemail notification popped up. She listened to the update on Francesca's declining condition and deleted the message.

What if mom really is declining?

Charley stared at the phone before pushing it across the table, dismissing the idea.

What I really need to get my head around is the fact that she's not my mom. She's nothing to do with me, family by blood but no other ties.

A pain crossed her chest as she looked out to the garden, bathed in glorious sunshine this afternoon. Francesca was useless and lazy, greedy, and entitled, and Charley could go on, but she was still the only mother she knew. Her sisters were the same. Evelyn, Kate, and Rue, were each as bad in their own right, and they drove her to distraction on a regular basis. But they were her sisters, and to think they were anything else caused an emptiness in her heart.

On the one hand she was ecstatic that she wasn't tied to them, ecstatic that Elizabeth was her birth mother, although she had still seen no proof other than the will. -*Was that enough?*

But on the other hand she had lost an entire family. The girls she had grown up with, laughed and cried and argued with, the ones that she had shared stories of the witch with. They didn't belong to her either. They were still family of course, but cousins, and that felt so distant from sisters it may as well have been Pluto from the Sun.

The ache in her chest grew. If what she had learned was true, then she was an only child, and both of her parents were dead. She felt the weight of it like she was being encased in concrete. She couldn't breathe from the pain some days.

This is all so fucked up, Aunt Elizabeth... mom... what the hell am I supposed to call you? Why didn't you tell me when you were here so that I could at least thrash these feelings out with someone? Thanks for leaving me alone with this. I'm not sure you were any better a mother than Francesca.

She felt an immediate stab of guilt. Elizabeth had never had a chance to be one.

But why?

'Stuff the poisoning,' she said to the empty kitchen. 'What's with the shipping me off to live somewhere else if you really wanted children? What the hell went on Elizabeth - mom? It's driving me nuts!'

She ran her hands over her face determined not to cry again. She had cried so much over the last few weeks, for things that were and things that could have been. Sometimes she looked at the will again just to see if she hadn't imagined it. She was in a tailspin that didn't seem to want to stop, and Francesca denying everything last time they had spoken had just made her spin faster.

The copper taste of blood seeped into her mouth. Charley frowned, sucking the blood from her lip. She thought she may just go up to bed, pull the covers over her head, and hope she woke to find this nightmare was just a dream.

The ping of a message came across the table and Charley pulled the phone toward her with a finger. She didn't know whether a message was better or worse than a call, until she saw it was Theo.

Hey, finishing early, if you're not busy how about we pick Belle up from school and take advantage of this weather in the boat?

Charley smiled, thank God for Theo, anything to get out of this hellhole. She text back.

Let's have dinner out tonight too, I need a break. Ready when you are.

Chapter Thirty-Eight

Theo said he would be another hour, so Charley grabbed her camera bag, locked up and drove to the beach. She sat in her favourite place on the rocks to wait, the gentle lap of the sea brushing all thoughts and staleness from her head as she took photographs of the bay. By the time Theo messaged from the harbour, an hour and twenty-five minutes later, she was calmer and more relaxed than she had been in months.

The boat was quaint. Brown and white, with a small open backed shelter at the front containing the wheel and brown benches running down each side and across the back. Theo and Belle were chatting animatedly as they worked together stowing bags on deck and Charley found herself grinning as she made her way towards them, around the harbour wall and down the steep stone steps onto the wooden planks of the jetty.

At the creak of the wood, Belle's head swung her way.

'Charley!' she called, putting down a bag to run toward her. Charley wanted to close her eyes as the jetty wobbled and bobbed on the water.

Please god, let her get to me without falling over the side.

Theo looked up from the boat, raising a hand in greeting as he continued to stow the box and bag under a bench, and then Belle reached her. Charley circled her arms around the little girl, blowing out a breath of relief.

'Hey Charley! We're having a picnic, dad brought lots of goodies, are you ready for the boat ride? Do you get seasick? Do you like scotch eggs? Do you want to see the castle? I can show-'

Charley stepped back and held up her hands laughing.

'Belle, it's good to see you too, but I can't even remember the first question.'

'Belle,' Theo warned, hands on his hips as he watched them. 'give Charley some space.' Then he looked to Charley. 'I figured we could go to the castle if you're game?'

Charley felt her mouth stretch into a bigger grin as she walked with Belle to the boat.

'Absolutely! Belle says we have a picnic?'

Theo shrugged with a grin.

'It'll be a cold one but at least the sun is out for a while longer, eh?'

'It'll be perfect, thanks Theo.'

'No problem. I figured you could do with a treat, it's nothing fancy, only shop brought stuff, but thrown together we won't go hungry. The island is pretty cool too.'

Belle grinned up at her.

'He said if we didn't have to get back for dinner then we'd get more time in the boat before dark.' She giggled as Theo lift her into the boat, tickling her sides as he set her down.

'That was our secret, blabbermouth.'

Charley laughed as Theo stretched out his hand to help her in. The small boat dipped and rocked on the waves and the smell of fresh paint filled her nose as she set her camera bag down on a bench.

'It'll be safer on the floor unless you're going to hold it.' Theo said, holding out a life jacket with a smile, 'I was going to remind you to bring the camera, there'll be an opportunity for some great shots out there.'

'I'm hoping so.' Charley said as she put the life jacket on. She stowed the camera under the bench as Theo secured a life jacket to Belle. Then he unwound the large rope from its post and pushed the boat away from the jetty before starting the engine.

'Are we ready, Skipper Belle?' He yelled.

'Aye, aye, captain.' she replied with a grin and a salute.

Charley sat back onto the bench as they slid away from the harbour. The sea was calm, a mere gentle swell caught the boat which Theo angled into the waves so that it cut through them like butter. Charley pulled her coat around her enjoying the breeze which cooled her cheeks and tousled through her hair as Belle chattered next to her.

Halfway to the island, Theo slowed the boat and cut the engine. Belle's Beauty bobbed gently on the waves as he joined Charley and Belle in the back. Belle dipped her hand into the water and began to sing, as Theo brought Charley's attention to the coastline, pointing out the parts of the village she knew, and then two further bays which had been exposed from out here.

Entranced, Charley pulled out her camera and clicked off some shots of the little village, and Fortwind house. The dipping sun lighting the facades of the buildings until the sandstone glowed golden. She lowered her camera and turned to Theo with a smile.

'The sun really sets off the village doesn't it? It looks almost ethereal.'

'It's pretty special,' He said with a nod, 'but this may be better.'

Hands on her shoulders he gently turned her, showing her the view from the other side of the boat. The low sun, the sky with a hint of red just brimming the castle ruins in the foreground. Charley gasped and brought the camera back up, clicking off more shots, taking time to adjusting the settings as necessary.

'Wow, this is amazing! The light is beautiful. You have fantastic scenery up here.' she said.

Theo nodded watching her.

'I've been digging around on your website. You have some really good stuff on there. Do you take all the pictures yourself?'

She took a few more shots of the castle and lowered the camera, turning to him.

'Yes, all mine. I was at a loose end one summer so I took a photography diploma and found something I was good at, and really enjoyed. The whole business spiralled from there. I don't want it to be all cute kitsch stuff though, I want to move on. As I said before, I want to make the camera really catch a moment, a scene, a smell, a taste, an emotion.' She looked at him, he looked back with wide eyed amusement, and she grinned as she packed the camera safely back into the bag. 'I know you don't get it, it's fine, it must sound really weird to you.'

'Not at all,' he said pulling back his lips and raising his eyebrows. 'Whatever floats your boat.'

She rolled her eyes and he laughed as he moved back into the shelter and turned over the engine, moving to boat on toward the island.

'I'm sure whatever the heck you're on about, it will look good.' He shouted over his shoulder. 'Want to drive Belle?'

Belle, who had been hanging over the side holding her arm out to catch the spray jumped up with a grin and joined her father at the wheel. Charley watched the two of them with a smile. Belle between her father's arms as they steered together. And then she basked in the last of the cool sun, spray hitting her cheeks, until they arrived at a small jetty on the west side of the island.

Chapter Thirty-Nine

The wind was brisk, and Charley shuddered as Belle ran up the cliff-side steps ahead.

'Careful up there, Belle.' Theo shouted as she ran, then he turned to Charley with a grin. 'It's our thing, we always have a fire, she loves to collect the sticks. The wind is cold up top, but the castle walls will shield us from the worst, I promise. The fire is an added bonus.'

'Sounds good to me,' Charley said, zipping her coat as her teeth chattered.

They grabbed the box and bags from the boat and carried them to the cliff edge, where makeshift steps led to the top. Each step was uneven, carved from the cliff itself, and with no handrail quite perilous although the climb wasn't particularly steep or tough.

The wind was tough at the top, however. hitting as Charley stepped onto the grass, snapping her hair and placing cold fingers down her neck. She tucked her chin into her coat as she surveyed the little island. A scattering of trees huddled to her right, the end closest to the bay, bent almost double with years of prevailing wind. Charley saw Belle collecting sticks underneath the nearest one. The rest of the island was a carpet of grass leading to the sudden edges of perilous cliffs which reached down to the ocean below. The only structure here was the ruined walls, providing three 'rooms' of shelter before they crumbled away into the ground.

Theo stepped up beside her, placing the cool box down on the grass.

'Deceiving isn't it? It's smaller than it looks.'

Charley frowned and nodded.

'It really is.'

'Hostile too. The only access is from the small jetty here. It's the only side with a small beach and the old steps to get up here, and I guess whoever built the castle carved them. The rest of the island has sides so steep you'd need crampons and a rope to scale them. God knows why anyone would want to build a castle here.'

'It's a perfect fortress.'

'No-one would bother to invade.'

Charley giggled as she stood taking in the island and the view back toward the bay. Theo took the bags from her and strode ahead, setting them down behind one of the towering grey walls before coming back for the box.

'Looks like the bricks from the last fire have been moved. I'll have to collect more.'

'I'll help,' she said following him to the old ruin.

They gathered brick from the fallen walls as Belle brought an armful of sticks and Theo set about making the fire. The spot was perfect, next to a wall that gave shelter from the easterly wind and would allow them to catch the last dappled rays of the sun as it lowered. As the fire took hold they spread out a couple of blankets and set out the food.

Charley's stomach rumbled as more and more appeared from the cool box. Cakes, chocolate, scotch eggs, sausage rolls, spring rolls, pasta salad, chocolate chip brioche, crackers and cheese spread, and a bottle of wine to drink, strawberry fruit shoot for Belle. It was a certainly a man's picnic, but Charley enjoyed the meal almost as much as the sea bass at the cafe. Theo laughed when she told him.

'Could have saved myself a fortune.' He said.

Sitting on the blanket with their backs up against the wall, Theo and Charley munched the last of the picnic in the fire's warmth as they watched Belle play in the confines of the small ruin, chattering happily to Ted, as she pretended to stoke the remains of a centuries old fireplace. It was Theo who finally broke the comfortable quiet.

'So, anything to report?'

Charley shook her head as she munched on brioche. She swallowed.

'Nope.'

Theo raised his eyebrows, a mini scotch egg hovered mid way to his mouth.

'Nothing at all? Even with the chart?' He said lowering the egg.

'Nothing. I'm so sick of going over everything. I can't even find the link in the food she ate. It's impossible, she just didn't say enough in the book. I keep thinking I should just give it up but then I feel guilty for thinking it. I don't know what to do next, there are just no leads.'

The egg finally made it home and Theo chewed on it, thinking before he spoke.

'Hmm, well what other angles have you looked at it from?'

Charley frowned.

'Angles? There aren't any other leads to go at it from another angle.'

'Everything can be looked at from a different angle. We have the facts, they're there in black and white, but what about information around the facts?'

'Such as...'

'Well, I don't know, expand a little. Like, we know what food she ate and at what times. We also know, from what she has written, the quantity she ate is directly proportional to the seriousness of the attack she has afterwards, but maybe-'

He cut off and flung a hand out to grab her arm, his eyes wide.

'What is it?' She said, startled.

'Charley, the answer has been staring you in the face. You made the last thing she ate. You know what it was and the quantity, so let's chart it - what was it? What time was it? How much did she have? Who was around?'

Charley reeled as she stared at him. How could she have been so stupid? She had forgotten to chart the very last day of Elizabeth's life. She had been there when she had eaten the very thing that had poisoned her, if she had been poisoned at all, so wouldn't that have been the perfect place to start?

She slapped a hand to her head.

'Oh god, I'm an idiot! Elderberries, it was an Elderberry pie, and she ate a lot, like most of it. I guess she wasn't expecting me to poison her. Oh god-'

Theo cut off her train of thought before she went too deep down guilt road with a knapsack and a sleeping bag to boot.

'Okay, so she ate a pie. That's significant right? I mean, how many pies were there that caused her to feel unwell?'

Charley's brain clicked into gear as she realised the connection he was making.

'Loads, they were the main item of food.'

'Yes, so what if all of the pies were elderberry? What are elderberry's like? I've never had them. More to the point what if they are poisonous in large quantities?'

Charley shook her head with a shrug.

'Shit, I can't say I know much about them, and I didn't have any of the pie, I hate berries. I do know that Elderberries were one of her favourite things to eat though, she said as much. She said she hadn't had a pie for so long. That could have been since she stopped eating Nell's food I suppose. I can't remember the date off hand that she had the last pie on the chart.'

Theo's eyes were bright.

'Right, so there's a lead, it doesn't explain the other food, sure, and it's tiny, but it's a start.'

Charley's stomach flipped as she caught his excitement.

'I need to look into the berries.'

He nodded.

'Exactly, find out everything there is to know and see where it takes you, if it's nowhere then we'll try another angle. If berry pie killed her then maybe we need to find out all we can about the berries and see if we can trace the line backward from the end.'

Charley stared at him and shook her head, rolling her eyes.

'Christ, where have you been the last four days, Theo?'

He popped the last scotch egg into his mouth and licked at his fingers.

'Working.'

'While I've been banging my head up a brick wall that you just made vanish in an instant!'

Theo laughed as Belle came back from her imaginary fire to the warmth of the real one He stood to place a fleece blanket around her shoulders and she cuddled into it, orange light of the fire dancing on her face as she grabbed a sausage roll. The sun was lowering now, the light dimming. Charley looked at her watch. 6.25pm.

'Do you need to get back?' Theo said.

'Nope, just curious. There's nowhere I'd rather be right now than sitting a million miles from Fortwind House and the questions it raises.'

Theo smiled.

'Good, cold?'

'A little.'

He stood to get her a blanket placing it around her shoulders as he had Belle and then he made them each a coffee with the flask of hot water he had brought. They chatted and laughed comfortably as they sipped, talking about Belle's school day, what she had done, and about her friends. Then about Theo's day and what being a fisherman in a small village actually entailed.

They talked about everything except Elizabeth Kane and the many holes she had punched in Charley's life. Holes that had turned her a full one hundred and eighty degrees, as Elizabeth's days had ended. Charley was glad, she wanted to forget, and here on this island she was allowed to for a while. For this moment, life was perfect.

Chapter Forty

It was early evening, but the lowering sun was already spinning its last golden light across the harbour where it danced with elongated shadows. The cold was seeping back into the air after the warmth of the day, and after the last few evenings he had spent out in the cold Axl had wrapped up warm, putting on three extra layers under his coat.

He saw her as he walked around the harbour wall. She sat on a bench, catching the last of the dying sunshine in front of an old building that mercifully blocked the cool breeze from behind. She turned with a tight smile as he approached.

'Axl,' She said, turning to look back out across the water.

'Evening, Nell,' He replied, stuffing his hands into his pockets with a sniff as he sat down.

She looked well, he thought. Bleached hair immaculate, skin that seemed to glow under a light covering of makeup. Her features calm and relaxed.

Obviously doing better than I am.

He shuffled his feet to cross them at the ankles and she huffed a sigh beside him.

'What is it, Axl?' She said.

Axl looked down at his feet.

'I feel guilty.' He said

Nell looked at him sidelong, one eyebrow raised.

'I'd say it's a little late for that, wouldn't you?'

Axl rubbed at his beard and watched the swell lap at the harbour walls.

'Yes, I suppose it is.'

239

They sat in silence for a while, the sounds of the lapping waves and the screech of a seagull the only accompaniment. Finally, Nell looked to him.

'What are you worried about? Being caught?'

'No,' he said.

And he wasn't. He knew that he had tied up every loose end. This feeling wasn't frustration or fear. It was simply guilt. Stomach eating, all-consuming guilt.

'You don't have anything to worry about.' Nell said. 'There's no one to suspect anything now, nothing that Charley can find except the letters I suppose. I don't imagine they would mean much to her though, not enough to read them anyway. Maybe I should go up to the house and get hold of them for both of our sakes.'

Axl felt himself reel. He swallowed hard wondering what to say. A brisk wind bat his cheeks and travelled down the neck of his coat. He pulled the collar together, aware of Nell's eyes on him.

'You... you know about the letters?' he said turning to her.

Nell smiled, her gaze back out to sea.

'Oh, of course I do, don't be ridiculous.' She paused and then faced him, eyes serious. 'I know Elizabeth kept them, and I know they're the only shred of evidence left now. The only thing to-'

'Not anymore. I have them.' He cut in.

Nell's mouth dropped open, she snapped it shut with a click and a short nod of her head. Her eyes searched his and he saw a small bloodshot vein in her right eye, travelling from the pupil back into the socket.

'Right, well. I think they would be better in my care. You have more of a link than I do. If anyone comes knocking it's better they're not found on you isn't it? Nothing to put together.'

Axl reddened as he stared at her, and his heart began to bump a steady beat in his ears.

If she knew of the letters, then also she knew what he had said to Elizabeth. And if that were true what could she possibly want with them other than to have a hold over him? What was she planning? To hand him over?

She raised an eyebrow, expression unreadable, and he shook his head vehemently.

'No. No, they won't be found on me, I intend to burn them. As soon as possible.

Nell pursed her lips and Axl saw the red flush her neck. Anger.

'I... I just want a quiet life Nell,' he stammered, annoyed with himself for being weak, 'I'm fed up of the lies and the creeping around. I'm fed up of the part I played, and I'm fed up of the guilt.'

To his surprise Nell smiled, and then she began to laugh. She laughed so long he found himself joining her with his own uncertain smile. Finally she pulled a tissue from her bag and dabbed at her eyes.

'Oh, come on, Axl,' she said, voice now devoid of any mirth. 'don't give me that crap. You had as much reason to need this outcome as I did, you're already free. I'll take the letters, I need to check what Elizabeth knew, you're a free man. Go deal with your guilt and get on with your quiet life.'

'No.' he said. 'There's nothing to check. Nothing more needs to be taken apart. The damage is already done, just leave it.'

The smile fell from Nell's lips and fear circled in Axl's chest as she stood, smoothing down her coat and skirt and picking up her bag. She turned to face him, the fury under her reddened cheeks evident.

'Damage? Is that what you call it? I call it voluntary involvement. Willing assistance. Eager accomplice. This was your choice, Axl. Yours alone. And the letters are not yours to burn.'

Axl stood too, towering over the smaller lady. She didn't flinch.

'Nell...' he said putting a hand to her arm. She brushed him off.

'I don't think there's anything more to be said Axl. Have a nice life.'

Axl stepped back with shock.

'I... Nell, I didn't... but we have...'

But she was already walking away. Halfway to the lane she stopped and turned to look back over her shoulder.

'Oh, and Axl? You may want to check where your boy is. I'd say you'll have more trouble from him than a bunch of old letters. The quiet life isn't made for some. You reap what you sow unfortunately.'

She turned, walking briskly up the lane leaving Axl alone by the bench, sun almost gone from the sky. He frowned after her.

What is she talking about?

As Nell disappeared round the bend of the lane Axl turned his attention back to the harbour and saw his son's boat missing, not that this was anything unusual. What stopped his heart was the car parked next to Theo's. A yellow Mini. Not just any yellow Mini.

Charley's.

Axl sat back onto the bench heavily and stared out to sea. If Theo had taken Charley in the boat, then he thought more of her than he had let himself believe. His jaw clenched tight as he shook his head.

No. this can't happen. I will not let Charley come here and ruin our lives. Not now.

Chapter Forty-One

Although it had only been twenty past eight when they left the island the boat trip back had been cold and dark, so they had huddled in the tiny shelter together.

Theo steered them back to shore with his right hand, Belle, wrapped in a blanket, was perched on his left shoulder, thumb in her mouth, sound asleep. Charley helped Theo to dock the boat, and carried the cool box and bags, allowing him carry Belle. At the car he leaned in to lay her across the back seat and covered her with the blanket.

'We've only got two streets to go,' He said by way of explanation, 'The village is always quiet at night, I'll drive slow, she'll be fine.'

Charley smiled and waved a hand toward him nonchalantly. She looked at Belle snuggled in the car, and thought of that day at the beach, of her climbing the rocks while Theo was miles away. Running down the jetty boards today with no safety rails to stop her falling. Hanging over the side of the boat to touch the water. Running off alone on a small island with sheer cliffs.

Did it surprise her that he wouldn't strap Belle in for the ride back? Not really. He was a lackadaisical father for sure, but he was also a good, caring, and loving one, and Belle was a happy and carefree little girl.

Charley had never known a father, had never had a father figure in her life, and the more she hung out with these two, the more she wished she could have had a bond like theirs with her own parents. Just a loving mother figure would have done. She sighed and smiled sadly.

Too late now.

She looked back to Theo, who was surveying her with interest. She wasn't about to get into the mucky waters of absent parents and crappy childhoods now though.

'Well, Thank you for a fantastic afternoon, Theo. Not only fun, but productive too. You're good company, you two, you took my mind right off the crap. I have only one complaint, you brought me back. I could happily have stayed there until all of this is over.'

Theo shook his head.

'You couldn't. You're essential to driving this forward and fighting for your Aunt... sorry your mom. If you're not here, nothing moves.'

Charley grimaced.

'Can't you do this for me? you're so much better at it than I am, I can't see past the crap in front of my nose.'

Theo chuckled.

'I'll buy you a shovel. You can dig right?'

Charley punched at his arm lightly and he laughed.

'Just joking, listen I can pop up tomorrow if you like, Belle will be around but if I bring some toys with us, she shouldn't be any trouble. I've nothing planned yet.'

'Sounds good, just leave the sarcasm at home, eh? I'm fragile right now.'

He pulled in a breath through his teeth and wrinkled his nose.

'I'm not sure that part detaches, but I'll have a good go, like. I'm not promising anything though.'

Charley rolled her eyes and pulled him into a quick hug which he returned with a hard squeeze.

'We'll sort this, don't worry,' he said before letting her go.

'Thanks Theo, I'll see you tomorrow then.'

He nodded and got into the car, starting the engine and driving off with a wave much faster than she had expected.

He probably forgot Belle was even on the back seat.

She huffed a laugh and got into her own car.

Turning over the engine, the car lights flicked on outlining a lone figure in the shadows amongst the buildings that sat around the harbour. She surmised that it was a he by size and shape alone, tall and bulky, probably a mixture of size and extra clothing to keep warm as he watched the sea.

Charley sat a while longer, checking her phone, aware that she was drawing attention to herself but the person in the shadows didn't seem that bothered, maybe he had his own issues. Her eyes flicked back up to him. He hadn't moved an inch, still watching whatever had caught his attention. She narrowed her eyes, squinting through the windscreen.

Is he even watching the sea? Why hasn't he moved? Is he even real?

Charley felt a little shiver creep up her spine and she shuddered as she locked the doors with a click. The car park was desolate at this time of night, and apart from a small track, it was cut off from the village. She didn't know who this person was, but she didn't fancy tangling with them down here alone.

God, Charley, you think too much. He could live at one of the houses up the hill, he probably comes down here every night to watch the sea. I know I would, for sure. If you don't like it just leave.

The knot of tension in her gut released some of its hold and she let out a small laugh, shaking her head. She put the car into gear and moved toward the exit, headlights flashing over the figure as she turned.

She gasped, the car slowing.

Axl Maddox!

And if he had just been staring at the sea there probably wouldn't have been an issue, but he was staring right at the car. Charley had hardly moved since talking to Theo, who she had been parked next to, and Axl hadn't moved at all since she had noticed his form. As the car slowed to a stop he stepped backward into the shadow of the building, bowed his head, and walked quickly away from the harbour up the incline of the dunes.

Charley's heart thumped.

Was he watching her?

Her blood ran cold as she stared at his retreating back.

Looks like it, and there's a reason he could be watching too, isn't there Charley? If he knows you're digging around about Elizabeth's death, and he has something to hide, then he could have a very legitimate reason to watch you. And a very legitimate reason to hurt you to keep you quiet.

Charley swallowed hard. He had an excellent source for finding what she was doing, and how far she had got, too.

Theo.

He had been to his father's just a few days ago, and now Axl was tailing them, watching? Theo wouldn't know to keep quiet - he wasn't a suspect to him. Elizabeth had been Axl's friend after all and having information may explain why there had been no backlash from the poisoning yet. Axl was being careful, biding his time.

As his form disappeared from sight Charley pushed her foot to the floor, and with a screech of tyres, drove back to Fortwind house as quickly as she dared.

Chapter Forty-Two

Back at the house Charley was fired up and ready to go. If Axl knew what she was up to, and he was involved, then it was imperative she get on with the search. His suspicious behaviour only gave credibility to Elizabeth's claims, and that also put Charley in danger. She would have to be careful.

I also need to remember not to mention Axl to Theo. In fact, I should be careful telling him anything, which is shit, because Theo has all the good ideas.

It sucked, but it was necessary. If Theo wasn't aware his father was a suspect he couldn't say anything, but as of now, Axl was Charley's top suspect, and as soon as she had found out more about the Elderberries she decided to make pursuing information linking him a priority.

Pulling the little laptop toward her, she fired it up, entering the password and letting it load as she made herself a hot drink. It was more comfortable working at the kitchen table, but after the feeling of being watched, she had spent her evenings in the drawing room, pulling the curtains closed as the sky darkened.

She looked to the darkness beyond the French doors as the kettle boiled.

You realise it may have been more than a feeling of being watched? There could very well be someone out there. A large male someone, who could just be the father of your only friend in this place.

Charley shuddered as the kettle clicked off and she made her drink. All the more reason to get this sorted out, and if it did turn out to be Axl, they could cross that bridge when they came to it.

Folding the laptop down, she carried it through to the front room with her drink, setting it down onto one of the plush velvet chairs. She put her drink down on the table, closed the curtains, and checked all the doors were locked before going back into the drawing room.

Switching on the light, she sat on the settee, opened the laptop, and typed elderberry into the internet search bar.

Google solved much more than one problem for Charley that night. elderberries, it appeared, were everywhere. They could be made into jam, syrup, sauce, wine, and jelly amongst a variety of other things, as well as being added whole to a host of other dishes including muffins, and more importantly pie. Lots of pie's, all different, but all including elderberries.

Checking the chart Charley gave a small whoop of joy as she crossed off almost every item of food that had caused Elizabeth to feel ill. Every one of them could be made with, or accompanied by, elderberries.

The berries are the key, I think we have the murder weapon! Aunt Elizabeth was right! Holy shit!

She double checked the list, cross checking, and cross referencing everything neatly. As each item fit into the box she nearly cried with relief. Things were starting to click into place.

Elderberry. That was the culprit.

Picking up her tea she sat back with a smile. Now she had something to work with. She would look tomorrow and see if there were elderberries in the garden, but she was already pretty sure they'd be there.

So it just remains to find out who and why. Axl was the gardener, he was also watching us tonight, so he's first to be scrutinised.

Sorry Theo.

She looked back at the website on the screen, scanning her eyes over the picture of the little black berries that she had put into the pie.

And then the smile slipped from her lips.

Hold up, Charley. You're missing the bigger picture again, if elderberry is the murder weapon, then why is used in so many recipes? It doesn't make sense, it wouldn't be so widely advertised if it could kill.

She put down her cup and quickly typed a search into google, checking down the first three pages, slowly and meticulously. All of them said the same.

Elderberry was not poisonous. In any quantity.

Shit. What the hell?

Charley's shoulders dropped and she sat back in her chair. Her head ached with a connection that seemed mere millimetres from to clicking into place and yet seemed a million miles from the source connector.

How is this possible? How is this linked? There must be something you're missing.

She finished her tea and got the little book and chart spreading them out on the floor. She knelt above them thinking. Then she pulled over the little notebook she had brought down from her room and turned to a blank page.

Okay. What do I know already? I know Elizabeth was certain she was being poisoned, I know she was certain enough to write down all of her daily events, conversations and meals. All to prove what?

Well that was easy, to prove that she didn't have dementia. To enable the right people to confirm what she had written, for example Glen agreeing with parts of it. Well, lots of the later parts that she could remember better.

Charley noted it down on the blank page and added the fact that Glen had confirmed most of the later entries next to it.

What else? To prove she was being poisoned. She listed it underneath the first point. Elizabeth had linked her attacks to meals, and every attack, apart from a handful, had come within an hour of eating depending on the volume eaten. She also had drinks that had caused them too, but it all came down to one absolute certainty.

Something that was passing her lips was followed by her feeling unwell.

Elizabeth knew it enough to be bothered with doing this book day after day and describing things in such detail that it must have taken hours sometimes. She also thought so enough to hide the book, Charley hadn't known it existed until Glen had said she found it, although Elizabeth had referenced it in the letter, so she didn't want just anyone finding out she was keeping notes.

Right, so food and drink has a definite link. And all of the food, or most of it, can be attributed to elderberry in some form or another. Whether it was or not is an unknown because Elizabeth didn't write that bit down. But for now I know Elizabeth loved them, I saw how much she loved them by the way she reacted when I cooked the pie, so it is more than a possibility, and all I have to go on.

Charley wrote down food and drink on the next line and put elderberry next to them with a question mark, adding the fact that it wasn't poisonous in brackets alongside it.

Underneath she added the fact that the quantity Elizabeth consumed seemed to lead to a more serious attack, the longest one spreading over a couple of days. She also noted that as Elizabeth had become aware and began to eat less the attacks were less violent and lasted shorter periods of time.

Charley scanned the book and the chart again, but it seemed the line had been exhausted for now. That was all of the 'solid' information she had, and although the sequence of events smacked of poisoning, the food source didn't.

Another dead end.

She turned to a new page in the notebook and wrote.

Next:

- Check elderberry bush in the garden.

- Check for other berries in the garden.

- Check the times Nell was around against the food eaten.

- Check when Axl was around against the food eaten.

- Check other links for Axl and Nell.

Axl grew and picked everything Elizabeth ate fresh, that would include berries.

Glen saw him with the berries, putting them in the cupboard.

Nell cooked all of the food Elizabeth ate, using the ingredients Axl got for her.

Could they be in this together?

Charley rubbed at her eyes and sighed. It was half past eleven and a headache was beginning to thump behind her forehead. She could finish up tomorrow, for now, at least, she felt a little more organised, and ready to follow up in the morning. She picked up the book and chart and after shutting down the laptop she took everything up to her room.

Upstairs Charley undressed and switched off the light before peering out of the window. Not at the view tonight, but at the driveway and the front lawn. Was he there? Watching? Or had he given up for tonight?

With a shudder, she drew the curtains, before falling into bed and lying awake for the next hour with her mind whirring as she listened for noises, both outside and in.

Chapter Forty-Three

When the call came through the next morning Axl was absorbed in the paper, which seemed to be his only pastime lately. Ann was eating her breakfast in the small dining room at the back of the house. He knew she wouldn't move to answer the phone, so he heaved himself up and into the hall to pick up the receiver.

'Hello?'

'Dad? Hi, I just wondered if you would do me a favour and watch Belle for me today, just a couple of hours or so? I have something I need to do.'

Axl frowned at Theo's voice. It was unlike him to ask for help with childcare at any time, but twice in the last week?

Not that he minded. Belle was a blessing and good to have around when you had nowhere else to be. Especially when the only company you have is your wife of twenty two years, who has a face like a smacked bulldog, and only answers with grunts when spoken to - if she can be bothered to answer at all.

'I can have her it's no problem,' he said, 'I'm not doing anything else today, bring her over when you're ready. Bring some waterproofs too, I may take her out down the beach again if the rain holds off.'

'Brilliant! Thanks dad, See you soon.'

Theo disconnected the call and Axl stared at the receiver. He wondered just where Theo was going that couldn't involve Belle, he had never been known to hand her over easily. Axl and Ann usually had to ask to spend time with their granddaughter, and it took a crowbar to prise Theo away when he dropped her off, this wasn't usual behaviour. A flutter of fear made its way into Axl's chest.

Was he going to see Charley again? Their friendship was an unexpected and awkward turn of fate, especially as Axl wanted to be as far away from Charley as possible right now.

Replacing the receiver with a click, the door to the hall swung open. He turned to see Ann, hands on hips, her face stern.

'You aren't going anywhere until you've fixed the cupboard door. I'm fed up of asking. Every time you scuttle off into the living room with the paper, or off down the beach. I don't want to see you either, Axl, but things need to be done in this house before it starts falling down around us.'

Axl looked at her. His wife. The large rollers in her hair, pink slippers on her feet. The dressing gown, which just covered her body, hung low over one shoulder. Since she had retired this was pretty much her day to day look, and he couldn't say he cared for it much. He didn't even understand why she bothered curling her hair, she didn't go anywhere.

'Theo is dropping Belle off in a while.' he said.

He fought the urge to add that if she did anything but sit around in nightwear all day, puffing on cigarettes outside the back door, she could help to keep the house in shape too.

Instead he moved past her into the kitchen to look at the cupboard door.

'Oh,' She said, her voice shrill. 'Doesn't he want to be a father anymore? She was here a few days ago.'

'He has things to do, and I don't. I will take care of her. He's a good father.'

'Too right you will, I'm busy this morning, Irene is coming to do my nails.' She held her hands in front of her, inspecting her fingers. 'In future, he needs to give us more notice. He can't expect us to drop everything to look after Belle on a whim. She's his responsibility not ours. We've done our bit, now it's his turn.'

Axl turned slowly toward his wife, whose face was now scrunched into the scowl that caused so many of the lines that had appeared there.

'He rarely asks, Ann, I will look after Belle, leave the lad alone he does a good job.'

'At least one of you does. Maybe I should ask him to fix the cupboard. He'd have it done in a minute, not six months later.'

'It hasn't been six months, and I've been working-'

'Working? Working on what? Elizabeth Kane's garden? That wasn't work, she didn't even pay you. I bet her garden is still beautiful, even all these weeks after her death, while I sit here in this shit hole you could care less about.'

Axl grit his teeth and turned away, ignoring her. He went out of the back door to get a screwdriver from the garage. The hinge had lost a screw, it would take seconds to repair and then she could moan about something else.

In the kitchen, he screwed the hinge into place, opening and shutting the door a few times, as Ann wittered on about Theo behind him. He wondered if she had stopped as he had left to get the screwdriver, or whether she had just carried right on with her rant, as if the kitchen was bothered.

'I don't know where he's going that he can't take her.' She continued, 'There's nowhere in my experience as a mother that children aren't welcome or tolerated, except the workplace, and he's not going to work.'

Axl sighed as he shut the cupboard and turned to her.

'All done.'

There was a knock at the door. Ann caught his eye and flicked her head toward it before looking back to her nails. Axl grunted as he rose.

Letting in Theo, he scooped Belle up into a hug, feeling his face crack with the first smile of the day, as she grinned at him and pulled at his beard.

That's better. Now the day can start properly.

He followed Theo into the kitchen, where he placed Belle's bag on the table. Ann had disappeared into the dining room, as she often did when visitors arrived.

Any second now.

Ann flounced through the dining room door on cue, hand to her chest.

'Theo! What a lovely surprise! I'd have made more of an effort if I'd known you were coming.'

Axl raised his eyebrows but said nothing. Her dressing gown had at least been straightened.

'My darling,' she cooed, 'how have you been? We just don't see enough of you or little Belle these days.'

She smothered Theo's face in kisses, and pulled him into a hug, which he responded to with a laugh.

'Mom, I'm fine. You saw me last week. Dad said you'd be okay to have Belle for a while today. Just for a few hours.'

'Well of course, 'she said, hands now cupped round his stubbled cheeks, 'You don't have to ask, we're happy to have Belle anytime, such a darling little girl. She's a credit to you sweetheart, you do such a wonderful job.'

Axl watched the display. She was like a peacock; it was all show. One day he may record the conversations before Theo arrived and show him just how different she had been just minutes before.

Ann came his way and he put Belle down before she got too close. Belle ran for a snuggle in her Nana's arms as Theo moved over to give his dad a man hug with a firm pat on the back.

'Thanks for this you two. Everything she needs is in the bag, I've even done her lunch, it's all ready for her. I'll crack on, I shouldn't be too long.'

He bent to scoop Belle into his arms raining kisses over her blonde head, making her giggle.

'Be good, skipper, I'll see you in a while.'

'I will.'

Axl followed Theo back up to the door. He hadn't intended to ask where he was off to, maybe it was better he didn't know, but Theo offered the information anyway.

'I'm only at up at Fortwind if you need me, dad.'

Axl's heart skipped and started to thud behind his ribs. He licked his lips.

'Fortwind House? What are you doing up there?'

'Just visiting Charley, you know Mrs Kane's niece? Surely you must have met her.'

Axl nodded keeping his eyes on Theo.

'I have, yes.'

Theo paused, obviously expecting Axl to say more but he couldn't force anything out. He may know Charley but if Theo was after his blessing he wasn't about to give it. He needed a way to keep them apart. For good.

'Okay,' Theo said as the silence stretched, 'I'm just helping her with a few things after Mrs Kane's death. She has a lot to sort, I said I'd help, that's why I thought Belle would be-'

'Where did you meet her?'

'Belle?'

Axl tried not to lose patience at his sons' confusion.

'Charley.'

'On the beach, a few months ago?' Theo's eyes were wide.

Axl felt himself reel back. A few *months* ago? A lot could happen in a few months and they had hugged yesterday. How far had this gone?

'Theo, you need to be careful. You don't know this girl and you have Belle-'

Theo cut him off with a laugh.

'Oh god dad, aren't I a little too old for the birds and the bees talk. Look, I'll save you the trouble, nothing is going on between me and Charley, we're just friends. I don't think of her as anything else. She's good company, that's all. But actually, even if I did think any more of her, Belle would not be an issue, she adores her. I'm sure she thinks about Charley much more than I do.'

Axl tried to nod and smile but he was like a coiled spring. His muscles were still tense, and although it appeared Theo was telling the truth, he couldn't let go of the fact that they were together. It was just too close for comfort. If Charley found out what Axl had done he would be in all sorts of trouble, and that would be bad enough, but if Theo found out, it was game over.

'Right, interrogation done, I'll be off, bye dad.'

'Bye.'

Axl forced a hand into a wave and watched his son get into the car and drive away. To Fortwind House. The one place he shouldn't be going. Axl thumped a hand against the door frame and brought the other fist to his head digging between his eyes with his thumb. This was all going so wrong.

But as he shut the door a thought occurred to him. The tension let go a little between his shoulder blades, and he brought his hand slowly back down.

If Theo is with Charley, then I have the means to find out how far she has got with her digging, if anywhere. Theo isn't the enemy, he's the spy in camp. I just need to be careful how I get the information from him.

He smiled, this time it came easily.

Chapter Forty-Four

Charley was back at the kitchen table surrounded by papers like some old treasure hunter, shoulder deep in maps that led to nowhere. She was about to double check another dead end, when she heard the bump of music and the scrawl of tyres on the gravel outside.

She rose, getting to the front door as Theo got out of the car with a grin that equalled her own.

'You're psychic!' He said.

'Nope, the music and screech of tyres gave the game away.'

He frowned.

'I didn't screech.'

Charley unfolded her arms and pointed to the dark lines stretching out from under the wheels. Theo looked back at her with a shrug.

'Gravel moves.'

'It does when you brake too hard, yes.'

He rolled his eyes and stepped past her.

'You going to let me in? It's cold out here today.'

Charley shut the door behind him and then opened it again quickly.

'Oh!'

Theo spun around.

'What?'

'I nearly locked Belle out,' She poked her head outside. 'Where is she?'

'Oh, I dropped her with mom and dad. I thought I would be easier to concentrate without her. It killed me though, I have to admit, I already feel like I don't spend enough time with her. I told them I wouldn't be too long.'

Charley shut the door and smiled.

'You should have brought her, it would have been fine.'

Theo shrugged.

'It's done. So, how are we getting on?'

Charley wrinkled her nose as she passed him and led the way to the kitchen. He chuckled.

'Fabulous, I knew you'd break the back of it after that revelation yesterday.'

'There was no revelation, Theo. I thought there was, but it was a big fat dead end. Again. How is your dad these days?'

'Good, I think. He misses this place, the garden, Elizabeth. He and mom haven't got on for years, they think they hide it, but the atmosphere can be incredibly tense if you're there for any length of time. I think staying in with her all day is driving him mad. I'll make the drinks.'

Charley turned to watch at him as he took cups from the cupboard and grabbed the coffee.

'I can't have him back up here, Theo. It's not my house yet, and I couldn't pay him if it was.'

Theo threw a shocked look back over his shoulder.

'No. no, I know that. I didn't mean anything by it, I was just stating a fact that's all. It is what it is.'

Charley nodded, relieved. Theo grinned and turned back to the coffee.

'He was quite interested that I was coming up here today though, digging for information. He thinks we have something going on and I just want Belle out of the way.'

He laughed and Charley joined him, but in the pit of her stomach lay a lump of lead.

So he had been watching them yesterday, and now he was already pressing Theo for information? I do need to be careful. Really careful from here on in.

Theo's laughter trailed off, and he turned to look at her.

'Charley, we are on the same page, aren't we? Because you seem a little uncomfortable. If I've led you to believe-'

Charley reddened, and a hand flew to her mouth. If her laughter hadn't seemed genuine, it was to do with Axl, not Theo. He'd read her wrong, but in the moment she couldn't resist winding him up further.

'Oh god, no, Theo. I'm completely on the same page. I love you too, I really do.'

Theo paled, and the spoon clattered to the ground. He cursed, stooping to pick it up and running it under the tap. Charley giggled as she moved to him.

'You look a little uncomfortable.'

'Well, I...'

He cleared his throat and pulled at the collar of his t-shirt. Charley laughed and swatted his arm.

'As a friend that is. I love you as a friend, idiot. I want nothing else, I'm sorry if I led you to believe I wanted more. I don't, really. I have enough to deal with right now, without some bloke hanging around.'

'Thanks, I think.'

Charley laughed, and Theo finally joined in with her, relief evident.

'Well, I'm glad we cleared that up,' he said. 'So why the fake laugh?'

Christ, he can see right through me!

She shrugged.

'Like I said, a lot on my mind that's all. Elderberries mainly.'

Theo turned to her serious.

'I don't understand. So, the berries went nowhere?'

'Nowhere. I got excited for about ten minutes as I read up about them. They go in everything, I cross matched them with most of the food on the chart, and probably they would match the other bits that I'm not sure of. You can also make tea and wine from them, so that accounts for the drink too. Everything cross references.'

'That's great, isn't it?'

'No, you're missing the point. Elderberries go into everything because they are a safe food source. They don't poison people. Not the berries anyway.'

Theo's face fell.

'Ah.'

'Ah, exactly.'

Theo poured the water into the cups as Charley watched him.

'I feel like there is some minute detail that would allow everything to click into place, but I just don't know what it is, or where to look to find it.'

'Right,' Theo said as he stirred the coffee in the cups and took them over to the table. 'So, we've gone from murder to no murder.'

'Not with elderberries anyway, unless they were being laced.'

Theo sighed as he sat down and Charley sat opposite him. He looked at the chart and the papers littering the tabletop, the chart now scribbled with connections that seemed to go nowhere. She knew what he would say even as he said it.

'Charley, I'm not sure there are any connections. This seems just a little too hard. No leads at all? Do you think maybe that's because there are no leads, because she was an old lady with delusions caused by dementia? Maybe the whole book was part of her illness.'

'I don't think dementia works like that, but I have thought the same. Maybe I'm making too much of it. I walked the garden this morning and found three elderberry bushes, big mature ones, which makes sense with Elizabeth loving them, and it could account for all the elderberry dishes on the chart. But it just doesn't account for the feeling unwell after them, so the major link is missing.'

'Could she have been allergic to them?'

Charley shrugged and sipped her coffee.

'I don't think you'd be allergic to the food you love, she must have eaten and enjoyed enough of them, if she'd have felt unwell she would have avoided them, surely.'

Theo looked at her, and she looked back into his green eyes.

'I can't think of anywhere else to go from here.'

He shook his head and pursed his lips.

'I'll have a think, but I really can't see where you could go either. I thought we'd cracked part of it yesterday, I really did.'

Charley smiled and cocked an eyebrow. She pulled the papers into a pile, blowing out a breath. Theo watched her.

'You said if you had found nothing after a week, you'd let it drop. Tomorrow is day seven. What do you think?'

'I think I may have to do just that. I've already decided to put things in motion. I want to take the will to the solicitor this morning so they can get things sorted, so I guess the shit really is about to hit the fan. I can't concentrate on this with what's going to blow up. It probably was part of the dementia, I suppose.'

Theo grabbed her hand across the table, giving it a small pat.

'I'm sorry, Charley.'

'Sorry it's not murder?'

'Yeah, that sounds wrong doesn't it. I mean, I'm sorry you've had to go through all of this for nothing.'

Charley smiled and hoped it looked genuine.

'Sometimes things aren't what they seem to be.'

'No, sometimes they're not.'

* * * * *

Three hours later Charley watched Theo drive away with a wave. They had taken the will to the solicitor together, and then she had offered to cook him lunch up at the house. He had refused, saying she might poison him, instead treating her to yet another lunch before they got back to the house. They had laughed, lots, and it had eased the tension tremendously.

As she watched him go, she sighed heavily.

He was a good friend, and he clearly looked out for her, but she couldn't let him know of the things she had found out this morning. He couldn't know because his dad was just too close, and if Axl was sniffing around, the less Theo knew the better.

It was a shame because his input and humour had been invaluable over the last few weeks. She just hoped that when this was over they could continue being friends, if Axl didn't drive a wedge between them with his part in this, anyway.

Charley really hoped not. She thought she had found a bit of a kindred spirit in Theo; he shared the same lines of thinking, and the same humour, they were very similar people.

She shuddered in a cold breeze as she shut the door and gathered her papers, taking them and her laptop back into the drawing room.

Right, let's get back to business.

She worked so hard trying to find links and openings, that she barely noticed that the doorbell and both the study and the cellar doors were closed and silent all afternoon for the first time in weeks.

Chapter Forty-Five

Over the course of the next morning, refreshed after the first full night with no chiming of the doorbell, Charley had investigated plants that could be mistaken for elderberry. Blackcurrant and blueberries came out top, but other than that her search hadn't thrown up anything useful. In the end she decided to do it the hard way, checking the garden to see if any of the bushes had a trace of berries left on them.

It was late September but an odd one of the right shape and colour may be all she needed. It would be time consuming. The garden was large, and Charley only knew a handful of plants, but she felt it necessary to cover all avenues. Otherwise she may as well just leave it as she told Theo she would, and she wasn't sure she could do that to Elizabeth.

She cursed when she saw the rain, but committed and determined, she pulled her hood further over her head and made her way outside, checking each plant and bush, one by one. She carefully looked both under leaves and on the ground for anything incriminating underneath. Some plants were immediately obvious, especially if they already had late berries starting to fruit. Some were small and some large, but they were all hard and red, so she had moved on carefully and methodically checking the fruit of all the plants and bushes in the garden.

After two solid hours in the rain, wet through, shivering, and frozen, she finally found a bush growing at the side of the greenhouse, between a large rhododendron and a camellia.

The plant itself didn't look suspect at all, but luck would find her a couple of bell-shaped flowers on the floor. Now a faded brown, but undisturbed they had kept their form. Charley had only taken any notice because they had reminded her of little Belle. She hadn't intended to look any closer until she noticed the rotting berries underneath the plant. They looked around the same size as elderberries, if a little larger, and from what hadn't rotted away she could see they would have been black. She stooped, lifting away wet leaves and putting a finger amongst the rotten fruit. It came out purple which only confirmed her suspicions.

Bingo.

She rocked back on her heels, almost whooping for joy that there was somewhere to go from here, and that she could get out of the blessed rain.

Taking out her phone, she struggled to press the camera icon with cold and wet hands, as she snapped off pictures of the plant, the berries that lay underneath, and the bell-shaped flowers. After few close-ups of the leaves and dying flowers she went back inside, where she fired up her laptop on the kitchen table, before going to get changed into fresh, dry clothes.

The cellar door was swinging open as she re-entered the kitchen, her heart gave a small jolt as she caught the movement. She paused, frozen, and then she shook her head.

Pretend it doesn't matter, shut the door.

'I'm giving it my best.' she said aloud trying to dispel the fear that was crawling up her chest. 'If there is anything to find, I'll find it, don't worry.'

She peered down the stone stairs. Cold air circulated but nothing else seemed out of place. Not that she was going down if her life depended on it. She pushed the door shut, checking the catch had caught properly after Nell's admission that it was broken.

Keeping a hand on the door Charley swallowed hard trying to slow her breathing.

'If this is you Elizabeth, you asked me to keep the study locked, I'm asking you to keep the cellar locked. Please.'

She moved back to the kitchen table, turning her back to the ominous feeling and set to work.

An hour later, sitting with her phone next to the laptop to view the photographs, Charley was starting to think it was impossible to identify a plant via dying leaves and dead flowers. Hundreds of plants had similar leaves, similar bell-shaped flowers, and hundreds of plants had black berries. She used all the descriptive words she knew to search the shape of the leaves, the colour, the bell shape, but none of them brought up anything specific.

She sat back in the chair frustrated, tapping her hands on the table. The phone buzzed, and the bell-shaped flower disappeared, Evelyn's name appearing on screen instead.

Charley cursed.

Just what I need right now. Should I answer it or not?

She watched the phone as it rang off and immediately began to ring again.

The will was at the solicitors now, there was no further reason to ignore them, it would all come out in the wash soon enough. With a huff she snatched up the phone and answered, hackles on her neck rising involuntarily.

'What?' She snapped.

'Excuse me?'

Evelyn's haughty voice made Charley's jaw clench, and her knuckles white with the pressure of squeezing the phone.

'Is that any way-' Evelyn continued, but Charley cut her off.

'I have found the will, it is with the solicitor.' she said, through gritted teeth. 'That's what you wanted to know, right? It's all in hand, what will be will be, so you can stop calling me.'

'Right, well, that's good news, anyway.'

There was a muffled scuffling in the background and a dull roar behind the line which Charley couldn't identify.

'What's good? Has the will had been found?'

'What does it say?'

Kate and Francesca's voice floated in the background and Charley realised she was on speaker phone. She rolled her eyes.

So they can all assess just how mean and spiteful I am. Evelyn proving a point. Brilliant.

'Yes, yes, the will has been found and is with the solicitor.' Evelyn said primly.

Charley kept quiet, assuming Evelyn was talking to her sidekicks. She listened as Francesca suddenly gave a loud wail.

'No, oh god, no! It wasn't supposed to go to the solicitor straight away. I need to see it first. I wanted to check that Elizabeth had got it right. Did you tell Charley that? Did you tell her when you phoned?'

Kate answered, muffled in the background.

'She wasn't taking our calls mom. I did tell her in the messages though.'

Charley frowned. They had left messages, but none that she could remember mentioning this little nugget of information.

'The little bitch, she's done this on purpose I know she has.'

There was a faint noise in the background and Charley knew the dramatics were coming on. Anger and hurt fired a response before she stopped to think.

'Gosh, mom, you sound so poorly. I had no idea just how ill you were.'

'Charley? Can you hear me? What did you do with the will? What did you do with it?'

Her mother sounded frantic and Charley smiled, winding them up made her feel so much more in control.

'I took it to the solicitor, as happens with these things.'

'I needed to see it!' Francesca screeched. Charley closed an eye and wrinkled her nose, holding the phone away from her ear.

'You're not the executor.' She said.

'Charley,' Evelyn cut back in, louder, she was obviously nearest to the phone, 'That's rude. Mom is concerned that Aunt Elizabeth has done something stupid. She had the complications of dementia, she probably didn't know what she was writing, especially after your ridiculous allegations the last time you spoke to her.'

So, she told them then. They all know now whether they believe it or not. They know I'm not part of their family.

Charley thought of the will. Was Evelyn right? Had Elizabeth done it under the cloak of dementia? She looked back at the laptop. She had to get off the phone and continue this lead. If her aunt was poisoned, and in her right mind all along, then she needed to know for both the sake of the will, and her sanity.

'And if she did?' Charley said. 'What the hell can mom do about it now, anyway? The will was written and signed by Elizabeth, it is withstanding whether she checks it or not.'

'What did it say? I'll contest it.' Francesca snapped.

Charley rolled her eyes and rubbed at her temple with her free hand.

'Contest it, whatever. The solicitor knew her, he wrote two of her wills with her over the years, he knows what he's doing, and he knows she knew what she was doing when she signed them.'

In fact, the solicitor had been overly excited to finally meet the daughter of Elizabeth Kane, so she had obviously told him everything too. Charley had been touched, and a little glad she had Theo there for backup.

'She knows something,' Francesca said, 'She forced her, Elizabeth was a sick old lady. What have you done, Charley? You're twisted, you're no daughter of mine you sick little bitch!'

Charley ignored the stab of hurt that punctured her chest. Francesca was shouting again, and this time it was Rue's worried voice that floated back...

Charley blinked.

Rue?

Have they really got together just to make this ridiculous phone call to me?

She pulled the phone away from her ear to stare at it as angry voices streamed out, tumbling over one another.

Oh my god, listen to them, this is pathetic.

Charley put the phone back to her ear.

'Evelyn, I'm busy, I have to go, the solicitor will be in touch if he has anything to say.'

But Evelyn was too busy shouting.

'Will everyone shut up, please, I'm trying to drive. Charley, I'm sure you are busy and I'm sure we can see the solicitor ourselves, don't worry your little head over it. I was actually calling to tell you we are on our way up. It's about time this issue was sorted and you seem so incapable of handling the responsibility.'

Charley paused as her stomach flipped over.

'Excuse me? What did you just say?'

'I said we're on our way up to Fortwind house. We're about an hour away now so we'll sort this when we get there.'

'I want that will from the solicitor.'

'Shush mom,' Kate cooed, 'We can sort it all out soon, everything will be all right.'

'I'll contest it if it says anything different from what we agreed. That bitch will get nothing.'

Charley narrowed her eyes as the conversation unfolded. It incensed her that they were coming up here with no prior warning. Not just to Aunt Elizabeth's house, but now to *her* house, and not just one of them but the whole bloody pack. What right did they have to think they could just waltz up here and stay in this house without even asking? And there was the bitch comment again.

'What you agreed?' She said. 'You haven't spoken to Elizabeth for the last twenty-odd years, why should what you agreed back then ever stand now? You cut her off. Not only that but you cut her off from her only child.'

The car erupted again, voices low and high bouncing over each other, Charley didn't bother trying to listen she was to wound up.

'The other thing is,' she continued, 'when Aunt Elizabeth, my real mother, was ill none of you could be bothered to get up here to look after her. Mom was too ill, Evelyn was too important, Kate was too busy, Rue was incapable. Every excuse was batted around the table but suddenly here you all are, together in the car coming up here to sort things out.

'Not so important after all Evelyn are we? And mom obviously isn't too ill to travel as she's now in the car, travelling to the very place that would kill her to get to just a few months ago. Except now she's *really* sick, apparently, but not sick enough to stop her contesting the last wishes of her only sister! You make *me* sick, all of you!'

Charley cut off the call with a guttural roar and slammed the phone onto the table. Putting her head into her hands she pulled in large deep breaths trying to calm herself down. She stared at the phone which was back to displaying the bell-shaped flower. This time, as her breath slowed, she noticed something she hadn't seen before.

Purple. The flower had been purple.

The cellar door clicked and swung open.

Chapter Forty-Six

A purple bell-shaped flower, combined with black berries, brought up a few hundred fewer plants than before, which was encouraging. By studying the shape of the bell, and then the shape of the leaf and its colouring, she finally got it down to just a handful. And then just two.

One of which was highly toxic.

Charley swallowed hard, her heart beginning to pump. Had she hit on something after all? Was this the break she needed? She typed the name of the plant into google and read through a few pages of results.

Oh my god, toxic is almost an understatement. This plant is venomous.

She searched along the lines of poisoning and found page upon page of people throughout history that had died, accidentally or otherwise, using the berries, roots and leaves of this plant. Clicking further, she found a page of symptoms and checked through the list with mounting fear and dismay.

Hallucinations, vomiting, confusion, loss of balance, slurring, thirst, vision problems.

A cold chill wrapped itself around Charley as she stared. This was the plant all right, there could be no mistake, surely. She clicked back to a picture of the plant in its glory, bright green leaves and contrasting purple flowers. Even the berries looked inviting, shiny and black at their peak. She wrote the name down on the chart, scratching it onto the top in large letters so as not to get lost in the mess was on the page.

Belladonna. Deadly nightshade.

But if it was so so deadly then why did Elizabeth live for so long?

She turned back to the laptop and scrolled down the page where she came to a disarming statistic. A couple to a handful of berries would produce nasty side effects but not death in all instances. To kill an adult usually took around twenty to thirty berries depending on that person's build and weight. Any amount or any part of the plant would induce side effects, but there was nothing anyone could do. Those unlucky enough to be poisoned were hospitalised and observed, some pulled through, many didn't. There was no antidote and no cure, the poison had to be ridden out of the system.

Charley held a shaking hand up to her mouth. If the berries she had baked in the pie were in fact Belladonna, not Elderberry, how many berries had she put in? She didn't know exactly, but it had to be over thirty, lots more than thirty, which is why it had taken Elizabeth down. For whatever reason Elizabeth had thought they were Elderberry, maybe the taste was similar? Charley had no idea.

Oh god, Elizabeth - mom - I'm so sorry. You trusted me and I let you down. Whoever was doing this I promise I will find them and make them pay. I won't let you down again.

She looked back at the screen and a thought occurred to her.

Why only slip her enough to make her suffer, not to poison her outright? It was as if, whoever it was, they were making sure she felt the horrific adverse effects, but then recovered enough so that they could do it to her again, and again, and again.

Charley shivered.

Who would be so cruel?

Again her mind flit to Axl. He had put the berries there, Glen had seen him, and she thought he had looked shifty when he had done it. As much as Theo wanted to protect his father, it wasn't looking like he was innocent. The berries were put there for Nell to use though, weren't they? Axl didn't feed them to her directly.

So were the two of them in it together?

It was looking more and more likely, but with what motive? What reason could Elizabeth's two longest standing friends have for wanting to make her suffer like they did? And who thought up the idea that dementia had similar symptoms and to play off the poisoning as a natural progression to death through a relatively common disease?

That one was easy,

Nell.

It had to be. Nell had been the one taking her to fake appointments and feeding the test results back to Glen. She was so careful that even a private, live-in nurse had been fooled. She had given Glen had no reason to suspect anything other than dementia.

The other thing striking Charley was that she had cooked the pie that had used the berries from the boxes. If Nell had still been cooking, would she have used them all at once? Was this supposed to be the finale, or would this cruelty still have been going on? Nell had hinted to Glen that Elizabeth only had weeks to live, wasn't that intent to kill? And surely leaving Belladonna berries in the house would be asking for trouble. They wouldn't be that blasé, would they?

Charley sat back and blew out a long breath. Her mind was whirring with the questions that this raised and the two people that it seemed to point to.

But what's the bloody motive? This doesn't make sense, there has to be more to it, something I'm missing. I need to look into both Nell and Axl's relationship with Elizabeth somehow, without causing suspicion. And if Axl wasn't already acting suspicious, which makes him less than innocent in my book, I'd have the perfect person to ask from one side, but Theo can't know, so who else?

Charley glanced at her watch, the wolves would be here soon, whatever she did she would have to make it quick for today. She couldn't let the rabble know what she thought either. Better to let them bicker about the will.

She looked at the name scrawled in red at the top of the chart.

Belladonna.

Then an idea struck her and she pulled out her phone, dialling Theo.

Chapter Forty-Seven

Theo answered on the second ring as Axl picked up the jigsaw, getting to his knees on the floor, pretending to occupy Belle as his son spoke on the phone.

'Charley! What's up? You found something?'

Axl's ears pricked up at both her name and the insinuation that she was searching for something, and until he knew what that something was, he was going to go insane. He listened intently as his son um'd and ah'd. Theo had turned serious, the smile slipping from his lips.

'Okay, I don't have a number for her, old ladies aren't really my style, but I know she lives at number four.' He paused. 'Yeah that's the one, it's the road that runs along the bottom of the driveway. Turn left, and it's the second house, I think. What do you need her for?'

Axl stiffened. Number four, High Street, was Avril's address. There could be no reason for Charley to want anything from Avril, could there? Unless she was on the trail, that was.

Axl swallowed hard. He had thought getting rid of the paper evidence would be enough. He was confident that, although it had been on the table, Charley hadn't seen it, or she would have been at his door by now. So where the hell was she getting new information from?

He sat back on his heels, wiping his sweat laced palms on his jeans as Belle put the last piece into the jigsaw and cheered. He stretched his mouth into a grin but put a finger to his lips indicating that Theo was on the phone. Belle put her hands over her mouth and giggled.

'Again Grandad.' she whispered.

He nodded and broke the jigsaw back up for her, lying the pieces face up.

'They weren't that close, I don't think, you'll have to see what she knows. I don't know her that well, only through dad really.'

Axl stopped in his tracks, heart hammering.

'Okay, Charley, well, if you need me to help out you know where I am.'

Belle sprang to her feet.

'Charley? I want to talk!'

She hopped from foot to foot, stomping jigsaw pieces, as she waited for Theo to explain that she wanted to say hello.

'Hi, Charley,' Belle said with a grin. Axl turned to face them, getting up shakily and sitting back on the chair opposite. Theo held the phone over Belle's ear and was smiling at her as she talked animatedly about what she had done at her nan and grandad's this morning.

Theo shot a look at Axl and rolled his eyes with a grin. Axl tried to smile back but the muscles in his mouth didn't want to stretch.

'Come on then Belle, wrap it up.'

'Dad says I've got to go.' She said. Then she paused, listening and nodding, 'Okay, good luck with your Elizabeth mystery. I hope you find the next clue.'

Axl's heart turned over. He thought Theo looked a little uneasy as he took the phone to say goodbye himself before ending the call and giving a short, nervous laugh.

'Right Skipper, 'He said to Belle, 'I guess it's time to go, come on.'

'What little mystery is this?' Axl asked, unable to help himself. He couldn't take the not knowing, and the not knowing if he should put a stop to the situation before it got out of hand.

'Oh, nothing,' Theo avoided Axl's eyes as he fussed around Belle, tidying her playthings up, 'Charley just has some stuff to sort out that's all.'

Axl rubbed his beard.

'Anything I can help with? Maybe I know a little about this mystery, Elizabeth was a good friend of mine after all.'

'Nope.'

Axl clenched his fists as he worked his jaw.

'Okay, well, if she needed information I'm sure I could have provided a lot more, and certainly more accurate information than Avril. Avril was only at the house twice a week. Nell and I were there every day.'

'I don't know what she needs dad, she didn't really say. I'm sure if it was something she thought you knew she would have asked. It's nothing important, I'm sure.'

Irritation gnawed at Axl's stomach. Theo was hiding something. He wouldn't meet his gaze as he got Belle's bag together and went into the kitchen where Ann was having her nails done for some non-existent event.

Axl watched Theo kiss her cheek and Belle followed suit, very aware of Ann's wrath if she knocked her hands, especially while Irene was working. Then he followed them to the door.

'You didn't have to rush off.' He said.

Theo finally met his eyes, and Axl thought he looked a little guilty. It was a look not dissimilar to one he had given when he had been younger; after flushing all the toilet roll down the toilet blocking the bowl and causing it to flood.

'I need to go, dad, I have a few errands to run before I go home. Thanks for having us, I really appreciate it.'

Axl nodded.

'Anytime son.'

Theo leaned in to clap him on the back, holding him perhaps a little too long, and then he busied himself getting Belle into the car.

Axl frowned as he waved them off.

What did Theo know that he was being cagey about? And what did that hug mean. Did he know something too?

Axl stood in the doorway for a few long minutes after Theo had left, trying to decide what his plan of action should be from here.

Things were moving. That was for definite. It was time for action.

Axl set his jaw as he shut the door.

Maybe Charley could do with a little visit, just to see how she's getting on up there alone, of course.

Chapter Forty-Eight

Rue Costin stared at the passing landscape from the back window of the car. She had sat with her hands over her ears as the argument with Charley had escalated until Francesca had told her to quit being a child and slapped at her left hand. She had missed actual contact, but Rue dropped her hands to her lap obediently anyway. She had long since learned that her mother's wrath was not to be messed with, and although Francesca's strength was diminishing with age, she could still crack off a good slap if needed.

With a sharp look, Francesca flashed the hand signal which told Rue she was walking a fine line. A warning if you like.

Rue didn't like.

She swallowed as Francesca quickly touched each finger in succession with the thumb of the same hand, travelling down from the forefinger to the little finger and back up. A subtle movement, subtle enough to be missed, and sometimes Rue thought that was part of the game.

She pulled herself in to the side of the car, legs pressed up the door and leaned her forehead against the glass, mindful of her large glasses. She knew Francesca - Rue never referred to her as her mother - would be furious at this wilful ignoring of the signal, which really meant sit up Rue, act normal Rue, there are other people around.

Under Francesca's cutting stare Rue would usually behave appropriately without question, she always had, but here in the back of the car she felt something let go. There was only Francesca back here to see, and she knew nothing much would happen in front of Evelyn and Kate. Her sisters knew nothing of the volatile relationship, Francesca wouldn't allow it, and besides, right now she was too busy playing her own part of the sick and needy mother.

Watching the landscape roll past, Rue marvelled at the pitiful mess that was her life. She sat in relative safety for now, but she knew she would pay for this small admonishment later.

A small sigh escaped her lips as she wished, as she had so many times before, that she had never found that stupid box.

She had been only fifteen. Evelyn and Kate had already moved out of the family home, only Charley had remained to oversee the jibes and abuse that had occurred after Francesca had caught her with the box. As Charley grew, Francesca became more cautious, conducting the snide remarks and punishments behind her back. She kept firm control of Rue, while outwardly keeping up the pretence that she was a loving, doting mother.

Rue left home at just seventeen thinking that she could escape, but Francesca only followed, getting a key to her house cut under the pretence of helping to clean, and to help with her 'illness'. Francesca was so thorough with her story that Evelyn and Kate never questioned whether Rue was anorexic.

She wasn't.

Her appearance and skinny figure were the sole work of their mother, not a disorder. It was part of Rue's day that she could do without, her only escape was work, and she enjoyed the long hours where she could immerse herself in anything but home and family life.

Family being her mother and sisters. She wasn't allowed any other sort of family, and men were out of the question, not that a man would look twice. Francesca vetted all clothing, banned all make-up, all hair products, including shampoo. When Rue had started to wash her hair with shower gel that was banned too. She was allowed a bar of soap. Period.

Rue had attempted on only two occasions to get help. Once, begging Evelyn to listen through frustrated tears, from which there were two outcomes; Evelyn reminding her with a pitying look just how serious anorexia was, and that only when she finally accepted her fate could she hope to get better. The other was the contact of Francesca's fist with Rue's nose so hard that it broke clean across the middle. In private, of course.

The second time Rue had attempted to tell a neighbour, a few years after the episode with Evelyn, the consequence had been an arm broken by a stamp of Francesca's foot. As Rue had screamed in pain, Francesca had simply laughed and said that there would be worse to come if she continued to be unruly. It was five hours of agony before Francesca finally allowed her to go to the hospital with a story that she had fallen.

Francesca was not only hot on excessive punishment, she was hot with the details of the disorder. Rue was always well versed in what she had to say, and how she had to act, and Francesca would use their alone time to reiterate exactly what would happen if Rue didn't stick to the rules.

Always.

* * * * *

'I need to get some circulation in these legs girls,' Francesca groaned kicking at Rue's ankle, 'I'll get a blood clot.'

Rue tried to ignore the bolt of pain. She stared out of the window as the countryside opened up around them.

'Shall we stop, mom, let you have a move about?' Kate said.

'No, no. I can move about here,' Another two kicks hit home and Rue closed her eyes and grit her teeth. 'better we get to Fortwind and clean the bloody mess Charley has got us in to. Who knows what we have to sort out. Keep going.'

Of course, Evelyn and Kate encouraged her to keep moving, giving Francesca more excuse to kick at Rue. A few times she had leaned into the middle to speak to Evelyn and Kate, using the position as an excuse to pinch Rue's thigh between her thumb and forefinger.

The pain of the pinches was worse than the kicking, filling Rue's eyes with tears, but she had known better than to utter a single sound, let alone cry.

As she pinched, Francesca whined at Evelyn that her hips hurt, and how much this journey was taking out of her. She couldn't *breathe.*

Rue glanced at her, hatred sliding down her spine.

Francesca. Mother. Old, grey, fragile, sick.

Apparently.

Apathetic, she slid her eyes back to the window.

Low self-esteem, threats, and constant management of what she ate, what she wore, where she went, and what she did, had worn Rue down over the years. She could no longer be bothered to try to fight it.

She did as she was told. Always.

Most of the time she wished Francesca would die.

All of the time she wished she had never found the box under the bed.

Always she wished she had never looked at the contents, and always, she wished her mother had never chosen that moment to enter the room.

Chapter Forty-Nine

After wrapping the small gift Charley left the house in a hurry, piling her laptop, the chart, and Elizabeth's book on the back of the settee. She could move them later. As she tugged the front door shut, there was a dull thud from inside and the doorbell chimed for the first time in days. The sound, dull and muted out here, instantly set Charley on edge.

'What now? What would you rather me do?' she said, unease picking its way through her stomach. But the house fell silent, offering no more, and with a shake of her head Charley turned to the car. Sure, she could have walked, but if the wolves arrived when she was out, they would have no idea where she was, and she had no intention of answering her phone.

Less than a minute later she pulled the yellow Mini against a kerb where she hoped it couldn't be seen from Fortwind's driveway. She took the bag from the front seat and walked the short distance back to Avril's house. The stone mid-terrace was small, the garden neat, the door painted a bright, cheerful red. A large number four sat dead centre, just above a silver door knocker in the shape of a horseshoe. Swinging the wooden gate open with a creak, Charley walked up the path and tapped the knocker twice with a metallic thunk.

Avril hadn't been around for enough of Elizabeth's episodes for her to be a major suspect. Or at least Charley hoped, because by talking to Avril she would arouse suspicion. Especially if the lady herself had anything to do with what had gone on. As she waited, she reminded herself to be careful about what she said, and how things were phrased.

Again.

Irritation wound in her gut. She was tired of having to hold her tongue and keep thoughts and ideas isolated in her head.

Pursing her lips, she glanced down at the small bag where she had stowed a small ornament that Avril had once mentioned she liked. She had brought it as a gift, wrapping it in some tissue paper she had found in one of Elizabeth's many shoe boxes.

A cheap stab at getting the old lady to open up.

Such a class act, Charley. Really.

Charley felt guilt flood over her as the door opened, just a notch.

Avril peered around the chain, eyes widening in surprise before she pushed the door shut, and then swung it open fully.

'Oh! Charley, What can I do for you?'

She seemed puzzled and Charley thought that was probably a valid response. They hadn't been in contact since Elizabeth died, last seeing each other at the funeral.

'Um, hi, Avril. How are you?'

Avril nodded slowly.

'I've been better. Been worse.'

She looked at Charley expectantly but offered nothing more, and Charley knew she was just going to have to cut to the chase. She swallowed hard, praying Avril would be compliant.

'Avril, I know this may seem strange, but I just wondered if I could come in and have a chat with you? About Aunt Elizabeth. There are so many unanswered questions and I... I feel a bit lost.'

The desperation of the question, and the stress of the last few weeks collected in the words, and her eyes filled with tears. Tiredness, frustration, hurt, longing all coming to a head. It caught Charley off guard and she swiped at a tear that ran down her cheek.

Avril seemed to stall, and then soften, giving Charley the encouragement to continue.

'I won't take up too much of your time, I promise. I have a gift for you too, for all the help and support you gave Elizabeth as the disease took hold. I know you meant a lot to her.'

Charley held out the little bag. Avril glanced at it before looking back up at Charley. It was obvious the hurt of her friend's death was still raw and Charley felt another stab of guilt for coming here, for bringing it all back up.

I have a purpose though, and if Elizabeth meant so much to her when the truth comes out she will understand.

Avril finally gave. She took the bag from Charley with a nod.

'Thank you. All right, come in dear, I'll put the kettle on.'

Inside they did the formalities, each asking how the other one was, discussing the funeral, and how Elizabeth would have liked the send-off. Avril finally looked at her gift, thanking Charley as she wept, and then they sat in the small, neat, living room and discussed Elizabeth.

Avril had met Elizabeth when she worked for the council. She had been in an administrative position when Elizabeth had been elected, and from there the two of them had struck up an instant friendship. Elizabeth had been well liked by all except her two fellow councillors, whose ideas she often strongly opposed. They were men, and as such their pride was always hurt when Elizabeth won a majority vote or pushed awkward proposals through. She was good at speaking, fantastic at putting across a valid argument, and adept at manoeuvring people to her way of thinking.

Avril said they had often celebrated together when there was a big win, such as proposals for the bypass to run alongside the village which Councillor John had said would bring in more tourism and expand the villages' opportunities.

A smile passed over Avril's lips as she recounted that Elizabeth had opposed furiously, saying that the greenbelt land it ran through should be protected, and that Fortwind Bay should keep its small fishing village status. The village was commercially viable as it stood, offering tourists a peaceful break with stunning views, a golden beach, and plenty of opportunities for boat trips, walks, and water sports. The town of Portsway was only four miles up the road if visitors wished for a little more activity.

Avril looked at Charley.

'Elizabeth thought Fortwind stood proud as its own picturesque bay. Its peaceful location and small friendly community were what drew people back. Numbers didn't matter to an already thriving village, but expansion and loss of community would affect everyone. The Bay would have been changed forever.'

Avril paused, looking to the window.

'She was right, of course,' She finally said. 'She worked tirelessly for this village, she really did. When she had a fight on her hands, she would do her research and come in coolly and calmly to state her case. I sat in on a few of the meetings as minute taker, things would usually get quite heated as proposals were passed or thrown out. Elizabeth was always calm, it was if the tense air couldn't reach her, and she always left with firm handshakes and a smile for everyone involved. She was an inspirational woman, I really admired her.'

Charley sipped her tea. The warmth with which Avril spoke about Elizabeth made her chest ache for the woman, the mother, she had never known. How different her life would have been if Elizabeth had kept her here and they had been a real family. For the umpteenth time she wondered what had happened, although she knew that she would never get any answers if Francesca was the only one who had information.

She sighed and smiled at Avril.

'I know she adored you, Nell and Axl too, you all did so much for her. She appreciated it, I know she did. How long have you all known each other?'

Avril chuckled. She took off her oval glasses and dabbed at her eyes, before cleaning the lenses with a small cloth.

'I'm the odd one out, I'm afraid. I've known Elizabeth over forty years, but I didn't know Nell or Axl until these circumstances threw us together.'

Charley raised her eyebrows.

'But this is such a small village, I thought-'

'Yes, it is, but whether you live in a village, town, or city your world is as big or as small as you make it isn't it? I've never been one for getting out and meeting people. I did my job, which I loved, and then I came home to my family. I know a few people; the families of my children's friends, people on the council, but to be honest, I've never been big on 'people'. I'd rather spend my time alone and with close friends and family. I knew of Nell and Axl, but I didn't know them personally, until fairly recently.'

Avril put the glasses back on and looked up at her. Charley frowned.

'I had no idea. So Nell and Axl, were they friends before?'

'Oh yes, and they knew Elizabeth from school, both of them. Axl was brought up here in Fortwind Bay. Elizabeth and Nell both hailed from Stoney Cove, which is a small village a few miles away. There is only one school that the two villages share so they ended up here together. I'm afraid I'm a little older than they are, but even so I grew up in Portsway, which has three schools to itself. I had no need to be schooled over here. I didn't move to the bay until the job with the council came up. I got it and moved here two years later. I've never had the desire to move since. I love it here.'

Charley nodded.

'So how did you end up cleaning for Elizabeth?'

'I offered. I had gone to visit her one day, Nell and Axl were both there. Nell was visiting, Axl had tended the bulk of the garden, and the vegetables, once a week since Frank's accident. After he retired, it was perhaps three times a week or so. This was one of his days at the house. It was early stages of the disease, and Elizabeth was annoyed that things in the house were lapsing. She wasn't able to cope with the cooking, and the cleaning, and the small amount of garden she managed herself, and certainly not to the standard that she set herself. She joked about it, of course, but I could see she was very frustrated. Nell had already offered to cook, and I offered to come and clean, just for a couple of days a week, so that she was better able to cope with the mess that accumulated in between. At the time she declined my offer, of course, I had expected nothing less, but a few weeks later Axl and Nell came to see me here.'

Avril took a slow sip of tea as she looked out of the front window. She seemed to be lost in a memory. Charley waited until her attention came back into the room and then put out a hand to touch hers. Avril looked at Charley surprised.

'So, Axl and Nell came to see you?'

Avril gathered herself and continued.

'Oh, yes. They came to ask me to help out. They had both taken over the cooking and gardening full time by then, although how they persuaded Elizabeth was beyond me. She had seemed very firm when it had been discussed before, but now they were almost constantly at the house. Of course I said that I would do the couple of days cleaning. They asked for no more and went away happy after agreeing Tuesday and Saturdays would be my days.'

Charley immediately felt alarm bells ring in her head.

'Hang on, so they came *here* to ask you? And they were already up at the house full time at this point? Only two or three weeks after the chat?'

Avril dismissed it with a flick of her head.

'I was surprised myself, knowing Elizabeth. But obviously they knew her a lot better, and they had forced the issue to make her more comfortable, I suppose.'

'I suppose so. Did Elizabeth say anything, or seem to mind when you were there?'

Avril sipped more tea, thinking.

'You know, I wasn't there enough to get the brunt of any ill feelings about the arrangement, but she wasn't always pleasant. Sometimes she told me I wasn't needed. In the early days anyway. I was up for leaving it, I didn't want to annoy her, but always, either Nell or Axl would convince me to stay. They would say it was the disease talking. And it was, I understand that now. They were with her a lot more, and they took the brunt of her moods themselves. They did an awful lot for her until Glen came to help.'

'So where does Glen come in? Nell and Axl? Or was it Elizabeth herself?'

'No, they had no say. The doctor, or the hospital, sent her I suppose.'

Charley frowned.

Nope, not if the hospital wasn't involved. So where the heck did Glen come from? Had Elizabeth hired her?

'Ah, of course,' she said, aiming for a lightness in her voice. She smiled at Avril wondering if she had pushed too far, but Avril seemed calm and ready to talk, so she pressed a little further. 'So they go way back then. Elizabeth, Nell, and Axl. I suppose they were very tightly knit when you came into the group too. That must have been hard.'

Avril looked at her over the china cup, eyebrows raised.

'Not at all. You've met them. They're lovely people. We seemed to hit it off from the start. I suppose we all had Elizabeth's interests at heart really, but I've met up with both Axl and Nell since Elizabeth passed. I'm happy to be able to count them as good friends now.'

Charley nodded.

'Yes, they are nice, I always felt welcome too.'

And she sincerely had, she thought as she sat back in her seat; it was all very conflicting.

So what is the issue here? What is going on? There must be a crack in this story somewhere.

She nod her head with a smile as Avril offered more tea and left to go to the kitchen. Charley stood, watching the ocean from the window. She ran a hand over her face.

How was it possible to feel more frustrated and confused now than when she had arrived? Where were the cracks, the fine trails of deception?

She wondered if there was anywhere left to go from here at all.

Chapter Fifty

It had been bad. It *was* bad.

Rue's fifteen-year-old self sat on the floor, contents strewn around her. Her mouth was open, slack, her heart pounding as she read the letters. She hadn't managed to read them all, Francesca had found her long before she'd had a chance, but she had read enough.

She wished had never read any.

She didn't like what she had found out, and now it couldn't be unread.

Rue knew the secret, and she knew the circumstances. She was the only one, other than her mother and Aunt. She had thought that would never change until they were both dead, but now the secret was out. Or part of it anyway.

Charley now knew what Rue had known all these years, and as much as Francesca denied it, scoffed, and pleaded innocence to Charley, Evelyn and Kate, Rue knew the truth.

Part of her wanted to break free and shout it to the world. Tell Charley that yes, she was Elizabeth Kane's daughter, and that she should be glad that the witch had been her mother. It was preferable to being Francesca Costin's daughter.

She wanted to help Charley, and she wanted to stop her own reign of terror, but Francesca was too close, too strong, too manipulative. Her mother, her keeper, was stronger than she had ever been, and that was why Rue would stay quiet. If she spoke out she no longer knew the extent of the consequences, and what could happen up in Northumberland scared her to death. It scared her what Francesca would do to Charley now that she knew the truth now that she knew.

Of course, Evelyn and Kate would be the antidote. Francesca had never said or done anything extreme in front of them. Ever. Rue hoped that both she and Charley could keep them close, but something told her Charley was not overly fond of either of them at the moment. She simply had no idea how this would play out.

A sign for services appeared ahead, half a mile. Rue felt a flash of inspiration, and before she could mull it over and reject it, she braced herself to make a small stand. Give Charley a little time.

'I'm hungry,' she said. 'It's after one, can we stop for lunch?'

Evelyn and Kate both made aggregable noises. Francesca cast a cold stare at Rue, and then she moved back into the middle to discuss what services they were, and how long it would hold up this horrendous journey. All the while her fingers poked and pinched.

Hard.

Francesca was outnumbered though. It seemed everyone wanted to eat. Both Evelyn and Kate agreed that the stop would do their mother's legs good, and that it was good that Rue wanted to eat given her condition. They would get some food at the next stop.

Ignoring the stabs of pain, Rue looked back out of the window as the world rolled by and chanced a small smile at her reflection.

A small win was still a win.

Chapter Fifty-One

Axl left his car at the bottom of the long drive and walked up to the house, sticking close to the shrubbery until he saw that Charley's car wasn't there.

Good.

Charley wouldn't be here without it, which could only mean that she was still at Avril's, or down in the village. He stepped out onto the gravel and crunched openly up to the house. The fact that she may still be at Avril's induced a sweat and jump started his heart. He tried to calm himself as he walked.

Avril knows nothing. There's nothing she can tell.

Still, she had been into the locked study to clean, hadn't she? Axl knew all the incriminating papers had been locked away, but what if she had found the safe? Found the combination? Just as Charley had.

No. Why would she? She hadn't found it up to the point Elizabeth had died, why would she find it after?

Axl had first jimmied the lock to the study not long after Avril had been given the clearance to clean, just to make sure the evidence was safe. He had approached Elizabeth about going in under the premise of checking over things for her, but she had shot him down.

No-one was to set foot in Mr Kane's study except herself and Avril, and finally Glen, who had taken over Avril's key when she had arrived, and so his hand had been forced.

How Elizabeth could trust a total stranger with the key to her most private possessions he had no idea, and he knew that Glen had been abusing her trust. He had caught her coming out of the study at least twice with one excuse or another, and just before Elizabeth had died Glen had looked flustered as she blocked the kitchen doorway, but even through the darkness of the hall he had seen the light from the room and the fall of the study door. Glen had been snooping again.

He had been so worried about Glen initially that he had taken to spending more and more time at the house. He liked to watch what was going on, see if she reacted strangely to him, or see if anything she said may indicate that he had been found out - that *they* had been found out - but as time went on he relaxed. Her snooping seemed to be bringing up nothing. And maybe she really had gone in there simply to read the books, because now she had left she hadn't accused him of anything. She hadn't even bothered to contact, and that was the way he liked it.

At the back gate he smiled as he found the gate key still where it had always been. He let himself in and decided he would wait in the kitchen for Charley. Sit there quietly until she came in. He was sure it couldn't be classed as breaking and entering if he had a key, and he wanted the advantage over her, the element of surprise.

Chapter Fifty-Two

Rue managed to draw out a full hour in the services. Feeling uplifted by the mass of people around her, she had gone against her mother's silent glares and ordered a steak and ale pie, with chips and gravy, and a huge blueberry muffin to follow. She had taken her time as she ate, savouring every delicious mouthful until it had all gone. Evelyn and Kate had been full of smiles and delight at her sudden about-turn.

Francesca had smiled too. But that smile was full of hidden malice. Rue could feel it across the table, closing down on her like the teeth of an alligator. She would be in trouble, not only back in the car with the silent pinches and kicks, but when they were next alone, and that would be the time Rue would dread most.

Francesca always used her old friends threats, violence, and the hand signal to make her play along with the eating disorder fallacy in front of her sisters. And to keep full control of her creation, she took everything from Rue's cupboards daily so that she had very little to eat. Everything Rue bought was immediately removed and taken away, the waste of both food and money had hit Rue hard.

Eventually, she had relinquished control and stopped food shopping altogether, which had been the worst mistake. Now, with Evelyn and Kate's blessing, Francesca also took a huge chunk of Rue's salary, under the proviso that she could shop for her and make sure she ate well.

The little money Rue had left each week would barely buy a take-out, and other than basic rations, food was not on Francesca's agenda. Rue had no idea what she did with the rest of the money she took.

'Want anything else?'

Rue looked at Evelyn. With a full stomach and the rich taste of pie still clinging pleasurably to her palate, Rue thought that she did. She was in trouble anyway, it would make no difference now. She went on to order a large hot chocolate with extra cream, and a chocolate flake. The gold of the moment being when Evelyn brought it back to the table. Francesca immediately reached for the flake, but Evelyn pushed her hand away.

'Rue is eating, she wants it. Let her have it, mom.'

Rue smiled inwardly. She picked up the chocolate from the saucer and ate it slowly, letting the heavenly sweetness melt on her tongue as Francesca fumed. She only managed one kick under the table before Rue moved her legs out of reach.

When they were ready to go back to the car, Rue told them all to go on ahead and hurried toward the toilets, disappearing through the crowds with the protests of her family in her ears. A moment alone, a single precious moment alone before the continued spiteful attacks in the back of the car. A moment to collect herself was all she needed.

After hiding in a cubicle for a few minutes, Rue opened the door and scanned the room. It seemed none of them had followed her.

Letting out a sigh of relief she spent time in the busy sink area, splashing water on her face and trying to sort out her lank hair.

She was a mess.

She looked awful, and it was all her mother's doing. The glasses had been Francesca's choice. They were huge and round on her pallid face, making her eyes look bulbous and haunted, and her hair, suffering from lack of nutrition and having only been washed with water for the last twenty years, was stringy and lifeless.

As she ran warm water over her hands, Rue sneaked a glance at the lady next to her. Glossy dark hair shone around her head like a halo as she inspected her face in the mirror. Rue watched, entranced, as she applied a bright pink lipstick, smacking her lips and sliding them together. Then, putting the lipstick back in her bag, she gave Rue a small smile and walked away, heels clicking below well-fitting jeans and a cream jumper.

Rue stared, the other people in the room fading away as the woman walked out of view. Then someone pushed at her back as they tried to find space to wash their hands, bringing the noise of hand dryers, and toilets flushing, back into the room along with crowds of other people.

Rue looked into the mirror, gaze travelling down to her oversized brown cardigan and the dungarees that hung past her bony hips, the bottoms ripped where she had walked on them.

She felt a sudden surge of sadness and anger.

How has it come to this?

Rue looked back at the mirror, at her pallid, sunken face.

More to the point, how had she *let* it come to this? All over a secret she would never have told anyway if Francesca had just asked nicely. Anger flared in her chest, flushing her cheeks with much-needed colour, and she vowed it would stop.

Here she stood, full and content for the first time in years, and she swore it wouldn't be the last. She lifted her chin, assessed the fire in her eyes, and strode purposely from the bathroom brimming with renewed energy.

The anger fizzled away as she saw the three of them waiting at the car. Matching scowls, shouts, and shakes of the head.

The questions came thick and fast; Why had she been so long? What had she been doing? Why didn't she wait for someone to go with her? What was the hurry? Now we understand why you ate so much!

The lightness and smiles were gone as Rue realised they thought she had gone to throw up her lunch.

Bulimia, they were now saying. She was very sick. She needed help. It had progressed; she needed help before the affliction killed her.

The pinches and kicks increased tenfold during the last forty minutes up to Fortwind house.

Chapter Fifty-Three

Axl was getting impatient, it was bad enough that he had to keep dragging up things that should be left alone, but the waiting around was driving him mad. He tapped his fingers on the table, trying to calm his beating heart as he breathed heavily. He ran his hands over his face and then he heard it.

The unmistakable sound of the key in the front door.

His heart rate trebled in an instant and a shot of adrenaline surged through him. He hadn't planned what he would say. He didn't know whether to come clean and then keep her eternally quiet, or whether to talk to her calmly, figure out what she was up to and take action from there. The trouble was he didn't feel very calm right now. He was anxious, frustrated, and desperate.

The front door shut, and there were voices in the hallway.

Voices?

Axl stood, straining toward the door as he listened. If Charley had come back with Theo, and even worse Belle, then he had to leave. Right now. Heart thumping in his ears, he forced himself to stay still and quiet. The voices were female, one even sounded familiar, although it wasn't Charley.

As he stood with his hands on the table, heart pounding in his ears, his mind slowly clicked reason together.

What am I still doing here? If Charley has company I can't carry out this plan, I need to get out. NOW!

He spun round, knocking the chair over in his haste. Within two strides he was at the French doors, but it was too late. He heard the hall door open behind him.

'Hey! What the hell are you doing here?'

He closed his eyes, hand gripping the handle, cursing himself as he breathed heavily. He knew that voice, it was one he had thought, no *prayed*, that he would never have to hear again.

Steeling himself, he turned to face Francesca.

'I could say the same about you,' he said gruffly.

Chapter Fifty-Four

Charley sat back on the settee in resignation. The information she had gleaned so far amounted to nothing. Axl and Nell were good friends, they had been good friends to Elizabeth, and they had accepted Avril into the fold with the same welcome and grace that they had accepted Charley. There was nothing to suggest that they were up to anything together, no suspicion other than Glen's own, and would they really be so blatant with the poisoning when other people were around? Including a nurse?

Nell had obviously faked the appointments for a reason, and Axl had placed the berries there for a reason, but those reasons didn't necessarily equate to murder.

She blew out a long breath, wondering where to go next.

Why do I always seem to be hitting my head against brick walls? One door opens, and the next shuts firmly in my face. Every time.

Avril came back into the room with the cups, handing Charley her tea, before sitting down herself.

They sipped in silence, Charley wondering what to say, and then Avril turned the tables.

'So how is it you ended up looking after Elizabeth? When Glen said that family were coming up to take over I expected Francesca, as did Nell and Axl. Although I suppose she's getting on herself now, isn't she?'

Charley pushed out her lips as she looked down at her cup. She could go to town with this one, but did she want to?

'She's sixty-seven,' she said, 'but to be honest she's fighting fit. She moans and complains like a ninety-year-old but there is nothing physically wrong with her. My sisters rally round her and she rarely has to do anything herself, so it was out of the question for her to come up here, apparently she is far too frail.'

Charley couldn't hold back the sarcasm, but Avril didn't seem surprised. She nodded lightly.

'Well, maybe that's a good thing. There were things in the past that shouldn't have been brought back to Elizabeth's doorstep when she was ill. You were probably the best deal for everyone, don't you think?'

Charley looked at Avril perplexed. The old lady looked steadily back, obviously thinking Charley would make a connection that she couldn't see.

And then she had it.

The feud! Avril was a close friend of Elizabeth's, and obviously that meant she knew Francesca. Maybe Avril would know something of use after all, even if it wasn't what she came here for. Charley broke eye contact and sipped her tea before speaking.

'Did you know her? Francesca? I'm sorry, I just... I can't call her mom right now.'

'The decision is still raw, I see,' Avril smiled and shook her head as she turned to the window. 'I didn't know her personally, no. I heard a lot about her over the years though. The arguments upset Elizabeth terribly, and when Francesca moved away with you girls she was devastated. It was the only time I ever saw her show any outward signs of personal stress, other than Frank's death later on. Elizabeth confided in me a little at that time.'

Charley's heart jumped and began to race.

'She confided in you? I know there was something big going on back then, but I know so little of it. Francesca hasn't spoken of the reason. She won't even speak Elizabeth's name. It's so confusing now I've met Elizabeth properly because I know she was well liked, and I think she was a really beautiful lady. I've often wondered what on earth went on back then. Do you know?'

Far from opening up as Charley had expected, Avril paused and pursed her lips.

'I'm afraid I've already said too much, Charley. Those things were said in confidence and I never break a person's trust.'

Charley felt everything in her slump under the weight of the statement. She understood and respected Avril's loyalty, but she couldn't lose this thread now. It wouldn't solve Elizabeth's possible murder, but it may hold the link to her own past. Unfortunately, Avril was holding firm, offering nothing more.

'Okay,' Charley said, an idea coming together, 'Well, how about I tell you what Elizabeth told me already, and maybe you can fill in some of the blanks?'

Avril looked unsure but Charley continued anyway.

'So, I know that Elizabeth and Francesca were close as children, and I know that it was Elizabeth's marriage, and Francesca's jealousy of it that caused the first rift. I also know Francesca married a bully, our father, but he left before I was born.'

Apparently.

She took a breath, trying to think how to put the next events. Should she tell Avril or not?

Maybe not yet.

'I know that I was a mistake, and that Francesca couldn't cope in her house with four of us. I know that Elizabeth tried to help her by getting her a bigger council house. I also know that Francesca didn't believe her, and that things got worse between them until she took us and left. And I know that she did that out of spite because we were doted on by Elizabeth, because she wanted children, but she and Frank couldn't conceive.'

Charley took a breath, heart pounding and her hands shaking. Avril watched her, the look in her eyes unsure, trying to assess whether she should say anything.

Then she turned back toward the front window in silence.

Charley grasped her arm gently.

'Avril, please. I'm begging you. This is my past, and I'm sure Elizabeth would have told me the rest had she had more time but, she

300

told me... she told me this just before she collapsed. She *ran out of time*, and this is so important to me. Please!'

Tears spilled down her cheeks, and she put down her cup to wipe them with her hands. Avril leaned over to pass her a tissue, and it surprised Charley to see tears running down her face. She dabbed at them with her own tissue.

'All right.' she said, 'Okay, I'll tell you what I know,' she flicked her eyes to the ceiling, 'God help me Elizabeth, I'm so sorry, but the girl is so upset.'

Charley let out a fresh barrage of tears in relief and Avril moved to sit next to her on the small settee, putting a warm, comforting hand over hers.

'Listen dear, I don't know the whole story, and I didn't push for details. Elizabeth was a very private woman, and an immensely proud one, but I think most of the stress started when Elizabeth was taken ill.'

Charley dabbed her eyes with the tissue and sniffed as she looked at Avril, eyebrows drawn together.

Elizabeth didn't say anything about an illness.

'At least, that's when I noticed that she was a little more down. She had months when she looked tired or unwell, and eventually she was granted sick leave from her position for six months. I didn't see her over this period, but I kept in contact via email and phone calls. I heard that she wasn't taking visitors, but the few people that went to see her said she was very ill. Axl was one of them. To this day I don't know what was wrong with her, but she eventually made a full recovery and was back to herself at work after the time she had off.'

Avril sighed and dabbed at more tears.

'Except, she wasn't herself.' she continued, 'She seemed preoccupied, her mind was elsewhere, and although she fought and made proposals with the usual vigour, her research lacked, and she lost several proposals that she would usually have won easily. I asked her about it one lunchtime, after over-hearing a heated phone call with Francesca, and Elizabeth broke down.'

Avril shook her head, tongue darting between her lips.

SHATTERED

'I had never seen her break down like that, but she admitted she was glad to have someone to confide in, it was eating her up keeping it to herself. She said that she had lost a baby, a miscarriage I presume, and that Francesca was also making things extremely hard for her. Francesca was at a hard point in her marriage, she had just had you, the house was too small, and they were on the verge of breaking up. Elizabeth wanted to help her, and it was me she asked to find new accommodation for her if I could. Quietly, of course, it could have cost us both our jobs.

'The fighting went on for a good couple of years if I remember rightly, but one day she called in sick. Elizabeth never called in sick, so in my lunch hour I went up to see her. She was in pieces, completely broken. She eventually told me that Francesca had upped and left. She hadn't seen or heard from her in a week, so she had stopped by the house to find it empty. No sign that she had ever lived there, except for a note, screwed up in the hallway. Elizabeth showed me that note, it was horrible.'

Avril swallowed hard and shook her head again. Charley held her breath.

'What did it say?' she pressed gently.

'Oh, it doesn't matter now. It's in the past. The point is Elizabeth looked for her, searched every avenue she could, using her position to push searches she would never have been able to otherwise, but everything turned up nothing. It was like you had all simply disappeared.'

'Did she say why she thought Francesca had gone? What the reason was?'

'No, only that they had been fighting, and that Francesca had been asking for money. Elizabeth was happy to pay, to help her out, but Frank found out and I think it had to stop. And rightly so.'

Charley looked at Avril. This was basically the same story Elizabeth had told her, minus finding out the big spoiler in the will, anyway.

More reason to suspect she was right about the poisoning?

Charley sighed heavily.

'That's all you know?'

Avril nodded.

'That's all I know.' She sniffed and looked away. 'But I have a theory - if you'd like to hear it. God help me for speaking out of turn, Elizabeth.'

Charley nodded eagerly.

'Please.'

'Well, if you want my take on it, I think Elizabeth had the time off sick for IVF. Frank, well, Frank was in a wheelchair after his accident, he had no feeling from the waist down, catheter and all, and I'm not sure whether... well, you know. So, I think maybe IVF was his only way of giving her what she wanted. Anyway, in those days it was a very delicate procedure, and she would have had to have rested well. To me it would explain why she looked tired and stressed. Having a child was the single most important thing to her. I think maybe that's why the stress showed through her facade. I believe she lost the baby, as she said, and it hit her doubly hard, especially as Francesca would have been pregnant with you at around the same time.

'I also think that's why she found it so hard to recover, and why she just wanted to be around you girls all the time. She loved you all, you were all she spoke about, especially you Charley. Oh, she adored you, she really did. But, looking back, she would have had a baby of a similar age. I think she was trying to hold on to you as part of the baby she lost.

'Francesca saw an opportunity, I believe. I'm sure it was around the time you were born that the bribery started. Francesca pushed and pushed, knowing how Elizabeth needed to be in contact with you all, especially you Charley. I think she took advantage of Elizabeth's loss and desperate situation. When Frank put a stop to it. Francesca did the thing that would hurt Elizabeth most, she took you all away.

'And it did hurt her, it really did. She was so broken Charley, and if you want my opinion, I think she would have been over the moon that it was you who came back to look after her now. Absolutely over the moon, dear... oh!'

Avril broke off as she saw the tears Charley couldn't keep back. Her body wracked with them as she sobbed.

Oh, Elizabeth. It's really true, isn't it? There's no mistake, no memory lapse, I am your daughter. In a roundabout way Avril has just confirmed it. So, if you are my mom, why couldn't I just stay with you?

Avril passed Charley another tissue and sat while the sobs abated.

'I'm so sorry, dear, I didn't mean to make you more upset.'

'No,' Charley stammered, 'no, it's not you. I think... I mean... Avril, I was only three when Francesca took me from here. I spent my whole childhood around stories from her and my sisters saying that Elizabeth was a witch, and that she hated children. I believed every lie they fed to me. I was terrified of her. I hated her, but I didn't *know* her. How could they be so nasty? They didn't *know* her, Avril!'

Avril looked taken aback, her mouth formed a little 'o' as she found Charley's hand again.

'Well, listen. I could tell you a little about where that probably came from-'

Charley cut her off, eager to make her point about who she really was, and how close Avril had it. The witch stuff was starting to feel dead in the water. Her sisters – cousins – were cruel and spiteful. It was that simple.

'It's okay, I understand now,' she said, 'Glen told me she was into herbal medicine, but that doesn't mean she's a witch or a monster. That means she wants to help people doesn't it? Not that she wants to lock children in her cellar and eat them. I get it-'

Charley paused as Avril squeezed her hand and gave a short laugh.

'No, Charley, there were no children in the cellar, and yes you're right. She did help a lot of people around here with her remedies. She loved to help to make others feel better, to find them a cure. It was her hobby, her release from the pressure of work, and of life I suppose. People would always be at her door asking for a cure for this and a remedy for that. It drove Frank mad that she always came up with something for them but never charged a penny. even if she had to look it up or buy something in. If you've been in the study you've seen the books?'

'yes, there are loads of them.' Charley nodded.

'There are. She brought every book that she came across. She hated the pharmaceutical world, said they were leading the world down a pill path simply for money. She thought most pills were placebos. Simply sugar and water. It was belief that healed people, she said, and she would rather them have something natural that they believed in, something that would do them no chemical harm.'

'Right,' Charley whispered, a glimmer of understanding piercing the terror of her childhood.

'But the cellar was strictly off limits to you children,' Avril continued, 'There were ingredients and remedies down there that would have done great harm if you had ingested them. Of course the girls, your sisters, they thought it a great mystery and a great game to get into the cellar. They were caught halfway down the steps once and that is when Elizabeth had to start coming down hard on them. It wasn't that she was angry, or wanted to shout, but if they didn't listen their lives could have been in danger you see-'

'And they never listened.' Charley said, cutting Avril off as she thought of all the times Evelyn had said they had tried to get into the cellar to free the children. 'Stupid!'

Avril sipped her tea and smiled.

'Not stupid, just young and curious. Most children are. Elizabeth was diligent about the cellar, and I witnessed her yelling at you girls. But you have to understand that she didn't want any of you harmed, she loved you all, and you were so very young then Charley. A lot of the items down there could have been fatal for you, if not the others. I should imagine that's where your stories originated, dear.'

Yes, that's probably exactly it. They pushed their luck and got shouted at one too many times. Sour grapes, eh, Evelyn?

'Yes, I agree,' Charley nodded, 'Thank you for that, at least I can put one thing to bed now. It was nice to see a different side to Elizabeth.'

'There were many different sides to Elizabeth, she was a good, kind and caring lady. Always put others first.'

Avril looked out of the front window again, warmth in her eyes that seemed to radiate from her soul, and Charley realised that Avril had cared for Elizabeth deeply. She looked back to Charley with a sad smile.

'And that's why this whole mess was such a shame. The promise of the IVF, if that's what-'

The IVF!

Charley grasped Avril's hand stopping the lady midway through her sentence.

'Avril! The IVF? I think you're right. I think your theory is bang on. Elizabeth and Frank had IVF, and it worked. They did have a baby, and the feud surrounding Francesca was because of that baby.'

'Well, now, it's all supposition, dear, I don't really know-'

'But I *do* know, Avril, because that baby was me. Everything in Elizabeth's will is left to her only child. And that child is me. It's in black and white, signed by Elizabeth and the solicitor.'

Avril paled, her eyes wide as her hand pressed to her mouth. Charley nodded wishing she had the will, or a copy, to show her.

'I know, it's difficult to get your head around. I felt the same when I read it, but things she said, and things you're now saying make incredible sense. I always felt left out of my family, just little things. I mean, I was cared for as much as the others, but I always felt a little odd, like Francesca didn't understand me, and didn't want to try to.

'She used to make little snide comments here and there, and I always seemed to be an afterthought. Evelyn said that all teenagers felt that way, but it's never changed for me. I still don't feel comfortable with her. It's like we're built of different stuff and she just doesn't seem to care.

'I got railroaded into coming up here. The four of them gave me no choice. I told them my fears about looking after Elizabeth. Especially when I feared her and with a disease I knew nothing about. The witch stories and her impending death terrified me, but they just told me I had to deal with it.'

Charley stumbled on her words, and paused, taking a breath. Avril sat looking at her, eyes wide, waiting for her to continue.

'I'm glad I did now, but at the time I felt like they didn't care, and it's been that way throughout my childhood. It got so bad recently that I was all for coming up here and never going back, it was driving me mad being around them, their energy is so draining. Avril, the more I think about it, the more I learn, the more I think I really am Frank and Elizabeth's daughter. Please believe me, it's in the will, I can show you...'

Avril shook her head, shocked surprise evident on her face, then she smiled, and then she cried. Charley cried with her. When they had both ran out of tears they sat looking at each other, and finally Avril voiced what had been foremost in Charley's mind since she had found out.

'Oh Charley, she had a baby? But they so wanted a child. If the IVF worked, then why did Elizabeth and Frank give you up? Why did Francesca raise you as her own? Elizabeth never said anything other than she had lost a baby, and I suppose that was the truth in a way, but why?'

Charley wiped at her tears and shook her head.

'That's what I can't figure out. I don't understand it either, all I can think is that Francesca bribed her somehow, or something. She was always jealous of Elizabeth and what she had, I would have made her life complete, Francesca was probably fuming. I need to try to find out what went so wrong, why Elizabeth gave in to her taking me?'

Avril sniffed and tapped at her nose with her tissue.

'I don't think that's what happened.'

Charley swung her head to Avril.

'What makes you say that?'

Avril looked at her and gave a little sigh.

'The note. The note Francesca left was addressed to Elizabeth. It didn't say a lot, but what it said didn't imply that Francesca was happy with the situation either. I don't think she took you out of spite. It would

307

appear, now I know more of the story, that Elizabeth handed you over for Francesca to raise as her own.'

Charley swallowed. This was getting more and more twisted.

'What did the note say, Avril, can you remember?'

'Oh, I remember it word for word, and the look on Elizabeth's face as she read it back to me too. It simply said; You will pay for ruining my life. One day I will ruin yours. Watch your back. It was signed by Francesca, there was no mistake. So, it would seem that she didn't actually want to take you on.'

Charley blew out her lips, her heart sinking.

'No, it seems no one did.'

Chapter Fifty-Five

Axl stared at Francesca. It had been a long time, but she looked the same. Same hard face with trademark scowl set firmly in place, just a few more lines that the years had added. He cast his eyes over the rest of the brood. The two women flanking Francesca's sides, Evelyn and Kate he presumed, had the same hard look on their faces. A veritable inheritance. The one at the back stood with her head down, staring at the floor, stands of hair hung limply over her face.

'Well?' Francesca said, 'I asked you a question Axl Maddox, what are you doing in my dead sisters house?'

He smiled calmly, utterly composed now that he remembered he had a valid reason to be here.

'I do the garden for her, Francesca, I know it's been a long time, but surely you remember that?'

Francesca smiled back, a smile that said she could have found more intelligence in a pebble. Axl didn't like it. Who the hell did she think she was?

'Elizabeth is dead, Axl. What are you still doing in her house?'

'Charley said that I could continue on here, as a testament to Elizabeth.'

Francesca curled her mouth into a sneer.

'Charley? And why would you take orders from her? It isn't *her* place to say who can be here now Elizabeth has gone. This house should be sealed shut to all but her family, and that would be me. I have things to sort out, and this house is one of them. Consider yourself fired, you can leave now.'

Axl felt the anger rise like bile in his stomach.

'I can't be fired, it's a goodwill gesture. And that's what you're doing here, is it? Sorting the estate? You couldn't be bothered to attend the funeral, and don't look particularly upset at your sisters passing, but you're happy to come and take what you think you're owed?'

'Why should I be upset, Axl? After all she put me through? Swanning around here like lady muck? Throwing money at the town and expensive parties, whilst all the time I'm living in a squat bringing up her child? She cut off the maintenance, did she ever tell you that? Cut me out cold, and you expect me to be grieving? No, Axl, I just want what's mine.'

Axl saw the faces of the two women flanking Francesca register shock and the one with red-rimmed glasses, turned to her.

'So it's true? Charley isn't our sister? But you said-'

'Oh, shut up Evelyn, keep your nosy beak out for once.'

'But mom-'

Francesca turned to her.

'No,' she barked, 'Charley isn't your sister, she wasn't my baby, I didn't even want her. Perfect Elizabeth fell from her pedestal and had to give up the thing most dear to her. Serves her right. Karma is a bitch, right Axl? She certainly got hers, didn't she? You made sure of that. Both of you did.'

Axl stepped forward, anger spiralling upward. His fists clenched and unclenched at his sides but there was nothing he could say without incriminating himself. Francesca was a hard bitch, and she was on a roll. He stood, torn between wiping the hard smile off Francesca's face, or chasing down the threat he had come here for.

Charley could be on her way back right now, surely she couldn't have been this long at Avril's. He had to find out where she was, get to her before Francesca, before everything spiralled out of control.

He took another step toward Francesca who stood solid, staring him in the eye.

'This isn't over, Francesca.'

310

He left through the door he had come in. As it slammed behind him he heard Francesca laugh and caught her shout.

'Oh, no Axl, you're right, this isn't over by a long shot. I know what went on up here. You've been a very bad boy Axl, a very bad boy indeed.'

Axl passed through the gate, letting it slam shut behind him as he ran for his Land Rover at the bottom of the drive. With every step he expected Francesca to come out after him and shout things that should never be said out loud. What had been so perfectly executed, and perfectly covered up, seemed about to come tumbling down.

He clutched his chest as he reached the car, trying to calm his rapidly beating heart, as a stitch lodged painfully in his side.

Think, Axl, think.

But his thoughts were crazed, his brain racing a million miles an hour. Francesca had caught him off guard and her being here was a game changer. After her absence at the funeral he had never expected to see her again, but she knew everything, and it appeared she wouldn't be afraid to shout it from the rooftops.

With a surge of pure terror he got into the car and started the ignition. Avril was a stone's throw away, and hopefully so was Charley, but he had to calm himself. If Charley was getting any further with her investigation, he could well be a suspect by now, he didn't need to ruin things by frightening her off with a madman act.

His phone sprang to life in his pocket, registering on the car's display. Theo.

His heart plummeted into his stomach. Was he with Charley? Had they put it all together?

He rubbed his hands over his face. He had to know. He pressed the button on the steering wheel to answer the call, trying to sound as normal as possible.

'Hi, son.'

'Dad?'

Axl was immediately alert. Something was wrong. Theo sounded cagey, not his normal jovial self.

'Yes? What is it, Theo? I'm in kind of a rush, are you okay?'

'Not really. I mean, I suppose you may be able to explain. I'm at yours, I'd left Belle's scented crayons. She has more at home, but you know how she is, she just wanted these back.'

Axl went cold and felt himself holding his breath.

'Okay, that's fine. Is your mom there?'

'She was, she's gone to bingo with Irene. It's Sunday, remember?'

Ah, of course, that's why she was getting her nails done. Each day seemed to roll into the next when you were retired.

'Okay. Theo can we get to the point, I do need to go.'

Theo paused, and Axl heard Belle's voice in the background. He screwed his eyes up and laid his head on the steering wheel, waiting.

'Well, dad, I found something. Letters? I mean, I suppose it was private, but Belle picked the envelope up from behind the bookshelf. It was on the floor. I didn't mean to read them but... Dad, I don't understand. What the hell is going on? Did you write this stuff? I can't even believe it. It's not like you. Charley said-'

Axl thumped the steering wheel with the heel of his hand.

'Are you with Charley?'

'No, I haven't heard from her-'

Axl cut off the call. His heart was back to pounding up a storm. He put the car into gear and floored the accelerator, wheels screeching as he shot onto the road. Rounding the bend at Avril's he saw Charley's car. She wasn't in it, which probably meant she was still inside the house.

Damn it!

He pulled up in front of the Mini. He'd have to wait. But also needed to move. The waiting around was infuriating him.

SHATTERED

You need to get Calm, Axl. Use the time to get calm. You're going to ruin everything.

His phone rang. Theo again.

He shut it down with a grunt of frustration, wishing he'd had chance to burn the damn letters as he intended to. If Theo had found them, then it was all starting to unravel with lightning speed. Theo had information one end, and Francesca had information the other. They were literally a mile apart, like comets waiting to collide. In the middle sat Charley with however much she now knew.

Axl swallowed hard, finding himself close to frustrated tears.

This is wrong, so damn wrong. It wasn't supposed to end this way.

He hit the wheel again as the phone buzzed over and over. Finally, he switched it off. There was nothing he could say to Theo now. Nothing that would make any difference.

He caught sight of Charley in the rear-view mirror walking toward her car. Dizzy with relief, he waited until she was at her driver's door and then he got out quickly, registering her shock as he took her arm.

'Theo has had an accident, he's in a bad way but he's asking for you. Come with me, I'll take you.'

It surprised him how easy it was. She let him lead her to the passenger side of the Land Rover, got in and put on her belt without question. Axl got into the driver's side and locked the doors as they moved off.

He was in a situation now. He had effectively kidnapped Charley. When she knew that Theo wasn't hurt she would be angry and scared, he had to get her somewhere she couldn't shout out for help or get away from him. Fortwind house would have been perfect, or his house at least would have been empty for the afternoon until he could decide what to do with her, but both of those were off limits now.

He drummed his hands on the steering wheel as he drove, breathing hard, aware of Charley watching him. And then he had it. The perfect solution.

He turned the car one hundred and eighty degrees with a screech of wheels and headed back toward the harbour.

313

Chapter Fifty-Six

Charley felt the first flutter of fear when Axl turned the car around with such a screech and a lurch she thought she may fly right out of the seatbelt. She held tight to the door handle, while sneaking a glance at him. His face was pinched in a worried frown, and that made her worry too.

'What happened, Axl? Where is Theo, is he in hospital? How bad is he? Will he be okay?'

Her questions fell on deaf ears and eventually she sat quiet, heart pounding against her ribs.

Axl swung the speeding land rover down a small side street, passing parked cars with millimetres to spare. Charley scrunched her eyes closed and gripped the door handle.

'Axl! Please slow down!

He ignored her, careening to the stop sign at the end of the junction, and swinging left onto the main road without pause. As divine luck would have it, nothing else had been in the vicinity. The land rover creaked and rolled on its suspension as Axl fought to counteract the oversteer, struggling with the wheel. The car swung wildly, and Charley put her free hand over her eyes as Axl now turned hard right forcing her against the passenger side door.

Terrified, she took a peek between her fingers. A lane. They were on a lane. Was this the way to the hospital? Something about it seemed familiar, and then they broke out into the small harbour car park.

It was deserted, as always, only three boats were moored today, one of them Theo's little motorboat.

They screeched to a stop and Charley blinked before looking to Axl. There was no sign of Theo's car and no sign of Theo or Belle.

'Axl? I thought Theo was hurt? What are we doing here?'

Axl flung open the door, running around to Charley's side as it slammed shut. He wrenched it open and helped her down, although rather more forcefully than she would normally allow. Today, Axl Maddox was a worried man.

He grabbed Charley's arm and practically ran her down to the little boat where he immediately started to untie the mooring rope.

'Get in.'

Axl motioned to her to enter the boat and for the first time Charley was uncertain of his motives. She stood on the bobbing jetty, making no move toward the boat.

'Why? I thought we were seeing Theo? What's happened? You're scaring me, Axl.'

'Get in the boat Charley, Theo is on the island. We were spending the afternoon there with Belle when he fell. He was shouting for me to get you, I took Belle to her nan and came straight away. The air ambulance might even be there now. We need to hurry.'

Charley stepped back, still unsure. There were no helicopters overhead, the island seemed deserted in the murky grey distance.

'He's on the island? But it's freezing over there. You left him alone?'

Axl dragged a hand down his face and turned to look at her, holding the mooring rope as the boat swung slowly away from the jetty. He looked pale, his jaw was working under his beard.

'I called the ambulance and then did as he wished. We need to get back as quickly as we can. Get in the damn boat, Charley, time is ticking.'

Charley sensed his urgency. Not knowing if she was doing right or wrong, but doing it for Theo anyway, she jumped into the boat as Axl tugged it back to the jetty with the rope. He followed quickly, throwing the rope inside before him and turning to push against the wooden planks. He put some distance between the boat and the platform before going to the little covered wheel shelter.

Charley swallowed hard as she watched him from the back of the boat. He checked inside the little pockets under the windows and then in the pocket in the sun visor. Key located, he started the engine and pushed the throttle. The boat lurched forward and Charley screamed, falling onto her backside with a thud.

Grey clouds plumbed over the sky, and the wind was biting cold out on the exposed ocean. Axl turned directly toward the island, and the heavy rolling waves immediately battered the left side of the boat. Still on the floor, Charley grabbed a bench to hold herself steady as the boat rocked alarmingly. She thought she remembered Theo turning into the waves so they caused the boat less stress, and she began to crawl up to the cabin to tell Axl.

A large wave crashed and boomed, sending a spray of water over the side, and over her. She sucked in a breath, shocked still by the freezing cold, before crawling again, hands and knees now in water.

He's doing it all wrong, he'll tip the boat over. How did Belle stay in the boat like this? Did he even put on a life jacket on her?

Another flurry of water crashed at the side of the boat, sending fresh spray over Charley. She closed her eyes and spat the salty water from her mouth.

'Axl,' she shouted, 'slow down and turn the boat, please. It'll be wrecked.'

Her voice was lost in the roar of the little motor and the crash of the waves. She stood up, wide legged, holding the little side benches for balance, and took the three steps to the cabin quickly, bracing herself against the wooden sides of the open doorway.

'Axl!' She screamed.

His large back filled the cabin, hands tightly on the wheel.

'Axl!' she screamed again.

This time he turned, his face was white, eyes wild.

'Charley! Can you drive? I can't handle this.'

Charley nodded. She had no idea, but she had seen Theo, she could only give it her best, which would surely be better than Axl was doing.

He shuffled around her to the doorway, leaving her room to move forward as an extra-large wave smashed the side. The boat was knocked almost ninety degrees before righting itself. Axl grunted behind her and Charley's heart started to pump as she staggered. She put a hand on the small wheel, trying to keep it steady as she lessened the throttle. The boat slowed, and she assessed the path out of the front window. The island was straight ahead, but the waves were buffeting from the left. If they carried on toward it, they would be shipwrecked before much longer. Working on instinct, she turned away from the island and into the waves as Theo had done. She had no idea if that was what she was supposed to do; she had never driven a boat in her life - had no boating skills at all - she only hoped it would work.

The boat turned slowly to the left, out toward the open ocean. The island dropped to their right and the ride suddenly became much easier. The bobbing on the waves was certainly less dramatic as they flowed into the tide, but Axl wasn't happy.

'What are you doing?' he shouted. 'The island, Charley, we're moving away!'

He tried to grab at her arm but missed as the swell tipped the boat. Charley turned to look at his ashen face.

'We can't go straight to it, the waves will wreck the boat, this is the only way.'

'Ridiculous! you're lying. Boats cope with rough sea all the time, turn it back.'

'Axl, this isn't rough sea and boats *sink* all the time, especially small ones, this is the only way. Can't you feel how much better the ride is now?'

But Axl was panic-stricken. He grabbed Charley's arm. She pulled it out of his grasp, knocking the throttle back to full. As he grabbed her again, Charley was acutely aware that they were now going full speed out to sea. She grunted as she fought to keep control, but he was just too strong. He grabbed both of her arms at the biceps and ripped her off the wheel, swinging her back out of the small doorway. She didn't quite make the opening, her head and shoulder bouncing off the side of the cabin. Pain exploded down her left side and across her eye, and she felt herself falling through the doorway to the floor of the boat. Back in the wet, and at the mercy of the wind, she glanced back to Axl who was turning the boat back toward the island without slowing the throttle. The boat angled precariously and for a short time waves were almost buffeting the underside of the boat.

Shaking with fear and cold, Charley knew there was nothing she could do. Axl didn't trust her and she couldn't fight him. All she could do now was huddle as low to the floor as possible, brace herself, and hope that they reached the island before poor 'Belle's Beauty' was smashed to pieces.

Chapter Fifty-Seven

As Axl was having his big idea to take Charley to the island, Rue was watching the pandemonium unfold around her. Kate and Evelyn were horrified. Not at what their mother had done, but the fact that the secret had been kept from them. After Axl left, Francesca had set Rue to work finding tea and coffee as they all sat around the table to fight it out.

Rue watched them quietly from the counter.

Why did it always end up with arguments around a kitchen table? This family had always been the same. It didn't matter whose house, usually Francesca or Evelyn's, but the kitchen table was always involved. If tables could talk, theirs would have some stories to tell, but this table would learn the biggest kept story of all.

She pushed out a breath and looked out of the French doors to the garden. It looked unkempt, the grass long, bushes wiry, weeds in the path. But Axl had said that he was the gardener, hadn't he? Had been for years. Was this his idea of gardening? Or had he been here for another reason? Rue thought he had looked shocked when they arrived, but then again, that was normal wasn't it? They hadn't been here for years.
Even so, the feeling that something wasn't right stuck with her, it hadn't only been shock she had seen, there had been something more; agitation, nervousness.

'I always knew there was something different about her,' Kate announced loudly, pulling Rue's attention back to the table, 'she just isn't like us. I always found it weird that she was completely opposed to everything we said or did. I thought she was merely obstinate, but maybe this is why instead?'
Rue felt her heart sink. They were already pulling Charley apart, talking about her as though she was some foreign object to be examined. She had grown up with them, and to Rue she had been more

caring and considerate than her real sisters ever had.

'It's obstinance either way.' Evelyn chimed in, 'She grew up with us. How much do genes play a part? Her character is hers, but we have moulded her, surely.'

At this Francesca slapped a hand on the table which shut the two of them up instantly. Rue turned back to the kettle with a sigh.

Family dynamics and roles, how I would love to break out of the mould.

'She's stubborn and obstinate because Elizabeth was stubborn and obstinate.' Francesca said, 'She had bad genes, that's all, Charley can't be blamed, the poor child didn't ask to be born. That was because of the selfish wants of a rich lady used to having everything handed to her on a plate. The matter at hand isn't whether Charley is or isn't like you, the fact is that she is not your sister, she's your cousin, and therefore has no reason to be like you.'

Evelyn looked away, but Kate, who would speak out when she had something to say regardless, sat back in her chair and looked at her mother.

'So, what happened and why is it such a big secret?'

Rue's heart picked up a steady drum as she wondered if Francesca was ready to let everything out. Surely she couldn't, it was the reason Rue had been so hen-pecked all these years.

She watched her mother flick her hard eyes to Kate.

'It was a long time ago, and nothing more than a silly mistake that Elizabeth paid for the rest of her life. I did her a favour, and when I did she cut me off. That's why we left and that's why I haven't spoken to her since. Gratitude. That's what it was, and that's all it would have taken, and she could have seen her daughter every day if she'd wanted to. Self-righteous, pompous, do-gooding bitch. How she could ever have handed a child over to someone else is beyond me. If you make a mistake, you live with the consequences. She chose not to, and so I made her live with the consequences of that decision. Every decision in life has *consequences,* you'd do well to remember that girls.'

Rue rolled her eyes as the kettle boiled. It seemed Francesca wasn't about to tell everyone the version Rue knew at all. More and more lies.

This family was so tangled in a web of them, with the poisonous Francesca spider in the middle, Rue didn't know if she would ever be able to free herself.

As she set about making the tea Evelyn and Kate murmured their agreement and Rue wondered if Francesca even knew what the truth was anymore, she had lied so much.

'That's a massive favour,' Evelyn said importantly, sitting upright in her chair, 'That's not just picking up some milk from the corner shop for her, that's a life changing thing. Mom, I admire what you did, and I think I understand why you did it. You couldn't leave an unwanted baby on the street, especially not family, so you took Charley in as your own and made sure that we were all unaware so that she didn't feel she wasn't part of us. All of us, including Charley thought we were sisters, there was no reason to doubt it. That is a noble and honourable thing, you gave your life for us, mom, and I love you for it. I hope I convey as much kindness and caring as you have over my life.'

Francesca smiled.

'Well, my caring sister has already tried to break the bonds I worked so hard to create, I only hope Charley is okay. As always, I'm left to deal with the fallout of Elizabeth's mess.'

Evelyn and Kate nodded, concern in their eyes, identical expressions of pity on their faces. Rue wasn't surprised.

They're minions, or lemmings. Where Francesca will lead, these two will surely follow.

She took the tea over to the table and placed it down, pushing the cups to each person before pulling the chair out to sit herself, as she knew she would be expected to do.

And then Evelyn let out a large sigh and reached a hand over the table to clasp her mother's.

'I forgive you for lying, I really do.' she said.

Rue felt her heart jolt as she stopped in her tracks, half ready to sit down, half ready for a war to break out. She saw Francesca's Adam's Apple bob in her throat.

'Lying?' Francesca said, 'I haven't lied to you.'

Rue held her breath.

Oh but you have, not just a small one either mom, a huge juicy one, and now Evelyn has seen through you, finally.

And then her bubble popped as Evelyn shook her head with a smile.

'You did, when Charley rang and confronted you about being Aunt Elizabeth's daughter, you said it wasn't true, but now I know you only said it to protect her.'

Francesca visibly relaxed, shoulders dropping, but her face was ashen as she smiled.

'Yes, well, even at the end of her life that miserable old woman still tried to claim what was hers. Well, it was too late wasn't it, and it's too late now. If I'd have known she was well enough to stir up trouble, I'd have come up here myself and Charley would have been none the wiser. Poor, poor child.'

Rue saw her mother gulp and look down. There would be tears any moment. Francesca was adept at producing them on demand if she wanted to stop a line of conversation or induce pity.

On cue, a large tear slipped down Francesca's face and Kate and Evelyn grabbed a hand each, only Rue sat unaffected. She looked down into her mug, tired of the theatrics already.

'No-one could have known, mom.'

Francesca looked at Kate and smiled sadly wiping the tear away, Rue saw the hardness creep back into her face.

She placed her hands on the table and sniffed, sitting upright. Mood gone as quickly as it had appeared.

'No, they couldn't. Right girls, there is work to do before Charley comes back. We don't know whether she believes what Elizabeth said so she could be feeling hurt and angry, or she could be upset. It's better that we throw ourselves into finding what I need before she gets back, then we can devote the time to making sure she is okay.'

'What do we need?' Evelyn looked confused.

Francesca looked from Kate to Evelyn. Rue was glad that she kept her attention off her.

'There are some letters hidden somewhere here. I don't know where, but I'm sure Elizabeth would have kept them together in an envelope, she always kept things in blasted envelopes. I don't know where they are, but I know she kept them. She threatened that she could use them as leverage if she ever wanted to take Charley back. I tried to keep this from you, to protect you all, and this is the reason we moved away, they were my answers to the bribery she put me through over the years,' She ran a hand over her face and closed her eyes, heaving a dramatic sigh, 'girls, they're not nice because I was responding in anger. She won't have kept her side of the letters to show you of course, but the point is I've written things that I'm not proud of and I want to get rid of them. They are a link to a burden I no longer need to bear, and they could get me into trouble for nothing more than helping my rude and arrogant sister. If you find them, please don't read them, bring them straight to me and I will check they're the ones I need. I don't want you seeing that kind of insensitivity from me, it wasn't right, and I shouldn't have said what I did.'

Evelyn nodded and Rue closed her eyes briefly at how easily they thought their mother was incapable of cruelty.

'So what kind of envelope are we looking for?' Kate said.

Francesca pursed her lips and shook her head.

'I don't know, but I should think it will be large and bulky because there were a lot of letters over the years. Elizabeth will have hidden it, and I don't know where it will be, so we need to look everywhere. Every little nook and cranny. They're highly important so I suggest we take a room each, Evelyn, you take the front drawing room, and Kate you take Elizabeth's bedroom, you'll know it from her prissy things. It doesn't look like Charley has sorted much out yet, which is good. I'll take the study at the bottom of the stairs. Rue, you keep a watch out for anyone coming, especially Charley, I don't think we'll have much time.'

Rue looked at Francesca whose hard gaze and subtle hand signal were telling her to keep schtum or there would be repercussions. An extra kick under the table helped to get the message across, although this table was big so she didn't get quite the hit that Rue thought she would have liked to. Rue nodded lightly and looked back down at her hands with a sigh.

'Oh, and one more thing girls,' Francesca said, 'If the letters are mentioned at all, especially in the will we will simply say we didn't come across any such thing. Are we all clear?'

The three of them agreed and went to work in their respective rooms. Rue hoped the envelope would be hidden in the kitchen, because if it was, she would find it and take it before anyone else could. She didn't know what she was going to do with the information yet, but just to have it would give her some power over Francesca.

As the others left the room, Rue started her own search, diligently checking every space and every cupboard in the kitchen as quickly and quietly as she could.

Chapter Fifty-Eight

The saving grace was that the boat had passed above the island a small way as it had hurtled out to sea, so when Axl turned it back around, heading for the wooden dock, he was driving with the waves at their back.

With the boat a little more stable Charley pushed herself off the wet floor and stumbled back to the cabin for a little warmth. She sat herself up the corner just inside, pushing herself back against the wall and using her foot against the door frame to steady herself against the rocking. Her head pounding, she winced as she pressed her fingers to a bump that had risen like an egg.

It hurt like hell to touch, but seeing no blood she thought she would live, and her shoulder was just a small ache now.

She looked up at Axl. He had no idea she was behind him, he was too preoccupied handling the boat.

And isn't that weird? I know he's worried, but what's the problem? He got it back from the island with Belle, so why is he flailing around trying to drive it now? The sea is choppy, sure, but it's not...

Charley watched his huge back, and the second ripple of fear ran through her as a thought hit her.

At the harbour Axl had untied the mooring rope before getting into the boat, which Charley knew was dangerous. The boat had started to float away before they had even got in. Inside the cabin he had searched for the keys, but surely he would have known exactly where they were if he had just driven the boat back. It could have been worry and pressure, sure, but one thing was ringing not only alarm bells, but an air-raid siren in her head.

The boat had been dry.

The bottom boards and the seats were all dry. There was no way they could have dried out that quickly if things had happened as urgently as he had told her, especially with the chill of autumn fast approaching.

Which meant Axl hadn't been in the boat.

Which in turn meant that Theo wasn't on the island and possibly wasn't even hurt.

Charley's heart flew into her mouth and her heart thumped in her ears.

And what if Axl was the murderer? He was still one of the main suspects. If he knew the things she had found out there was no way she could call for help on the island, and there was nowhere to run.

Maybe that's exactly his intention, he's going to finish you off on the island where no one can hear you scream.

Charley gulped in breath after breath as terror welled inside her, adrenaline flooding her veins. She was stuck, trapped. Theo didn't even have a boat to get to her now...

Theo.

Maybe he didn't have a boat, but that didn't mean she couldn't alert him to what was going on, he could at least get help over here.

Axl was grappling with the wheel as he turned the boat back toward the island's jetty, sidelong into the waves again, and Charley braced herself as they battered the boat with renewed vigour. She reached into her coat pocket and pulled out her sodden phone, swiping at the screen as she watched Axl. It took a while to come to life and for a second she thought it would be too wet, but the screen flared up in the impending gloom of night.

It seemed glaringly bright in the dull of the late afternoon. Charley grimaced and glanced at Axl, but he was too busy fighting the wheel.

She quickly tapped out a message to Theo.

On your boat with your dad. He's taking me to the island. Says you're hurt but I'm starting to doubt it. Are you ok? I'm scared.

She sent the message, locked the phone, and braced against another wave as she blew out a shuddery breath of relief. If nothing else, at least Theo would know where she was. Then the phone screen lit up and Charley almost cried as a message pinged straight back.

On my boat?!!!! He's never driven a boat! Charley, he's up to something. It may be bad, and you may have been right about Elizabeth, I can't explain now, but I'm on my way. Be VERY careful.

Charley felt icy fingers creep down her spine as Theo not only confirmed that he had no idea what was going on, but also that she was right to suspect Axl, and now he had lured her out here under false pretences. She quickly typed back.

Please hurry.

She sat back and closed her eyes. Help was at least on the way. How Theo was going to get to her she had no idea, but she didn't doubt that he would.

A sudden crash boomed around them and the boat lurched with a squeal of wood. Axl yelled as planks flew up the small front windows of the cabin, smashing one of the glass panes. Charley screamed, scrabbling to her feet.

Out of the now glassless window the island loomed too close and then she was thrown off her feet into Axl as the boat ran aground, the front end splintering against the rocky shore. Wooden planks from the makeshift jetty fell into the back of the boat, propelled right over the roof of the cabin. Axl stepped back with a grunt, almost on top of Charley as sand and water appeared around his feet. Charley lurched into the open back of the boat and looked over the side.

The boat had crashed right through the small structure and ran up into the sand and rocks beyond. She felt a moment of horror that Theo's beloved boat had been wrecked, and then she saw an opportunity.

Axl was just behind her coming out of the cabin as he mumbled. He looked shaken and white as Charley vaulted over the side of the boat and into the shallow sea. She gasped at the cold washing up her legs, heard Axl yell, and then a wave buffeted the boat, knocking her from behind onto her hands and knees in the water. She crawled quickly to the dry sand and looked back to the boat. Axl had been thrown over with the wave too and was now pulling himself up inside the boat as another knocked him off his feet almost immediately.

Charley shivered, her heart knocking against her ribs. It was now or never.

With one last glance at the wrecked boat she turned and ran for the steps up to the island, her ragged breath coming quickly in her ears. Axl's angry voice propelling her stiff, cold body forward. Her feet pounded the soft sand and stone underneath her and she heard each breath that tore in and out of her body, but she didn't dare stop or turn to look.

She reached the grassy top of the island and bent over, hands on her knees as she drew ragged breaths into her burning lungs. She looked around, quickly remembering that there was absolutely nothing up here but the ruins of the old castle, and a small cluster of trees.

The trees were too far, and it seemed insanely obvious, but the only place to hide were the castle walls themselves. Breath slowing, she looked back down to the small cove. The boat was now empty. Axl must be on his way up the steps.

Swallowing hard, she ran for the castle, tucking herself behind a wall where she could watch the grassy top. At least this way she would have the advantage of knowing where Axl was first. The wind blocked by the wall she felt a little of the warmth she had generated running reach her body. The wet parts of her she thought would never thaw.

She shuddered, cold quickly setting back into her bones, the warmth short lived.

Chapter Fifty-Nine

After checking the driveway for the umpteenth time, to find that no one had arrived, Rue turned from the front door and caught Francesca's decimation of the study through the partially open doorway. Books, ornaments, and papers were strewn over the floor, it was like a whirlwind had hit. The door itself had obviously been locked, now it was splintered around the handle with the force Francesca had used to open it.

Gazing at the destruction, Rue felt shame colour her cheeks at Francesca's lack of appreciation for other people's things, dead or otherwise. Not that it came as a surprise. Nothing Francesca did came as a surprise, and Rue knew damn well just how much she had to find the letters. If she was so sure that Aunt Elizabeth had kept anything at all, Francesca would be in a flat panic right now.

And that was why Rue had to get her hands on them first.

Appalled at the mess of the little room, Rue quickly went back to the kitchen. Spurred back into her own search, she emptied or moved the items in each cupboard and carefully put them back again. She was no longer bothered if Francesca caught her at it, she would just say she was looking for the letters too. It was the truth, after all, and it would be what Francesca wanted to hear, she would simply think Rue was on her best behaviour after her rebellion at the services.

With the top row of cupboards done, Rue turned to the bottom row. She paused for a moment, listening. Bangs, scrapes, and rustles of the others at their search floated down the hall.

Good.

She started to work her way along. Cutlery, plates, utensils, pots and pans, cereal boxes, pasta, vegetable baskets with potatoes and a few onions.

329

In the cupboard by the sink she found an old Tupperware box stuffed right to the back, sitting amongst the cleaning agents and cloths. Pulling it out with curiosity, she peered through the cloudy plastic lid, and saw a purple looking substance. Opening the lid a small way, she wrinkled her nose, and gagged as the smell hit her.

Berries.

Or what had once been berries she thought, although only a couple on top retained any form, the rest of the box was a mash of purple slush and mould that had formed as the berries had decomposed.

She gagged again, and replaced the lid tight, putting it back inside the cupboard and pushing it back where it had been.

I'll dispose of them later, right now I need to concentrate on the letters. They may be my way to freedom.

Butterflies fluttered in Rue's stomach. She moved to look through the last two cupboards, and finally the full-sized cleaning cupboard, tugging out the ironing board and hoover, and pulling the baskets off the shelves to check inside.

Nothing.

She had been almost certain the letters wouldn't be hidden in the kitchen anyway, but the force of the blow still hit her in the gut. She huffed out a breath, close to tears.

Why can't something go my way? Just for once, can someone up there give me a break?

Across the room the cellar door clicked and opened with a low groan. Rue stared and swallowed hard.

Is this my break or is this a joke?

She made her way to the open door and looked down the familiar stone steps. Damp, cold darkness filled the space below. There had been a window and a light down there, she recalled, either the window had been patched up or more likely the dull day wasn't letting much light inside.

As she stood she felt a circle of cold air at her back. It was just air, not heavy, not forceful, and yet she felt it was urging her down the stairway. It *wanted* her to go down.

Going down wasn't the issue for Rue, she had never been scared of the cellar. Her own investigation at twelve years old had told her there were no children down there, just lots of weird bottles, what she now knew to be a pestle and mortar, and many hanging and draped dried herbs and plants. If she had thought Evelyn's stories were fallacy and a hefty helping of imagination before, she had certainly known it then, and after seeing the poison sign on some of the bottles she had also understood why their aunt had forbidden them from being down there.

After that she had lost all fascination for the cellar or the stories, although Evelyn had managed to place reasonable doubt in her mind on more than one occasion, especially after they had moved house, and were no longer in the vicinity of Aunt Elizabeth.

Even so, right here and now Rue wasn't scared of the cellar, she was scared of Francesca's wrath. Could she get away with being down here if she was caught?

The air swirled and pushed and she found herself on the top step, heart pattering.

What if Francesca comes in, finds me down here?

But what if the letters are down there? It would be a good place to hide them surely.

Rue chewed her lip uncertain and leaned back to listen to the sounds of the house. The sounds of searching, bangs and grunts came back to her, and thinking there may be no better opportunity she felt herself propelled forward. Pushed gently down into the murk below.

Chapter Sixty

Axl kept below the ridge of the grassy top of the island. He tucked himself in to the cliff and worked his way slowly up the rugged ridge to the left of the steps, hoping he didn't slip and fall to his death.

He knew the island well enough to know that there was nowhere Charley could hide. She would be at the castle watching the steps if he had to take a guess. He didn't want to give her the satisfaction of emerging at the top of them. He wanted the element of surprise. She was much younger and fitter than he was, and if he could obtain the advantage by staying out of her line of sight, he would save himself the trouble of chasing her round the island, and probably giving himself a heart attack in the process.

When he thought he had traversed the steep-sided rock slope far enough, he heaved himself slowly up on to the grass, breathing heavily. He saw he was level with the south wall of the castle and almost collapsed with relief. The climb had been hard, but worth it. With no low window openings Charley would have to be at the edge of this wall to see him, and hopefully that meant he would see her too. He kept his eyes trained to the wall edge for movement as he got to his feet and jogged to the wall, keeping low. He placed his back against the cold stone catching his breath while assessing his next move.

To his right were the remnants of the back of this room, a small broken wall that jutted at a right angle to this one. There was room to get around it but Axl knew that behind was just the rest of the south wall and a drop to the sea. There was nowhere to go from there, no room to get behind the castle, which had been built almost onto the cliff edge. Charley would be stupid to be behind it. Trapped.

He checked anyway.

There was no-one behind it. Nothing but the crashing sea, sixty feet below. The drop was sheer and vertical. It gave him the sweats just looking at it. Wiping his mouth shakily he returned to the south wall, The safe wall, he thought, and made his way back to where he had started. He peered slowly around the thick brick.

The next room was large and open, the remains of two rooms. A brick line in the grass hinted at a former dividing wall reduced to ground level. Two large fireplaces, one for each room still sat either side. Both were large, open stone ranges built into the thick walls. A person of Charley's size could possibly keep out of sight in one of those. The back wall was split into two smaller rooms. One was partially open due to a collapsed wall, but the other was still fully concealed through a small arch doorway. The space behind it revealed only stone wall from where he stood.

Three places she could be concealed and watching.

Axl's heart thud in his chest as he scanned the area. He heard nothing and saw no movement. Taking his chance, he moved into the big space, glad to get behind the shelter of the large wall, out of the biting cold of the wind. There were the remains of an open fire here. Probably kids. He half wished it were alight so he could warm his bones and wondered why he had thought the island such a good idea.

He checked the fireplaces first, scanning the open front of the castle for movement, before going to the back rooms. Again, if she was here she was trapped, and he didn't think she was that stupid.

He poked his head around the more eroded room, taking in the small roofless space. The back wall had fallen in a little here, the disruption starting a cascade of bricks, most of which had fallen into the sea. Axl didn't need to look behind the back wall. He knew it was a sheer drop behind.

Turning back to the open rooms, he gazed over the grass and across the sea to Fortwind Bay. It was late afternoon but already the lights of the village were blinking on against the impending dusk. It was getting dark, the dullness of the day moving evening closer earlier; he assessed he had about an hour before the sky turned black, and then he would only have the moonlight to find her by, if the racing clouds gave him the grace.

Plenty of time.

He hurried to the small arch doorway and peered inside. This room was complete apart from the ceiling, the lack of roof left it open to the elements, but the smaller fireplace was intact, and a small flight of worn spiral stairs still rose most of the way up on the left-hand side of the archway. With a quick backward glance, he moved into the room, checked the fireplace, and the little nook behind the stairs as they wound upwards.

Both recesses revealed nothing.

Axl grinned. This middle space held the only places to hide. If she was past the next wall, there was nothing but bricks, grass, and sea. The rest of the castle had crumbled to foundations.
Grunting with satisfaction he strode back to the open front of the castle with more confidence to peer around the last standing wall. The back wall here ran in step like fashion down the ground, exposing the sea behind, and the North wall of the castle had gone completely. Grass had grown over the remains of the old wall and fallen bricks.

No Charley.

Axl frowned.

How have I missed her? Unless she went for the trees after all.

He put his hands on his hips and stared at the open land. The trees were sparce, so thinly spread that a mouse would have trouble hiding there. There was clearly no-one.

Where the hell is she?

He felt anger bubble at her uncanny ability to outwit him on an island so small. There should be nowhere to go. Hell, there was nowhere to go. The cove allowed the only access to the island. The cliffs were too dangerous everywhere else, and if she wasn't at the cove, she had to be up here it was as simple as that.

The cove.

Had she gone back to the boat while he had been checking the rooms? If she had, she would be trapped there too. The boat was no longer seaworthy, that was a fact. With a small chuckle he turned to the cove as a dark form rushed at him. He flinched and ducked, but his reflexes weren't quick enough and pain rebounded through his head.

334

He fell to his knees with a thud.

Chapter Sixty-One

Rue tugged the old pull cord at the bottom of the steps, with a 'tick-tock' it filled the room with a ping and an electric hum. Dull yellow light slowly lit the area around her.

The cellar was small, nowhere near the size of the house, and the small window remained just as she remembered it, the growing darkness outside pressing against its crossed pane.

Under the window a long workbench ran the length of the room, it's stone top cluttered with small bottles and the leaves left from some sort of plant. String, labels, knives, scissors and even an old pen still sat next to an old saucepan and the same age-old ceramic pestle and mortar. The shelves behind held a multitude of bottles and jars and hanging from the ceiling were plants and herbs, bound and tied with string,

Rue felt herself transported back in time. The room sat almost entirely unchanged from when she had been down here before. It was as though Elizabeth had been down here just yesterday, and yet, with the dust covering the clutter it could have been centuries ago.

She moved to the table seeing her Aunt's neat writing on the labels. Weird and wonderful names passed before her eyes.

St john's wort, lemon balm, belladonna, peppermint, aloe vera, calendula, chamomile.

Alongside the saucepan was a list of the strange names and a method not dissimilar to a recipe. Rue realised what had gone on down here.

Herbal remedies. Elizabeth liked to make herbal remedies.
Evelyn's witches' potions, of course, not such an imagination after all.

She picked up the paper, dust and the old musty smell coming together to make her want to sneeze. She held it in for fear of bringing Francesca and the others down here.

Francesca. I'd better get moving.

As quickly, but as delicately as she dared Rue looked behind, under and around the clutter in the room. Moving bottles gently and moving bunches of plants which showered dust and husks which only made the impending sneeze ever more likely. She crouched under the desk, scaling the uneven redbrick floor but came up with no envelope. No letters. Nothing.

Oh well, it was a long shot. I guess this was a joke, not a break after all.

She turned back to the steps and for the first time noticed the small white freezer sitting in a recess by the back wall. Clean. Which was strange in this dusty time warp.

Curious Rue lift the lid and peered inside the immaculate white space to see hundreds of small, loose frozen black berries. No, make that thousands. She frowned.

Wow, that's some stock! Must have been something for the remedies maybe?

Then she remembered the box in the kitchen cupboard. Were these the same berries? She was about to put a hand inside to pull one out when there was a bang upstairs. Rue jumped startled as the doorbell rang.

'Rue! Damn it, what are you playing at!'

Francesca's yell almost turned her blood to stone. Heart rate tripling she quickly shut the freezer lid, flicked the light off and ran up the steps as Francesca hollered her again from what she hoped was the hallway and not the kitchen.

Chapter Sixty-Two

Charley had chanced going back to the boat as Axl had been checking the castle, hoping against hope that he wouldn't see her cross the expanse. She had thought herself lucky when he hadn't, but a good look at the boat revealed just how broken it was. Belle's Beauty wouldn't be sailing anywhere for a while, if she ever sailed again.

Dismay falling over her, Charley had been stumped, feeling trapped and lost, until sight of the docking rope and broken jetty had given her a plan. Not one she liked, but one that would have to suffice. Now the boat was wrecked, there was no other option. She untied the rope from the boat's stays, and rolled it, putting it over her shoulder like a cowboy. Then she had picked up the heaviest piece of wood she could carry and headed back up onto the island.

She caught Axl coming out of the most complete bit of the castle where she, Theo, and Belle had sat for their picnic just a few days ago. He headed left, his back to her, as she jogged toward him, head tumbling with thoughts, stomach swirling with fear.

Why had she let Axl lead her here so willingly? He hadn't even had to try. She had got into his car and onto the boat without reservation. It was stupid. She was stupid.

You were worried about Theo.

She had been, but the reservations had been there. She should have listened to her instinct before she got on the boat. At least at the harbour there had been somewhere to run and people to get to. She could have outrun this large, overweight man easily.

Close enough now she swung the plank before she could question her decision. As luck would have it, Axl chose that second to turn and stride toward her meaning the wood had extra impact. It collided with his head perfectly with a dull crack that sickened her to her stomach and brought him to his knees.

Horrified, she hesitated, staring down at him as she gulped heavy breaths. Had she really just done that?

He groaned, placing a hand to his head. Not knocked out, just shocked and dazed.

Terror spurring action, she pulled the rope from her shoulder, but lost precious seconds as she tried to get to grips with it. Grabbing his hands firmly behind his back she tried to tie the rope around them, but her hands were frozen, the ropes thick and hard to work with. She cursed herself for never having learned knot formations. As she fumbled with the rope Axl regained his senses, disparaging of it as though it were strings of spaghetti, as he got to his feet and swung to face her.

He grabbed at her hands, catching her by the wrists perfectly, and holding with a vice like grip. It didn't seem to matter what she did, he took it with indifference. Now she looked at him, terror rising from her stomach like a wave. He could do whatever the hell he liked out here, she thought. No-one *would* save her. No-one would hear her scream.

She shook, cold and fear collecting in her stomach as she glanced at the lights over in the bay. Safety. Disheartened, her shoulders slumped with assent. Out here, with no boat to get back, she was trapped. Trapped and at Axl's mercy. Even if she escaped his clutches now, she could only run in circles for so long.

Oh God, please hurry Theo.

Axl held her wrists tight but had made no other move since she had stopped struggling. Sensing his hesitation, she looked up to find him staring at the wall just above her head, working his jaw.

'What are you intending to do with me?' she said, voice wavering.

He blinked, looking at her with mild surprise, as though just remembering she was there.

'I don't know yet Charley, I need to think.' he said, tightening his grip.

Charley winced at the increase in pressure, and then the realisation hit that he hadn't come here with a plan.

No plan? Surely that's good news. Or at the least it buys you time. Talk to him, see if you can talk him down.

She felt a flicker of hope. If she only had this one shot, while he was uncertain, then she had to try.

'Axl, why am I here? And why lure me here under false pretences? I don't understand, what have I done?'

Axl worked his jaw and heaved in a breath.

'It's not what you've done Charley, it's what you know, and now I need to think what to do about it.'

Charley felt herself reel, gasping a swift exhale as though someone had given her a punch to the stomach. She swallowed hard.

Oh shit, he actually did it. And he knows I've been following up because of Theo. How much does he know? Oh god, I'm in real trouble out here. So much trouble.

'I... I don't understand.' she stuttered, 'I don't know-'

He tightened his grip on her wrists and pulled them upward. Pain shot into her already numb hands.

'Don't make me out to be an idiot. You *do* know. I know you've been digging up information, putting things together. A lot of people could be hurt by what you know. I need to weigh up whether it's worth my suffering or yours. What do you think you would you do in my shoes?'

Charley closed her eyes as the pain rolled down to her shoulders. She whimpered.

'I don't know, I don't know what I'd do.'

'Of course you do,' He said with a harsh laugh, 'Self-preservation. That's what life is about, isn't it? That's what biology is. Survival of the fittest. And now I have to do what's right for me, because if this information gets out my life is over. I lose my granddaughter, my son, my wife, not that she's much of a loss, but they are my life after all, by

340

preserving myself I am also preserving them. I can't let you loose with this Charley, it's too dangerous for me.'

Charley began to shake as his words sank in.

'So you're going to keep me here? There are people waiting for me, they'll report me missing. Axl, please do the right thing and call for help. We can go home and carry on as normal. I promise I won't say a word. We can put this all behind us, we don't even have to see each other again. Please, I'm begging you.'

Axl laughed, a deep belly laugh, like she had just told the funniest joke in the world. His eyes looked a little wild as his grip tightened.

'No, Charley,' He sniffed, 'see you don't get it, it's not that easy is it? You seem to have struck up quite a friendship with Theo and Belle and that, I'm afraid, is just a little too close to home for me. So, you see, the right thing for you, and the right thing for me, are very different things right now.'

Panic surged in her chest at the insinuation that he may need to do something other than let her go.

'I can leave, Axl,' She pleaded, 'I'll leave. I have a flat in Harrogate. I'll go straight away, and I'll never tell a soul what you did, I promise.'

Axl chuckled and glanced over to the Bay.

'What *I* did?' He said softly, 'Don't put all this on me, Charley. It was both of us, both of us did it, but you know that anyway, it's obvious, like two plus two, isn't it?'

Charley swallowed and stared at him. She had been almost certain both Axl and Nell had been involved, but his confession made her blood run cold. And the fact that he knew that she knew gave her no other option. She couldn't deny it. Had Theo been so sure of his father's innocence that he had told him everything? Given the game away?

Even if that was the case, it was a flood of relief that flowed through her veins as she realised it was at an end. The game was over. They had poisoned Elizabeth, as she had said all along.

From here on who knew what would happen, but she would fight to get off this island and she would expose Axl and Nell when she got back. Elizabeth - her mother - deserved that. They would pay for the life that had been cut short and the little time that Charley had with her too. Who knew how many years Elizabeth could have had left if these two despicable individuals hadn't made her suffer for over eighteen months before she finally met her end.

Self-preservation. He had that right. Now it was all about her own self-preservation and the dignity of a mother she had never really known. There was only one piece of the puzzle that she was missing, one last piece to slot into place.

'Why?' she whispered, 'Why would you do it to her? She was an old friend, a best friend, she trusted you.'

Axl faltered, his determination seemingly caught off guard. His eyes almost registered sorrow. Charley curled her lip.

Too late to be sorry now, you murdering bastard.

She held his gaze, daring him to look away before she had answers. Finally he did, looking up at his hands on her arms. Consciously, or unconsciously she didn't know which, he loosened his hold a little. The relief was phenomenal. Her fingers were completely numb from the tightness of his grip and exposure to the bitter air, but she felt the blood rushing back into her upturned arms.
'I had no choice.' he said with a shake of his head, 'I couldn't do anything else. She wanted it, and what Elizabeth Kane wanted she got. I was a friend enough to grant her wish.'

Charley gaped at him, wind whipping hair around her face. She pulled some strands free from her mouth.

'She didn't ask for this, Axl, she didn't want it. I have proof. And even if she did, did she ask you to make her suffer beforehand too? If you think that, then you're a sick old man.'

She knew she had spoken too hastily as the words left her mouth. His head snapped up and he re-established his grip.

'You know nothing,' he spat inches from her face. 'You come up here out of nowhere and think you can dig into a lady's past and know everything about her from the few scraps that you find? You didn't know her, Charley, you knew nothing about her.'

The words rang in her ears, and she felt hot tears spring into her eyes.

'I didn't get a chance,' she shouted back into the wind. 'You took that from me, you and Nell, and I'll never forgive you. And for your information Theo knows you've done it too, I messaged him and he's on his way over. It doesn't matter what you do to me, Axl, the bond is already broken with Theo. Self preserve all you like, but the truth will out, in whatever form it comes.'

She looked out toward the harbour and like an angel on the sea's surface there bobbed a light. A small boat.

Theo. Please, please let it be Theo.

She gave a small whimper of relief and Axl turned to see the same bobbing boat. She saw the panic in his eyes. His grip grew tighter, and he seemed to go into overdrive. Shoving her back against the wall, he placed an arm across her chest and leaned in close.

'Don't think he's coming to save you, Charley, he's only halfway, you won't be here when he arrives.'

Charley looked back at him, struggling to breathe from the weight of him across her chest.

'I won't?'

Axl shook his head, eyes now cold, dead... resolute.

'I'm sorry Charley, I'm not normally this kind of man, but I'm desperate. You have to understand there isn't any other choice.'

Adrenaline fired through Charley and as Axl looked back across the sea to the boat she knew there would be no other moment. Pulling her hands free of his loosened grip, she brought up her knee, hoping to connect where it would hurt most but ending up driving it into his overhanging stomach. He grunted in surprise as she pushed at his chest as hard as she could, just giving herself room to duck underneath his arm and run like hell.

Chapter Sixty-Three

Rue shut the cellar door with relief. The kitchen was empty.

She ran into the hall to see Francesca open the front door, glance outside, and shut it again with a curse. She scowled at Rue as she passed back into the study.

'Will you get out here and do your damn job Rue,' she spat, 'I don't have time for these games.'

'I'm done in here, there's nothing, mom.' Evelyn called from the drawing room as Rue reached the door and checked outside for herself.

No-one.

Avoiding the decimation of the study, Rue turned toward the drawing room instead. Her stomach sank and her mouth dropped open with a gasp. It was tidier than the study, but not by much. Evelyn had obviously been as careless as her mother had.

Are we really going to trash an old lady's house like a band of money crazed criminals?

Evelyn looked up, catching Rue's expression with a huff.

'What's the problem, Rue? We're looking for something in a hurry, what do you want me to do? This mess can be tidied afterwards, unless you'd like to have a go now, while I look through the kitchen?'

The sarcasm in Evelyn's voice was belittling, but Rue let it slip. She didn't want to witness Evelyn making a mess of the kitchen, she knew there was nothing to find in there, but in here she saw the opportunity to have a good look herself as she tidied the room.

Rue gave a quick nod to Evelyn, who strode past her, shouting her intention to Francesca as she went. Rue entered the large drawing room

344

and shut the door quietly behind her, sealing her off from the rest of her destructive family.

With a heavy sigh, she surveyed the mess. Absolute. Every book, every ornament, was off every shelf and thrown to the floor. She stooped to pick up an ornament that had been broken in Evelyn's search. Small, white, and smooth, luckily it had only broken in half. She placed the broken edges back together to form faceless figures, a mother and child. Rue shook her head as she ran her hands over the ornament with a frown.

The doorbell rang. Three loud chimes, and Rue flinched. She carefully put the pieces on the carpet and ran to the front door, flinging it open.

'Who is it?' Francesca said, coming to the study door. 'If it's Charley, tell her to get in here.'

Rue frowned and looked outside and down the driveway.

'No-one.' She said.

'No-one?' Francesca cocked her lip. 'Again?'

She shook her head and Francesca disappeared back into the study with a roll of her eyes. Rue shut the door and went back to the drawing room, picking the broken ornament up and placing the pieces carefully back together.

Mother and child.

The sentiment hit, and a sadness welled in Rue as she thought how much it would probably have meant to Elizabeth. She thought of the letters, how Francesca had bribed her Aunt and finally taken Charley away. Not only that, but she had also read a heart breaking letter of Elizabeth's that had begged Francesca to let her see Charley. The first page of the letter had brought tears to Rue's eyes even at fifteen, but the second had stopped them before they fell.

This page had been defaced, Rue knew the writing, it was Francesca's. Red pen had been slashed through Elizabeth's neat writing, and foul words had been scrawled with thick hard strokes. It had been written in anger. The emotion of both sisters, so vastly different, literally pulled from the page.

It had been this page Rue had been reading when Francesca found her, and Rue knew why she had been so angry. She had seen the real Francesca. Knew her plan. She didn't understand it then, she loved her mother as any child did, but as she grew up and the real person revealed more of herself through her actions and control, Rue had been more and more convinced that Evelyn was wrong.

Elizabeth Kane wasn't the witch at all.

Francesca Costin wasn't a witch either, and nor could she be called a monster. Francesca was something far, far worse.

Rue looked back down to the ornament in her hands.

I'm so sorry for what she did to you, Aunt Elizabeth.

The anger Rue had felt in the service station surged again as she placed the ornament pieces into the pocket of her dungarees. This one she would fix, the rest she would tidy. Out of respect.

One way or another, a storm was brewing, Rue could feel it forming inside her chest. She'd had enough. There would be no more poor, browbeaten Rue.

It was time Francesca Costin paid her dues.

Chapter Sixty-Four

Charley knew she had run the wrong way as she sprinted along the side of the south wall. There may have been more cover, but she was trapped up here unless there was room to get around the back of the castle, or place to climb the cliffs from behind the broken bit of wall. Cursing her stupidity as she heard Axl huffing behind her, she flew around the wall.

The edge of the cliff caught her by surprise, mere feet beyond the wall, the ocean pounding below. Charley tried to stop, but her feet slipped from under her and she came to a halt inches from the edge, face to face with the drop as her heart hammered.

It was a straight drop. All the way down to the crashing sea below. There were no jutting edges, nothing to grab on to, certainly no way to climb down. She looked at the rest of the south wall, built right into the very edge of the cliff. There was no way out from here. The wall itself towered above her straight and solid.

I'm trapped!

Her mind whirled. There was only one option, and that was to run back past Axl. He may have the strength, but she was more agile. She could give him the slip, surely. There was just enough room at the side of the south wall if she hurried.

Scrambling away from the edge and to her feet she turned to run out of the small area as Axl rounded the bend. He slowed and grinned at her, panting heavily. He knew there was nowhere she could go. There was no room to run here, the cliff edge too near to skirt around him.

'You're making this easier, Charley.' He puffed.

Backing up to the wall now behind her, she placed her shaking hands onto the cold rough stone, felt it dig into her back, and wondered if it would be the last thing she ever really felt.

Trapped. She was completely trapped, between the very real devil and the deep, raging grey sea below. Her mind screamed and something inside clicked loose. Her breath came in ragged gulps of panic, and her heart banged in her chest.

No way out, Charley. THERE'S NO WAY OUT!
 She watched in horrified slow motion as Axl ran the few paces between them with a guttural roar.

Chapter Sixty-Five

The pile of books Rue had balanced on the back of the settee slipped and fell with a bang. She grimaced and froze, not wanting to draw attention to herself. She was enjoying being on her own, putting her Aunt's things back where they should be. It was far preferable to being with any of the others right now.

Opening the door gently, she poked her head out but everyone was still busy with their own searches. There were bangs and scrapes from upstairs, in the kitchen, and across the hall where the real danger was in the study.

Taking the opportunity, Rue checked outside the front door again and relayed the news to the others loudly.

No-one replied.

Satisfied that they were all busy, she went back into the drawing room and shut the door.

She picked up the books that had scattered across the settee, placing them directly onto a shelf, before going back for the ones that had fallen on the floor. She got all except two, which had fallen behind the large sofa. She would need to move it to get those back, which she would do, she was in no rush to leave.

She pulled on the arm of the large chair, but it wouldn't budge. Dropping to the floor, she ran a hand around the bottom of the sofa where she found the problem. The plush carpet was doing all it could to hold on to the feet of the chair. There was a large indent where the foot sat, the carpet fibres rising around it stiffly.

Blimey, this can't have been moved for years.

Trying a different tactic, she stood and placed her backside against the arm and pushed backward. The chair moved slightly but fell straight back into position as she took her weight off the arm. Annoyed, she pulled with her hands, crouching backwards to ensure all of her weight was behind her, and then she turned and pushed backwards at it again. All with the same result. The chair moving millimetres before falling back into place.

She stood, breathing heavily, hands on her hips.

Leave the books?

And be beaten by a damn chair, the way you've been beaten by everything else in your stupid life?

The surge of anger came back, and inspiration struck. She forced herself into the small space at the back, pushing her body between the chair and the wall. The chair gave a little, as it had from the side, but now she had leverage. She pushed against the wall, ignoring the pain in her ribs from the back of the chair. The chair tipped forward, back legs rising off the floor. When she could push no more, she let it back down with a grunt of frustration.

She thought she had made no difference, but now the chair was further from the wall, she was standing in the gap quite comfortably. Looking down to her right, she could see the indent of the foot in the flattened carpet. The chair was now fully down, so if the back foot was out then so must be the front. Spirits lifting, she tried again and found the chair scooted forward. It was still hard, but not as it had been, and with another shove she moved it out further.

The triumph she felt at defeating the chair was euphoric and she gave a little giggle of delight.

See, Rue, you're not as weak as you thought!

She leaned down to get the books and came across some other things which had fallen. Frowning, she picked them up and put them onto the seat. Papers. And a small laptop.

There was no way that Evelyn had moved the chair, there were no marks in the carpet that said so, which meant that these were things Evelyn hadn't found. She glanced at the door quietly, listening to the others as her heart thumped.

She put the books on the shelf out of the way and sat on the settee, one of the large cushions placed ready to pull over the things she had found if anyone came in while she was investigating.

The laptop she now recognised as Charley's. She set it aside and picked up the papers, which turned out to be one large sheet made of a few smaller ones stuck together. The writing was Charley's, although there was someone else's hand she didn't recognise on there too, and the paper was a mess, it had scribbles and marks, and random words all over it.

Intrigued, and instinctively aware that this was something the others shouldn't see yet, she pulled the chart open and tried to make sense of the information. Dates, times, people, symptoms, and food.

Why would Charley do this? What was it all about?

The words scribbled all over the paper seemed to be various types of fruit. She ran her hand over them - blueberries, blackcurrant, elderberry.

Berries? What is Charley up to?

At the top of the page in red pen and circled across the top entries of the chart was Belladonna. Rue had seen that word written in the cellar.

Belladonna. Another berry?

Rue frowned and shifted her weight to lay the paper out more fully. At her side something shifted down into the fold of the chair, and looking down, she found a small leather-bound book. With a last look over the chart, She folded it and opened the book.

The emotional writing of the letter she had read at fifteen years old, seared into her memory, matched the writing on the page. This was Aunt Elizabeth's book. She flicked through the pages carefully, not daring to read it and take her mind off what the others were doing just outside the door, but she skimmed her eyes over the first few pages. At a glance it seemed to be a diary Elizabeth had kept of her moods, psychotic episodes, and thoughts. Not only that but food, drink, times, names...

Hang on, is this what Charley has condensed into a chart?

Rue closed the book, heart racing. Her breath coming faster as she felt precariously balanced just on the cusp of something big. Something Charley had been searching for.

Where did Charley get the diary? What prompted her to do the chart? What is going on here?

Whatever it was, Rue got the impression that this was vitally important. She carefully placed the folded chart into the book and put it back behind the chair where she could get to it but it wouldn't be seen. Then she pushed the chair with relative ease back into its carpeted slots.

Only the small laptop remained. She could have hidden it with the book for now, but Rue had an almost insatiable urge to see what was on it. The machine had been with the chart and diary, which surely meant that Charley had been working amongst the three. If the others came in now, they wouldn't be interested in Charley's laptop, she only used it for work, but maybe this would hold the connection she was looking for.

The screen came to life instantly when she opened the lid, and the battery icon flashed in the corner. The screensaver, a panoramic shot of ocean with white beaches, filled the screen. Rue pressed the spacebar and the prompt for a password appeared. She cursed under her breath, there was precious little time for guessing passwords now.

The banging from across the hall escalated, and she heard Francesca curse.

Rue closed her eyes. The mess the study and the rest of the house would be in when they had finished their search was unthinkable. So many of Aunt Elizabeth's things would be broken. So many of *Charley's* things would be broken. She was the rightful owner of anything that was Elizabeth Kane's surely.

Come on Rue, Concentrate. Think. You know the password.

Her eyes flew open as she realised she did. Or had done, anyway. She sat back in the chair, mind whirring, fingers poised over the keys.

Think, Rue. The old laptop. Charley gave you her old laptop when she brought this one, she gave you the password and told you to change it so they weren't the same. You wrote it down, remember?

Rue wrinkled her nose in frustration. She may have written it down, but the trouble was since that day, Rue hadn't been able to use the machine. Francesca had found it at the house and had seen fit to smash it and file it in the bin, cutting off ties to anyone she could contact for help Rue supposed. She hadn't thought of it since then. Hadn't even told Charley.

What was it?

She flung herself forward, staring at the sea scene hard, as though she could conjure the word from the very screen. Almost on cue, it suddenly came, surging forward like a wave.

Ocean, of course! It had been Ocean and a series of numbers. Ocean... 153... no 4, 154... 96? 15496! That's it!

Rue typed the password quickly, blinking when the screen remained locked.

She tried to recall the scene of Charley sitting with her, writing the password down. She tried a few other number combinations, but nothing sat right.

It was 15496, I'm sure. She must have changed it.

Rue sat back with a sigh, and then she slapped a hand to her head.

The colon! There was a semi-colon in the middle!

She tried the password again and the screen sprang to life just as the door to the drawing room flew open.

Chapter Sixty-Six

Rue sprang to her feet, slamming the lid and throwing the laptop onto the chair behind her. Francesca narrowed her eyes as she stalked into the room and shut the door quietly behind her.

'What are we up to Rue, dear?'

Rue swallowed hard as she shrunk back, her calves hitting the settee behind her.

'Nothing.'

'Nothing? You should be up to something, I asked you to keep a watch out for Charley arriving back didn't I? That at least should have been your answer.' She gestured to the chair, 'What's that?'

'Just Charley's laptop...'

Rue trailed off as Francesca pushed her aside and grabbed it, prising open the lid. Rue held her breath, lips pursed. Francesca frowned and then turned her hard eyes back to Rue, turning the screen and holding it aloft in front of her.

The password box sat across the centre, the panoramic beach scene behind it. Francesca raised her eyebrows.

'Password?'

Blood thumped in Rue's ears.

'I don't know.' She whispered as she looked down, her fingers found and pulled a brown thread that had come loose from her cardigan.

The smack caught Rue off guard, the palm of her mother's hand catching her under the chin and snapping her head back. She staggered at the force of the blow, catching a foot on the settee and falling onto

354

the arm of the chair. Her chin began to burn where Francesca's hand had connected. She brought her own shaking hand to the spot as she looked up to meet Francesca's gaze. She stood with the laptop at her chest, a look of pure contempt skewing her features.

'I don't know what happened to you, Rue, the bad seed. Always awkward, always having to make things hard, always making my life harder. And now, now you're going to start lying to me as well. I saw you, sitting on the chair with the laptop, you hadn't just picked it up Rue, you were looking at the screen, so what is the password?'

Rue said nothing, the brown thread snapped free under her grasp as her heart thumped in her ears. She hadn't seen what was on the machine and she didn't want to incriminate Charley, or compromise what she had found if there was anything on it. The laptop had been with the book and the chart for a reason, she was sure. She couldn't tell Francesca, she had to stay strong.

A swift kick to Rue's ankles caused her to cry out with pain, but she didn't look up, or meet Francesca's eyes. She did, however, when Francesca grabbed a handful of hair, twisting it in her vice like grip and forcing her to meet her gaze.

'Password.'

Francesca growled the word into her face and Rue's shaking hands flew up to her head where the pain was bringing tears to her eyes.

'I don't know,' She whispered as tears started to run down her face, but her resolution was fading. She hadn't wanted to cry, but the pain from her jaw, ankles and hair was just too much. Francesca yanked harder, forcing Rue's head right back. She put her face inches from Rue's, bending over the top of her, and Rue could smell the staleness of her breath as she spoke.

'Keep going if you like, but if I have to ask you again, you'll get what you had last time you defied me. You thought I'd broken your nose, remember?' She paused with a smile. 'Well, this time maybe I'll go ahead and do just that. I will punch you, not just once like last time, but over and over and over, because you *know* damn well how important it is for me to get hold of what I need. I could go to jail, Rue. *Jail*. I won't let that happen over some insolent little slut with an attitude. Tell me the password.' She hissed.

Rue let out a sob as the door to the drawing room opened. Kate was quick and smart, but Francesca was quicker. She pulled Rue to her chest, immediately putting on the theatrics as she pressed a kiss into her hair, and stroked a hand up her back, murmuring quietly and gently.

'It will be okay, Rue, I promise. We'll find it, don't worry yourself.'

Kate entered the room and placed a hand onto Francesca's arm.

'Nothing in the bedroom, I've turned it almost upside down. What's the matter with Rue?'

Francesca pulled Rue closer, hard grip on the back of her neck filling her mouth with knitted jumper so that she couldn't have spoken if she had wanted to. She didn't want to. Right now, she was struggling just to breathe.

'She's fine, she's just a little upset that we can't find the envelope and that I might get into trouble. I've not found anything in the study either and Evelyn is going through the kitchen. Listen Kate, put the kettle on, we could all do with a break. Give us a couple of minutes here, then we'll regroup and see where we go next.'

Kate nodded and left with a stroke of Rue's hair, the pressure of her touch hurt the already sore scalp from her mother's pull. She shut the door behind her.

At the click Francesca grasped Rue's hair again.

'Do I need to repeat myself,' she hissed.

Rue tried to shake her head as she gasped for breath, but the pain on her scalp was too much.

'N... No,' she whispered.

'Good. Password.'

The hold released on Rue's hair, and her hands immediately went to the painful spot, as Francesca threw the machine at her. With some phenomenal luck, it bounced off her thigh and landed lightly on the settee. Rue sat down next to it, opened it up and put the password into the machine. The screen changed, and a web page appeared.

'Belladonna; Deadly Nightshade has a poisonous past.'

Underneath was a large photo of a bush, with a closeup of the berries and flowers down in the lower corner of the picture. Rue's heart sank. She felt like crying as Francesca whipped the machine away and looked for herself.

Did Charley think someone had poisoned Aunt Elizabeth? If so, a look at Francesca's face told her she also knew of this poison. Her face had dropped, all colour drained from her cheeks.

'How did she... Why was she looking at this?' She spat, as though Rue had been here all along and party to what Charley had been up to.

Rue shook her head, expecting a blow. When one didn't come, she looked up to find her mother still staring at the screen. Finally, she shoved the screen back to Rue.

'Delete it. Now.'

Rue's heart flew up into her mouth. She didn't want to delete it. It was Charley's search, and obviously Francesca had been rattled by it. Just what that meant Rue couldn't quite piece together at the moment. Still, with all the will in the world she didn't want a punch to the face, so she scrolled to the search history and cleared everything that came up. Francesca checked the internet and came up with the home screen, which was all she knew how to do. Satisfied Rue had taken the page down, she pushed the machine back to Rue and stalked out of the room, looking for all the world like she had seen a ghost.

Rue barely had time to draw breath before she was back, taking her by surprise as the full force of Francesca's fist connected squarely with her jaw, which clicked loudly.

There was a moment of dreamlike quality *-Did that really happen?-* Before the pain rocketed around her head and face, and Rue slumped shell-shocked on the settee, hands holding the place her mother's fist had connected.

Not the nose, though. Thank god, not the nose again. Small mercies.

When she mustered up courage to look to the doorway, Francesca was already gone.

Chapter Sixty-Seven

As Rue was busy getting a thump to the jaw, Axl was half-heartedly lunging at Charley, who stood with her back against the castle wall, horror etched on her face. There was nowhere to go, no way to get around him, but as he rushed toward her, arms outstretched, he almost wished there was. Right at the point where he had an almost fool proof opportunity for an accident, Axl wobbled.

This was no accident, it was murder. *Murder.* Even if he could forgive himself, he was absolutely certain Elizabeth would never forgive him. Charley was blood.

Oblivious to his change of heart, momentum and driving wind propelled Axl forward and he grabbed her arms crushing them against the back wall. Charley screamed and struggled under his grip as his mind floundered.

What do I do, Elizabeth? Tell me, what can I do?

If she was out there she gave no reply, but as he looked into Charley's terrified, defiant eyes, it was Elizabeth he saw staring back at him. The same defiant look, same sharp, clear oval eyes. Her eyes.

But his eyes too.

Theo's eyes.

That green belonged to him. Axl blinked and faltered, shaking his head, trying to clear his thoughts. Charley took control of his hesitation immediately.

'What's the matter?' she said, disgust amongst the fear on her features 'Lost your nerve? Can't handle it on your own? Such a big tough man aren't you, Axl. Obviously, Nell was the brains behind the poisoning, eh? Is she the one with the nerve, or did you think you could just pretend it was nothing to do with you? Plead ignorance with

358

yourself. After all, you weren't the one doing the actual *feeding* now, were you?'

'What?'

'What?' she mimicked, 'I *said* is it too hard to kill without a sidekick?'

'I have no idea what you're talking-'

'You admitted it,' She screeched, face inches from his as the wind roared, no shelter here on the cliff edge, 'You as good as told me the both of you poisoned her.'

Axl flinched, aware that he was loosening his hold as he reeled from the accusations. Charley's angry face contorted in front of him, but it was as though she were speaking Chinese, he couldn't make head nor tail of what she was saying, or what the heck Nell had to do with it.

'Poisoned who?' He yelled, wind whipping the words from his mouth.

Catching him off guard Charley pressed her hands to his chest and pushed hard. He staggered backward, heart thumping as he fought to regain his balance, knowing he must be close to the edge but not daring to take his eyes from Charley.

'Elizabeth, who the hell do you think? You murdering bastard.'

'Elizabeth?' He stuttered, trying to focus. 'No-one poisoned Elizabeth, Charley, she was ill.'

Charley spat a laugh.

'Don't deny it, Axl, she knew it herself. She wrote it all down in a diary, almost daily over the last eighteen months. She recorded everything. Everything. It's all in a book, in black and white, in her hand. Even the time she overheard Nell making up her visits to the hospital and the test results after she had taken her to the beach. She linked her confusion and illness to things she ate, things that all have a link to the food she loved so much. Elderberry.'

Charley came forward, forcing him to step back, gaining momentum, and the upper hand, as he struggled to process her words. He wondered where the cliff edge was, wondered, ironically, if she would force him over. Panic tumbled into his already muddled thoughts.

Charley pulled wayward strands of hair from her mouth and the wind forced them back. She continued her assault regardless.

'It wasn't elderberry, though, was it, Axl? You know damn well that it wasn't because you picked the berries for her. You picked them from her own garden.'

'What?... Yes, Elderberry,' he managed to mumble, confused. She huffed a breath throwing up her hands and he took the opportunity to shuffle away from the edge.

'No, not Elderberry!' she screamed, fists now balled at her sides, 'When are you going to give this up? It was Belladonna, Axl. Deadly nightshade. I know it, and you know it. You picked the Belladonna berries in replacement of the Elderberry and gave them to Nell to cook for her. A little at a time, just enough to cause confusion, upset and hallucinations. Just enough to make her think she was going mad. Enough to convince everyone else that her dementia was real. Well, you managed it, both of you. You had everyone convinced. Everyone except Elizabeth herself. If she hadn't been sound enough of mind to write it all down, you would have got away with it, wouldn't you. The perfect murder.'

Axl's heart drummed behind his ribs as cold wind whipped the back of his ears. Where had she got this from? And was it the truth? It was obvious why Charley thought it may have been him and Nell, but what really upset him was that Elizabeth may have believed that too.

A small stitch pain dug behind his rib, the breath sucked from his lungs. He put a hand to his chest.

'You have nothing to say?'

Charley glared. Her bottom lip quivered with cold, but her face was set and hard. Defiant. Certain. Axl shook his head.

'No Charley, you have it all wrong. Elizabeth had Belladonna in the garden for her remedies. I had no idea that she thought this. No idea that she may not have dementia. It pained me to watch her go through it. I would never...'

The ache grew in his chest, and he took small breaths, closing his eyes. When he opened them, Charley was eyeing him with uncertainty, arms crossed tightly across her chest.

'She believed it Axl, she knew it. If it wasn't you, what's your alibi? Because it sure makes sense to me. Theo also said that you had been up to something. Hell, you can tell me you're not that person all you like but you brought me here, you alone, and you did that to kill me. An Accident.' She stepped forward, jabbing a finger at him, '*You* said that. And if you did that, then you are most certainly capable of killing off an old lady.'

Axl rubbed a hand over his eyes.

'Charley, I didn't...' he swallowed, unsure what to say because she was right. He had seen no other way. Frustration filled his eyes with hot tears.

Christ, Axl what were you thinking? Did you honestly think you could kill Charley, Elizabeth's one big dream and wish?

'I didn't know what to do.' He said. 'I still don't. I don't know what to say.'

Tell her the truth?

'Just admit it and do your time Axl,' Charley said, 'because that would be the right thing to do, not bring me here and add to the body count. What did I ever do to you? -'

Before he could change his mind Axl grabbed her arm cutting her off. Charley immediately snatched it from his grasp dodging out of his reach. He nodded in acceptance, regret washing over him as he understood that even if everything could be worked out now any relationship was now over before it had begun. He held his hands up signalling that he wasn't interested in hurting her further, she eyed him warily.

'Okay, listen,' he said, 'Yes I am hiding something, of course I am. And if Elizabeth really wrote all of this I understand what you think you believe, but it's just not true, Charley. I'll tell you the truth, I could never have hurt Elizabeth. I... I loved her.'

There was a moment when only the wind seemed present. Continuing to push and pull as though nothing had happened as they each eyed the other. And then Charley broke the spell, curling one side of her mouth she looked away, shaking her head. Axl faltered, he had expected shock, even anger, but he hadn't expected disbelief.

'Charley, please!' He said, fumbling for any way to make her believe. 'It's the truth, I loved her, and she loved me. We were in love, we just couldn't be together, it wasn't right. Frank was ill when we became close, and although the illness changed him, she loved him just the same. But he could no longer satisfy her as a woman, and certainly never provide her with a child.'

Charley stared at him with an angry frown. He implored her to fill in the blanks herself, but it seemed she wasn't going to give him an easy way out.

'Charley, you are Elizabeth's child and she loved you like nothing else, but she couldn't keep you. To keep you would mean admitting her infidelity, she couldn't proclaim you to be Frank's. He was well aware that you couldn't be, as were most of the folks in the village. To have the secret ever come out would be to ruin her life, integrity, and her name. Mine too of course, but for her sake, and yours, you had to be passed off as Francesca's child.'

Charley shook her head, disdain and disgust crossing her features.

'I can't believe you would be sick enough to use this-'

'Charley, please.' Axl's hands came into prayer before him as he cut her off. 'I know it's a lot to take in, but the reason I brought you here is, well... I knew you were hunting for information, and when Theo told me you'd found things, I panicked. This is one secret we need to keep Charley. Please. For Elizabeth. For your mother, who loved you so very much ... And for your dad, who also had no choice but to give you up.'

He pleaded with Charley, his entire body shaking with anticipation. If she didn't agree, then what other option would there be other than to follow through with his plan? And that suddenly seemed ludicrous. He couldn't kill his own long-lost daughter, any more than he could kill Theo. She was his, and she was the only part of Elizabeth that remained. The only part of their secret life together and their love for each other.

'Charley?'

His heart ached, and his voice cracked with emotion. He was almost at breaking point when she finally spoke.

'LIAR!' She screamed and before he had chance to react, she lunged to the right.

Surprised, he stepped toward her hands out. His only aim was to catch her, to calm her and ensure her it was the truth. But as he did, she dodged further out of his reach, forced to the edge of the cliff, and then she was over.

Axl's heart stopped, and the breath caught in his throat as he tried to reach her too late. Her arms flailed as her feet hit air, and then she was gone, down past the cliffs into the darkness of the pounding sea below.

'Charley!' he screamed.

An inhuman sound left his throat as he fell to his knees, the wind whistling past him as she plummeted into the water. Staring at the swollen inky blackness, he roared her name into the wind again and again as though he could use it to turn back time. His hands clutched at his head as he rocked back on his heels and howled.

Just one more chance. There had to be just one more chance to do things over. With Elizabeth, who thought she had been poisoned, and with his only daughter, who had just plummeted over a cliff edge into freezing ocean.

Both now irrecoverably lost.

Chapter Sixty-Eight

'She's just taking some time out, she's a little upset,' Francesca said from the kitchen.

Appalled at the lie, Rue grabbed the laptop and forced her shaking limbs behind the chair to collect the little book and chart. With the three gathered in her arms, she peered around the drawing-room door into the hall, heart thudding in her ears.

Francesca's form passed across the open kitchen door and Rue took her chance, crossing to the stairs and making her way quickly to the first floor, her ascent almost silent thanks to the thick carpet under foot.

She saw the bathroom almost dead ahead from the top of the stairs. The perfect place to take the time she needed in private. Heart thumping, and expecting to be caught at any moment, she entered and locked the door behind her, pressing her back to it. She held Charley's things tight to her chest and listened, breathing hard. Francesca was starting to rant downstairs, but Rue heard no-one call for her.

Thank God.

Gulping in a breath of relief, she closed her eyes and swallowed hard, before lowering herself to the cold tile floor. She placed the book and chart beside her, and opened the laptop, ignoring the throbbing ache in her jaw and neck. She had been dealt worse and had survived worse at the hands of her mother.

In the kitchen downstairs Francesca's voice, raised and shrill, was punctuated by soothing undertones of Evelyn and Kate telling her it would be okay, she would be absolutely fine, there was no need to worry.

Oh, I wouldn't be too sure about that.

Fingers trembling, Rue typed the name of the web page that she had memorised into the search engine, reloading the page Charley had left on the screen. The one Francesca had been so rattled by. Rattled enough to vent her frustration at Rue's jaw for no reason, which was extreme - even for her.

Extreme is an understatement. Apart from my nose, she's never punched me. I did as she asked down there. That might get me a pinch, but never more.

So what is going on here? What did Francesca see?

Rue skimmed over the information, reading right to the end of the article before she understood. Her mouth dropped open with a gasp as she grabbed the chart and looked at the word scrawled in red at the top.

Belladonna. This is the same plant.

Frowning, Rue looked back to the screen. She re-read the article, taking note of the poisonous properties of the plant, as her heart began to thud. Looking more closely at what Charley had scrawled over the chart, it was obvious that she was trying to attribute a food source to the meals Elizabeth had eaten. If Belladonna was that source, then she would certainly have been poisoned. Rue shuddered.

Poisoned? But she had dementia. Why poison her? How can that be right? What do you think happened, Charley? And why?

Remembering the book, Rue folded the chart and picked up the small leather-bound diary. Aware that she may be short on time, she read the first couple of pages, skimmed through to the middle and read a few more there. She was painfully aware that the others could discover her gone at any time, and in here there was nowhere to hide the evidence - if that's what it was.

Keeping an ear on the commotion downstairs, she read through snippets of her Aunt's days. Meals, conversations Elizabeth had with her nurse, and graphic descriptions of her feelings, thoughts, and visions, through her confusion and hallucinations. The undertones of the writing seemed to lead somewhere, but Rue still had no motive as to why Charley would think this was anything other than a diary.

She licked her dry lips and then cursed herself as the ache in her jaw started up in earnest. She sighed.

Come on Rue, there must be something that Charley hit on for her to be searching for information.

Focus back on the diary, she turned the page and came across an entry that almost made her heart stop. Charley wouldn't have picked up on this blinder, but it sure hit a nerve with Rue.

A very raw nerve.

Elizabeth had overheard a conversation. Between Nell, who Rue knew was the cook from earlier pages, and Glen, who was her private nurse. Nell had told Glen of a visit to the hospital. A visit Elizabeth wrote she had never made. Furthermore, Elizabeth overheard Nell giving Glen results of tests she swore she never had. Elizabeth had written it all down, adding her insight and clarity to a day she had actually spent at the beach.

A cold dread crept up Rue's spine as pieces of a macabre puzzle started to slot together neatly her mind. She could have passed this off as an old lady's dementia inspired ramblings, but the description hit a nerve.

It appeared to run in the family.

Made up doctor visits, and fake test results ruled Rue's life. Francesca researched and made up everything to explain the state she kept her in, attributing it to a disease Rue didn't have, and now it seemed Elizabeth had the same problem over the last couple of years too. Rue's breath caught in her throat.

Surely this is no coincidence?

The book shook in her hands, knocking against her knees. Not only would it be a very large coincidence, but Elizabeth's fate could well be hers one day too. If Francesca decided that Rue was too much trouble, she could pop her off quite easily without an issue. Starve her until she died, and blame anorexia, or bulimia. It would be an undiagnosed catastrophe, and she could see her mother's weeping face as she told everyone how the system had let her poor ill daughter down.

Could she do that? Would she?

Do you really doubt it?

No. Rue had no doubt that Francesca was perfectly capable. She would have no issue at all.

And to poison Aunt Elizabeth?

After what she had found as a child, and what she had experienced at her mother's hands ever since, Rue knew this approach was one at which Francesca was adept. In fact, this was remarkably similar to her own story.

Too similar.

But Francesca was down in Harrogate the whole time. She had an opportunity to come up here. She chose not to. And yet the whole thing screams her style. And where does Nell fit into this, why would she lie to the nurse?

Thoughts muddled in Rue's head. She couldn't piece together the whole picture, but if this poisoning had taken place, she knew exactly who was behind it. She knew with the confidence that a spider knew dinner had landed in its web.

Heart thudding wildly, Rue sat back against the door, trying to catch her breath as her head spun with this new information. Elizabeth's diary had provided the information. Charley had put it together. Rue knew that she most certainly had a capable suspect, and a very clear motive.

Which suddenly made Francesca Costin dangerous. Very dangerous indeed.

'Shit,' she whispered, and closed her eyes.

Chapter Sixty-Nine

The water hit Charley like knives. Sharp, unrelenting cold seeping painfully into every pore. Water bubbled past her ears and then she broke the surface, gasping for air, while her chest simultaneously felt so constricted that she was sure nothing would fit in her lungs.

She bobbed on the swell, dragging in breath after painful breath as the tide jostled her back to the island's cliffs.

The cliffs.

Her mind clicked into gear.

Move, Charley, you'll be as wrecked as the boat!

The voice in her head, clear and sharp, snapped her out of shock. She finally began to move her arms and legs, swimming away from the cliff edge, pulling hard, trying to pump some warmth into her body.

It was dangerous to be in the water in these temperatures; she knew that, but she had seen no other option. The gap had been too small to get around Axl, and she had a feeling his little 'accident' would have involved her leaving the edge of the cliff anyway. So, she had jumped rather than be pushed. At least that way she could control her leap from the edge, pushing herself as far away from the cliff face as she could. She'd had no idea if there was any part of the cliff waiting to snag her lower down, or if there were any rocks lying just under the surface of the sea. She supposed if there had been, she would have been dead by now.

But she wasn't dead, and that left her two priorities. Get away from the cliff and get to somewhere she could get out of the water. Vital warmth was being sucked from her body with terrifying speed, and Charley knew it would be mere minutes before she lost body and brain function.

A large swell of icy water loomed and pushed, forcing her back toward the cliff, even as she moved forward. She worked harder, swimming against the tide, pulling her arms and kicking her legs hard. Her strokes, initially strong and sure, fast became weaker as she battled the large waves, and fatigue set in.

An icy cold penetrated her limbs, and though Charley knew she wasn't getting far, she fought to keep moving. Knowing it was useless. She knew the sea. Knew how ruthless the ocean could be. Her body couldn't generate enough warmth to stop it from shutting down in here.

No! It has to. There has to be a way!

Adrenaline pushed Charley forward again, strong strokes, until her arms and legs felt like lead. She stopped, looking back to the cliff face.

Too close, Charley, you're still too close.

She was, but she couldn't find the strength to turn and battle the waves again. It was too much. Her arms moved weakly, treading water, as she bobbed and swayed on the swell.

I'm too tired. It's too cold.

The island rocked, lulled by the waves before her, and Charley felt her vision start to glaze over as her mind sludged through random thoughts. She shook her head, trying to focus, but finding it impossibly difficult.

By choosing to jump, I think you've done Axl a favour, Charley. You can't survive this, you'll shut down like a wind-up doll. And there's no key to this doll. No second chances. This is how it ends. You're going to die tonight.

*You're actually going to **die.***

Charley's frozen heart jolted and started to pump. Another surge of adrenaline turned her, and she pulled into the tide again, frozen limbs screaming with pain. As the swell dipped, there was a mirage on the crest of a wave close by. A wooden mirage with a small light headed straight toward her.

There's a boat! Oh God, there's a boat! I'm going to be okay.

Renewed hope surged through Charley. She waved a laden hand, trying to shout, but her words were muddled, her brain not able to get them from her head to her mouth. She tried to scream, anything to make some noise, but barely forced a whisper before a crested wave swamped her. Swallowing a mouthful of salty water, the outside world disappeared. Her eyes stung with salt, and the world bubbled around her, muffled and quiet as the water closed over her ears. She broke the surface coughing, her blurry vision catching the little boat's light in the dusk, before the next icy wave topped her head.

Legs kicking feebly, Charley's clothes felt heavy, laden with rocks that pulled her under as her muscles grew stiff with fatigue. She pulled back up to the surface and gasped frigid air with lungs that screamed in pain.

The boat was too far. She was too far.

It had been a mistake to jump. She had survived, but only minutes longer than if she had hit the rocks and died instantly. Charley almost wished she had. It would have preferable to the slow and painful death she was about to endure. Everything felt too slow, too much effort, too painful. Even her thoughts had slowed and gone fuzzy. At some point she became aware that she had stopped moving and was bobbing thoughtless, helplessly on the water. She was caught in quicksand, the turbulence of the water sucked at her legs, tugging her tired body down.

Just a little rest. I just need...

Charley closed her eyes, and let the tiredness wash over her, as the next wave rushed over her head, dragging her under.

Chapter Seventy

Downstairs in the kitchen Francesca was brewing a storm the like of which Rue had never witnessed, screeching and wailing as Evelyn and Kate trying to calm her. Their own yells and squeals adding to Francesca's shouts, as bang after furious bang came from below. In the bathroom Rue sat with her hands over her ears, feeling her heart thump furiously between them.

Francesca had never let herself go this far in front of Kate and Evelyn, and if she was getting this lapse with them around, she was obviously running scared. Knowing the implications of what she had just pieced together, Rue had a horrible feeling she knew the reason why, and she didn't like to think what her fate would be later if they didn't find that damn envelope.

She sat up with a jolt, diary still in her hand.

That's it! That's the only way. The only thing to save me now. I have to find the envelope, even if it holds damning evidence. We can deal with the rest when Charley gets here, as long as I hide the book and laptop. I just hope that's enough.

Rue whispered an apology to Charley, deciding then and there that if she found the envelope she would hand it straight to Francesca, get back on her good side. The hell with trying to stand up to her, it would never work. She didn't know what she had been thinking.

So, what's the next move?

Rue picked up the laptop, folding the chart inside the book, as Francesca's voice roared from the kitchen below.

'You don't understand Evelyn, you never did, those letters will be the end of me, I may as well shoot myself right now. I need them! Now!'

Someone spoke. There was a bang and Evelyn screeched.

'Oh, they're here all right, Nell would have told me if she found them. So, where the hell are they?'

There was another crash from below. Rue listened, standing stock still with fear, as Kate tried to sooth her, but Francesca was too far gone.

'Oh, shut the hell up, both of you. Nell doesn't matter. I need this house turning over before Charley gets back. I want those letters in my hand, or all of you will get it. All of you! What the hell is Rue doing, anyway?'

Rue's stomach turned over so fast she thought she may be sick. Trying to combat the tremors and sweat on her hands she pushed Charley's laptop, the book, and the chart awkwardly inside the cabinet on the wall. Shutting the mirrored door, she was instantly struck by the scared wild look in her own eyes. She swallowed hard.

Tearing her gaze away from the image she moved to the bathroom door. It took her a moment to grasp the small gold lock with her trembling hands, and then she turned it with a click. *What's the plan, Rue!* Her head screamed as the door unlocked.

Go down. I have to go down and help, keep them from this bathroom before Charley's things are found.

At the thought of going downstairs a small whimper escaped her lips and the urge to cry was overwhelming. She pulled in deep breaths, her hand still on the lock as she checked herself.

Stupid Rue, stupid. Breathe. Calm down or you're going to trip Charley up.

Rue pulled the handle and opened the door onto the landing, just as the doorbell rang and the kitchen door opened downstairs. There was shuffling in the hallway. The back of Francesca appeared at the foot of the stairs, moving toward the front door.

Rue's stomach somersaulted at the sight of her mother and with a knee-jerk reaction and another whimper she quickly pushed the door shut and locked it again. Fear now completely in control, she got Charley's things out of the cabinet and climbed into the bath, pressing herself behind the shower curtain, the laptop and book hugged to her chest.

The front door banged shut, and then Francesca's furious voice roared up from the stairs.

'Rue? Rue! Where the hell are you? Are you up there? Get downstairs, we need to re-group. I said NOW you insolent strip of shit!'

Chapter Seventy-One

Charley's body smacked something hard and cold. The waves jostled and pushed, bustling, bumping and pressing her against it, her back, her face, her chest alternately bumped and scraped.

Rock.

The word seemed to drag for minutes in her head.

If her body and mind hadn't been so numb, she may have felt pain. As it was, she felt nothing but the sensation. She bobbed in the water as the bustling went away, and then it was back, pushing against her ribs with a strange sound, like a cat slowly lapping milk.

There was another sound. A voice? From somewhere far away. And then pressure under her arms and around her chest. She felt her body lifting, slowly, heavily, up and out of the water. Water which felt warm compared to the frigid air she was now exposed to.

More voices. Hands holding her upright as she was sat on something solid, dry. She coughed up mouthfuls of salty water. A hand at her back, throat raw. A rustle, and something was wrapped around her, more hands rubbing her legs and arms, and more things wrapped around her, furry things, cosy things. She smiled as she finally pulled sweet cold air into her aching lungs. No effort needed to breathe now.

I'm dead. Nothing cosy in the sea. Nothing warm.

'Come on now, drink up.'

Did people talk in the afterlife?

She supposed they did.

There was a warmth at her mouth, and liquid touched her lips. She took some of the warm fluid into her mouth and swallowed. The heat seemed to travel from her mouth to her toes. She gulped it greedily, relishing the heat, as a hat was pulled over her head, and another blanket was added to her layers. Completely disorientated, Charley sat huddled, back propped against a wall, drinking liquid warmth from an invisible hand.

I have no idea what is going on, and I don't care. If this is heaven, it's perfect... apart from the pain.

The pain wrapped itself around her limbs as the feeling started to come back to her body. With the next lot of tea inside her, she finally felt alive enough to open her eyes.

She saw blurry blankets wrapped around her, the blurry wooden bottom of a boat. She blinked and saw her feet come into focus. She moved them and winced at the pain. She tugged the blankets further round her hearing an odd crinkle. She frowned, trying to place the noise. Still uncertain where she was or why.

'Foil blanket,' a voice said. 'It will keep the warmth in. Charley, you scared me to death. What the hell were you doing? You could have died! If Mr Thomas hadn't seen you jump, you'd be a gonner by now. It's a bloody good job we were so close.'

Charley blinked up at Theo, seeing him and the other man for the first time since being pulled into the small boat. A boat much the same as Belle's Beauty.

'You're certainly a very lucky girl.' The older man said. Grey hair and tanned wrinkled face orange in the lamplight. Mr Thomas, she presumed.

Looking back to Theo, she tried to process his questions, but they had come too fast. She shook her head, trying to clear her brain, which seemed to be unable to catch up and make sense of what was going on.

Theo sat next to her with a sigh and put an arm around her shoulders rubbing both of his hands up and down her arms hard.

'You're all right Charley, you're picking up fast, you'll be okay. I need you to think now, it's important. Where's dad? What happened?'

Dad?

She blinked, and then things slowly started to appear from the fog in her brain.

Dad. Theo's dad. Axl. The island. They had been on the island.

She swung her head around toward the island, her neck stiff.

'He's still on there,' She said, her voice low and croaky, 'He said there would be an accident and I jumped. I jumped so that he couldn't push me.'

Theo followed her gaze to the island, and then his head snapped back, eyebrows raised, incredulous.

'Push you?'

Charley nodded lightly, noting the amused disbelief in his eyes as her senses made a return.

'He said there would be an accident, that I had to be removed, and that you wouldn't be able to save me. We saw the boat, but he said you wouldn't get here in time.'

Theo took his arms away with a frown and shook his head, mouth in a firm line.

'No, Charley, he's not capable. I told you-'

'Yes, you did tell me. You also said he'd done something bad...'

Theo held a hand up for her to wait. He threw a look at Mr Thomas, who was at the wheel in the little hut. Theo shouted instructions to dock on the island so they could find Axl before they sailed back to the harbour. Mr Thomas gave a nod and started the boat, steering toward the broken wooden jetty on the island.

The Deja-vu was strong as the boat tipped and rocked alarmingly as it turned. Theo held onto Charley with one hand; his foot and the other hand supporting them both on the small wooden bench. When the worst of the turn was over, Theo turned back to Charley, his voice low.

'Yes, I know I said he'd done something bad, but it wasn't him, I got it wrong. I'm sorry if I scared you. I would like to know why the hell he took you and my boat over to the island though.'

Confusion fogged Charley's mind. She had just told him, hadn't she?

'To get rid of me, so I couldn't tell the world what he's done.'

Theo shook his head and pressed his lips together.

'No, Charley, you've got it wrong. He didn't poison Elizabeth. He wouldn't, I know that for a fact because he loved her.'

'That's what *he* says.' Charley said with a huff.

Theo frowned.

'You know? He told you?'

'Of course he told me. He was trying to throw me off the scent. He as good as admitted his guilt. Just before I jumped he changed the story. He said no-one knew there had been an affair, so how long have you known?'

'Not long, that was what I found out from these.'

He pulled an envelope from his pocket, full and bursting at the seams. Charley looked at him in puzzlement but made no move to come out of the small warmth that she had to take them. What difference would they possibly make now?

'What are they?' She said.

'Letters. Bribes. I thought that dad was bribing someone at first, I confronted him, but he cut me off and wouldn't answer his phone. When you messaged, I actually thought he may have done something, or at least had a part in something bad. I took a closer look on the way over here and I realised it wasn't his handwriting. Close, but not his. This was someone bribing him. Not just him, Elizabeth too... because they were having an affair. I haven't read them all obviously, but whoever wrote these mocks the fact that they have obviously said that they were in love at some point... but that's not all.'

Theo swallowed hard and glanced to Mr Thomas before looking back at her. Charley saw the worry in his eyes.

'Charley, these letters, they're sick. Whoever wrote them is sick. It's bad shit, really bad shit. What I don't understand is why this person had such leverage over dad and Elizabeth? What was it for?'

Charley stared at Theo as the altercation on the cliff top came back to her. She had called Axl a liar, but now these letters suggested otherwise? Axl had been serious and adamant, as was Theo now. She looked at him. He was so similar to herself. Not only his green eyes, but the dry humour. She had noticed it before. Thought it an amusing coincidence. A brother from another mother... but the father?

She blinked back confusion and frustration at what that meant, and somewhere in the background, but gaining speed, was anger at the fact that she still had no damn leads on the poisoning if this was the truth.

'I just don't get it.' Theo said, slapping the envelope back onto his knee. 'Any of it. Didn't he mention anything else? Anything at all?'

Charley swallowed the lump in her throat as Theo rubbed a hand through his hair with a sigh. He stood up, staring at the island which was looming close now. Mr Thomas slowed the boat as they neared.

'He said that no one could know. He said that it would break his world, that he would lose you and Belle-' Charley started, hauling herself up off the bench to stand next to him. She planted legs that felt like jelly onto the floor to keep herself upright in the swell and placed a hand on his arm. Support for both him and herself.

'But why?' Theo said, turning to look at her, 'I don't get it. I don't blame him for having an affair. I'm angry he went about it that way, behind mom's back. He should have just left her. They haven't got on for so long, they would probably both have been happy by now if he had just done the right thing, I just don't understand the big deal, people fall out of love all the time.'

Charley bit at her lip and stared at the floor as he sat back down, pulling her down next to him. He rubbed his face, head in his hands before dragging his fingers through his hair.

It was Axl's story to tell, but watching Theo suffer, Charley found it spilling out anyway.

'Your dad not only had an affair, Theo, he fathered another child.'

Theo's head snapped up to look at her, eyebrows so low they were almost pulled together into one.

'A child? He told you that?'

Charley nodded.

'Yes. There was a child born between him and Elizabeth. If what he said is true.'

'But Elizabeth couldn't have chil-' Theo looked at her, mouth dropping open as the penny dropped.

'But Elizabeth did have a child,' he finished, still staring at her.

Charley nodded. He blew out a breath and ran a hand through his messy dark curls.

'Shit, So you're...'

He broke off with a shake of his head, and Charley nodded again.

'That's what he said. I'm his. His and Elizabeth's.'

Theo stared at the island, looking thoroughly shell shocked. When he looked back to her, she held his gaze, hoping he wouldn't laugh her off the boat, or throw her off, but he just nodded lightly as he watched her, gathering his thoughts.

'What do you think, Charley?' He said finally.

Charley licked her salty lips and glanced to the island before looking back at him.

'I'm not sure. I mean, we do have the same colour eyes, and we do have the same humour. Maybe…' she said with a feeble shrug.

Theo sighed. Then he nodded and gave her a small smile, as he placed an arm firmly back around her shoulders, rubbing hard. Charley felt tears spring up out of nowhere and she swallowed them back down quickly.

'Okay. If this is the big secret, this is okay, right? It's okay. It's fine. Absolutely fine.' He mumbled to himself.

SHATTERED

Charley knew he was trying to make sense of what she had told him. It had shocked him as much as it had her. She sat quietly borrowing his warmth as she waited for him to continue, but they were out of time. They bobbed with the waves gently as Mr Thomas let off the throttle and the small boat bumped gently up to the sandy shore. 'The dock's gone, we'll have to pull it onto the sand,' Mr Thomas called over his shoulder. Theo nodded and rose. He hopped over the side of the boat into calf high water to untie one of the ropes. Charley got up unsteadily as Mr Thomas jumped out to untie another rope. She climbed slowly out of Theo's side, the frozen water hitting her calves as she caught a wave. Her breath caught, and she shuddered, moving quickly onto the sand as the men pulled the ropes together.
A bulky form caught her eye to the right. She turned her head toward it.

Belle's Beauty. Theo's boat. Oh god, I forgot the boat.

She closed her eyes, drawing in a long breath. She kept them closed until the scraping of the boat up onto the sand stopped, and she felt a presence beside her. She instinctively knew it was Theo, and without looking at him she already knew he had seen his beloved boat.

'Theo,' She started, opening her eyes to find she was right. 'The boat, it's-'

'How bad?' He whispered at her side, eyes not leaving the forlorn bulk being pulled back and forth with the tide.

She nodded and pursed her lips.

'Bad. It won't be leaving the island for a while. We crashed into the jetty.'
Charley turned to look at him as he lowered his head and ran a hand over his mouth. She put a hand on his arm lightly through the layers of cloth and foil around her.

'Let's find dad and get out of here.' He said, turning toward the small steps up to the castle.

It was only then that Charley noticed him, a dark form, sitting solitary, almost indistinguishable in the dark. Axl sat in the back of Theo's boat, staring out to sea as though he had seen and heard nothing of the commotion going on just down the shore. Within three steps Charley had Theo's arm. He swung back to her and she gestured at huddled form in the boat.

Theo stared momentarily, and then he strode toward his father.

Chapter Seventy-Two

The bathroom began to spin and Rue sank to her knees. Pulling in long breaths, she hugged the laptop close, the book slipping onto the floor of the bath with a thud that sounded like blown mortar to her ears.

'Rue? Where are you? Answer me!'

Francesca's voice was near, and Rue knew that she had climbed the stairs. Her mind screamed to pull herself together, to answer Francesca, to act NORMAL, but she couldn't move. At least the bathroom was slowing its infernal spin. Rue put the laptop down with the book and dragged her hands over her face.

Get it together. For Charley. Pull yourself together.

Loud rapping on the door, made her jump. She was glad she had put the laptop down or she may have thrown it across the bathroom. The tremors started in earnest at Francesca's voice just outside the door.

'Rue? Are you in there?'

Rue pulled in more breaths, calming the shakes but not Francesca who was now tugging the door handle. It was locked, but Rue remembered the state of the study door after Francesca had broken through it. Horror filled her every pore.

If she gets in, it's all over. Charley's stuff is sitting in the bath. Stop being weak, Rue. Get your shit together and help Charley out for God's sake!

With a surge of adrenaline Rue grabbed the book and the laptop and climbed shakily out of the bath.

'I'm on the toilet.' she called, trying to keep the tone of her voice even without success. She hoped Francesca wouldn't notice.

382

'On the toilet? Open this door! Since when do you need to lock the door when you go to the toilet, Rue? Get it open where I can see you.'

Rue heard Kate shout something up from the kitchen.

'Mind your own damn beeswax!' Francesca shouted, 'Rue, I said open the goddamn door!'

Rue quickly placed the laptop and book in the small cabinet, flushed the toilet, and unlocked the door.

She pulled it open to not only Francesca, but Evelyn and Kate as well. She blinked in the light of the landing, straightening her glasses with a shaky hand.

'My God, Rue,' Evelyn said. 'You look like hell.'

She almost sounded normal, but the fact that she didn't step forward to bustle around her spoke volumes.

'I'm sick,' Rue said, her voice cracking.

'I'll bet you are,' Francesca said with a sly smile. Her sisters behind her, Rue knew the smile was hers alone. She plastered her face with annoyance as she turned back to Evelyn and Kate.

'Bulimia. I told you. Look at the state of her.'

Rue's heart gave a jolt.

Jesus, Rue, why didn't you just say you were taking a crap. Now she has more ammunition to get rid of you. You're feeding it to her.

She floundered, trying to backtrack, holding a hand out to Francesca in plea.

'No, no. It's not, I promise. I just feel unwell, that's all.'

Kate pursed her lips as Evelyn finally moved Francesca aside and placed a hand to Rue's head. Rue's eyes shifted to Francesca, who was back in concerned mother mode, a worried look on her face.

'Rue,' Evelyn said, 'You're shaking and soaked with sweat. Listen, it's okay. If you have Bulimia, we can sort it, don't worry. You just need to tell me the truth. Did you throw your lunch up at the services?'

The condescending tone jarred through Rue. She clenched her teeth and looked to the carpet.

'No.' She said.

'They never admit it, she probably has no idea,' Francesca cut in.

Evelyn put her hands on Rue's shoulders.

'Rue. You need to tell the truth or there is nothing we can do. Now, did you throw up at the services?'

Rue looked into Evelyn's eyes.

'No.' She said, louder.

Evelyn sighed and rolled her eyes.

'It's no use, Evelyn,' Francesca said, adding her own sigh. 'This is all my fault. The stress...'

Francesca put a hand to her head, and Kate placed an arm around her shoulders.

'It's not your fault, mom.' She said.

Francesca nodded.

'Yes. Yes, it is. If I had come here instead of Charley, this trip would never have had to take place. The stress of the trip, and now the stress of my possible trouble has compounded her illness. Bulimia... oh God, Rue. My poor, poor baby.'

Francesca gave a sob and turned her face into Kate's ready hug. Rue panicked.

Was this part of her big plan? Did she bump off Elizabeth as a practice run for her?

She had to turn the conversation around, look in control before everything spun *out* of control.

'I'm fine! I do not have bulimia. I just felt ill. I'm good now, and I did not throw up at the services. Listen, I think we're all forgetting the situation Fr... mom, is in here. Don't we have some letters to find instead of standing around here worrying about me?'

384

At 'letters' Francesca's head snapped back, and she dried fake tears as she gave a sniff.

Evelyn started to object, but Francesca put a hand on her shoulder.

'Leave it Evelyn, Rue's right. The letters are the most important thing right now. Let's get them found, Rue can be dealt with afterwards. We're just wasting time.'

Rue raised her eyebrows but said nothing.

'Come here.' Francesca said, gathering the three sisters into a tight huddle where she tried to encircle her arms around them. Rue was glad to only receive the tips of her fingers.

'Listen girls, I'm so sorry about the way I have been behaving. I'm so worried about these letters, and now with Rue... I feel so weighed down with all of this. I'm too old for it, and I'm too old to be getting into trouble for something that happened thirty years ago. I'm scared, girls. That's all. I'm so sorry if I worried any of you.'

Kate smiled at Francesca.

'It's understandable, mom. It's fine. If you're that worried about these letters then we have to find them.'

Evelyn nodded, and Rue forced herself to play along, bobbing her head with Evelyn's aware of Francesca's gaze turning to her.

'Right,' Evelyn said, 'we haven't checked up here except Elizabeth's room. We'll take a room each. Mom, go down and put the kettle back on. I'm sure it'll still be working. We'll take care of things up here.'

But Francesca shook her head, keeping her eyes on Rue's.

'No, I want to check Elizabeth's room again myself, and I want Rue with me. She shouldn't be left alone. We'll look up here together.'

Rue swallowed hard. She had wanted to formulate a plan to get everyone downstairs and away from Charley's things, but by diverting their attention away from her, and back to the letters, she had inadvertently given them a reason to stay up here and search. Which would include the little cupboard where she had just placed the book and laptop... and, after this bulimia pa-lava, Rue didn't think she would be allowed back into the bathroom by herself anytime soon. Charley's things would be found. It was simply a matter of time.

Rue felt her heart sink as she realised she hadn't even shut down the page she had been looking at on the laptop. Everything was back there to see again.

If Francesca had poisoned Elizabeth, she would put two and two together. Then there would be real hell to pay.

Chapter Seventy-Three

Charley shivered, pulling the blankets tightly around her, as Theo helped Axl onto Mr Thomas' boat before returning to his own. As she watched he lit the torch on his phone, running the beam of light slowly over the damage, his despair evident when he finally sank to his heels, torch lighting only a small circle of sand at his feet. He stared at the battered boat for some time, silent and unmoving, as darkness crept around them. A gust of wind set Charley's teeth chattering, and she began to wonder if she should interrupt him before she froze to death on the sand. Then, Theo rose and motioned that they were to go.

A tug of anxiety rippled through Charley, the cold preferable to sitting with Axl, but she said nothing as Theo stretched a hand to help her aboard. He had been through enough, and there was no other way, she had to get off the island. The boat bobbed as she climbed in and Axl looked up. She met his gaze warily, confused when his face registered shock, then disbelief, and finally utter relief. He stuttered her name but could say no more. He sobbed loudly, head in his hands, elbows on his knees, shoulders shaking as Mr Thomas and Theo pushed the boat back into the water and maneuvered it away from the shore. Charley clutched her blankets tightly at her chest as she watched him from the bench opposite, the island finally growing smaller behind them.

'I'm so sorry, Charley, really I am,' Axl said, tears disappearing into his beard in the orange light. 'I would never have hurt you, you know that don't you? I didn't mean it. Any of it. I don't know what I was thinking. Can you forgive me? Please?'

Charley stared at him, feeling very much like the proverbial rabbit in the headlights. She understood that he had taken her to the island to hurt her, but also now understood that he had loved Elizabeth and that she most probably *was* his daughter. She didn't understand his side of the story any more than he understood what she had been digging for.

They had stabbed at each other from different directions without obtaining the facts, but Charley didn't want, or need, his apology. What she was desperate for were answers. She looked into his watery eyes, full of plea and regret, and quickly smothered a pang of remorse for the big man.

'I don't know you, Axl, I don't know the lengths you would have gone to, and I'm not sure why. If what you said up there is the truth, then this whole sorry mess doesn't make sense.'

Axl sniffed again and dragged his thumbs underneath his eyes.

'It is true, Charley. You are...' He paused with a glance to Theo who was leaning against the tiny cabin, arms tightly folded. His face was hard. Set. Showing no emotion and no acknowledgement that his father had spoken. 'You are my daughter.' Axl finally continued looking back to Charley. 'Mine and Elizabeth's. I can promise you I had nothing to do with whatever you were going on about on the island. That's all I thought you'd found out, nothing more.'

Axl looked back at Theo who was now staring at the wooden floor of the boat as his jaw worked.

'Theo? I'm sorry son, I'm so sorry. This mess... the boat... I... What can I do?'

Even with his father close to more tears Theo said nothing. He merely heaved a sigh and moved to sit beside Charley, elbows resting on his knees, hands clasped, He was still working his jaw as he looked at her and she saw the anger and hurt in his eyes. He needed the same as she did. An explanation. Charley placed a hand on his arm and turned her attention to Axl.

'You could tell us the truth, Axl. Why the drama? Why take Theo's boat? Why the madman act? Elizabeth has gone. What difference does all this make now? I want to know everything. The truth. All of it. Help me to understand, and *maybe* I can start to forgive.'

Axl looked helplessly to Theo, who raised his gaze to his father and nod his head.

'Go ahead. I want to know too.'

Axl glanced at each of them before dropping his gaze to his hands.

388

'I guess I owe you both that much,' he mumbled.

As the story unfolded it turned out that Axl had been very much in love with Elizabeth, Charley saw it in his face when he spoke about her, about how they had got closer as Frank's ill health took hold, and how Elizabeth had been torn between the two men.

'What happened to Frank?' Charley asked.

Axl stared out across the ocean.

'She loved Frank,' he said. 'She had loved him with all of her heart, but there was an accident at the harbour. Frank was paralysed from the waist down. Confined to a wheelchair he wasn't so much bitter, as *snappier*. He couldn't do or get where he wanted as quickly as usual. He still got there, don't get me wrong. Frank didn't let the wheelchair, or his disability stop him, but when his health declined, he became frail and dependent.'

Confused, Charley tried to grasp what Axl was trying to say but couldn't find the thread.

'If she loved Frank so much, then why...?'

Axl nodded and stared down at the boat floor before looking back to her.

'Me. I pushed her. I insisted I take care of the gardens as she cared for Frank, although for my part it was entirely selfish. Frank was a friend, but it was Elizabeth I wanted to be around. I put myself in her way. Frank couldn't satisfy her. You know, like a man should. He wasn't able after the accident.'

Axl ran a hand through his hair, and his tongue darted to lick his lips.

'Anyway, we started the affair around four years before Frank died, but both of us knew we couldn't go anywhere together openly. She made it clear that she would never leave Frank, and even if she had, Elizabeth was a councillor. She was well loved and had a lot of integrity. An affair with the treasurer, hah! What a scandal. No, it couldn't have happened any other way, it wouldn't have been right.'

Axl's voice cracked and Charley struggled to smother the sympathy that was forcing its way through her. Whether it was an affair or not, four years was a long time together. Especially to have to keep things behind closed doors.

'It was my fault.' He continued. 'I was in the loveless marriage. I had nothing to lose in that sense. I was happy to be her lover in secret. She could carry on living her life with Frank, I was happy to stay in the background as long as we were together. It wasn't to work out that way though. Elizabeth fell pregnant.'

Charley swallowed hard.

'I wasn't planned.'

Axl shook his head and looked out across the sea.

'No, you weren't planned at all, that's for sure. We'd been together for two years or so at that point, and you were a huge shock. We discussed abortion, but Elizabeth couldn't bring herself to do it. We also discussed adoption, but they couldn't guarantee the access Elizabeth wanted. It was torture. A child was the one thing she really wanted, yet still couldn't have, even though you were here, alive, inside her. It broke her. It really did. Broke both of us.'

He shuddered a sigh and wiped fresh tears from his cheeks. Charley held her breath, the intense emotion, obviously still raw, made her heart ache for him and Elizabeth.

'So that's where Francesca came in.' He said, gathering himself with a sniff. 'If Elizabeth could use something she did have – money – to help with anything you needed, then maybe Francesca would bring you up as hers. That way Elizabeth could have the access she wanted, and she knew you would never be far away.' He rubbed his nose and huffed a short, mirthless laugh. 'But that didn't work out either. Francesca asked for more and more, and when Frank found out just how much Elizabeth was giving to her, he put a stop to it. That's when Francesca took you away and-'

Axl's voice caught. He paused, running his hands over his face, clearly struggling. Theo gave a sniff beside her. For a second Charley thought he was crying too, but a glance his way found his face still dry and emotionless.

'On top of that,' Axl continued, 'When Frank died just a year later, he hit Elizabeth where it hurt. He had suspected the affair all along.

Elizabeth had been ill for the period when she had been carrying you. He hadn't seen her much at that time, she made sure of it, but I can vouch that she was grouchy and uncomfortable. She told me Frank noticed that she had put on weight and was asking questions. It terrified her that he would find out why, so she left him to his carers more and more. After your birth she wasn't able to tell Frank about the deal with Francesca, for obvious reasons, so he believed that Elizabeth's stress was over his illness and disability as opposed to Francesca becoming difficult. As she drew back from him, he thought she had given up and was looking elsewhere. And where else but the gardener? Especially as we were whispering together a fair amount at that time.' Axl paused to look at Charley with a small shrug. 'We denied it, of course, but he was right, all the same.'

He turned to look across the sea, wind tugging at his dark hair, pain and regret on his face as he sighed. Charley tried to take in the horror of what had happened, along with the knowledge that her whole life had been a lie. Not just a bit of it. All of it. She looked at the man before her. Her father. Dad.

He looked back at her in turn, giving her a sad smile, no mirth in his eyes, just deep pain.

'Frank was a very proud man, Charley. After his death we found he had a clause put into the will that if an affair came to light, even after his death, all money would be pulled away from Elizabeth and donated to the council and to charity. Elizabeth couldn't afford to have that happen, at that point she was trying hard to locate Francesca to build bridges and restart payments so that she could see you. Alone she didn't earn nearly enough to pay what Francesca asked, the money was key. You were the sole reason she couldn't ever let the affair come out. To be destitute together wouldn't have been so bad, but she had you, and you were at the forefront of everything.'

Charley stared at Axl. She wanted to believe him, but something didn't add up. She shook her head.

'I just don't understand why he would do that. Elizabeth said that Frank was a great man, and that they were deeply in love-'

Axl closed his eyes and licked his lips before giving a small nod.

'They were, he adored her as much as I did. It must have cut him to the core to suspect such a thing, especially not having full function of his body. He never turned outwardly bitter but he must have been cut up inside, I know because I know how much it hurt me to understand that she would never love me like she did Frank. Not back then, anyway.'

'But he would have wanted her to find love again, wouldn't he?' Charley said narrowing her eyes. 'Why would he deny her that after he had gone?'

'He wasn't saying she couldn't get with another man, Charley, just that if there had been an affair…' Axl swallowed hard as his voice hitched. 'Payback I suppose. He did it because his pride didn't want it to be true whilst he was alive. Anyway, we couldn't be together after his death either, it would have spelled disaster for us both.'

'Not after a few years, surely?'

Axl met her eyes.

'Yes, Charley, even after a few years. Francesca found out about the clause. God knows how she ever found out, I have no idea, but she wrote Elizabeth a letter saying that if we were ever to publicly come out as a couple, she would put you back into the mix, send you back to us as ours. To do that would mean that two and two would make four, and that everyone would know you had been born when Frank was still alive, and Frank couldn't have children remember. It would have been obvious she had strayed.

'Elizabeth wasn't bothered about the money in that instance so much as the moral implications. You thought of Francesca as your mother, she didn't want to up-heave your life with fighting and court cases. And Francesca *would* have fought, Charley. Tooth and nail. Elizabeth and I discussed it many times. She would have declared you ours and then fought to take you back. Double the damage, and you would have been in the middle. You would have been the one hurt.'

Axl swallowed and dropped his gaze with a dismissive wave of his hand. 'Anyway, we were all but through by then, it was never quite the same afterwards, so the affair never came out after all, until now.'

Charley stared at him, unsure what to say as tears gathered in her eyes.

So that's it? But what about me? Was I not worth fighting for?

Theo put an arm around her shoulders, and she revelled in the warm comfort as small as it was.

'So… so she just left me?' she whispered.

Theo tightened his grip but Axl looked startled.

'Oh, no. no, of course not, Charley, there was a lot more to it than that. Elizabeth never really stopped trying to find you. Don't think that for a second. It was... complicated.'

Easy to say.

Charley sighed pushing down the hurt. She supposed it didn't matter right now, there were bigger things to discuss.

'Okay,' She said. 'so, if this was the information you thought I had found out, why did you bring me to the island? I don't understand?'

'Panic,' His answer was quick, his eyes shifting out to sea, 'the problem is that even now, after Elizabeth's death, I couldn't be certain that you would get the inheritance that you should have. If I had declared you mine and, again, the whole affair had come out, even after Elizabeth's death, I don't know what would have happened. I'm not sure whether Frank's clause goes as far as to illegitimate children, but I didn't want to find out. You have been denied a life with a mother and father already, you deserve to get what little Elizabeth has left don't you?'

Charley stared at him.

'No. I don't buy it, Axl, you didn't know me. You *don't* know me. Why would that matter to you?'

Theo squeezed her shoulder. He had listened to the story in silence, but his voice was soft as he spoke, no trace of anger left.

'Blood is blood, right dad?'

Axl nodded, visibly grateful that his son had given him a way out.

'You're my daughter, whether I know you or not, right?'

Charley narrowed her eyes.

393

'No. No, that's not it. You said on the island that this couldn't come out-'

'Yes, Charley, for your sake it can't.'

'If you're so bothered about my inheritance, then why would you try to kill me?'

Axl opened his mouth to protest, closed it, and stared at her running a hand over his beard. Finally, he nodded slowly. Theo merely stared at him, a look of confused horror on his face.

'All right. Okay. You have to know that while that may have been in my head, it was panic, Charley, I stand to lose everything, but when it came to it, I couldn't have pushed you. I couldn't do it. You're my daughter. A product of myself and Elizabeth, of our love.'

'Congratulations.'

'Charley, I know it sounds like a yarn, really, but when you went over the edge, and I thought you'd gone forever, I realised... I realised it had been a terrible mistake. I would have done anything to bring you back right then. Anything. I love Elizabeth, and Elizabeth loved you. I do too, of course, but you're right, I don't know you. I thought I'd be able to do it, convince myself that it would be an accident and that it wouldn't matter, but I couldn't, because it does.'

Charley shook her head. She wasn't about to let him off the hook that easily.

'But why Axl? Why did you need me out of the picture?'

Axl huffed a breath and looked to the floor of the boat, running a hand through his hair. Next to Charley Theo stared at him, mouth now hanging open in horror.

'Alright, listen. The truth is I was scared. Elizabeth approached me back in July about changing the will. She knew that you were having trouble with the family and she wanted to tell you the truth, she wanted you to be free to have a fresh start, if that's what you wanted. She seemed to think you did. I was initially opposed. I didn't think she was thinking straight, as she often didn't with the dementia, you know. She had become lax with a number of things, her mind wasn't as sharp, and I didn't need this bringing back up after all these years. But we spoke about it, and she agreed that as far as she was concerned you didn't need to know that I was your father. In the end I agreed, my name had never been on the birth certificate anyway and I was there to witnesses the will. I hoped that would be the end of it, but hearing that you were searching for something more after Elizabeth's passing, I panicked. I immediately thought you were looking for your father and I couldn't have that.

'If this came out now, I'd have nothing left, Charley. Before was easy, I had Elizabeth, and she was strong. She had to be with all she's been through. She was my rock, my reason to get up in the morning, even with all she was going through over the last couple of years. She was there. And I saw glimmers of her, glimmers amongst the dementia that she was still my Elizabeth. She was still in there.

It's selfish I know, but I knew that if news came out that you were mine my world would change, and I'm seventy-two years old. I can't start life again now, it's too late. I'm terrified of being alone and I didn't want to lose everything over a mistake that had happened nearly thirty years ago. My life would be ruined. I'd lose friends, I'd lose credibility in the village, my reputation would be shattered, Anna would leave me, Theo would probably take Belle and never speak to me again-'

He gestured at Theo, who shook his head vehemently.

'No dad, it wouldn't go that far. Is that what you think of me? I may have been angry, I suppose I am that you went behind mum's back, however long ago it was. And maybe things wouldn't be as bad between the two of you now if you'd just given her your all and worked things out instead of playing away.'

'Theo, things aren't bad-'

Theo laughed, a harsh, clipped sound.

'They are bad! Dad, you hardly speak to each other. The atmosphere is so tense sometimes I feel we'll all suffocate under the weight of it. Maybe if you hadn't-'

'She was doing the same, Theo. She may never have known about me, but I knew about her.'

Theo stopped, his mouth dropping open again.

'What?'

Axl pursed his lips and looked out to the inky black sea.

'She was having an affair long before I was.'

Axl let the words sink in and Charley found and squeezed Theo's free hand in a small gesture of reassurance that she knew would make no difference. Her world had already fell apart, now Theo's was doing the same. They had to try to swim together, to help each other through it.

Is he really my half-brother? Axl really my dad? Is this what remains of my family, right here?

She stared at Axl, feeling a little like she was in a dream until Theo spoke again.

'If that was the case why didn't you leave?'

'I couldn't. You were just two years old when I found out. I came from a broken home, my parents constantly at each other's throats, and when they finally split they continued to do the same, using me as leverage for each other's spiteful battle. I moved out on my own as soon as I could, and I hadn't seen either parent for a good many years before they died. That's why you never knew your nana and grandad. I didn't want that for you, or Belle. Hell, I didn't want it for me, and I didn't want you to see the fighting as I had. I just thought if I could keep quiet and sit on what I knew, for your sake, it would all be okay, at least until you grew up.'

'But it's not okay, I've known things haven't been right for years. And I'm grown up, it's still the same dad.'

'Yes, but times goes on. The affair your mom had stopped after ten years or so, and after the trouble when Charley was born Elizabeth and I couldn't continue either. Our respective worlds collapsed, but we still had each other, no matter how bad things seemed.'

'You didn't have each other. You *don't* have each other dad, you hate each other. It's obvious. You barely tolerate being in the same room together. I feel it, and soon Belle will too, surely we'd all be happier if you both just went your own ways.'

Axl shook his head.

'No, Theo, I can't take that upheaval, Not now, it's too late-'

'It's never too late,' Charley said, 'Do you think Elizabeth - mom - would ever have said it was too late that I came up here only a few months ago? Happiness can hit you at any moment, but you have to find the balls to make the shift, not try to bury it all under the carpet... or push it off a cliff as the case may be.'

Axl looked at her with an odd expression of mixed regret, pain and horror.

'I know you must think I'm weak, Charley, but I'd lose everything. Anna would never speak to me again, Theo and Belle... the relationship would be broken at least, I know I've ruined things with you and... Elizabeth is gone. I'd have no-one. No one!'

He tried to continue, but an eerie sobbing yowl left his throat. As she watched him cry, Charley saw him for what he was. The grey flecks she had never noticed in his jet-black hair, the lines on his face, the overhang of his belly. He was an old man. An old man scared that he would be alone and estranged at the end of his life.

It certainly didn't excuse him trying to take hers, but he was right, in the end he hadn't really tried to. Even by the cliffs, he had held her arms, but he hadn't tried to throw her over, he'd faltered, he hadn't got what it took to do it. He was a decent man, but a very scared one, and Charley knew that fear did strange things to decent people. She had seen it in the way her sisters - cousins - were around Francesca. Rue had an eating disorder, for god's sake. Was that because of the tension that Francesca had brought them all up in? And now that Charley knew what had been going on, she understood why everything had always felt so fraught, and why Elizabeth was always made out to be a monster, so that the girls kept well away.

Which they did. It worked. And maybe Francesca held the others over a barrel and made them scare Charley until they believed it themselves. It didn't matter now. Either way, the witch story had served its purpose for nearly thirty years.

Theo sniffed beside her and, taking his hand from Charley's, placed it onto his dads, which was resting on his knee. He looked up at Axl.

'Dad, I promise you no matter what happens, or what has happened, there is no way Belle and I would ever cut you out of our lives. She loves you, and she needs you. So do I. People make mistakes and I think after a lifetime living with a woman you didn't want to be with, and not able to be with the one you loved, even when her husband has died? I think you've probably suffered enough, it's not for me to judge. And mom the same, I love you both, it matters more to me that you're happy than what you've done in the past or if you're together.'

Axl looked at Theo, and Charley saw the tears running down his face. The relief was palpable. She almost saw the weight lift right off his shoulders. After a moment's hesitation, she placed her hand on top of Theo's, on top of Axl's. She didn't know what she wanted to say, she didn't really know how she felt, but she knew Axl loved her mother, and if Elizabeth had loved him as much as he said she did then there had to be a reason, and maybe she wanted to learn more about that reason. Her mother was a smart woman. Everyone said so, right?

Axl looked up at her and gulped a sob.

'Charley, sweetheart, I'm so, so, sorry, I'm so sorry for all I've put you through. Please give me another chance, I was so worried, so scared. And when Theo was spending more and more time with you, well... given the circumstances it only made me more desperate. I'm sorry.'

Charley looked at Theo's tear-streaked face and grinned at the insinuation, especially after the conversation they had had at Fortwind House just last week. Theo raised his eyebrows back at her.

'Not a chance.' They said in unison before breaking into surprised laughter.

Axl put a hand on each of their arms making a little circle in the boat, and then he sobbed, wretched and with abandon. So hard, and so heart breaking, that for a second Charley thought she might just sob with him.

Chapter Seventy-Four

Rue sat on her aunt's bed folding the jumpers Francesca had thrown. It seemed that Kate was the only person not intent on ruining everything in their Aunt's house. When Francesca and Rue entered the bedroom it had been fairly tidy, with none of the mess that was strewn around downstairs. Rue watched that change as Francesca's arms reached into the wardrobe and emerged with silks and fine fabrics, which she dumped on the floor beside her until the shelves were empty. Finally, she stood, hands on hips, breathing hard before swinging to Rue, face red.

'What the hell are you doing Rue? We don't have time for that, check the drawers.'

'I just thought I'd tidy as...'

'Tidy?' Francesca hissed, 'Rue, you know as well as I do what these letters mean for me, and believe me if I'm going down, you're coming with me. This is your life as well as mine. You'd better search and search hard, do you hear me? Get on the damn drawers.'

Francesca moved from the wardrobe and stooped to place her face inches from Rue's. Rue wondered if her mother could hear her heart thudding behind her ribs.

'Do you hear me?'

Rue nodded quickly and placed the powder blue jumper onto the folded pile on the floor. She rose and headed for the chest of drawers next to the bed.

Opening the first one, she heard a scuffle and Francesca began to laugh behind her, no - *giggle*. Rue turned to see her throw the stack of neatly folded things into the air with a small 'whoops'. A small silky almond jumper landed on Rue's head, causing Francesca to laugh harder.

Rue pulled it off and turned back to the drawer to hide her tears from Francesca. Why did she have to be so nasty? It wouldn't have hurt to have left the pile of things to be put away later.

The wardrobe door closed and Francesca moved to the dressing table next to the chest of drawers. Rue's heart sank. She opened the top drawer fully and pushed her hand through the underwear inside, feeling from corner to corner, finding nothing but cotton and silk.

'Oh, for pity's sake Rue, quicker. Like this.'

Francesca used a bony elbow to push Rue aside and grabbed handfuls of underwear throwing it across the room as she pulled it out.

'There, see how easy it is? Drawer empty! Next drawer.'

Rue fought the urge to gather them all back up and put them into the drawer.

'I just, But...'

'Just, But what, Rue?' Francesca stared at her, spiteful amusement in her eyes. 'What? Do you have a problem looking through a dead old lady's underwear?'

She crossed to the pile and pulled out a pair of lacy knickers, holding them up to her stomach, stretching the lace from hip to hip. Rue heard them tear.

'I mean, what the hell does a seventy-year-old want this kind of knickers for, anyway? Axl Maddox? Dirty whore. She always was.'

Rue blinked and turned back to the drawers, pulling out the second drawer to keep from having to watch Francesca's lack of respect.

She put a hand back into the next drawer. Belts and winter wear. Hats, scarves and gloves.

'Not like that Rue,' Francesca screeched in her ear. 'Like this.'

Francesca tugged the drawer right out of its housing and threw it across the room. The contents flew as the drawer crashed against the bed frame and came to rest on the floor.

Rue gasped as Francesca laughed again, clearly enjoying the time she had to torture her further.

'Get it, Rue? Harder, faster, quicker.' she clicked her fingers in beat with the words. 'I suppose you were never that 'quick' were you?'

Francesca peeled into laughter again, and Rue felt herself shrink back to the drawers as Francesca stepped forward. She kicked Rue's shin, hard and fast, bringing the heel of her small court shoe forward. Tears sprung into Rue's eyes again as she pressed herself against the wood behind. Inside her jeans, something warm oozed from the wound. Francesca held a hand up as Evelyn called from across the landing.

'What's the joke?'

'Oh, Rue doesn't know her own strength, silly billy. She threw one of the drawers right across the room, contents and all!'

Francesca gave Rue a nasty smile and moved back to the dressing table just as Evelyn entered the room.

'Rue did what?'

Francesca looked back at her, cool as a cucumber, an affectionate smile now on her face. She gestured to the drawer by the bed.

'Pulled the drawer right out of the chest...'

Francesca continued but Rue heard no more. Her heart all but stopped at the sight of the laptop and book tucked under Evelyn's arm.

She's found the evidence. Do something, Rue!

But Rue was frozen. She felt the blood rush past her ears and her heart jumped into her throat. The rest she saw as though in a movie.

Evelyn held the laptop and book aloft. She said something to Francesca, a puzzled look on her face, although it was as though the sound was on mute. Rue couldn't hear a word; she could just see Evelyn's mouth moving in slow motion in front of her. As though turning on a rusted old thread Rue's head forced itself slowly right to see Francesca leave Evelyn's gaze to glare at her and mouth something, also in slow motion. She held an arm out for the items, all the while staring at Rue. Evelyn began to hand them over and then Rue felt herself propelled toward them, the world turning back on in high definition.

Rue snatched the laptop and book from Evelyn's outstretched hands before either Evelyn or Francesca could stop her. She grasped them tightly, just managing to hold on by the tips of her fingers as she ran from the room and onto the landing.

The bathroom, Rue!

The voice in her head screeched instructions, and dodging past Kate, who had appeared in a back bedroom doorway, she ran into the bathroom and slammed the door shut, turning the lock. There were shouts, bangs, confusion, and then the loud thump of Francesca's fist arrived on the bathroom door and a tear slipped down Rue's cheek.

Chapter Seventy-Five

'I have something for you.' Axl said, wiping the last of his tears with the heel of his hand.

He shifted on the bench, reaching into his pocket and pulled out a familiar brown paper bag, although more worn, creased, and folded than it had been all those months ago in the kitchen. He handed it to her across the boat. Charley hesitated, and he nodded at her to take it.

'I didn't want you to find it,' he said seeing the recognition in her eyes, 'It was before Elizabeth changed the will. Back then I selfishly didn't want you ever to find out, but it seems daft to keep it from you now, and it may help you understand just how much she wanted you. I know you must be confused, and this story is far from short and simple.' Axl gestured to the bag and Charley took it from him, 'Elizabeth intended you to have it when she told you the truth herself. And believe me, she fully intended to tell you when the time was right. She wanted a relationship with you Charley, she rehearsed what she would say many times, but you never came back, she never got the chance.'

Charley stared at Axl, her heart thumping behind her ribs. Back in the kitchen that day she would have killed to know what Axl was hiding, but right here and now, with the truth at her fingertips the weight of the bag loomed heavy with emotion she wasn't sure she was ready for.

'Open it.' Theo said, nudging her gently with an elbow.' The suspense is killing me.'

Blood pulsing in her ears, Charley carefully opened the bag and peered inside. At first glance it appeared empty but a little digging around inside revealed a delicate gold chain. She pulled it out to reveal a necklace. A small angel, wings spread, glittering stone in the centre of her chest, hung on top of a larger thin gold heart. Charley held her breath as Axl turned the heart over to reveal an engraved message so small she had to squint to read it in the low light. Axl helped her out, reading from memory.

'It says 'Charlotte. My angel, my heart. Always in my thoughts and dreams, until we are together again, and I am complete. My eternal love. Mom.' The angel's heart is a diamond if I remember rightly.'

Charley couldn't speak. Tears filled her eyes as she felt a rush of connection with Elizabeth so strong that she couldn't breathe. She may not have been planned, but she was absolutely wanted and loved. It radiated from Elizabeth's writing, the necklace, the will, and the people alive to speak of it. There was nothing more that Charley could ask for, and at the moment nothing more she needed.

Thank you, mom, this means the world.

She blinked and hot tears fell onto her cheeks. It still felt weird to call Elizabeth that, and yet it felt more comfortable than giving the title to Francesca.

'Here,' Theo said, holding out his hand, 'Want me to put it on for you?'

'Um...'

Charley considered the necklace, blurry through her tears. It was beautiful, but as much as she wanted to keep the sentiment and Elizabeth close, wearing a real diamond around her neck was so far moved from reality that she thought she may just put it away instead. Keep it safe.

It was Axl who swayed the decision.

'It would have meant the world to her to see you wear it, Charley. That was to be the ultimate confirmation that you believed and accepted what she said as the truth. For her, anyway.'

Charley looked up at Axl, the tears in his eyes matching her own. She nodded and handed the necklace to Theo, keeping one hand over the angel and heart long after he had fastened it around her neck.

'There's something I don't understand,' she said. 'If Elizabeth was so intent on telling me the truth, and having a relationship with me, why not track me down? I'm not a child anymore, Francesca wouldn't have been able to stop her, surely.'

Axl sighed and pursed his lips with a sniff.

'It wasn't quite that simple. Maybe I'd better finish the story, 'he said. 'After you were born things spiralled out of control. Francesca, recently left on her own, found it hard with three children and a baby, and obviously Elizabeth couldn't help with night feeds, sickness, making bottles and all the other stuff that comes with having a small child. It was Francesca who took you to the doctor when you were sick, made sure you had your immunisations, weaned and potty trained you, because Elizabeth couldn't do any of that. She wanted to, Charley, believe me. It killed her to see you brought up to call Francesca 'mom'. But she was not to be seen as your mother.

'The only hold Elizabeth had was that she registered your birth at 3 weeks old, naming you and stating that she was your mother. That way she thought she could retain some rights for the future. Unfortunately, this only caused problems for Francesca who then had to pose as Elizabeth for anything official, such as nursery and school.

'Francesca felt hard done by I suppose, she kept her end of the bargain for only a few months before getting bored. Then she dropped the time Elizabeth could spend with you, from a couple of hours, to an hour, to half an hour a day, finally to every other day, and then once a week as time went on. Elizabeth kept her end of the bargain, paying Francesca more and more each time she asked, but seeing you less and less for her efforts. It hurt her immensely, but her hands were tied. There was nothing she could do. She had to keep the peace or risk losing you altogether.'

Axl took a shuddering breath and let it out slowly. Charley watched him feeling her sympathy grow. He hadn't wanted this any more than Charley or Theo wanted it now. He had just wanted the woman he loved, on whatever terms.

'So, eventually Frank noticed the money going out of the account and asked Elizabeth about it. She couldn't tell him the truth, of course, but she did say she was helping Francesca. It was the wrong thing to say. Frank had always been at odds with Francesca, they hated the sight of each other. He immediately ordered Elizabeth to stop paying the money, told her that Francesca had to learn to make her own way in life. Elizabeth did as he said but was trying to find another way to pay her on the side. Francesca was kept informed of the whole process, through either myself or Elizabeth, but one morning she decided to just take you and go. Elizabeth never saw you after that, I guess you would have been three, maybe four years old, but the contact didn't stop there.'

Axl ran his hands over his face, the distress evident and Charley felt a flutter of nerves in her stomach.

'Dad? Are you okay?' Theo asked.

Running a hand over his mouth, Axl gave a nod, dropped his gaze and continued.

'After that letters arrived at Fortwind House, lots of letters. Elizabeth was distraught by the content. Initially, she kept them secret, but I met with her one afternoon and she seemed distressed. I eventually got her to tell me why and insisted she show them to me. I think she was glad to talk about them, she had no-one else to confide in, and the letters weren't nice. They ranged from plain nasty to death threats.'

Charley looked at Axl, perplexed.

'From Francesca?'

Axl nodded.

'Yes. All of them. Elizabeth wanted to track Francesca down, to pay her any amount to put this behind her and see you all again but she couldn't locate her. It was as if you had all vanished, and yet the letters still came. Letters with no forwarding address.

She threatened everything. From leaving you on the steps of the orphanage, starving you, keeping you from school, locking you in the cellar. She told Elizabeth that she would never see you again, and that you would never want to see her now that you knew what a conniving, nasty piece of work she was. Francesca said she had made sure you were terrified of her, made sure you had no intention of visiting 'Aunt Elizabeth' ever again.

As the months went on, the letters got more and more extreme. Some stated that she would dump you in the middle of the forest and leave you there to die, she also threatened to strangle you. Some of her letters stated that she had carried out her threats, and how free she felt without you burdened around her neck, which obviously left Elizabeth distraught. Usually, there would be another letter a few weeks later saying that she had been joking.'

Charley's mouth dropped open. She couldn't believe what she was hearing but couldn't stop herself listening either.

Francesca? *Mom?* *Really? But why would she go this far?*

'On more than one occasion Francesca threatened to expose the affair,' Axl continued, 'to confirm that there was a child born before Frank had passed away, especially after she learned about his clause. She also threatened Elizabeth, her life a few times, and countless times she said that she would get her revenge for the hardships she had put her through. The letters always ended with Francesca telling Elizabeth to leave you alone, and to watch her back.'

Charley shut her mouth with a snap and her eyebrows flew up to her hairline.

'Francesca?' she said. 'Are you certain they were from Francesca?'

Axl reached for her hand, pain in his eyes, which held her gaze steadily.

'Of course I'm certain, Charley. And there was so much more than that. Ultimately, it ruined the relationship between myself and Elizabeth. We stayed good friends, and I never stopped loving her, but things were never the same after that. Francesca forced so much guilt and so many threats at Elizabeth that she backed off completely. She became paranoid and jumpy for a good many years, but eventually, thankfully, the contact became less, and she gradually put those horrible years behind her.'

Axl looked down to her hand in his.

'She always thought of you, Charley, but she couldn't pursue a relationship with you, even when you were an adult. She could possibly have located you, technology has come on so much, but part of her knew that she would turn your life upside down, and the other part didn't want to stir Francesca up after she had gone quiet. I think it was Francesca that ultimately swung the vote for her. Elizabeth had been through hell for too many years. She didn't want to fight or be threatened anymore.'

Charley felt ice crawl down her spine as he spoke.

Francesca? The same woman I've called mother all these years? Axl has to be making a meal of this, doesn't he? Was she even capable? She was too busy with four kids, surely.

But even as her thoughts ran, Charley wasn't at all certain. Francesca had been cold and detached with all of the girls at points over the years, and she knew the jealousy that Elizabeth's lifestyle had provoked, she had witnessed it first-hand. She had seen the twist in Francesca's face each time she had spoken about it.

But not as far as death threats, that's ridiculous!

Charley stared at the harbour as it came into view, watching it rise and fall with the rhythm of the boat. She was only vaguely aware of Axl still talking until he spoke her name.

'Charley? I know it's a lot to take in.'

Charley shook her head and pursed her lips.

'Axl. Before I knew you were Theo's dad, I accused you of poisoning Elizabeth. Theo told me point blank that there was no way. That you weren't capable. I wasn't so sure at the top of the cliffs, but ultimately he was right, you didn't push me, there was no accident. I feel the same way about Francesca. She can be a hard, cold, and jealous person, especially where Elizabeth is concerned, but death threats? No, I don't think so. She wouldn't be capable. There has to be another explanation. Are you sure you didn't read them wrong? Were the letters from someone else, someone else who knew about the affair, someone else who had a vendetta?'

Someone else who wanted to poison her?

Charley's heart jumped.

Of course! Whoever was sending death threats back then could be a possible suspect now, even all these years later, couldn't they?

Axl looked crestfallen as he implored her to believe him, but it was Theo who stood quickly, reaching into his coat pocket, losing his balance a little as the boat rocked. Charley looked up at him.

'What's the matter?'

He handed an envelope to her, an envelope Axl paled at. He began to protest, but Charley took the envelope and opened it, pulling out a pile of letters, as Theo sat back beside her. Her heart thud and her mouth dropped open as she recognised the handwriting straight away.

Francesca.

She read through a few of the letters, the hateful spite almost jumping off the page with the words Francesca had chosen to write and the pressure of the pen. In just the first few Charley read she found one where she had threatened her life, and with mounting horror found another two that threatened Elizabeth's.

Charley couldn't breathe. Her hands shook. Axl had been right. Avril had been right. And at the end of each letter was a warning, just as Axl said, to leave Charley alone and watch her back. A few more threatened that one day, when Elizabeth had let her guard down, Francesca would come for her revenge.

Revenge.

Goosebumps littered her body. She swallowed hard and looked up, immediately meeting Axl's eyes.

'Charley,' he said, looking anxious, 'you said on the island that you thought Elizabeth had been poisoned, that you had proof? Now you ask who had a vendetta?'

He motioned to the letters. Charley nodded, swallowing hard.

'I think we may have a prime suspect,' she finished quietly.

Axl nodded lightly, and she knew the same thought had crossed his mind. She put the letters back into the envelope and gave it to Axl with shaking hands.

'Keep these safe,' she said, 'Francesca may well be at Fortwind house by now, I don't know what's going to happen when I get there. If she's been sitting outside for hours she'll be furious, and so will her minions, I don't want possible evidence ruined in the fray.'

'She's already there.' Axl said, placing the envelope carefully in the inside pocket of his jacket. 'She's inside the house, with the others. I went by to see you earlier, before... well, all of this.'

'Wait, she's at Fortwind house?' Theo said grabbing the cabin's frame for balance as the boat turned, catching the swell. 'Charley, she may be dangerous, you can't go back there alone.'

Charley's heart pumped harder. She licked her dry lips as she looked at him.

'Well, as far as she knows I still think I'm her daughter. She denied it when I asked her, so much so that I questioned Elizabeth's sanity. I just have to tread carefully, but if she has done this, she will pay. I will make sure of that.'

'Charley, please. Come home with me or Theo tonight. I can't see Francesca again, I don't want to, but tomorrow we can-'

Charley cut Axl off. 'No, it's okay, I'm not asking either of you to come with me. I'll be-'

'Well, you're not going up there alone, that's for sure.' Theo said, 'So let's see if we can work this out without any bloodshed, eh?'

Axl lunged to his feet, grabbing Theo's arms.

'No, Theo! She may be dangerous. Charley, lets just call the police, let them deal with it.'

'Deal with what?' She said, 'We don't even know she did it? And we have no evidence to give. They won't do anything.'

'Round in circles. I'm getting Deja-vu,' Theo said helping Axl back onto the bench before sitting next to Charley.

Charley nodded wryly, fingering the necklace.

'Well, let's make sure this time we get enough steam to go forward.'

The small boat purred its way safely into the harbour walls as Theo and Charley went over how they could find out the truth. Axl looked like he may be sick, but Charley had no time to console him. Her adrenaline was pumping. She wanted to get up to Fortwind House and try to solve this whole sorry mess for Elizabeth.

If she was right, Francesca may well have finally got her revenge all right; in a perfectly orchestrated murder.

Chapter Seventy-Six

After a quick goodbye, Charley and Theo left Axl at the harbour with his land rover. Charley thought she had seen real fear behind his eyes, but she had no time and no inclination to go into what that meant.

Her own car still by Avril's house, she jumped into Theo's Renault. He turned over the engine and thrust the car into gear, barely giving her time to shut the door before driving far too quickly back up to Fortwind house. Charley's heart began to pump as she kept replaying Axl's look of fear in her mind; even knowing that they were going to face a family that had put no fear into her just a few months ago. Now was different though, she felt she would be dealing with a whole different Francesca to the one she had grown up with.

Charley peered into Evelyn's car as Theo pulled to a stop beside it. Axl had been right, it was empty. She turned to Theo, her blood starting to boil as white-hot anger settled in her stomach.

'They must be inside, like your dad said. How did they get inside, Theo? Who the hell do they think they are?'

She threw open the door, climbing out as Theo threw open his own door and ran around the car, stopping her in her tracks. He stood, palms out, between her and the front door which was only feet away.

'Charley, calm down. Don't go in guns blazing, be smart. We could be dealing with a murderer here.'

Charley smirked.

'She's hardly Charles Manson Theo, she poisoned her sister through someone else if she did it, and she'll let someone else take the flack if it's ever proven. She's a coward, whether her threats said otherwise or not. And besides two months ago they were my family, I wasn't scared of them then, and I won't be scared now. Nothing has changed.'

Charley flung an arm toward the door and made to move around him, but Theo grabbed her, forcing her to look at him.

'*Everything* has changed. And Francesca knows you know Elizabeth was your mom. You can't play it the same, and remember, she will think she holds the cards.'

Charley glared up at him.

'She doesn't hold the cards Theo, I do. She won't be expecting me to come at her with the poisoning, she will be expecting a fight about parental responsibility, and my irresponsibility with the will, which for some reason she thinks she has a right to check out and approve.'

Theo nodded sagely.

'Right, and that may be so, but you still need to be careful. Please calm down.'

Charley huffed a breath. They were wasting time, and although a small part of her knew there wasn't any need to rush, she had to get to the truth. Two simple questions were all it would take.

Had Elizabeth really been poisoned? And had Francesca done it?

It was all Charley wanted to know, and yet she knew it wouldn't be that easy.

Pushing past Theo she lead the way to the front door which was unlocked. She pulled the handle and stepped inside.

The mess hit Charley first, the open door of the study catching her eye. She was used to seeing the dark, solid door, but now yellow light spilled out into the dark hall, exposing the chaos that was inside. Her breath caught as she swung her gaze to the left. The door to the drawing room was only open a fraction, but she could see that this room was also in a similar state.

Back lit by light from the kitchen, Evelyn, who was directly in front of her in the hall looking upstairs through the spindles of the bannister, snapped her head to Charley as they entered, wide eyed behind her red-rimmed glasses. Her gaze now flit between Charley and upstairs, as if she had no idea what the hell was going on.

Well, for once I'll give her that, she has no idea. No idea at all.

Beyond Evelyn, Kate was hiding behind the open kitchen door, half of her face peering out into the hall which struck Charley as amusing. These two, of all people. So big, so important, so responsible. So very aware of how much their elderly mother needed to be pampered and looked after; now so frightened and unsure.

Charley paused, wondering what the hell was wrong with this scene, and then Francesca shouted from upstairs, loud and threatening.

Threatening? Evelyn and Kate were down here, which meant that she could only be threatening one person. Rue.

Charley looked up the staircase where Francesca's back presented itself to her in the light of the landing. She bristled as she caught the violent stream of words and started forward, but Theo grabbed her hand, pulling her back.

'Charley,' he whispered.

His voice was fraught with fear that would probably encompass her too if it weren't for the anger. She knew that Theo was warning her to watch her step, but at the threat to give Rue what she deserved, something in Charley's brain clicked, the flood of anger washing over her like a tidal wave.

Chapter Seventy-Seven

Francesca's shouts shook Rue to her core. She could hear the ragged scrape of her own breath pulling in and out in fast gasps, the small whine which escaped her lips with each exhale.

She whimpered. And then she hated herself for being so weak, for giving in so easily, but she knew there was nothing she could do. When Francesca broke into the bathroom - which she would, because Rue sure as hell wasn't unlocking the door voluntarily - she would have to hand over all of Charley's things, all of the possible evidence of an injustice would be quashed in an instant.

'Rue? You will damn well open this door, or so help me god I will make sure you never have the ability to open a door again.'

Rue sank down into the empty bath and closed her eyes, cold sweat breaking out over the goose bumps that littered her body.

'I'll break every bone in your no-good body until you realise how wrong it is to go poking your nose where it doesn't belong. Nosey, spiteful little cow. You won't get away with it any longer.'

This is getting away with it? Jesus Christ, mom.

When Rue didn't answer, Francesca rammed on the door again. Thud after thud, making the door shake in its frame. Rue flinched each and every time wondering if her heart would give out in fear before Francesca made it inside.

'Mom, please calm down. We can find out what Rue is up to without all of this. Please!'

Evelyn's voice floated from beyond the doorway. It sounded quieter now, like she had retreated downstairs, and to top it all Rue thought she sounded unsure. A flicker of worry had entered her tone, and in turn that worried Rue. A lot.

Evelyn always had full control, and Francesca had always been fully in control of the game around both her and Kate, but it seemed the game was escalating. Francesca no longer seemed to care about her behaviour and Rue knew that if she didn't open the door soon, her mother would be completely out of control.

The door rattled, straining into its lock as Francesca pounded thud after thud. Kate let out a scream from downstairs, and Rue struggled for breath.

They've both left me up here with her?

And then, low and menacing through the door:

'Rue, come out you little shit, you think life has been bad until now? I'll show you what bad is, I'll show you just how bad it can get. You think a broken nose is the worst you can get. You are so wrong. You'll get what you deserve for ruining my life, for poking that grubby nose into my business and thinking you can get away with it.'

Rue whimpered, and then her breath caught in her throat as another voice joined the fray. This one confident, bold, and angry.

'Just like Elizabeth did, eh? Got a taste for revenge now? Getting good at it?'

Rue's head shot up in the bath, eyes wide.

Charley?

Charley was back. Not only back but going for broke. Rue was terrified, appalled, and exhilarated all at once.

Oh God, Charley, please be careful.

Rue sat frozen, listening, her heart thumping. She could have cried at the sound of Charley's voice. Charley was the only one who wasn't patronising, the only one who didn't get on at her about the affliction she didn't have, the only one who offered any sort of support. Rue thought maybe Charley didn't really believe her diagnosis at all.

Rue swallowed the lump in her throat. She had missed her, missed the support she had given her at home.

Sitting in the tub, she half wondered if Charley's presence would shake her mother back into the pretence that had been their lives, but Francesca had crossed that line already. Evelyn and Kate had been witness. There was no going back from here, only forward, and that scared Rue to death.

She sat, hugging the book, chart and laptop to her pounding chest as the thuds stopped reigning on the door and all was quiet.

Chapter Seventy-Eight

Francesca swung around at the top of the stairs, and the hateful, twisted look of anger etched on her face took Charley aback. Now silent, she descended the stairs looking like a very capable, very monstrous looking Medusa. Charley marvelled that such an apparently fragile and ill woman had suddenly seemed to morph into someone so able-bodied and full of strength that she appeared able to turn someone to stone with a single glance.

Not if I get to her first.

Francesca stopped on the bottom step, giving her height, never taking her eyes from Charley's, a small, nasty smile crossing her lips. From the corner of her eye Charley saw Evelyn retreat into the shadows down the hall.

'Charlotte, how nice of you to grace us with your presence, going out when you knew we were coming wasn't very courteous now was it? Anyone would think you didn't want us here. Have you been for a swim?'

Charley stood tall as Francesca scanned her eyes over her now drying clothes. Venom poured from her controlled voice, but Charley's anger right now matched Francesca's beat for beat.

'What the hell are you doing in my house?'

'Oh, your house? Last I looked it was my sister's house, and I'm here to deal with my sister's death. I have a key that she gave me personally. I've done nothing wrong, Charlotte.'

'Really? Nothing at all?'

She let the statement hang, Francesca held her stare, her hard eyes holding amusement.

'Her death is dealt with,' Charley said, 'and that key was probably from thirty-odd years ago, I don't think she'd appreciate you using it now.'

'Then she should have changed the locks. You weren't here to greet us, it's cold outside.'

Charley grit her teeth, heart pumping behind her ears. She shook, barely able to stop herself lunging forward and pummelling the smug look from her face.

'So you let yourself in and saw the need to trash everything in the house while you were waiting? You couldn't just grab a cup of tea like normal human beings?'

Francesca raised an eyebrow.

'It's all trash anyway, who the hell wants to live in the past?'

'Elizabeth did. She was proud of this house.'

Francesca laughed, a bitter, spiteful sound. She stepped down from the bottom step, hand resting on the mahogany finial. Charley resisted the urge to step backwards, pushing her chin higher, certain the move was supposed to intimidate her.

'Oh, she was proud.' Francesca said. 'She loved to rub it in just how much she had compared to everyone else. How rich and important she was. Not so important now, is she?'

Charley took a step toward her, unable to help herself, and anger flared hot and white in her stomach.

'No, you saw to that didn't you?'

They were almost nose to nose now, and there was a tense silence as Francesca's narrowed, knowing, eyes searched hers. Charley's heart drummed noisily in her ears.

She knows. She knows I know. How did she find out?

Theo grabbed her hand and tugged, squeezing another warning. Charley swallowed hard, trying to assess where this left her. If Francesca knew, then this would be a different ball game, and the fact that she wasn't remotely surprised or unclear about what Charley was talking about suggested she at least knew something, even if she wasn't directly involved.

It was Evelyn that broke the spell. She came out of the shadows, hands in front of her chest, and turned to Charley. She looked calm, sounded calm even, but it was all pretence, Charley could feel the fear and uncertainty radiating from her like a beacon.

'Charley, listen,' she said, 'I'm not sure what you think has gone on, but there's something here mom needs, I know the place is a mess-'

Charley couldn't be bothered to listen. She had spent years bowing to Evelyn's reason, backing down when she had been forceful with her opinions, and she had a very good idea just what Francesca had been looking for too. She smiled at Evelyn.

'A mess? I'd say it looks like it's been ransacked. And the door to the study has had the lock broken. Indicative of a break in. Which usually only happens when there's something incriminating to be found. Something no-one else should know about. Evidence?' She turned back to Francesca, eyebrows raised. 'Did you find it?'

Francesca's face hardened and coloured, waving a hand that cut through Evelyn's statement of their mother's innocence. Charley wondered if Evelyn had any idea what their mother had done. What line had Francesca spun to get them to help find and destroy such damning evidence? And now Francesca was playing coy. It was for show, Charley saw the depth of anger playing in her eyes.

'Well?' she said.

'Find what? There's no incriminating evidence Charlotte because I've done nothing wrong.'

'Good, then you won't mind that it's already been found and removed from the house. The envelope is gone.'

Francesca's eyes blazed wide, and her mouth dropped open. She appeared about to lunge, or fall, forward but caught herself just in time. Her face turned beet red as she tried to control her rapid breaths, but she pulled herself together with phenomenal speed, her voice smooth and controlled.

'I have no idea what you're talking about.'

Now Evelyn interjected, a mixture of puzzlement and what Charley thought was relief on her face.

'Of course you do, mom, the envelope we were looking for! I told you it would be okay. Charley knows where it is see? She can give it to you now and all-'

'Oh, I don't think that will be necessary.' Charley said.

Evelyn swung to her, face slack with disbelief.

'Charley,' she said, her tone almost begging. 'You don't know the trouble that mom could get into! She needs it, and while I get that she may not be your mother anymore, and that you may not care, she's still ours and she's still an old lady. It's not fair Charley, just give us the envelope, it doesn't mean anything to you.'

Throwing in the guilt card again.

Charley turned to look at Evelyn. She was flustered, strands of hair hanging from her ordinarily neat bun. Cheeks rosy with frustration or exertion, Charley didn't know which. Her eyes were wild with worry behind the large lenses.

She's out of control for once, and she doesn't like it. She thinks the damn envelope will switch Francesca back to her normal frail mother, but there's no going back now. She's shown her true colours.

Evelyn faltered under her stare, dropping her gaze, and glanced back to the kitchen where high-profile horse mistress, Kate Attingham, was still hiding behind the kitchen door like a small child.

No help for her there.

Charley raised her eyebrows unsurprised and turned back to Evelyn, who was now watching her, eyes pleading.

'Well,' she said, 'as it happens Evelyn, the envelope means a fair bit to me, and the only people who will get their hands on it are the police. We can see what they wish to do with it, or whether they think it's important, eh, *mom*? Oh. sorry, should that be Aunt Francesca now?'

Francesca laughed, but it was an almost hysterical sound, and Charley noted the edge of uncertainty.

'The police?' Francesca said, her voice an octave too high, 'Charlotte, I don't know what the heck you think they're going to do with them, they're just letters I wrote to my sister. There's nothing in there they will arrest me for. What a waste of police time you stupid girl.'

'I disagree, those letters show a very different woman from the frail old woman you pretend to be. In fact, they show a hard, cold, calculated, unstable woman with a vendetta. A vendetta to get revenge on her sister, whatever the cost.'

Francesca clutched at her heart dramatically as she laughed. Making a play of wiping non-existent tears from her eyes.

'Oh Charlotte, I wrote those letters such a long time ago you really think they'll carry any weight now?'

'They will show the character you are when people aren't around to see. I think they will be very important to the investigation, don't you?'

Francesca dropped her hands and snapped her head up at Charley with a nasty grin.

'Investigation? If you've got nothing on me apart from a bunch of old letters I don't think there will be one, do you? We both know that's not enough.'

'I have more.'

'There is no more.'

'Elizabeth knew. She knew what you were doing.'

Francesca sighed dramatically.

'And what was it I was doing, all the way from Harrogate?'

'Poisoning her.'

Francesca laughed as Evelyn gasped. She was about to start in on Charley, but Francesca beat her to it.

'Oh dear. She really did have you taken in, didn't she? She had dementia, Charlotte. It's a brain eating disease. Lots of people get suspicious and paranoid when they have these diseases.'

'And you would know that because of your research.'

'What research?'

'To pull off that she had dementia instead of her having the effects of Belladonna poisoning. The test results and hospital visits were all fake. She never went to a hospital, never had a test. You had all the answers and test results she needed. Even her nurse had no access to her records. Because she didn't have any. You made it all up and watched her suffer from afar while you poisoned her slowly. Getting your revenge for having to take me in, bring me up. Don't you think she suffered enough just by you taking me away?'

Francesca huffed and stepped back, Charley thought she had paled at least a shade.

'Ridiculous! I'm glad you credit me with such brains, Charlotte, plotting and planning with such careful thought. I wrote those letters in anger, and why shouldn't I be mad? Don't you think I suffered? I already had three young children and no room in the house. She was up here in a palace whilst pushing you onto me for her one indulgent mistake that she should have just admitted like an adult. She had the affair, she had the baby, she should have taken the consequences. But no, she had to hide it, to keep her adoring public on side, to act like Frank was the only man on earth she loved, to keep the lifestyle and money that she knew he would have taken away.

She was nothing on her own, *nothing,* and she knew damn well she would have been destitute and alone with a child had she kept you. Axl would have wanted nothing to do with her when the money was taken away. He didn't care about you, he jumped ship not long after you were born.'

'You made him. You threatened them, you bribed and blackmailed. You pressured them so much that they couldn't have a relationship, even years after Frank died. Axl was happy to go with what Elizabeth wanted because he loved her. And he loved me. *You* broke them, it was you!'

Francesca smiled calmly and her colour returned.

'Well, that's his version now he's met you and the story is out. Frank knew about the affair, he put a clause in his will-'

The truth hit Charley like an iron fist.

'I know about the damn clause, and I know that it was you! It was all you, you told him. He didn't believe you, did he? He knew what you were like and he didn't believe you, but you put enough doubt in his mind that he saw fit to do something about it if it turned out to be true.'

'It was true. She was a liar and a cheat! She deserved to have all of this go to shit. She deserved it!'

'Like she deserved to die?'

Francesca shook her head, and Charley cursed. She had been too quick.

'No, you won't put this on me, Charlotte. I did nothing. Elizabeth was old, she had dementia, many people do. She knew nothing. She was ill. She had a disease of the mind. Whatever you think she knew, whatever she said, it was all in her head. Why would I be bothered enough to find out crap about some illness and cross reference the details to kill her off? I have a life to live too.'

'Yet you bothered to do exactly that with me.' Another voice cut in.

Charley looked past Francesca towards the landing.

Rue.

The same lank hair, big glasses, torn dungarees, years old brown cardigan, scuffed shoes. But something about Rue was different today. She stood tall and straight. Today her face was no longer expressionless. She looked focused.

Ready to do battle.

Chapter Seventy-Nine

Rue stood shaking at the top of the stairs. The whole stairway was rocking a little in her vision, and she sent up a prayer that she wouldn't faint and fall down them. Beads of sweat clung to her forehead, and she felt physically sick as her stomach swirled with nerves. She forced her shoulders back as she stared at Francesca's venomous eyes glaring into her own. Rue was terrified, but Charley was also looking at her, and she was on her own here. Charley had stood up for her more than once. It was time to pay her back.

'What did you say?' Francesca spat, flashing the hand signal.

Rue ignored it. She knew it was perfectly plausible for Francesca to have studied the disease and plotted and schemed. She'd had a lot of practice, and let's face it, with Elizabeth she wouldn't have had to foster control as she did with Rue, she just had to slip a little something in her food that she was unaware of. Easy. She would have help, and after looking over the chart she knew that Nell and Axl had been around the most. Axl wouldn't be compliant after the whole affair with Elizabeth and the things Francesca had said to them both. So that left one helper. Nell. The cook. Perfect.

'You do that with me.' She repeated, her voice wavering. Francesca looked furious, but Rue had started now she had no choice but to go on, and hope that everyone would believe her.

'Stay out of this Rue, you know nothing,' Francesca spat, shooting her a warning look and another hand signal. Rue flinched as the shakes set back in with earnest.

Keep going for Charley. For Charley.

Charley, who was now looking up at her, wide eyed, completely ignoring Francesca.

'Do what, Rue? What did she do?'

Rue glanced to Francesca and then back to Charley and the man. She didn't know who he was, but if he was a friend of Charley's he was a friend of hers too. Kate she couldn't see at all, but Evelyn was wide eyed in the hallway, staring at her through the spindles of the bannister.

So many eyes, so many watching.

She wobbled and then fixed her gaze back onto Charley.

Concentrate on Charley.

'My whole life is a lie.' She said, barely more than a whisper.

She saw Francesca ball her fists and bare her teeth, Charley frowned and shook her head, her gaze focused on Rue.

'What? I can't hear you.'

Rue took a breath, raised her voice.

'I said, my whole life has been a lie. Don't listen to her, she could take the time to research and plot the disease, she would be good at it, and the reason I know is-'

Francesca cut her off with a loud laugh.

'Oh Rue, you are such a drama queen, why would you say such a thing?'

Rue saw a slight smile appear on Evelyn's lips, and Kate appeared from wherever she had been hiding, to peer at her with pity too. She knew she would lose them all if Francesca continued. She had been effectively shutting Rue up one way or another for too many years.

'I didn't even finish.' She whispered, losing confidence as Francesca barred her teeth again, face set into a scowl that only faced Rue, her back conveniently to the rest of the gathering. Both hands now showed her the signal.

Shit. I'm in for hell if I don't continue, and even more so if I do.

She felt tears form behind her eyes. She wished she had never started. They would never believe her. This was pointless - and dangerous.

Charley pushed past Francesca and climbed the stairs, taking her by the hand at the top. Rue looked at Charley, drawing strength as Charley spoke out.

'Then finish Rue, we're listening.'

Francesca also climbed a few stairs, Rue automatically tried to take a few steps back, but Charley had a hold of her hand.

'No-one is listening, it's all dramatic nonsense. Rue has always loved the drama.'

Charley swung around to Francesca.

'Rue? Drama? I've never known anyone less into drama,' She looked toward Evelyn and Kate, 'And if you say otherwise, you're worse than she is, Rue never even gets chance to-'

'Charley, leave it alone.' Evelyn said, 'We need to clear things up, get hold of mom's letters. This is nothing to do with Rue, let's not start a silly family argument when there are more important things to discuss.'

'No, not until Rue has had the freedom to say what she needs to.'

'Rue does not understand what she's saying, she's as bad as Elizabeth.' Francesca spat.

'Oh, really?' Charley said facing Francesca. 'Does Rue have dementia too? How convenient.'

'No, Charley, she does not. But lack of food means lack of attention, lack of brain function-'

Rue felt the moment trying to slip away as Francesca spoke. It had always been the same. They would argue around her and the matter would be put to bed without her input, but not this time, this time was different. This time the stakes were too high, both for her, Charley, and possibly for her Aunt who no longer had a voice. Taking strength from Charley whose warm hand was still in hers, she felt the surge of anger rise up from her stomach and out.

'Oh, cut the crap, *mother*.'

The large hallway was a shocked into silence and Rue noticed that even Francesca's eyes widened momentarily before she expertly fixed her mask back into place. For the moment all attention was on her and she decided she had better use it before she lost her nerve, or Francesca broke through the block. She took a shaky breath and Charley squeezed her hand, urging her on.

'I don't have anorexia, and I don't have Bulimia, there is nothing wrong with me. She made it all up to keep me quiet. She looks up the symptoms and the medical diagnosis, the tests, and outcomes of the tests, and she keeps me like this to prove her theory, her diagnosis. To prove I'm ill. But I'm not, I just... I know something I shouldn't-'

Francesca snorted down her nose loudly.

'Ridiculous! Rue, why would you say such a thing? Are you trying to get me into trouble? I do everything for you. Everything to help you. I don't understand.'

The attention swung back to Francesca, which is exactly how she wanted it. The scowl and sneer dissipated in an instant as she paste a worried and devastated look over her features for the attention of the hall.

'Why would I want to pretend my daughter is ill? I only want the best for you, Rue. Surely you can see this is laughable.'

'-and she wants to keep me quiet.' Rue finished softly.

She looked to Charley, whose face showed concern and empathy, but not shock. Rue also knew, by the narrowing of Charley's eyes, that she understood exactly what she was trying to say, and the implications of how it tied Francesca to both her and Elizabeth. Out of the corner of her eye Rue saw Evelyn shake her head, opening her mouth with a frown, but Charley spoke first, urging her on.

'Keep going, Rue. What do you mean?'

Francesca huffed a breath.

'Oh, for crying out loud, it's all nonsense. She's being-'

Charley swung to Francesca.

'Will you shut up and let her talk? You never let her talk. Everyone in this god-damned family speaks for her. Rue deserves an opinion too, and this is one I want to hear.'

'There's no point, Charley, 'Evelyn said, 'We're wasting time. Rue, we all know that you think-'

'It's not what I think Evelyn, there's nothing wrong with me. Mom made up the diagnosis, the-'

Francesca put a hand to her face, shaking her head as the other hand clutched the banister.

'There is no diagnosis Rue, that's the point.' Evelyn continued. 'And we all know that people in your position often think or feel there is nothing they're doing wrong, but you are ill, just because the tests-'

The rage that had started as a simmer in Rue's stomach bubbled and churned.

'I'm not ill!' she shouted. 'And I've had no tests. This is the whole point!' She pointed to Francesca who in usual fashion was now preparing to step back and let the girls fight it out until they made her out to be the one wronged. 'She made the whole thing up. She never took me to any Doctor, because I don't need one!'

Charley squeezed her hand again. She saw Evelyn and Kate exchange pitying looks, and Evelyn even put her hand through the bannister to touch her mother's thigh. On cue, Francesca let out a loud sob.

'Rue, look at the state of you.' Evelyn said, 'You're not well, you're hardly the picture of health. With all due respect mom could make up all the diagnosis's she wanted, but the evidence is plain for all of us to see-'

'She makes me like-'

There was another loud sob. Rue knew if Francesca looked up now, there wouldn't be a single tear shed. Evelyn shook her head.

'You're too thin, Rue. Far too thin. How can you say mom has anything to do with your appearance? You choose-'

'No, Evelyn. I don't. She limits my food, controls what I eat, she takes my wages, buys my food, my clothes, my toiletries. She says I've been to appointments that never existed. And she took the prescription and got these stupid glasses.'

Francesca now let out a loud wail, and Evelyn rubbed more vigorously at her thigh.

'Rue, that is ridiculous, you're upsetting her. Mom does her best, she comes to look after you, help you clean, cooks for you. She picked up those glasses for you out of the goodness of her heart. You were too weak to go.'

Rue huffed a breath, dragging a hand through her hair. What else was she supposed to say? There wasn't anything she could say that would convince them. And then Charley's friend spoke up from down by the door.

'You said she took your wages?' He said looking up at her.

The hallway swung to him, and although Rue was uncertain where he was going with it. She nodded.

'Yes, all of it. Every month. I'm not allowed to shop for myself. She controls everything.'

Evelyn snapped.

'You are too ill, Rue. For god's sake-'

'And yet she works?' the man said. 'How much time do you have off work, Rue?'

The hall erupted, and Charley shouted above the fray.

'Everyone shut the hell up! If there's nothing going on, then why don't we let Rue answer.'

'What's it got to do with him?' Kate said, anger in her voice, and Evelyn nodded her agreement.

Theo shrugged, held up his hands, and Charley took the baton from him.

'He has a valid point, don't you think? How much time do you have off Rue?'

Rue knew very well that Charley knew, but she said it out loud anyway.

'None. I never miss work.'

Theo nodded and pursed his lips. Kate piped back up.

'What does that have to do with anything? This is pathetic.'

Theo answered her calmly and quietly.

'I'm just getting a handle on this bear with me, so she never misses a single day of work.' He looked back to Rue, 'full time?'

Rue nodded, she liked this stranger who was giving her a helping hand. 'And overtime most days.'

Charley smiled at her as he continued, the hall dropping into silence.

'Full time and overtime? Not bad for someone too ill to shop, cook and pick up their own prescription for glasses don't you think?'

'I think this has nothing to do with you,' Evelyn said, averting her eyes as Francesca let out a few more sobs for good measure, but Rue knew he had hit a chord.

'I'm stating a fact, that's all.'

'It's not fact, it's supposition. And even if that were true, why the hell would mom want to do this to her? It makes no sense. It's ridiculous. If we're all so interested in listening to Rue, then let's see what she can come up with for that one.'

That's easy, easier than talking about me.

'I knew about Charley. I knew she was Aunt Elizabeth's daughter. I found some things a long time ago-'

And that's when the world came crashing down. Rue heard a roar and saw Francesca come up the stairs, not running, but seeming to glide, teeth bared in a growl. She heard Charley call out, felt herself falling as her hand wrenched from Charley's grip. She bumped down the stairs in slow motion, past Francesca, elbow knocking on the wall, hip bouncing her painfully and turning her backwards to face the top. She caught Francesca's face set in a nasty smile and then she was flipped again. Her glasses whipped from her face, and she closed her eyes, waiting for the inevitable end.

Chapter Eighty

Charley's heart lurched. Frozen in horror, she sent a small prayer of thanks that the stairs were wide enough, and the carpet plush enough to cushion Rue as she bumped down the stairs, twisting and tumbling over herself. Theo stepped quickly away from the door and in a smooth motion scooped Rue into his arms before she hit the floor as though she was featherweight.

'I've got you.' He said to Rue, who mumbled something back.

Charley let out a breath of relief, hand to her heart. There was a moment of calm, silence, but only a beat, and then Francesca was on the move, crashing back down the stairs.

Charley plunged down after her, grabbing Rue's, thankfully unbroken glasses as Theo set Rue on her feet.

'Oh my, Rue. Rue darling, are you okay?'

Evelyn and Kate stood with their mouths open, unmoving, horror on their faces as Francesca reached the bottom and offered a hand to Rue, who stepped back behind Theo.

'You... you pushed me.' Rue said, eyes wide as she faced her from behind Theo's shoulder.

'No, no, I didn't. Rue I saw what happened, darling. It was Charley, Charley pushed you, not me.'

Charley felt the wind sucked out of her lungs. She stopped just short of the bottom of the stairs and stared at the woman who was once her mother. Lying so easily and effortlessly.

'It's a lie, I would never push you.' She said.

Rue shook her head.

'I know you wouldn't, she did it.'

She pointed to Francesca whose mouth dropped open, hand fluttering to her heart, an expression of shock and disbelief over her face.

'No, I...'

'I saw it too.' Theo said, his arm out protectively between Francesca and Rue. Francesca turned on him.

'You saw nothing, you jumped up little idiot. I ran up because I saw Charley, I wanted to stop her, to stop Rue from falling, I didn't lay a hand on her.'

'I saw you,' he repeated, 'you ran up, pulled her, watched her fall, nasty little smile of glee on your face. You know, in private, you may get away with that look but when someone is watching the action, you'd better be telling the truth or keeping a straight face, neither of which I think you've done since we've been here.'

Normally, Francesca would have her daughters running around her, giving admonishing looks to whoever had hurt their mother, but now no one uttered a word. Francesca changed instantly, her face back to the kicked dog look.

'I'm an elderly lady, I don't have the strength to be pushing people around.'

'You took the stairs fast enough. Plenty of energy to stop someone saying something you don't want said out loud.'

'Oh,' Francesca put a hand to her brow, the other on the bannister, 'Oh, I don't know what you mean. Oh, Oh, I feel unwell, I've had a little turn. Evelyn?'

Evelyn seemed torn between going to help and being lost in the horror that was unfolding before her. Her tongue darted between her lips as she looked to Francesca, whose head snapped up in anger.

'For god's sake Evelyn! I don't feel well, are you going to help me or not?'

Charley saw Evelyn step back as Francesca glared, and she smiled inside.

SHATTERED

You're losing it, sweetie. No-one flits through emotions like that, it's not normal.

'Don't blame Evelyn,' she said, 'You're making yourself look really unstable with all this emotional hoo-har.'

Francesca let go of the bannister and stood up tall. She turned, taking a step toward Charley.

'If I am unstable, is it any wonder? Look at you, all of you.' She swung an arm at the small group in the hall. 'Not one of you willing to stand beside your mother against awful accusations by this stranger. The one who has given up her whole life to make sure you are all taken care of, the one who would go to hell for any one of you. All of you willing to send me to the slaughterhouse with no conscience.'

She grit her teeth and flung both arms out with so much force it lift the hair from her forehead.

'It's Pathetic! How I've put up with you for all these years is beyond me. I tried. I really tried to bring you up right, to be good, kind, hardworking girls, but it looks like I got to stand on the shit pile instead.'

She pointed to Evelyn.

'You. You, Mrs prim and proper headmistress, always self-righteous, too busy, too important. You're a headmistress, not the bloody prime minister. And now that your old mom is asking for help you're backing off like the pitiful excuse for a human being you are.'

She turned to Kate, who now reddened rapidly beside Evelyn.

'And you miss high and mighty; miss look at me, I'm a superstar businesswoman. I've got news for you, anyone can run a business. If I had been given a wedge of money from my husband like you, I could have done what you did too. I could have had all the nice things in life. Hell, I could have been just like Elizabeth and sat on my throne doing nothing, throwing lavish parties with all the money he rained down on me. I could have done that, that could have been me. You think you're so special, so clever, so savvy.'

She pointed to Charley.

'You with your holier than thou smart-ass mouth. Always stirring up trouble. Couldn't wait to get that will off to the solicitor and deny me everything I've been waiting patiently for all these years. I've brought you up good, gave you everything you needed. You never went without, and this is how you repay me? Even with the knowledge that your own mother chose her lifestyle over her child?'

Charley opened her mouth, but Francesca was already onto Rue.

'And you,' she said jabbing her finger in Rue's direction, 'If your big nose hadn't been poked into my business without a care you could have been leading a very different life now. You had to go poking around through my private things, you couldn't have just put them down. Oh, no, not miss nosey herself. No, she had a right to read them, a right to go into her mother's personal things and scan her grubby eyes over each one. This is *your* fault. Actions have consequences, and as your mother it's up to me to teach you that. You can't go grubbing around with personal information and expect to get away scot free.'

'How-' Charley tried, but Francesca was on a roll, barrelling right over her words.

'What Charley? What? This wasn't just my important secret to keep, was it? Oh no, your mother, my so-called sister, who promised so much if I looked after her sweet little longed-for baby that she couldn't be bothered to take the rap for and keep. This was her secret, too. Her dirty laundry. Do you think she would have been any less angry to find that one of you had learned the secret and may expose it for what it was? I was protecting her, again. I was always protecting the self-righteous old witch. It was her fault you had to be restrained Rue, not mine. Elizabeth and Charley, they are the ones to blame. They are the reason you had to be kept quiet. Had to be kept under such strict conditions. Do you think I enjoyed it? Do you think I've got a kick out of doing this all these years? I had to research eating disorders like no tomorrow to make sure that the story was convincing, to limit your food, limit your self-respect through appearance, to make sure you looked unreliable should you have blabbed your little mouth. I've gone to great lengths for this family, for her family.'

She jabbed a finger at Charley.

'Elizabeth Kane. Hah. What a darling she was, so well loved, such a dirty little whore. No one saw that coming, did they? No, but if I'd

435

had my way, everyone would have known. She would have gone out with a bang, but she had me tied see? She promised me all of this, all of her lifestyle and her money when she went, in return for looking after Charley. All of it! But what does she do?'

Her arms flinging back up in the air, she looked around the hallway at them. No one spoke. The silence was thick and tense as each one of them took in the weight of her words, the insinuations, and the truth that Rue had spoken. Each was reaching their own conclusion about Francesca Costin. Only Charley was whirring way ahead. With Francesca ranting with abandon, she only had to poke her enough for a confession. She had poisoned Elizabeth; she was capable, there was no question, all Charley needed was an answer. A definite, I did it, to put an end to this whole shambles of a family.

'I'll tell you what she did.' Francesca continued. 'She cut me off, left me to fend for myself with my three children and her baby too. She promised me money that stopped coming before you were three years old.'

She pointed at Charley, and Charley shook her head.

'No, she would have paid you all the money you wanted. You took me away, took all of us away from her.'

'The money stopped before then Charley,' Francesca spat.

'Yes, Frank found out, but Elizabeth told you she was working out a way to be able to pay you without him knowing. She told you that, and you knew he couldn't know. You were the one that took us away. She would have given you the money-'

Francesca spat a harsh laugh.

'And in the meantime? I had four children and a cleaning wage to bring you all up with, I couldn't hang around until she had finished faffing around. I was sinking in babies, I had to go where there was work, and that meant Harrogate back then. I did everything I could for you all.'

'That's very noble, but you never let Elizabeth know where we were. Ever. Why was that?'

'She didn't deserve to know! She wasn't getting her claws in again. I would not have her see you without keeping her end of the bargain. I still wrote to her, what more did she want?'

'You bribed her. You told her I was dead. More than once. You threatened her life. It's all in the letters. Letters with no forwarding address so that she could never write back!'

Francesca laughed again as Evelyn drew in a breath, and Kate pulled a hand up to her mouth. Only Theo kept his eyes firmly on Francesca, not the slightest sign of surprise at what the old woman was saying.

'Oh, fiddlesticks Charley, you make it sound so sinister. I was having fun, just winding her up until she saw fit to play ball and start taking care of us again.'

'Winding her up? That's a sick game to play.'

'I was trying to get her to take responsibility! She had you, you were the product of a sordid affair, and yet, she felt entitled to just hand you over. For someone else to do all the work with no input? I don't think so. It's not a recent game anyway, I haven't written to her now for over fifteen years.'

Five pairs of wary eyes were now fixed on Francesca. She shrugged her shoulders.

'I finally got her to accept some responsibility. She said that she would leave her fortune, this house and her possessions to me when she died, now that Frank had gone, she had no one to leave it to anyway, and she said that it would make up for Charley.'

Theo huffed a breath.

'Make up for Charley? Charley is next of kin, she deserves all of Elizabeth's things, as an only daughter should.'

Francesca waved him off with a flick of her hand.

'Well, of course she would have all of this through me. She would have lived here with her family, as she should have.'

Charley spluttered a laugh.

437

'Except I'm twenty-seven and have my own life and flat in Harrogate.'

Francesca turned a hard gaze to Charley.

'Well, I didn't ask her to take so long to die now did I? If I'd had my way she would have gone all those years ago and allowed me to have a life, but as it stands now she squandered all of her money, and the house is like a time machine. She has done this on purpose. Selfish bitch. I couldn't sit back and keep watching her throw all of my things down the drain, now could I?'

Charley saw her chance.

'So, you killed her and had done with it.'

Francesca's eyebrows came up with a curl of her mouth.

'I didn't say that, now did I?'

Charley felt anger burn as she mentally kicked herself.

'You implied it.'

'That's not a confession, Charley. And just how did I murder her with dementia? She had tests, a Doctor diagnosed her, she had horrible episodes of hallucinations, confusion, sleepless nights, she was fine one day, not the next. How did I manage to give an old lady a disease? And more than that, I was in Harrogate Charley!'

'Sounds familiar,' Rue whispered, clearing her throat, Charley caught it and her mind clicked into gear. What Rue had been saying, and what Francesca confirmed she had done.

'What?' Francesca narrowed her eyes.

'Familiar,' Charley said, 'yes, exactly. This is exactly what you have been doing with Rue. Faking a disease, moulding Rue to the perfect anorexia victim, researching and honing the facts, faking tests and results with research. Exactly. Exactly the fucking same.'

'Don't swear Charley, I brought you up to be better than that.'

'Maybe I should have been a calculated killer instead, more to your liking?'

438

Francesca took a step to her facing her square on, Theo moved to Charley's side, leaving Rue by the front door. Evelyn and Kate wore identical looks of horror on their faces.

'I'm not a murderer Charley,' Francesca said 'whatever you may think I've done I haven't. Elizabeth had dementia, that's the long and short of it, big deal, such a shame, that's life.'

Charley leaned into Francesca, refusing to be intimidated.

'You didn't know what dementia was when you sent me here. Forgetfulness was it? And yet you've just reeled off her symptoms as though you've rehearsed and memorised a list. How the hell do you know what she suffered with? You weren't here, remember? Haven't seen her for years and yet, so sure, and so accurate. Something is wrong here, isn't it?'

'Nothing is wrong. I did my research, that's all.'

'I think you did yes.'

Francesca was now almost nose to nose with Charley, and she felt her heart thumping behind her ribs. If Francesca had done it, she was eyeball to eyeball with a cold-blooded killer.

'If you're so certain, prove it.' Francesca said, 'I can't see what evidence you can possibly have. You've come to this conclusion out of spite.'

'No, I've read the letters, I know how cruel you've been. No normal, sane, person would be able to say such things, especially to family.'

'Pah, so that proves I murdered an old lady with dementia.'

'Murdered your sister for revenge. To get back at her for your decision to help cover the one big mistake she made. To make her pay for the hardship she caused you. To make her pay for not giving you the ludicrous payments that you demanded each week. You said at the bottom of each of those letters that you would be coming for her. In one way or another you threatened her life at the close of each vile letter you wrote.'

Francesca nodded slowly, a nasty smile forming on her lips.

'Ah, so the letters are your proof, are they? That and a website. I'm not sure they will stand up in court as murder evidence, and the lady who was supposedly the victim is dead, she won't be filing any charges against me now.'

'I have other things, little things that point in the right direction. Alone they stand for nothing, but together they will add up to a fair amount I should think.'

Charley saw Francesca pale and falter slightly, and then Evelyn snapped the tension between them like a rubber band breaking under pressure.

'Website?' she said. Her voice was dull and unsure.

No one replied, no one took any notice. But it hit Charley like a sledgehammer.

The website. Crap. The laptop.

Charley's heart skipped a beat as she glanced into the wrecked front room. She had left all of her work on the back of the settee. Out in the open.

Charley, you idiot! Shit! How did she get through the password?

Francesca raised her eyebrows and smiled.

'Oh, you look a little anxious Charley, was that all the evidence you had? Oh, dear.'

 Charley felt like punching the smug smile off her face, but then she realised it didn't matter. Francesca had found the laptop, and she had obviously seen the website and put two and two together. And if she had seen that, then she had found the other stuff. The chart, the book. She would know full well that she was onto her. She had probably destroyed everything, including the computer. Charley's heart dropped through the floor.

Oh God, if she's destroyed all that I have nothing but vague speculation and a Belladonna bush in the garden. I've lost, and she's won. There's nothing but circumstance left.

She's got away with it.

As Charley faltered and her mind raced, Francesca smiled, colour coming back into her cheeks. It was a smile that said she would happily breakfast with Satan himself and tip him on the way out.

To Charley it was a smile that said she was guilty as hell and she knew damn well she had got away with it.

Chapter Eighty-One

Francesca raised her eyebrows at Charley.

'Nothing else to throw at me? Well good, because it would be a real shame if someone innocent went to jail over false accusations now wouldn't it? That just leaves the will then.'

Francesca smiled as she watched Charley lose her conviction and Evelyn and Kate gain confidence and start to back her up. They were starting to get into a fray, it was time to sit back and watch, let them run the show.

She was proud of herself.

Proud that she had been able to orchestrate this to within a degree as to leave no evidence at all. She knew it would be hard to pin this on herself, and yet they couldn't pin it to Nell either. Perfectly done. And yes, the letters had been a slip-up, an oversight that should have been dealt with years ago, but she could deal with that. She had disposed of her sister and no-one had suspected; the letters would be easy.

At the earliest opportunity she would get them back and deal with them. They weren't with the police. Charley wasn't stupid, she had no reason for the police to be interested, but it had been close. She was thankful that she had come up to Fortwind Bay when she had, left a little longer who knew what else Charley would have uncovered.

A small flutter of fear travelled across her abdomen.

How did Charley figure it out? No one knows but me and Nell, and I didn't speak to her when there was anyone else around, not even Rue.

Francesca turned to her youngest daughter, still wide eyed by the door, even after her outburst. Francesca had to admit she had been a little impressed by Rue's confidence, but the reigns would need to be tightened from now on. She couldn't risk Rue having another outburst.

A surge of satisfaction flooded her.

Ah, Rue.

She understood that her youngest had been sent as a gift. Francesca had needed to control Rue to understand that she could do this. She could absolutely research a disease to such a degree as to fool everyone that someone had it. Hell, she could give herself a big pat on the back. Other than Rue opening her mouth just now, not one of her daughters had any idea that Rue wasn't ill.

She was malnourished and hen pecked maybe - not abused; never abused - but she wasn't ill, not even so much as a cold from one year to the next. Francesca was actually impressed with just how well Rue was. Still, the making up of appointments and test results and keeping Rue in line had all come quite naturally. It had even been an outlet for all the pent-up frustration at how her life had turned out. And Elizabeth had certainly been a big part of that.

Francesca smiled inwardly at the commotion and arguing going on around her. Rue would get her just deserts later, but for now there didn't seem to be much harm done, she hadn't even said very much and only Charley had been willing to listen. The others didn't seem too bothered, and that was good. Once this whole messy scene was over, she could get Rue back under control and sway Evelyn and Kate that she had been lying.

Maybe Rue could be getting loss of brain function through malnourishment?

Something to look in to certainly.

Francesca felt a warmth and excitement at the next challenge, although she didn't think anything before, or after this, would ever match the thrill of Elizabeth's death.

Well, if Rue gets too much to handle, or pushes it too far...

Francesca was jolted from her thoughts by Charley's friend, shouting and waving his hands in the air above the girls.

'Enough! This is not getting us anywhere, stop!'

She looked at the tall young man with wild dark hair that stood in front of her by the front door.

If he thinks he can stop the arguing that way, he doesn't know Costin girls.

But there was a hush that fell over the hallway, and the man lowered his voice.

'Right, enough ladies, please. Listen, let's all calm down, maybe get a cup of tea and talk this through like adults. I haven't got a clue what's what here, everyone's just shouting and screaming over each other.'

Francesca felt a smug satisfaction as she saw Charley swing to him with a look of incredulence.

'Tea? Theo are you serious? I can't have tea with-'

The man, Theo it appeared his name was, cut her off sternly with the palm of his hand.

'Charley. Enough. Of course you can. Look, you can't come at this like a wrecking ball at a paper house when there's obviously no evidence either way. Elizabeth had dementia as far as anyone knows, and as far as I can see, there's nothing solid to suggest otherwise aside from the brain of a sick woman getting paranoid. Just calm down and we can go over it properly. Whatever happened to innocent until proven guilty?'

Charley's eyes widened. She began to protest as Evelyn and Kate mumbled their agreement.

'Yes, Charley, he's right. Let's go and make some tea, calm down, and see where our wires have got crossed.' Kate said turning to the kitchen.

Francesca shrugged and smiled at Theo, while taking immense pleasure in the horrified look that Rue gave Charley. Charley put an arm around Rue's shoulders, an equally shaken look on her face, as they made their way to the kitchen. Francesca and Theo brought up the rear, and like a gentleman, he motioned her in first.

Francesca, a pensioner no less, stood at the counter, one hand holding her up, as she surveyed the tribe around her. Evelyn and Kate were already being the dutiful daughters, Kate asking if she was okay and moving the chairs back to the table, sliding mess from the cupboards out of the way, Evelyn retrieved the kettle from the floor where it had fell, or been thrown, Francesca couldn't remember which, and rinsed it before filling it and setting about making hot drinks. Rue was her usual self, although a little pale, but then her story had fell on deaf ears, however much she had thought it like Elizabeth's.

Something I must be careful of next time... if there is a next time...

A pattern would definitely cause suspicion that she could do without. At least this episode had enlightened her to the fact.

Charley was by the door whispering something angrily to Theo, who had the best head on his shoulders as far as Francesca was concerned.

Imagine if I had been innocent? He would be the only one defending me. Innocent until proven guilty? Ah, yes, I like him a lot.

And he was right. Even if Charley thought she had done it, there wasn't a scrap of evidence. She couldn't carry on the argument and accusations because she had run out of things to fire at her when she had mentioned the website.

Good foresight get in there first. Shock and awe, wasn't that what they called it in war?

She heaved a satisfied sigh. Everything would be alright. Her faculties were way ahead of this lot.

After whispering something angrily back Charley heaved a sigh and, with a shake of her head, slumped down on one of the chairs. Rue followed like a lost puppy, sitting next to her. Francesca noted Charley's sullen face with amusement, before looking back to Theo, who smiled warmly at her.

'Do you want to sit down?'

He gestured with a hand toward one of the chairs at the table. Unable to stop herself, and not wanting to, she smiled back at him and moved to the chair opposite Charley, who glared at her. Theo sat himself at the end of the table next to her.

'What a night.' He said running a hand through his curls, Charley huffed a laugh and Francesca smiled at him.

'Indeed, although it's not long into evening.'

445

He nodded and smiled to Evelyn, who handed him a mug of tea.

'Thank you.'

Kate and Evelyn finally sat down, Evelyn opposite Theo and Kate next to Francesca.

It stood to reason. Evelyn had always thought she controlled the family, controlled the meetings. She was a good girl, but she had absolutely no idea about real control. As she glanced nervously around the table Francesca realised that she was stuck, tongue tied. Evelyn had no idea how to begin, showing just how incompetent she was when a real crisis hit.

Evelyn finally looked at Theo.

'Um, could you maybe objectively talk us through this? As you have no ties, no emotion about it. How do you see it?'

Theo took a sip of tea and sat back, pushing out his lips and heaving a sigh. Charley stared stonily at him, and Francesca felt a small jump of glee. This was perfect. If there was a fight between Theo and Charley, this whole thing would be over faster than snow on a warm day. Francesca wondered how she could stir it up as Theo spoke.

'Well, I don't know about the whole Elizabeth stuff. I mean, she had dementia, right?'

'Apparently,' Charley snapped.

He gave her a nod.

'Of course, but the Doctor agreed. She had tests. She had a private live-in nurse. Surely she would have picked up signs. She was qualified to the hilt... apparently. See, unless someone checks her credentials and follows up whether she just added them to her resume, or legitimately earned them, who can really say.' He shrugged, 'It's the same with Elizabeth, right, the Doctor said she had it, prescribed the medication. Unless someone follows through her care, test results, and whatnot, then the given is that she probably did have dementia.'

Francesca fought to keep the smile off her face. Damn, he was good. Really good. He almost had her convinced, and she was the one adding poisonous berries to Elizabeth's food. Charley's face was like thunder.

446

'Theo, Elizabeth said countless times that she was being poisoned. She *knew*.'

'You can't say she *knew*. We all know that paranoia is part of the disease. There is no evidence that this is the truth, Francesca is right, all you have is a website and a few angry letters. It proves nothing.'

Francesca had been about to interject, but she kept her mouth shut and sat back. This Theo lad would do all the work for her if he carried on. Silence would serve her well here... oh, and a small look of anxious disappointment on her face. She immediately looked down at her hands, adopting a wide-eyed, worried look for effect. Charley slapped her hands on the table, her mouth a firm line.

'It proves everything.' She snapped.

It was hard to keep quiet when Rue spoke up too, but Francesca bit her tongue and kept her head down.

'What about the similarities between my treatment and Elizabeth's?'

Out of the corner of her eye, she saw Theo shake his head and shrug his shoulders.

'I can't see the link Rue, if there is one it's a tiny thread. You are in close proximity to Francesca, Elizabeth was miles away. She had dementia, she was never getting better, you have an eating disorder which can be healed...'

Evelyn straightened up and lifted her chin.

'I just don't understand you, Rue. It is ridiculous to think that mom would poison Elizabeth or want to keep her own daughter under such controlled circumstances for all these years, anyway. She's an old lady. She couldn't do it.'

Kate nodded agreement, as she usually did in these situations. Francesca grit her teeth and closed her eyes, pushing the anger down. Evelyn could be so patronising in her effort to be right.

She's on your side, that's the main thing.

Theo held up his hands.

'I agree, objectively, from where I'm sitting I don't believe Francesca poisoned Elizabeth, at all.'

'What?'

Charley scraped the chair back as she stood, and Theo immediately stood with her.

'Charley, listen. Please. If you want my honest opinion. No, I don't think Francesca did it, I think Elizabeth had dementia. It was just her time.' He looked at Francesca who chanced a timid flick of her eyes up to him.

This is getting better and better.

'But,' he continued, 'I do think something is going on with Rue. Putting Elizabeth aside, we should probably work that out.'

Francesca's stomach flipped over, and she snapped her head up.

'There's nothing going on with Rue, she has anorexia. It hasn't been diagnosed by professionals, but I'm with her most of the time when she's not at work, and I take her to tests for her diagnosis. I see her. I cook the meals she hides, the ones she throws back up in the toilet.'

Rue's mouth dropped open, but falling back into the familiar routine, the hand signal pushed her back into place easily. Rue looked back down at her hands.

Control felt good right now, and Francesca felt herself calming as Theo continued.

'Yes, you see, this is what's not making sense with me, if she's so ill how is she working? And never missing a single day?'

Francesca's stomach went over again as the question caught her by surprise. She struggled for a satisfactory answer.

'I... well... she, um-'

'I'll tell you how, because I'm not ill, because I get food from co-workers at work, because I get to be alone, I get to feel appreciated, I get to achieve something for myself. Because she's not there!'

Rue jabbed an angry finger across the table, and Francesca felt anger rush up from her gut. She pushed it down firmly.

'She's a Costin, she's made of strong stuff,' she said as though Rue hadn't spoken.

Theo narrowed his eyes in thought, looking at both her and Rue in turn.

'So what's really going on here? If she really has Anorexia, then she wouldn't be able to turn the bad times on and off. If there are no good times, she wouldn't be able to work, surely. And the way she looks, it seems she hasn't had a good time for a while. Sorry Rue.'

Rue shrugged lightly.

'I don't choose to look this way.'

Theo nodded, and Francesca struggled to keep up. Was he saying that he didn't believe she had Anorexia? If so, she needed a different tac. She required this man on her side. Evelyn and Kate were readily hanging onto his every word. Rue was controllable, and without anyone else Charley was a mere whine in her ear. No threat at all.

She thought furiously.

The truth? Even though it did tether her to faking Elizabeth's disease? But if she could be truthful about one, she would surely admit the other too, right? It may go in her favour. Not all the details of course, a sugar-coated version, one where she was the victim, not Rue.

'So, what is going on, Rue?' Theo said.

Francesca put out a hand and looked up, pretending to wipe a stray tear. If she was lucky, she would be able to produce a few real ones through her speech.

'All right, all right, I'll tell the truth. I'm to blame, I know. I panicked.'

Chapter Eighty-Two

Charley sat in quiet horror as Francesca went through Rue's tragic adulthood from the beginning. How she had found the letters and how awful it would have been for Elizabeth if the whole story had come out. It would have ruined her life. By keeping Rue quiet she was protecting Elizabeth, she said, which contradicted everything Charley had been hearing growing up, and all the angry vibes and the unwillingness to have Elizabeth's name mentioned in the house. The witch story, which seemed now to have been derived and fed to keep the girls afraid.

Nothing rang true. It was all an act. Charley wondered how it had gone so far as to become such a mammoth task. Why Francesca had made the illness up - and gone to great lengths to keep Rue looking such a state, making up Doctor appointments, even if she said nothing came of them. If Rue had been asked to keep it quiet, she would have. If Charley knew that, then surely Francesca knew it too. Charley was getting an overwhelming picture of exactly the kind of tendencies her former mother had. A need for sadistic control which it appeared had spiralled to murder as she had become more comfortable with the process over the years.

Charley felt a chill run up her spine. Francesca could have killed Rue too. Anorexia. Starvation. All she had to do was not get the medical care she needed when she had gone too far. Rue lived alone. She could profess that they had found her dead or dying.

With a shudder, she squeezed Rue's hand under the table. Rue looked up at her with huge, haunted eyes, and suddenly Charley was appalled. How had she never figured this out? Why had she been so quick to believe the illness, especially when Rue had insisted she was well? The same as Elizabeth, she realised. She insisted she was being poisoned, but everyone believed the dementia tale. At least she had listened to Elizabeth. It was of some comfort, if this hadn't happened they wouldn't be discussing Rue now and maybe she would have been like this until Francesca had died, or she had killed Rue.

Finally, she could keep quiet no longer.

'How could you do that? To your daughter, to your sister, to your flesh and blood?'

Theo flashed her a warning look, but Charley couldn't hold back the tide on her tongue which lapped ashore like a freak wave.

'The similarities between Rue and Elizabeth are striking, you must see that.'

Theo only shook his head, lips pursed, and she bit back the rest. She was aware that he had his own agenda, but she wasn't entirely sure what it was, or that it was working. If she could just get Francesca to confess, this could be over in a matter of minutes. It was so frustrating.

'Charley,' Kate said, 'Do you realise what you're accusing mom of? This is murder! She's not capable.'

Where have I heard that before? Except it appears that Axl really wasn't.

'A few hours ago I would have said she wasn't capable of fabricating the whole life of one of her daughters but here she is admitting the whole thing.'

Francesca choked a loud sob, a hand over her mouth.

'I'm admitting it because... because I know it was wrong, and because I own up when I've done something I shouldn't have.'

Charley ground her teeth and looked back down at her hands, taking deep breaths to keep from leaning over the table and punching Francesca full in the face. How had she called this woman her mother just a few months ago?

Evelyn heaved a sigh and rubbed at her eyes under her glasses.

'Nor would I, but it's done now. The main thing is that it shouldn't continue.'

Charley reeled back as Kate nodded.

That was it? They were just going to let her get away with it so easily? Prepared to let her completely off the hook, even with the nature of what she had done? Francesca nodded as a tear slipped down her cheek.

'It doesn't need to now, the secret is out anyway, I am so very sorry Rue. Can you forgive me?'

Charley felt Rue tense beside her and knew that she wasn't buying into it either. She knew that between the two of them they must have seen more acting from this woman than Judi Dench had done in her entire career. She held onto Rue's hand.

Hang in there, Rue, you won't be going anywhere with this woman now anyway. She won't hurt you again.

'Rue?' Kate said

Charley looked up and saw everyone's gaze on Rue.

Oh God, they want acceptance? Are they serious? This isn't some playground spat, this is abuse.

She blew a breath and kept quiet anyway, nudging at Rue to go ahead. Soon. Soon. It would be over. She heard Rue swallow hard.

'It's okay.'

And it was like the room breathed. The tension in the air dissipated and within seconds Kate and Evelyn were laughing, and Theo was congratulating Francesca for her bravery in telling the truth.

Rue looked up at Charley and gave her a small, hopeful smile. Charley smiled back and put an arm around her shoulders as more tea was made.

Chapter Eighty-Three

Francesca breathed a sigh of relief as she wiped the tears from her face and a concerned Theo turned to her, placing a hand on her arm with a smile.

'That took some guts. Well done.'

Francesca smiled a little too much and had to dip her head to hide it, pretending to wipe more tears as she hid her face.

'For what it's worth,' he continued, 'I don't think you killed Elizabeth.'

She snapped her head up to meet his eyes. Glee filled her soul, but she kept her face sorrowful.

'You don't?'

He shook his head as he glanced at Charley.

'Of course not. You don't have it in you, your daughter is right, you're an old lady. The past is the past. Those letters were from many years ago now. I think Charley is giving you too much credit, I mean, a murderer! How would someone like you be able to premeditate and carry out such a task? And like you said, from Harrogate? It's just not possible.'

He laughed, and she tittered with him, a little indignant at his words.

Old lady? Someone like her? And what exactly did that mean?

'It's laughable really, isn't it? You? Premeditating murder and carrying it through? From over a hundred miles away? Who does Charley think you are? The Yorkshire Ripper?'

He laughed loud and long, and the stab of indignance increased. Francesca narrowed her eyes as she glanced around the kitchen. Charley was talking quietly to Rue, and Kate and Evelyn were putting some of the things back into cupboards.

Perfect.

She dipped her head toward Theo.

'And what if I had more brains than the Ripper? I didn't get caught, right?'

Theo laughed more.

'Nope, because it's impossible to be caught for something you couldn't possibly have done.'

Anger rose in her chest at the insinuation that she wasn't clever enough to pull this off.

'Not so impossible,' she said through gritted teeth.

Theo's laughter turned to chuckles.

'Seems it to me.'

'No, young man, it's actually quite easy, especially for someone like me. Someone who has managed to orchestrate and control a person for so many years with just jibs and jabs to keep her going in the right direction. You think I couldn't do it?'

'I know you couldn't. And why would you go to all the trouble? Why not hire a hit man? It would be so simple to bump her off without all the agro, wouldn't it?'

The anger was dangerously close to spilling over.

Oh, he knew it, did he? She was as untraceable as the hitman would have ever been... and she had had fun into the bargain.

'Alright, listen.' She said. 'You have a vendetta; you hire a hit man. How appropriate, and how very expensive. Just as an example of course, let's see just how my mind would work in this situation. I have a vendetta. Elizabeth ruined my life, I want to ruin hers, or end it in this instance. She made me suffer for many years, bringing up a child who wasn't mine and stopping all payments for her that she had promised. It was hard to even take them on the one holiday a year they got. We were all squeezed into a two-bedroom house. I couldn't afford to move and the council put me to the back of the list as I was already 'housed'. We were okay, apparently. I struggled. For money, for work, for childcare, for time, for fun, for romance. I struggled for everything while she lived up here in luxury, skirting her responsibilities.'

Francesca was aware of her voice rising and stopped to take a breath. A pain was building up behind her chest as the anger built. She had to breathe some out or she would explode with the unfairness of it all. Theo was nodding at her with narrowed eyes. He placed a gentle hand back on her arm.

'Right, so the motive is clear, and very real. Let's not get any more upset, it's in the past now. So, let's have some fun. Theoretically, how would you pull it off? I wouldn't know where to start.'

Francesca looked at him. He was right, it was fun. She was enjoying this, enjoying showing this pipsqueak just how clever she really was, but not having to admit her guilt.

'Starting is easy. At the beginning. Research, research, research. What, when, where, how, and why. After months of research you find that Belladonna is perfect. Too much will definitely do the final deed, but just a few is not usually enough to kill outright, just to cause suffering and hallucinations, mild bodily discomfort. All of which, when cross checked with Dementia, could be passed off as those symptoms. And no account of Dementia is exactly the same, so no-one should bat an eyelid. Perfect. Of course you would need to start off small, just a few at first to check the symptoms and check how much she can tolerate. As a matter of fact, tolerance to them increased over time. Who would have thought?'

Theo was watching her raptured. He was impressed, and that spurred her on. It was only hypothetical, of course, it wouldn't hurt to spell it out just how clever she actually was.

'Anyway, at the beginning, I could source the berries from an online natural remedy site, it turns out that in some countries they are used as medicine in certain mixtures. I could buy them frozen and packaged ready to use easily and not too expensively.'

'Ah, intriguing.'

'Right, and after Nell agrees to her half of the plan, and locates the bush in the garden here, well, what a surprise? It suddenly makes buying a lot of berries cut by half, far less suspicious. If Nell could harvest and freeze her own during the summer months, that makes everything so much easier. And a little convenient, wouldn't you say? Almost too perfect.'

'Well, that's the how of course, but this was a well-documented disease. Everyone brought into it, even the Doctor here was prescribing medication.'

Francesca waved a hand at him.

'Pah, when you know someone who used to be a nurse, and is still working voluntarily at the hospital, it's easy to get a couple of forged forms for the Doctor's records. As soon as he is prescribing, there's no more need for any formal visits to anywhere. It's even better if that person is now the cook too, so she has credibility to take her for testing. I told Nell all the information she needed about the tests and the results that should come back from each visit to the hospital. She relays it back to the nurse, who doesn't suspect a thing. Only four visits needed, Doctor's prescribing the medication, a live-in nurse on site, a couple of good friends helping out and voila. Dementia well and truly set in and the plan commences into phase two. The fun bit where we watch her suffer for a while before phase three, the end. The only bit I didn't plan for was the live-in nurse.'

'Because of her training?'

'No, because of the cost. Elizabeth had promised to leave me this house and the rest of her fortune when she passed, as recompense for all I had been through, and for bringing up Charley. I didn't bank on her spending that fortune before she went. It wouldn't have been quite so bad if she hadn't frittered it away on the nurse and had spent some money doing up this shoddy old place. Honestly, if I didn't know her better, I would say she did it on purpose.'

Theo nodded slowly, completely entranced with her story. Maybe he was going to bump someone off one day. She could help him with it. She liked this affable young man. Heaven knows why he was a boyfriend of Charley's, he appeared to have more brains than that, but then there was no accounting for taste, and at least he had sense enough to follow his gut instinct and wasn't listening to Charley right now.

'Hindsight.' He said, 'So how could you be so certain the berries would still be frozen and store-able too when they got up here. They have to be delivered to you first? Or straight here, but then you'd have no control over that, and surely someone would notice them in the freezer right in front of their noses? There would need to be somewhere else, surely.'

Francesca, caught up in his interest, happily told him what he wanted to know. Not so old lady-ish now, huh?

'The cellar. There's a freezer in the cellar, Axl thinks it's for extra Elderberries. He knows the freezer is Nell's business, an extra place for food storage, so he leaves it alone. Nell deals with the packages and transfers them quickly. I tell her they're in transit and she bustles everyone out of the way with excuses and waits here for it to be delivered. If the berries unfreeze or go off, they are unusable, Elizabeth would taste them, so it's an intricate operation. Theoretically, of course.'

Theo nodded. His eyes narrowed in concentration.

'I like you're thinking, leaving nothing to chance. And the gardener just thinking the freezer is food storage? Priceless! It's a very tight plan Francesca, I'm impressed. But to leave no evidence after all that? That's what's really impressive.'

'I know, that's where I was really clever. Nothing points to me. There are no links, except the damn letters that provide a motive. I should have asked Nell to look harder for them, then I wouldn't even have been here in person right now. It was a silly mistake, but the only one.'

Theo raised his eyebrows.

'But you didn't do it right?'

Francesca was pulled from her reminiscing.

'What?'

'That sounded like present tense, not hypothetical tense.'

Francesca waved a hand at him as her thoughts ran.

'That was my downfall, I should have pushed Nell to look harder for the letters.' She muttered.

There was a gasp and Francesca looked up to find the room silent. All eyes on her.

'What?' She said, angry that she had clearly missed something.

Kate had a hand to her mouth.

'Mom?'

'What? Spit it out for god's sake.'

'You really did this? Didn't you?'

'Oh, how ridiculous, look at me, I'm an old woman, at the end of my life. How could you think such a thing?'

Theo looked calmly at her.

'You just told us the whole process in very minute detail. Astounding detail. We all heard it. And what's more, no one told you any theories, or who may have been involved, but you just managed to hit the nail on the head with the Belladonna, the bushes, the pies, Nell, the symptoms, the Doctor's records. All of it. It's a huge coincidence, don't you think?'

Francesca felt a stab of fear, but then she remembered.

No evidence. Nothing pointed to her, and unless the house was bugged, she would be walking away today whatever they thought they knew.

'Not really, I have a very precise mind. A minute attention to detail. I may be old, but I am most certainly not stupid.'

Charley and Rue stared at her, and Kate pulled her hand away from her open mouth.

'Mom! No, no, I can't believe it...'

Francesca let it go. Her daughters clearly needed to remember who had been wronged here.

'Look,' she snapped, 'at the end of the day I did nothing wrong. There's no evidence to suggest otherwise now is there? I was in Harrogate, I had nothing to do with any of this except to ship the frozen berries up here. Nell put them in her food, and Elizabeth ate them. No-one forced her. She made my life hell, I just wanted to repay her the favour, let her suffer a little. It's not my fault Nell put too many berries in the pie now is it?'

Evelyn's jaw hit the floor.

'Mom! Oh god...'

'How do you know it was pie?'

Francesca looked at Charley.

'It was mostly always pie, Nell rang and told me, every time she ate something, and exactly what the reactions were. I needed to be just in line with Dementia, without killing her outright, for a while anyway. I was surprised when Nell told me she had died. We were supposed to go on a while longer. I wanted to be more involved with that part.'

Theo looked at Charley, and Francesca struggled to understand the look that passed between them.

'It's still premeditated murder, whether you were here or not.' Charley said.

'Oh, please, I just had an idea, Nell implemented it, Elizabeth ingested it. It's nothing more serious than that.'

'Nell implemented it under duress, duress of the kind you placed Rue under, probably.'

'No, Charley, don't be ridiculous. How could I control what Nell did from Harrogate? If you want the truth, Nell had been shit on as much as I had by Elizabeth Kane and her perfect life. Nell had her own reasons for agreeing, one of which being swiping the love of her life from under her nose and living the dream with him. She was scorned, it never left her, especially when Elizabeth did the dirty with Axl Maddox. I simply provided the plan, and the berries when there were none available. The rest of the time Nell was the instigator. She picked the berries from the garden, froze them when she could, and I provided what she couldn't.'

'But Nell was a friend of Elizabeth's,' Theo said, brows pulling together.

Francesca laughed.

'And what a good friend she was. She allowed Elizabeth to live the life she should have been living, staying close to Frank in case he ever realised what he was missing. Of course, when Elizabeth wasn't around, sometimes he did, but he wouldn't leave for her. Nell's pain and anger were vented at me. Her best friend. Nell knew where I was all along, she knew where we lived. We've met up lots over the years, she knew exactly where I was coming from with my plan and was happy to help out. Every good woman deserves a good friend. Don't you think?'

The table was silent, and for the first time Francesca felt she may have said the wrong thing. She had told them too much.

Then Theo yawned, stretching his arms up in the air and said he was going out to get some air. He left via the front door. Francesca watched him, a niggle of doubt in her stomach. She looked at her three daughters, and one former daughter, around the table. Their faces horrified. She smiled.

It may be time to turn on more tears.

'It wasn't me really, girls, there's no evidence, it's hypothetical, that's all. You believe me, don't you?'

The table was silent, and then Rue put a hand on Charley's arm.

'It's okay Charley, I have all of your things. The laptop and the other things too, I kept them safe.'

'Other things?' Francesca said, 'What other things? The website is useless and there's nothing else. You haven't got enough to incriminate me, however you scrabble together against me. I didn't do this.'

Rue ignored her and Francesca felt hot white anger flood her veins. Then Rue spoke again, and the anger was replaced by a trickle of fear.

'I don't know whether they're the right ones,' She said, 'but I found some berries stuffed in a box too. A little worse for wear now, but given the conversation, maybe they'll be of use.'

Francesca nearly laughed with relief.

'Old berries from months ago, they'll be worthless, I didn't touch them, and I wasn't even in the vicinity. So, you see, it was the perfect murder, and when the will is read I shall finally get what I deserve.'

'I also found the freezer in the cellar, still full of berries. I don't know if they're the right ones of course but the story matches.'

Francesca opened her mouth to say that Elizabeth had them for her silly remedies when the sound of sirens in the distance froze the words before they made it out.

He hadn't, had he? The little shit.

It was ridiculous, but she could still be cleared. The only problem would be the lack of hospital notes pertaining to tests and results, but she had the faked ones and was sure if the local Doctor thought she had dementia and was happy to prescribe medicines, then he would be believed. She would still be all right.

Theo came back into the kitchen and whispered something to Charley. She looked at Francesca with a broad smile that made her heart jump.

Francesca forced a smile right back.

'I don't know what you're smiling at, they may take me away, but they still have nothing. They'll let me go and you'll forever be the girl who cried wolf. Let them come.'

'Oh, we will, we have your whole confession recorded. That plus the motive and evidence should lock you and Nell away nicely for some time to come, I think. Oh yes, you will finally get what you deserve alright. A nice healthy dose of karma.'

Epilogue

One Year Later

Hands shaking, Charley unwrapped the parcel at the kitchen table and carefully took out the two large canvases encased in bubble wrap. She looked at Theo across the table as he stuffed the last of the sandwich into his mouth, completely unaffected by her shakes.

'What are you waiting for?' he garbled around the bread.

'I'm not sure, I feel like I'm so over this emotion thing. I can't do it Theo. It sucks, but I can't. I know you're trying to help...'

He wrinkled his nose and rolled his eyes, reaching over to un-peel the wrapping himself. It was a large canvas, taking up over half of the large kitchen table, and Charley caught her breath as she looked at the scene before her. The one she had photographed from the boat, the first time out with Theo all that time ago.

She scanned the picture from left to right, taking in every detail. The roll of the hill with its glimmering lights, softly blurring, the play of the dipping sun on the water, the muted colours of the small houses as they rose up, barely a hue as the sun lowered in the sky. And, oh God, the sky as it lay beyond, the streak of colour, red, orange, yellow, purple, and silhouetted in perfect contrasting darkness at the top right of the picture, Fortwind House, the curve of the bay perfect under its sweeping gaze, proud and tall as it watched over Fortwind Bay like a sentinel, and somehow, although she didn't remember it being there, the moon perfectly captured above the left hand chimney of the house.

Goosebumps littered her arms, the composition was perfect, the effect awe inspiring on such a large scale.

She looked at Theo and tried to speak but found she couldn't as tears sprang to her eyes. She blinked back down at the picture, vision blurring.

'Hah, now tell me that didn't evoke emotion.'

Charley looked back to him, still breathless,

'Was this the one I took from the boat?'

'Yep, when you were blathering on about smelling photographs or something.'

'Why?'

'Look at it. Charley, I was so sick of you telling me you don't get enough emotion through, I got the picture off your laptop and got it printed. Look at what you can do, it's amazing. The emotion is all there Charley but I think you're looking in the wrong place. The emotion is in the beholder, not the actual picture, but in how it takes your breath away when you look at it. How it has the ability to bring someone to tears. Your photographs do all of that and more. It just has to mean something to the person looking at it, and everyone will interpret it differently.'

Charley shook her head blinking the tears away.

'You don't get it?' he said.

She sniffed.

'No, I do get it. Yes, I get it.'

She laughed as he flopped over the table in mock relief.

'Thank God for that. I agree with you, your earlier photos are good but they lack the wow factor. These later ones are fantastic, the next one may have reduced me to tears too.'

Charley raised her eyebrows at him, her heart skipping a beat, and he pointed a finger at her.

'If that gets out I will have to kill you. I have the perfect plan all set out and ready to go, some old lady told me all the details once.'

She snorted down her nose.

'It's missing one vital ingredient. You don't have an accomplice; Nell is locked up too.'

'I can enlist Rue.'

'She'd never go for it, I've let her stay here, given her a home, somewhere to be herself. She wouldn't bump me off.'

'You never can tell with sisters. The wounds go deep.'

Charley threw some bubble wrap his way rolling her eyes as the sound of laughter drew her gaze to the garden, full of flourish, summer colour in full bloom. At the small fountain by the rose bushes Axl, who had been pruning, was busy splashing water at Belle, she laughed as she splashed back and then he chased her round the bushes out of sight. Charley smiled and narrowed her eyes. Another perfect picture, there were no limits to the beauty up here, and Belle and Axl would be the perfect subjects to practice on today. She held up a finger to Theo and ran to get her camera from the newly decorated drawing room before stepping into the warm sunshine.

As the camera snapped and clicked and the world existed only through a lens she thought about how perfectly things had worked out now that the dark cloud had moved on and she felt she could finally breathe again. Perfect under such tragic circumstances anyway.

The court case had dragged for seven long months but ultimately the outcome was good.

Francesca ended up getting fifteen years for the murder of Elizabeth Kane, Nell, ten for being an accomplice and being the one to put the berries in front of Elizabeth. It was unlikely either of them would get out alive given their ages, even with early release.

Francesca had been right, the Belladonna information, berries, Elizabeth's diary and the letters would have meant nothing without the confession, which had convinced both police and jury that she had known what she couldn't that day. Charley couldn't thank Theo enough for his charm and persistence which paid off beautifully in the end. It had been tense, but she was glad she had let him do his thing, without him Francesca may never have admitted anything. As it was, not only did she confess to the crime, but she also led them directly to the Belladonna bushes in the garden and the freezer in the cellar. The berries under the sink, although mouldy mush, tested positive for

Belladonna, as did the berries in the small freezer. If that hadn't been enough, Nell crumpled and confessed everything as soon as she had seen the police at her door. Her story almost directly corroborated with Francesca's.

Evidence of both the planning of Elizabeth's demise and Rue's faked illness were found on a hidden hard drive in Francesca's house, their childhood home. It was a no win for Francesca and as the evidence kept coming there was less and less chance of her getting out of going to jail, except on a charge of diminished responsibility. It was futile as she was proven to be both sane and very aware of what she had done, even breaking into a fit of anger at her injustice on the stand.

Rue decided not to press charges against her mother. The police had pressed her to, and the evidence had been there for her to be tried for the crime but the murder trial had been long and hard for all of them and she had just wanted to put it all aside and finally start living her life, which she did on the day their mother was sent down, celebrating by attending the small ocean cafe and eating all she could at the expense of Charley and Theo, before ditching her glasses outside the opticians and walking in to buy a new, modern pair.

After the official reading of the will and the signing over of possessions, Charley had invited Rue to stay with her at Fortwind House. It was her home now and Rue's too if she wanted in. As it happened, she did. She immediately sold her house in Harrogate, quit her job, and moved to Fortwind Bay permanently, getting work in the local estate agent's and doing very well at it. These days she was the picture of health, no more bony frame and lank hair. She was rounded and curvy, making the most of her figure with stylish clothes and a shorter modern style for her refreshed, shiny locks. She was an altogether different woman, confident and self-assured, willing to speak out and have her opinion heard. It amazed Charley that this woman had been inside all along but had never been allowed to flourish.

Evelyn and Kate were harder to get around. They blamed Charley for exposing their mother 'at her time of life' and getting her sent to jail. They seemed to forget that their mother had committed the most cardinal of crimes and that an old lady's life had been taken forever. At least they could still visit Francesca in jail. And she supposed they often did. Neither Charley, nor Rue had seen or heard from them since the day their mother had been taken to her cell, her new forever home. It was no big deal to either of them after the way they had supported

Francesca through the trial, choosing to believe her innocence and supporting her even as the evidence mounted up.

Glen had come back to stay in the Bay for the trial, giving evidence and taking the stand herself with her own account of Elizabeth and what had happened, she had stayed in her old room at Fortwind House at Charley's insistence and the two had become good friends. Glen visited regularly when her job allowed, although there had been no more live in jobs since and Glen wasn't keen to take any. She felt horrendous guilt for not believing Elizabeth and for allowing the poisoning to carry on under her nose.

Avril and Axl both felt similar guilt, being around when this was going on, and not suspecting a thing, but they were learning to live with the outcome. Avril helped to clean the house after the mess that was left the night Francesca was arrested, but that was the last time she cleaned Fortwind House, she now visited every week, coming up to a much busier and more joyful house, but only for a cup of tea and a chat. Charley knew that she missed both Elizabeth and Nell in her own way, and with Axl spending most of his time at the house now it was a bit of normality and friendship that she knew she enjoyed.

Theo and Belle were an almost permanent fixture. Charley took over the looking after of Belle when Theo was at work, it suited both Belle and Charley who loved each others company. Charley found she could work around her if she involved Belle who was becoming quite a keen photographer at the age of six. She took her own kid proof camera around with her taking the same shots as Charley and mimicking her as she took them. She also mimicked what she called her 'work' when Charley had to be on the computer, Axl had brought Belle a kid proof tablet on which she pretended to work like Charley while watching you tube videos or playing games, leaving Charley to get on with her work quietly for an hour, two if she was lucky.

Most of the time Axl was around though and could pull her away if she became too much, or Charley was extra busy. After the fiasco on the island and then the revelation of Elizabeth's possible poisoning Axl had found his old life pulled away from him whether he had wanted it to or not. He found his patience with Ann had worn completely and he had finally left her, renting a small house further up the hill. Charley had found a gentle giant in her father and a very knowledgeable and kind man. She enjoyed his company and as they had bonded, she had invited him back up to do what he missed most. Fortwind garden. He had cried when she had asked if he wanted to come back and she had been touched by the emotion but she understood that he was looking after something that had been Elizabeth's here, keeping a part of her close, while keeping close to the newest addition to his life. She understood and appreciated it.

Charley laughed as she moved to take a photo of little Belle peeping from behind a pink rose bush, the colour picking up the flush of her cheeks as she panted for breath. Axl came at her again roaring like a bear from around the bamboo. Belle screamed and ran as Charley stood and stretched. She watched for a while before going back inside where Theo was polishing off a tub of Quality Street.

'Help yourself,' she said.

He turned to look at her, box in his hand, still chewing.

'Thanks. I knew you'd say that, so I thought I'd spare you the interruption.'

She grinned as she placed the camera onto the table, the smell of baking filling her nostrils. She stooped to look in the oven.

'Should be ready soon,' she said.

He brought the box to the table and Charley pulled one out, unwrapping it and popping it into her mouth.

'Ready for the next one now?' Theo said, unwrapping the bubble wrap on the second canvas and holding it up in front of her.

Charley sat down with a sob as the tears spilled over.

This picture was the one she had taken of Elizabeth, very much alive and in good spirits, sitting in the cast iron patio chair, stick at her side. Her hair perfectly coiffed and make up perfectly brushed, signature cream shirt and bottle green skirt contrasting with the white frames of the window behind her. Her gaze was confident and happy as she smiled, head tilted slightly up and to the left. Her gaze straight at the lens so that she would be forever viewing the world from the picture, seemingly watching over events with her sharp, piercing hazel, eyes.

Theo chuckled and placed the canvas down before coming around the table to place an arm around Charley's shoulders, squeezing her close.

'See?' He said wiping a tear of his own, 'That's real emotion, right there. I don't want to hear any more of this I can't do it lark.'

Charley huffed a laugh, wiping at her tears.

'Thank you. This one, this means a lot. Really.'

'I know, but all I did was order it, you took the picture. Where are you going to put it?'

Charley already had a good idea.

'Next to the hallway door, where she can look over the kitchen, and out to the garden, where she can watch dad and Belle.'

Charley picked up the canvas and held it up to the wall for him to see. Theo nodded and grimaced.

'What's the matter? No good?' Charley said over her shoulder.

'It's perfect, but Charley, she's bloody watching me. I'll never be able to steal another quality street in this kitchen again without feeling guilty.'

Charley laughed.

'Good.' She turned to the picture of her mother, who seemed to be smiling a little more if that was possible. 'We'll keep him in check together eh, mom?'

The beeps on the oven signalled that it had finished doing its work and Theo called Axl and Belle inside as Charley got the Elderberry pie out of the oven and some ice cream from the freezer.

'For you mom,' she said as they all tucked in at the table, then she looked at the canvas, propped up the wall ready to be hung. Looked right into her mother's bright hazel eyes.

'Oh, don't worry,' she said, 'I've made sure they're all freshly picked. We won't be making that mistake around here again.'

THE END

468

If you enjoyed this book it would be fantastic if you could leave a review.

Reviews help to bring my books to the attention of other readers who may enjoy them too.
Help spread the joy… or indeed, the fear!

To leave a review click the link on Shattered's book page at
Www.Amazon.co.uk.

Thank you!

SHATTERED
I wasn't there when my sister died... but it was my fault she came back.

The third paranormal thriller from Rebecca Guy coming 2021.

HAUNTED

Sign up to my mailing list to read the first six chapters for FREE

You also get access to exclusive behind the scenes content and extra's, and you'll be the first to hear about promotions, discounts, forthcoming titles and competitions!

Signing up is completely free and you will never receive spam from me.

To sign up visit - www.rebeccaguy.co.uk

You can opt out easily at any time.

*Working title and cover subject to change.

Enjoyed this book? Check out the previous release by Rebecca Guy available at all major retailers now!

RUIN

She will have to enter the darkness to find the light.

Darkness. Paranoia. Isolation.

Determined to start a new life as far from her shattered marriage as possible Emmie Landers purchases 'Bruadair' – an isolated ruin in the highlands of Scotland. A place where children are safe and angry fathers are absent.

But safe is not a word that applies to Bruadair. This is a place of uneasy darkness, where a deep cold penetrates the walls, shadows linger, and the intense feeling of being watched leaves Emmie unnerved. To add to her unease, chilling photographs of the family, her family, are appearing in odd places around the house, and three-year-old Grace is talking to empty rooms.

Down in Surrey, Scott Harvington is whipping up a storm. Furious that Emmie should get to start over so easily, he is determined to hunt her down and force her to face the consequences of tearing apart his family. She ruined his life, and now he will ruin hers. Hell bent on revenge, he is resolute. He will reunite his family – at whatever cost.

As events spiral out of control, Bruadair's secret is blown open with devastating consequences. Mentally broken, Emmie must face her worst fears as the full force of a terrifying past ensures the family's future is destroyed beyond repair.

Ruin.

Visit www.rebeccaguy.co.uk for more information.

SHATTERED

What readers are saying about Ruin

A story of love, loss and suspense that will give you chills. A fabulous spooky read that you will struggle to put down!

*****

My emotions were on a roll, scared, wanting more, anxious, frightened, CRYING, and happy. BRILLIANT story, great imagination.

*****

Sooo creepy, sad and happy. A real page turner, kept me guessing right up to the end.

*****

My heart jumped out of my chest so many times... really had me gripped

*****

Creepy, atmospheric, and fast paced. I would never have guessed the twist at the end!

CPSIA information can be obtained
at www.ICGtesting.com
Printed in the USA
BVHW032304261120
594293BV00003B/25